VIXEY

& THE DAMAGED GOODS

by J.X. Alexander

DEDICATIONS

Jeanne and all the others who have faced the Louis' in their lives and survived, though the scars remain for a lifetime.

May the Adam's never despair of being termed Damaged Goods.

My devoted wife, Sheryl, who has always stood by me through the good and bad times, fortunately, more of the former than the latter.

ISBN-13: 978-0622794814
LCCN 2016918297

CAST OF CHARACTERS

Cast of Characters

Anthony J. Murray: unsuspecting savior to Adam Magassey. Murray along with his wife, Sheryl, operate an insurance agency and have other investments, including boutique Texas hotels.

Adam Magassey: survivor of abuse and head of MABB, a multi adult entertainment corporation.

Bill St. George: the organizer of a Hungarian vigilante group, and Murray's longtime friend.

Michaeleen Ventura: CEO of a billion dollar empire and Murray and Sheryl's benefactor.

Carol Sue Winters: alias Carol Sue 'Vixey' Miller, a past instigator against Murray.

Louis B. Kolezy: Unscrupulous high profile attorney, and the stepfather of Adam Magassey and driving force of the Houston Hungarian Mafia.

Ilona Magassey-Kolezy: alcoholic and pill chasing wife of Louis B. Kolezy.

Melanie Magassey: sister of Adam and play toy for Louis B. Kolezy.

Rich Fedor: Secret Service and FBI trained and the owner of Moonlight Investigation, who is also a close friend of St. George.

Sevrin Fedor: former Soldier Of Fortune and Green Beret, acting as an operative for Moonlight Investigations and Rich Fedor's cousin.

Ernie Petrovich: born again attorney and would be novelist, who has reluctantly gone in with Bill St. George, Rich, and Sevrin Fedor to bring down Kolezy.

Ron Tanski: one time Special Forces agent, Green Beret, and Viet Nam veteran. High school friend and classmate of Murray's and now joining forces with Moonlight Investigations.

Wes Winters: president of Miller, Inc., the son of Carol Sue, and son-in-law to the Murray's by his marrying one of their daughters, Gina.

Carla Davis: Louis B. Kolezy's kept woman in Las Vegas.

Dimas Cavazos: Houston police lieutenant investigating a series of murders linked to Adam and Kolezy.

Zeke Cavazos: Houston police sergeant and brother of Dimas co-investigating the murders.

Kerry Yanek: psychotherapist and friend to Carol Sue.

Tom Zizka: venerable, local reporter at Houston's Channel 77.

Drago and Dimitri: hired killers and henchmen for Louis B. Kolezy's Hungarian Mafia.

Alicia Gonzalez: Melanie Magassey's love interest.

C.W. Roberts: United States attaché in Budapest and Murray's close friend.

Doctor Anton Horvath: renowned Houston internist and early friend from Hungary to both Ilona Magassey-Kolezy and Louis B. Kolezy.

Arnie Kaplan: Murray's corporate jet's co-pilot, known for his nervous antics on their air travels.

John Irion: the corporate jet's pilot and husband of Kerry Yanek, who was a veteran of the Iraq war.

Toth: inspector of The Budapest police and the head of the investigating team to apprehend Louis B. Kolezy.

Szilard Szabo: free-lance model, Adam Magassey's former "partner" and willing decoy in this case against Louis B. Kolezy.

ACKNOWLEDGMENTS

TO THE NOVEL

Sheryl Murray devoted wife and business partner of Murray. The mother of their three wonderful daughters.

Peter Beene and his Jorns Chevrolet dealership, in Kewaunee, Wisconsin, gave the shot of that great Corvette for our front cover.

My brilliant editor and beautiful wife, Sheryl, who found the time to work on this story and always had faith in the project. She feels that the reader needs to be broad minded due to the subject matter.

Karen, who placed me in the right direction on most of the aspects of this novel

Andy Hunter, artist, who illustrated a great cover, making it all come to life.

Hoss Fatemi, the design expert, who put the cherry on the cover and rear of the book.

The fabulous Hungarian crew, Bill, Rich, Sev, and Ernie, and of course, Ron, a great Polak, former classmate at CLS, all from our beloved city of birth, Cleveland, Ohio

Published author, Frank Cawley, of Ironmen, who gave a bundle of good advice

Gail Dawson McNally, published author of The Return, encouraging our work and steering us to publication.

To the fantastic Houston Police Department, who lay their lives on the line for the citizens of the fine city of Houston.

Tom Zizka, a dynamic reporter and fine family man, who allowed this author to lend his name to the novel.

The Adam's who continue the challenge of changing their lives.

As the 2008, crystal red, Buick Enclave rambled along Gessner Road traveling north, Anthony J. Murray, everyone called him, Murray, along with his lovely wife, Sheryl, were still thinking of the fine meal, earlier, at their favorite restaurant, Rudi Lechner's, where they traditionally, celebrated their monthly wedding anniversary. The early fiftyish couple recalled how their fortunes changed three years earlier when Michaeleen Ventura, a daughter of Murray's early love, Bobbie Jean Miller, came unexpectedly into their lives. She came in unannounced as they were working in their second floor paper milled insurance agency. Though moderately successful in their business while raising three daughters and a son, they had lived a middle class existence in a multi-cultured area, Alief, part of Southwest Houston. Sheryl, his devoted wife of over 30 years, served as his licensed secretary and partner. It was only the two of them living at their one story Spanish style home on a tree lined street. Two of their daughters Renee and Gina, had married and started their own families. The youngest, Karen, was finishing up an undergraduate degree at University of Texas, in Austin, then planning on obtaining a Master's Program later at the school. At the time, they had a son, Troy, who worked as an oil trader in the downtown section of the city, living in the midtown area.

Michaeleen definitely changed all that, as she was instrumental in bestowing upon them a huge fortune Murray had been cheated out of three decades before, from Bobby Jean's family, the Millers. Michaeleen became the majority stock holder and president of the company which was previously directed by her unscrupulous grandfather, the late Tex Miller. Among Murray and Sheryl's changes was moving to a custom built home in fashionable West Memorial. Later, purchasing a large insurance agency and making other multimillion dollar investments, including a private Gulfstream jet.

What transpired when Michaeleen walked in and dropped a life changing, body pinching story that day was still etched in their minds that night. It was almost an unfathomed belief that this tall, slender, blue eyed, early thirties, woman was kin to Murray's arch enemy, Tex and his family. Murray had become involved with their daughter, Bobbie Jean, when he was stationed with the United States Air Force at Wichita Falls, Texas. He felt an unquenchable love for Bobbie Jean Miller, an identical twin sister to Carol Sue. Carol Sue, a vixen, along with her father, mother, Donna, and brothers, Russell and Robert, conspired to place a wedge between the two lovers. They felt the Second Lieutenant, a military person, coming from a modest means life and not from a prominent, rich family that they were accustomed to would not fit into their own life styles. That, and he was a "Yankee" from the North and not a Texan irritated them even more. Though the face of Texas was changing in the 70's one who was not bred on the cattle and oil fields or who did not have that old money was considered a total outsider even though Tejas or Texas meant "Friendly".

Murray had an ally in Bobbie Jean's grandfather, Mike Miller, who took a liking to the Air Force Second Lieutenant, lending him money to buy stock in a new start up airline whose stock soared to three figures per share. Mike guided him through the early grasp of the market, directing him to sell his stock, subsequently; the crusty grandfather offered him a 10% interest in a North Texas oil and gas field. None of this set well with Tex and his family. Mike was a wildcatter in the fifties and was always going against the grain much to his children's dismay.

When that oil and gas field came in, Murray knew his Air Force days would be a thing of the past. He and Bobbie Jean celebrated the future windfall, making love in a Burkburnett, Texas motel, one hot August afternoon. As they were departing the love nest, Tex and his two sons, Robert and Russell, confronted Murray threatening him with bodily harm. Bobbie Jean just stood there not saying anything and walked away. He returned to Wichita Falls and attempted to contact her, with little success. Presumably hidden by her family from him.

Mike meanwhile had a stroke and later died in a questionable fire at his ranch. Tex voided any agreement in the lucrative oil and gas field even though Murray pursued it only to have the local judge, who was in the Miller's pocket, to rule against him in a tumultuous civil trial.

Bobbie Jean was sent away with her sister, out of state and hidden from Murray, even as he contacted Mike's widow, Lula Bell, who could not tell him where his love went. Unfortunately, he felt beaten and gave up the search for Bobbie Jean, always running against a solid wall.

Feeling that he was a total outcast northerner in the southwest, the young Air Force Lieutenant separated , honorably, from the Service, leaving Wichita Falls and bitter memories. Murray headed back to his original home town of Cleveland, Ohio, wishing to forget the past months and what he thought was the loss of Bobbie Jean and definitely, The Millers. A month after returning to Ohio, he received an anonymous letter at his job, postmarked Wichita Falls. In it was a wedding announcement from the local paper with Bobbie Jean's picture showing that she wed a Brett James a week before. Murray was heartbroken yet something told him that all would be better in the future. He believed it, but still wanting to return to Texas, knowing from his time in the Air Force and observing that the state was economically better than in Ohio, he could restart his life. Returning was his goal, although not wishing to look up any of those individuals from that past. His feeling for Bobbie Jean may have changed. He recalled that she never appeared to find him later on, and perhaps was no better than the rest of her family. In his mind, his desire for Texas was greater than a lost love that may not have existed for a young woman he thought had deserted him. Murray managed to work his way back to The Lone Star State. Two years later, he met and married Sheryl in Houston. Together, they started an insurance agency and a family, seemingly moving on with their lives. That is until Michaeleen came in that unbelievable day, giving them good and bad news. While Murray was at the beginning of gaining the riches of the past, Michaeleen suddenly told him that her mother Bobbie Jean and stepdad, Brett James, were killed in an auto accident when she was eight years old.

Murray was temporarily stunned by the loss of someone, from that past, who was still deep in his soul, yet no longer someone he totally loved. Sheryl comforted him for that moment as he regained his composure and wanted to know more of Michaeleen's background.

Michaeleen was now in control of Miller Corporation through inheritances and stock manipulations. After finding the original papers that her great grandfather, Mike had drawn showing Murray was entitled to the lucrative returns she confronted Tex, in his Wichita Falls office, with the intention of going to the authorities exposing him for the fraud he was. What she did not divulge to Murray and Sheryl was a hidden incident at Tex's office. A heated argument began, between the two. He drew a .38 special and threatened her. Although he was larger than Michaeleen, she earned a brown belt in self-defense She kicked the gun from his hand, causing the revolver to discharge striking Tex in the head, ending his long, despicable life. Michaeleen and Tex were the only occupants in the room and no one knew she went there to expose him. When the police came to investigate the shooting, she stated that Tex was already dead after she found him. No fingerprints other than Tex's, on the gun, made it easy indicating he died by his own hand. She offered no other statement on the case and it was closed as a suicide.

As majority stockholder in the vast corporation, Michaeleen wanted to undo the wrongs caused by her scandalous family as she set out to sell off large assets of Miller Corporation and pay not only Murray but a dozen other lesser investors Tex had duped the past 30 years. While the other individuals were cheated out of millions, Murray was the recipient of over five hundred million dollars. Michaeleen had paid off the back taxes assuring that each defrauded member would receive the entire amount that had been withheld from them all those years. With that Michaeleen left the couple, advising them to start their new life changing journey.

While Murray and Michaeleen became close friends, it also drew the ire of Sheryl when she discovered that Carol Sue Miller, who legally went by her married name of Winters, manipulated the relationship of the Murray's daughter, Gina, with her son, Wes, ultimately leading to the marriage of the couple. As uncomfortable as it was at their wedding Murray and Sheryl gave their blessings to the newlyweds.

All appeared to be going well for Murray and his family when tragedy struck, two and one half years later as their 27 year old son, Troy, was found murdered in a cheap, hourly motel in The Montrose section of Houston. While the entire family was devastated, their faith in one another carried them through this ordeal.

Murray and Sheryl knew how fortunate they were, holding hands as he drove. Their prior home in Alief was just a pleasant memory to them, enjoying a totally new life in the upscale Memorial section of Houston. As they journeyed in their Enclave down their dark Memorial neighborhood of high priced homes with a now and then sentry light illuminating the rear yards of the narrow road suddenly, a set of head lights from what appeared to be a van of unknown make and model nearly blinded the couple as it stopped momentarily and sped past them in the opposite direction. Murray looked in the rearview mirror at the strange vehicle when Sheryl careened her neck around, yelling out, "Stop the car!"

Murray was still looking at the tail lights of the van, still puzzled, "What do you see, Sheryl?"

If it were not for a sentry light that bathed the spot where the object landed she would not have given it any thought. "They tossed a large object out. It's strange that anyone would do that in our neighborhood, don't you think?" She insisted, "Go back to where the security light shines on that part of the ditch."

The Enclave was a half block in distance away as Murray thought. "Alright, let's see what was tossed out of the truck." He quickly wheeled the Buick around heading back as he knew his wife was not given to this type of an outburst.

The SUV reached the area where the halogen headlights picked up a brisk movement wiggling in a bubble wrapped package of plastic and tied in duct tape lying on top of the leaf clogged ditch next to the road. The Enclave screeched to a halt surely waking some of the neighbors who had turned in by this respectable hour.

Barely waiting for Murray to get from behind the wheel, Sheryl darted out, flashlight in hand from their glove box, over to see what was trapped in the long bubble wrap. As she drew closer, flashing the light, she let out a shriek, "Murray, there's a body staring up at me, hurray and cut it open!"

He remembered that they were at a sporting goods store, that day, to purchase some hunting equipment for their son-in-law in Florida, Richard Goehring, an avid sportsman. One of the items they picked up for him was an all-purpose knife for filleting fish and small game. Murray knew that they still had the packages, quickly reaching in the back of the vehicle, retrieved the knife, running to the spot where Sheryl was trying to rip off the plastic with her hands. He bent down and began swiftly slicing the plastic away. The contents of the large plastic revealed that of a naked, young, white male in his late 20's, duct tapped on his wrists and ankles, gagged with a multi-colored bandana that Sheryl yanked off only to find another cloth jammed in his throat, reaching in his mouth pulling it out .

The man gasped as he attempted to clear his wind pipe with a choking cough.

Murray barked, "Sheryl, take out a bottle of water from the car and bring it here!" As she left, Murray discovered that the young man was wearing green eye shadow and reddish colored rouge in addition to his pierced ears.

She hurried back, uncapping the plastic bottle, handing it to her husband. He raised the head of the young man, "Take it easy, just drink a little at a time, partner." She did her best to drape the plastic around him for warmth and to shield him from any nosy neighbors.

The young man almost drank the entire bottle. When he appeared to be finished and hydrated he stared up at the rescuing couple. "Thanks, whomever you folks are, but could you untie me, please!" he moaned, "Oh, god, it hurts, Ohhh!"

Sheryl saw the pain in his face, "Cut him loose!"

Murray retorted, "Okay, already, I'm left-handed and this knife is for righties and takes longer." He finally broke the bindings on his wrist and ankles, turning the young man over he gasped just as the last piece was removed, observing that the young man's buttocks was bleeding heavily and a pool of blood had accumulated in the plastic. Murray bent down, cutting the tape on the victim's ankles finding additional blood. "Oh, shit, kid, what the hell happened to you?"

The man appeared passed out from loss of blood. Murray saw that Sheryl was about to throw up. "Hey, hon, get that blanket we have to wrap him in it and get over to Memorial Hospital, like yesterday! The kid is possibly going into shock, don't know, and we may not have time to call for an ambulance to show up."

She ran back to the car and dragged their heavy travelling blanket she used to cover up on long trips. The two rapidly but gently, began to roll the young man into the cover. They bent down and with all their strength carried him to the rear of the SUV pulling him in the back. "Make him as comfortable as you can, Sheryl, and just ride with him as I drive. Will you be okay, my honey?" as Murray's voice had deep concern for her as well as for the victim.

"I'll be okay, but what do we say about his toe nail polish and eye shadow at the hospital?"

Murray climbed behind the wheel shaking his head, "Hon, god if I know, just see if you can remove some of it, I am not positive if the ER people will give a damn to treat him, hopefully, they won't discriminate because of it!"

Sheryl rummaged through her purse to find the nail polish remover and with the rear light began removing the red glow off his hands and feet as the rescued man stirred uneasily looking up at her. "I don't know why you are removing this; a lot of men wear makeup and polish?"

Slightly miffed at him for what she thought was his own doing. "No, kiddo, your eye makeup and cheeks are getting the once over. We are not going through all this for you so you can lay on a gurney in the ER while they figure if you are male or female. Guys don't wear makeup unless they want to be a woman after all!"

"What's your name, ma'am?"

"It is Sheryl. What is yours?"

"Adam Magassey."

Murray was listening to every word as he drove the 10 minutes to the hospital. "Is that Hungarian, Adam?"

The man attempted to rise up to respond only to have Sheryl push him back. "Yes, sir, it is Hungarian. Are you a Magyar as well?"

In what passed for Murray's small knowledge of his heritage he uttered, "Egan, feui." Yes, son, in Hungarian. "My name is Anthony J. Murray. Although, I go by Murray. Our family was from Central Hungary. My great grandparent's name was originally, Maucklansky, taken from their village, Maucklak. Their kids, my grandparents, wanted to Americanize the name, hence, Murray."

The young man rested, once more, on Sheryl's lap as she took Kleenex and water from another bottle and began wiping off the eye shadow and rouge. He was somewhat relieved that these two strangers were caring for him and that he was not an enemy. "At least you don't appear to be with the Hungarian Mafia."

Murray thought that remark was strange. "Hungarian Mafia? What are you talking about?"

Adam did not respond to the question, passing out once more as Sheryl finished, the hospital was in sight.

Pulling up to the Emergency Room entrance, Murray laid on the horn for someone to come out and take Adam in. It only took less than a minute as two orderlies, one black, one Hispanic, came out. "We have a very injured man in our car and he needs medical attention now!" Murray shouted at the men in hospital garb. One came up to the rear passenger door where Sheryl was cradling the half conscious young man now cleaned up facially and foot-wise, by her quick beauty salon work.

Under the bright lights of the ER entrance, the black orderly asked what was the matter with the young man. She briefly gave the background of finding him on the road. The Hispanic orderly, was bringing the gurney and accompanied by a doctor in green scrubs and a stethoscope hanging around his neck. He poked his head in looking at Sheryl and then Murray. "What's wrong with this man?" he strongly questioned the couple, acting as they were at fault for the episode.

"Doctor, ah," Murray wanted to see the name tag of the physician and spotted it. "Doctor Abbott, we found this young man a few miles back on a road and he is very injured...." Murray at that point could only point to Adam's body. "He's bleeding in his behind, Doctor, losing a lot of blood."

Doctor Abbott at this time left the interrogations for later. Motioning to the two orderlies, "Okay, guys, get him in to an examining room now!"

The medics gently pulled him out of the back of the SUV and placed him on to the gurney as blood dripped all over the car and their scrubs. They swiftly wheeled him in to the ER entrance as Dr. Abbott quickly followed disappearing through the electric doors.

Murray looked in disbelief at Sheryl, "What have we got into?"

"Hon, we have to get the car washed, look at all this blood in the car!"

"Look at your clothes!" He grabbed a clean towel and helped his wife remove some of the stains. "Sheryl, please call Jeanette, our secretary, who is staying, temporarily, in the guest room over the garage and have her bring us each clean clothes".

"What about Adam?" worried Sheryl.

"Stay here if the doctor needs anything. I'll go over to that all-night car wash and be back in thirty minutes, by that time Jeanette should have our clothes."

Sheryl went in to the waiting area as Murray left, unaware that he was being observed by others in the cargo van which had dumped off Adam less than 45 minutes earlier.

At the car wash Murray had the attendants wash all the blood out of the back and off the Enclave. As he got back in after the last wheel was wiped he looked over to the street to see the mysterious van parked at the convenience store parking lot. Quickly, Murray got in and dialed Sheryl. "Did Jeanette get there, hon? Don't want to alarm you but the van we saw tossing out Adam might be tailing me."

"Yes, she just arrived but only with my clothes. She forgot yours. For now, contact the police. Those people could be very dangerous; I am very concerned for you."

"Sheryl, I'll be very careful. Remember Cleveland? I've been through this before," boasted a confident, Murray. "Any news on Adam?"

"Too early to find out. He's been in there awhile. Please hurry and get here and be extremely watchful."

With that Murray put the SUV in gear heading back to the hospital while watching the van in his rear view mirror. It pulled out behind him slowly following. Nervously, he arrived in the ER parking area where a security guard was posted. He hailed him as he got out of the Enclave. "Sir, there is a van following me that may have been involved in a crime earlier tonight. Can you call the Houston Police?" He pointed to the van that parked fifty or so yards away.

The occupants in the van saw that Murray acknowledged them to the guard, so they drove off quickly, screeching their tires as in a salute of things to come. With that he hurried into the ER waiting room to find Sheryl already changed, although sporting a concerned look. "Dr. Abbott came out and told me that he removed the object from Adam's butt and contained the bleeding stating that he will have to remain in the hospital for a week or better. Adam is fortunate that his encounter was major, but the outcome was not as bad as his tormenters intended. The nurse with the doctor asked me to admit him and I was going to do that as you came in".

Murray blew out his breath in relief. "Happy that it turned out. You appear to have some heavy thought on this, though, what else did the doctor tell you?"

"This has to be reported to Houston Police Department as it is an attempted harm to a person thing, he told me. They will most likely interview both of us because of it."

Murray expressed his uneasiness on the events, "We need to talk with our young friend to see how deep we are getting into, as I feel that those people in the van meant business and I don't want you to be in the middle of all this crap."

Sheryl was even more upset. "We have no idea why Adam was left to die in that ditch. Maybe he was into drugs or even murder. You have to wonder why he was wearing makeup and nail polish?"

Murray looked at his wife, trying to assess the past hour and a half when they were wistfully driving home reliving their good fortune and suddenly, in the middle of a possible major crime they had nothing to do with. "Yeah, for now, let's put Adam in a private room and talk the talk with him. I hope there is some reason for all this and where we don't need to get involved. Rethinking, maybe with the police involved we may not wish to go further on it."

As they stood there, the tall, gaunt looking, goateed, Dr. Julian Abbott, came out of the emergency room with a grim look. "Mr. and Mrs. Murray, I will be reporting this incident, on Mr. Magassey, to the Houston Police Department as soon as I get into my office here at the hospital. His case is extremely warranted to do so, as this was not a childish prank. The police definitely will want to question you thoroughly on this matter."

Murray attempted to defuse the issue. "Dr. Abbott, we have no idea why Adam was in this condition and really cannot add anything to what we told the nurses and you."

"I am sorry to put you both through this; however Mr. Magassey's case is not an explainable auto or a fall in a home accident. His ankles and wrists show abrasions. And how do you explain a six inch pipe thrust in his anus? This is a felony case and will be investigated by the proper authorities. I know you are planning to admit Mr. Magassey into a private room. We want your information so that HPD can be in contact with you both. Is that clear, Mr. and Mrs. Murray?"

Murray looked away for a second, thinking how to respond, yet he knew they were boxed in. "Yes, Doctor, it is crystal clear."

As the doctor walked down the hall toward his office Murray turned to Sheryl. "Let's admit him into the private room. Have Jeanette take you home. You always can read my mind and knew I would stay here tonight. In the morning, after you get some rest and breakfast in you, bring me some casual clothes and tooth brush, tooth paste and all the goodies to make me smell okay for HPD. I'm camping next to Adam's bed in a chair. If those goons want to kill Adam, I can stop it. They will be back since they figure we brought him here. I picked up my .38 Smith and Wesson, in our secret compartment of the Buick, and have it in my coat. If they want to boogie with me, watch out."

Sheryl was more concerned. "YOU watch out. I wish in many ways we would have gone a different way, as not to be a part of this."

"It was fate that we should save him. Go home for now. I am going to contact Bill St. George. Remember the episode in Cleveland, a year and a half ago, where we went to help our Hungarian friend who was being terrified? Bill will bring Ernie, Rich and Sev. They all "pack"." He offered nonchalantly.

Sheryl did not know the term. "'Pack?', 'Pack' what?"

"You know", as he pointed to his inside pocket where the .38 was nestled.

"I remember that trip to your old Hungarian neighborhood where your friend's bakery was the target of those evil people. You and Bill and those others cleaned it up. You were so heroic."

He looked away, "Yeah, I was very heroic."

With that they went in to admitting and took care of Adam's extended stay at the hospital. Sheryl left with Jeanette for the drive to the Murray home in Cannon Village. Murray went back and hunkered down in a chair next to Adam, who had been sedated and was resting peaceably with three monitors hooked to him. Murray would not have trouble catching some sleep time as he was already totally gassed out. The gun was under his coat now lying across his chest. He slept light and if trouble ensued, he was going to be quick to respond.

On an unseasonal, sticky warm, late March night, the locale unfolds in Houston's gay community, The Montrose. A middle age woman walking her terrier, Hans, came across a grisly find. She was a collector of odds and ends peering through the trash strewn vacant lot. Spotting an item, she picked up a soiled G.I. Joe doll and started to place it in a grocery bag. Suddenly, she eyed a pair of bare feet; duct tied at the ankles, splotches of red outlined the still, lifeless form. Instead of running away at the moment, she was somewhat curious. The lady's pulse began to rise, stifling her emotions, as the form was fully illuminated by a nearby street light that bathed the almost unrecognizable discovery of a male, naked body bound further at the wrists with duct tape, gagged with a colorful red, green and white bandana. She pulled on the leash of her dog, dropping her bag and began to flee the scene. Turning around, the woman recognized the magnetic inscription of a Houston Police cruiser coming her way and waved frantically as she pulled the terrier close to her side. The police car with a lone officer stopped, and he got out. The woman, without losing any breath, rattled on about her expose, pointing to the empty lot, less than a half block away. The cop calmed her down and escorted her and the canine into the rear seat of the police car. They got in and he slowly rolled in the lot's direction. From the back seat of the teal and white, she blurted out, hysterically, "This is it! This is it, officer! Yes, he is in there. Go check it out!"

The patrolman, only on the job two years, dressed in his light blue shirt with HPD on the collar, got out as he switched on the red, white and blue bubble on top of his car. The almost patriotic glow sped patches of lighting far into the field. A solar light in hand, cautiously, the young cop unclipped his glock automatic in readiness of any dangerous outcome. Looking around he spotted the lifeless form. After determining the demise of the corpse he returned to his car and radioed the location and description of call. The dispatcher asked if a doctor should be sent out. Not completely new to this type of issue, a little frustrated and saddened, "Not necessary, a coroner will do fine, Ma 'am."

Soon the entire block suddenly was filled with sirens, bubble lights of a half dozen teal and whites, bringing dozens of residents from their homes and apartments which surrounded the trash strewn lot to view with morbid curiosity on what has almost started to become a weekly occurrence of police intervention in their once quiet neighborhood. Twenty minutes later the medical examiner's van and ambulance rolled up. From the van out stepped late fifties, yellowed haired, veteran of scooping up the dead bodies. Now he encountered a new series of murders in this fourth largest USA city. Armed with his case of chemicals and swab sticks, appeared Dr. Sam Nelson, a close resemblance to T.V.'s Dr. Zorba, from the old series, Ben Casey. He was accompanied by his assistant, Frank Jenks, a hulking 6'6" man with piercing gray eyes that appeared to penetrate even a thick solid piece of steel. Jenks was a former pipefitter turned EMS technician, who wished to have a more adventurous life.

Dr. Nelson, sporting a yellow afro style hair, medium in stature, with semi-tired blue eyes peering over Ben Franklin type glasses, began to pull on the plastic gloves of trade. He bent down over the dead man, and began the grueling examination.

The once somewhat ill lit area now became to see the faint glimmer of daylight, drawing more neighbors and gawkers who were now being cordoned off by Houston's finest as their numbers started to swell. Some of the lawmen were there to see how bad the apparent murder was perpetrated, discussing the different choices among themselves as where the case of the citizens occupying the street and sidewalks. The men in blue had their favorite ideas, as to who may have been behind this ghastly deed. Crazed doper or a vengeful psycho, maybe an abused recently released jail bird.? This area had already been the scene of three previous bodies dumped almost in an identical spot, yet the police had no clear cut serial murderer suspect.

A wailing sound pierced the area, once more, as an unmarked police car screeched to a halt. Stepping out was a western Luchesse boot clad, pressed Levi jeaned with Armani tweed jacketed, Hispanic police lieutenant by the name of Dimas 'Dee' Cavazos, a 26 year veteran of Houston's powerful police force, spending the past 19 years in homicide. Multi-decorated for his numerous heroics, bringing in the worst of criminals that patrolled Houston's highways and byways, always on the job costing him two divorces in the meantime adding, at times, by his checkered personal life. He was astute at cracking the most difficult cases involving Houston's crime stories. With his coat now opened, sporting a .357 magnum strapped to his right side this was beginning to be an all too familiar case as he had officiated on two other times to The Montrose, looking over young, male prostitutes, who trolled the area for their 'Johns'. He ducked under the ever yellow and black lettered crime tape lumbering his near 200 pound frame approaching the coroner, who was almost through with his exam of this latest killing, who looked up at the Hispanic cop. "Well, Dee, it appears we have another weird one," as the doctor's blue eyes bulged.

Almost knowing the answer to an all too familiar question." Dr. Nelson can you give me what you believe occurred ?"

Dr. Nelson ran his hand over his hair. "Naked, bound, duct tapped, at the wrists and ankles, stuffed with a red, white and green bandana stuck down his throat, mouth duct taped. Just like the others, his severed penis, like a German sausage, was in a six inch pipe drilled up his anus.."

"Was he alive when he was assaulted?" the cop slowly asked as he was writing down what the doctor was telling him in his flip pocket notebook.

'Yes, unfortunately, the blood flow from his anus tells us that he was still alive while having it done to him. He was choking to death but probably knew.....oh shit", the doctor trailed off almost in tears.

"I don't even know why in the hell it should even matter to me, Doctor ?" getting tired of the same garbage that pollutes our city streets."

"You're a cop, Dimas, skilled in trying to solve a murder, I hope. You and I are a lot alike. We hate this piss ant thing but some crazy asshole gets off killing white male whores." The tears were wiped away, "Maybe, just maybe, you want to do something about it before..."

Cavazos knew what Dr. Nelson was telling him, the beaten down coroner had a son who was murdered four months earlier just five blocks away in an hourly type hotel. The twenty eight year old man was found under similar circumstances. Greg, his son, was the favorite of their four children and destined for a career as a fashion model. That along with this. Now the fourth body in the same field, all in the past six weeks. Doctor Nelson had a heavy burden and no answers. He knew they were all connected.

The cop felt that Greg and these four had a link but no clues as to tie the five murders together. Going through the motions sighing deeply, "Dr. Nelson, yeah, you're 100 per cent right on but meanwhile give me the sordid details, if you would be so kind."

The medical examiner filled in Lieutenant Cavazos. The body was dumped earlier the previous evening, although killed elsewhere. The bandana was made of European silk somewhere in Eastern Europe. The duct tape, American made, standard buy at Lowes or Home Depot. Similar ages of all the victims, gentlemen of the evening as it appeared. The last part was difficult for Dr. Nelson to say placing his own son in that category.

The Lieutenant heard enough and thanked the coroner who was shaking with grief. Dimas placed his hand on Dr. Nelson's shoulder patting it gently. As the cop moved away toward a half dozen uniformed police who were standing around looking down at the nude, abused corpse, one of the cops was munching on a Slotzskys sandwich while the others enjoyed a taco dispensed from a now parked taquirera truck where the driver was taking advantage of the notoriety of the early morning. The police seemed oblivious of the dead man, finding the matter as all too common. Some of them finding a little humor in this tragic discovery,

Lieutenant Cavazos, his chin jutting out in disgust, viewing his fellow officers standing around joking and eating fresh tamales and empanadas sold by the strolling Mexican vendor in a beat up multi-colored former bread truck. "You men, call yourselves the protectors of the public how can you enjoy eating here with this tragic event of finding another one of our citizen's dead?"

A pudgy officer wearing the chevrons of a sergeant only shook his head at Dee. "Cavazos this stupid ass deserved what he got coming to him. He knew of the danger in this deal and ignored it for what money he thought he would get. Just another tight assed prick or should we say 'prickless' prick? Do any of us care about this damn guy? Strangely, yeah. I am positive he had a family who once loved him and now will light candles in church for his worthless soul."

Some of the other officers echoed similar comments. Cavazos closed his eyes and shook his head, then looked over at Dr. Nelson who had heard the dreadful comments. Forlorn, they only cast similar looks and thoughts to one another, and then each returned to their own tasks.

The Lieutenant bent down to view the almost non-tattooed body, except for a small heart with the inscription 'M Luvs A' on his right ankle. This young man appeared to be in his mid to late 20's sporting a gold stud in his right ear lobe. There was a six inch abdominal scar on his right side, probably from an appendectomy. He had a deep, no tan line body. Maybe he was going to a tanning salon which the cop figured would give him a lead on this man and others who knew him. Scratches and bruises indicate his struggle to ward off his attackers before being subdued and tied. The white, red, and green bandana lay in a plastic evidence bag as was a bloody pipe in an even larger see through plastic bag. Dr. Nelson had just placed the copper colored, rough edged instrument of torture in it after removing it from the rectum of the murdered man. In an ice chest next to the bags, Cavazos almost lost his late enchilada dinner when he saw another clear plastic bag containing what was a bloody 7 inch penis. The cop bent down, once again, and carefully turned over the body and with his flashlight shined it in on the bright red groin area where a lack of organ for the young man had once been attached, now only a bloody dried stub remained. Even for his most dreaded find over the years these similar finds had to be the worst. This time, though, he almost began to vomit, but stood up quickly and looked to the star studded early morning sky. While Lieutenant Cavazos sympathized with Dr. Nelson's loss of his son, he wanted to escape this hell hole and head home to some tequila and a warm bed, perhaps with a woman beside him. As he turned to get into his car, a rookie blue came up to him. "Are you Lieutenant Cavazos?"

Dimas stood and looked at the slick sleeved officer, already tired of the bullshit there and waiting for some wise-cracking response of the scene. "Yeah, ok, I'm Lieutenant Cavazos, so?"

The young cop sensed hostility. "Just passing a message to you sir. I do not want to get in your face, alright?"

Cavazos softened his attitude. "Sure, go ahead."

"Captain Short wants you to come in at 9:00 this morning, Lieutenant."

The older cop looked at the young cop, sensing more work from his captain. "Hey, rook, with all this shit going on and here it's almost five, my captain wants my ear, and I probably am not going to get rest since a full report has to be on his desk. I've dodged bullets and fists of the streets the past 25 and counting years, missed my boys ball games, daughter's recitals, gone through a couple of divorces. Kid, you sure you want to be part of all this garbage?"

The young cop only looked at him with intensity now, unafraid of this veteran cop, "Look Lieutenant, I went through the HPD Academy, have had my share, in my early times with the bad guys, I have a wonderful wife, two kids, I'll make it without missing their ball games or dance contests and my wife and I will survive. It is a different time from your generation."

Cavazos looked at the young blue. "In this light, boy, I could swear I see you wearing rose-colored glasses. If so, keep them on" because you ain't seen nothing, yet." With that he got into his car leaving the young cop smiling in his dust.

As Murray awoke next to Adam's hospital bed, the young man greeted him, managing a smile as he ate a breakfast of toast, scrambled eggs, and coffee. "Well, good morning, Mr. Murray. Are you as hungry as I am this morning?"

Murray was a little put out with the question as he tried to wake up from the grogginess of the past eight hours, four of which, as he glanced at his Breitling/Bentley watch, were sitting upright in a chair guarding this smiling practical stranger. "I could use some of that coffee." He pushed up out of the chair and slightly staggered toward the carafe, finding an extra cup. "Well, the nurse was considerate thinking I may need some 'get up and go' liquid this morning."

Adam agreed. "Yes, I awoke from all these things in my arm and fingers and saw you peacefully zonked out. You were here to watch over me, weren't you?"

As the morning sun started to break through casting a yellow hue over the hospital bed and the young injured man, Murray looked at him as he sipped the hot, caffeine induced liquid. It seemed only hours before seeing Adam trussed up last night and now hooked to three or so vitals with the machines wheezing together. "Yes, Adam, I felt strong that those characters in the van were coming back. They followed us here and sped off when I pointed their truck out to the hospital security guy outside. "What is more important, partner, is what you were doing wearing makeup, nail polish, winding up tied, gagged, naked in that leaf clogged ditch?"

Adam finished the last of his morning meal, and as he peered over his cup of coffee, cleared his throat. "Since you and your wife saved me last night I figure you are owed that much. You may not wish to believe the entire story as it is surreal, but when I was tied up in that bubble wrap you came out of the blue haze of the night."

Murray was not up to an introduction, "You probably should cut to the chase on it as I know the police are going to question us both on this and our stories should sound on the up and up, okay?"

Adam nodded. "I figured as much as that Dr. Abbott was a stickler to the code of the hospital law or whatever governs a place such as this. I believe I owe each you and your lovely wife, who caressed me on her lap while stroking my hair, an explanation as you attempted to sort out things. I am not lily white and you know that. I heard you mention that you never met a male escort before. Do we have 20 minutes to hear my life story?"

"Adam, don't know if we have two minutes or twenty, shoot!"

The young man began by retelling his birth in a small village outside of Budapest in April, 1978. His father was Anthal. Mother, Ilona. The couple always wanted to come and live in the United States so they picked more conventional names for their children. Ilona had given birth to four children, his younger brother, Ryan, sisters, Melanie and Melissa. Anthal, a successful attorney, was killed in a boating accident near Szilad. Ilona struggled to raise the family after that as she had no professional skills. Reaching for a lifeline, she married his law partner, Louis B. Kolezy in 1986. Ryan committed suicide under suspicious circumstances at age 26. Melanie, 28, now living with her mother and stepfather, Louis. Melissa, 31, was living in Austin with her husband and two children. Three of the siblings had one thing in common, abuse by their step-father. Due to the over protectiveness of Ilona, Melissa was spared the physical part of his lecherous behavior. In 1987, Louis decided to come to Houston on the guidance of an old friend from his University of Budapest days, a successful attorney, who now resided in Houston and had a downtown law firm. The entire family immigrated to their new surroundings. Kolezy would become enormously successful and be known as a high powered attorney with many connections throughout the Southwest. Even the local judicial system as well as the authorities had great admiration for him. He was riding on top after winning a gigantic tobacco settlement followed by an even bigger oil disaster settlement. Little did anyone know of his physical abuse to Adam, Ryan, and Melanie? He also had a second life. The connections in Hungary and Czech Republic where he teamed up with his partner Imre Rabb in a large scale pornography industry, employing over 100 males grossing over 250 million dollars a year. At sixteen, Adam escaped his tortuous environment only to start and have a similar operation in the United States. His empire was divided among an adult movie company, video stores, provocative adult and clothing magazines, adult garment manufacturing, hotels and resorts, restaurants and 'meeting bars' all under the umbrella of his corporation named MABB which inferred as Mount A Buddy's Behind. The various businesses under this flagship, grossed annually, over $400 million dollars. Louis wanted it and Adam would not sell out to his stepfather. Kolezy devised a scheme to push his stepson out, in a deadly way. Through his step-daughter, Melanie, who resided with him and her mother, Kolezy learned that Adam had a will, naming at the time, his brother, Ryan, and two sisters to inherit MABB in the event he died. Allegedly, Kolezy faked Ryan's suicide. He was discovered by Ilona, hung in his bedroom closet. Even though the chair that was used supposedly by her distraught son was three inches longer than he could have ever reached. The police did not investigate that fact due to Kolezy's standing and his insistence that Ryan was taking illegal drugs that lead up to the incident. Melissa had two attempts on her life, where she lived, in Austin. One was a deliberate episode of an unknown driver running her off the road in the hilly section of the city. Then the break in by two masked intruders where she was saved by the home security alarm going off and her husband Alan Reynolds, pulling his Winchester and firing off a half dozen rounds staving off the attack and sending them running for their lives.

Murray listened intently to Adam's dialogue. "Why do you think Melanie will succumb to Kolezy's tricks on all this? From what you say, she is a grown woman and your mother won't allow this to go on. Right?"

"Murray, Melanie is a kept, irresponsible girl at 28. Louis is tapping her daily for sex. She gets a lot of perks for spreading her well-splayed legs. He has her doped up at times when she tries to avoid his advances. My mother hides behind tranquilizers and Tito's vodka. Besides, I know my brother wanted out of that River Oaks physical assault kingdom. He was going to move in with me in my West University home. Louis knew about it from Melanie and he wanted to continue his physical dominance over Ryan. Melanie heard them argue that morning before he was murdered. Once Ryan left, Melanie would follow, I believed at the time. Now, I am not sure about her."

Murray had an earful but needed to get more information on why Adam wound up in the ditch. "Okay, so you are this, former male stripper, gigolo, mogul at MABB where you are being pursued by your step-father who wants your business, your weak brother may have been murdered, your one sister is easy, and Momma Kolezy is a pill popping, boozer. Alright, so why were you dolled up as a male hooker with makeup and toe nail polish?"

Adam was put out with some of Murray's descriptions on his family. "You saved my ass. Okay, you just don't appear too concerned about what else is happening! Maybe you should head out and leave me to the task of bringing my step father to justice for all this."

Murray got another cup of coffee from the decanter, throwing some Sweet and Low in as he stirred the black leaded concoction, looked down on this slightly confused refuge in a white hospital gown. "Are you always going to be this defensive, son, and acting like no one gives a damn? Do you think if I wanted to wash my hands on all this, my back would not be stiff from trying to sleep in that chair next to you? I got The Task, once we pulled you out of the leaves and plastic. You were my responsibility to the end of all this. I don't know all there is to what you are about or The Whys." With that Murray went over and compassionately laid his hand on Adam's shoulder. I really want to understand what I am getting into, that's all. Coppice?"

Adam was disarmed at that. "I apologize for being so uptight when.... I want Louis brought to justice for killing Ryan and the attempt on Melissa's life."

Murray stepped back in." Hey, don't worry about my feelings being hurt. You have suffered a lot in the past, 12-13 or so hours. Let's get on with your story."

"I left River Oaks when I was sixteen staying with a good friend and his family. Again, my life is a shade on the dark side. Certainly, it has not been straight. Louis always said I was born to be a male whore so make the most of it. He called me Damaged Goods. No one would ever want me for anything good other than a bed partner. He wanted to send me to his partner in Pest, Hungary as late as Ryan's funeral. Sell MABB to him and make a lot of money at his clubs because my body was worth a million dollars."

"Kolezy sounds like a real sweetheart." Murray arched his eyebrows at that description. "Damaged Goods? Hey, no one is allowed to say you are right or wrong in judging you. I am not in that place. I can't tell you how to lead your life. Can't you just get out of what you are doing? What puzzles me now about your deal is why if you are this multi-millionaire stud, you wind up doing, I guess, a trick, for whomever you made yourself up for last night. Why do a cheap stunt like that when you can have the world by the gonads?"

"I haven't fucked anyone like that in years. My friend Mark is still in the business and who I am concerned about getting into too much trouble with all this and doing drugs could not do a $25,000 night with these two guys. He had the runs and you know how can one give a great performance when shit is running out your butt hole? Besides, it is a great rush to give pleasure to others. No one is supposed to get murdered or roughed up, although in my earlier days I had a close call or two from 'bunkhouse bullies' who wanted to tie me up with barbed wire while they wore their ten gallon hats and Tony Lama's with spurs, cutting into my thighs."

Murray was starting to wince very uncomfortably at Adam's intro to his lifestyle. Maybe he did not wish to hear about all of it but had little choice as he opened the door to it. More leaded coffee was needed. "Wait a little. Need some more java to hear this." He stumbled to the coffee pot and drained the last of the brown strong liquid, thinking how glad that Sheryl was not there to hear the sordid details of being damaged goods. Yet, he could sympathize at Adam's tale. Something he himself had pushed back into his memory of what happened to him as a nine year old.

Adam was playfully grinning at his new friend's uneasiness. "A little too tender for your virgin ears?"

Murray was being challenged. "I can take it, kid, spit out the rest before the cops come in and question us, although I am slightly confused, again. With your buddies getting killed and suspecting that your stepfather was behind it, why did you not go to the police?"

"That is something I was intending to do after Wyatt was found, the second of three. I figured that being the head of MABB, the police might just shrug it off as Louis is so highly thought of and with the cloud of how Ryan died, as he was judged as a drug addict. My chances of convincing the law would be nil. I made the wrong decision believing it was all coincidental because Wyatt was too wild and took too many chances with the wrong 'johns', ah, his clients."

"Too bad you did not go to the cops and try, though. Someone in HPD has to be not on Kolezy's side and they could have looked into it and questioned him, maybe stopping him from doing anymore killings. Or is it, Adam, you enjoy living with danger?"

"Murray, you probably are right. I was up to doing both guys at the motor inn on the Beltway, but intending to give the twenty- five grand to Mark, who always needed money. Maybe I did it to see if I could still go two hours or so, at a stretch. With three of my guys getting killed, for some stupid reason, being in danger of being the fourth never entered my mind. It is a high with me without being on wacked out drugs. Then after the first twenty minutes I knew they were there to kill me, not anything else. It got brutal with two other guys coming in and overpowering me. I blacked out after getting kicked and slugged all over. Last thing I remember was being trussed up like a Thanksgiving Turkey. I am such a lofus, or who yea, dumb fuck. I deserve what happened to me but God heard my prayers sending you and your wife to save me."

Murray was beginning to see the picture and his part in all this but asked, "Who were these guys? Could you I.D. them in a lineup?"

"Yeah, now that I can hindsight it. Hungarian Mafia."

Murray shook his head in disbelief at that. "What? You said that before in our SUV. What makes you believe it?"

"It was their accents, facial features and clothes. The first two were Eastern Euros, young, maybe 20, 21. One went by Luka, the other Janos who said he was John but let his Hungarian name slip. When the other two came in as we struggled, Luka referred to them as Drago and Dimitri and their speech gave them away. They were part of my beloved step father's Hungarian Mafia as Melanie told me he started up a few years back."

As Murray was trying to sort out this latest part of Adam's saga, Sheryl walked in, after Jeanette dropped her off. She gave Murray a kiss and handed him a duffle bag of his more casual clothes. "I certainly am rested after all that doings last night," she addressed to both her husband and Adam. "How did you sleep last night, honey and was yours, restful, Adam?"

Murray scrambled through the bag and looked up, "Thanks for the clothes and toiletries, Sheryl, I slept as well as can be expected. No problems from "THE HUNGARIAN MAFIA!"

Sheryl started to laugh, "That again? I have been married to this Hungarian for over thirty years and he has never mentioned that part of his heritage. Are they makers of chicken paprikash or dobos tort?"

Adam was disappointed. "Neither of you believe me."

Murray quickly filled his wife on what Adam related to him minutes earlier that caused her to strangely react to the fallen adult entertainment business person. She went over to him and tenderly touched his exposed arm gently massaging it, that he, too, was surprised. "You have certainly been through a lot Adam and my husband and I hope you will recover from all this."

He looked up at her smiling broadly, batting his brown eyes. "To answer your question, yes I had pleasant dreams of a very attractive woman aiding me, cradling me in her lap, stroking my brown hair."

Murray became a little jealous. "Adam, for now, stick to guys."

Adam looked over to Murray, stifling a laugh. "Actually, in my dream this beautiful woman kept telling me 'you have to change your life and become a Romeo to all women!' When I was in that bubble wrap I prayed to God that if he saved me from all this I would sell out MABB. It may have cost the life of my brother, and three friends, as well. Yes, even though I have made countless tens of millions, it has not been worth it."

"Worth it for what, Mr. Magassey?" a voice came through the door wearing a badge around his neck. It was Lieutenant Dimas Cavazos. "Yes, tell me what that last statement was about?"

Adam looked at the Murray and Sheryl perplexed that this booming voice was barging in on their conversation, and then spied the badge. Murray grunted, "The police have arrived, I assume."

"I am Lieutenant Dimas Cavazos!" He had a touch of hostility to his voice, one of disapproval. "Dr. Abbott from the ER turned in a report this morning and I am here to get the details. I want your full cooperation, if that is possible?" With that he took out his spiral notebook from his sports coat. He filled in the name, address and phone numbers of Adam. Turning to Murray and his wife, "Now who might you two folks be?"

Murray did not like the tone the cop was portraying. "For the record, it is Anthony J. Murray and this is my wife, Sheryl M. Murray. We met up with Mr. Magassey last evening and brought him to the hospital."

Cavazos nodded, 'ok' and began to focus on Adam and his monitors. "Do you believe in God, son?"

Adam knew this line as he heard it a dozen times before from so called 'do gooders'. "Yes, Lieutenant Cavazos, I do. Why do you ask?"

Placing the notebook down, with a snarl. "Boy, because you came extremely close to his final judgment last night. A person of your type that is, if I am not mistaken, a gentleman of the evening. Yeah, the boys in the local jail would like you. You would really find love."

Murray had heard plenty and sprang to Adam's defense. "Hey, Lieutenant Cavazos, what's the beef? Did you get up on the wrong side of the bed today? You haven't allowed this young man a chance to tell you what actually happened. You don't know him and here you are running to judgment. Are YOU, God?"

Cavazos lips quivered wanting to lash out to this defender but thought better of it. "I'll get to you later, Mr. Murray and your wife." With that he turned his attention to the main reason he was there, thinking in the back of his mind, 'Was this guy another near victim of the Montrose Murders?' "What happened, Mr. Magassey that placed you in this hospital bed?"

Adam hesitated looking over at Murray, shrugging his upper body almost pulling out the vital sign needles from his wrist. "I was at a venue with these men who wished for me to buy a painting they wanted to sell at my art gallery in The Montrose. We debated the cost for what they wanted to sell it for, an argument ensued, and voila, I wound up here."

Murray was surprised at that statement even though he hardly knew Adam, but an 'art gallery'? Cavazos looked at Murray.

"Are you bull shitting me, Mr. Magassey? C'mon, an art gallery? All this was due to selling a piece of artwork? You had a six inch pipe rammed up your asshole!"

Adam, at that insinuation, became visibly angry. "So far, Lieutenant Cavazos you have come in here spouting off instead of trying to understand things. You have to be a great piece of work at the station house!"

The Lieutenant softened his approach. "I don't hang around the station house much, too busy investigating persons who get murdered or wind up like you. So, you own an art gallery. Where?"

"It's Duffy's on Westheimer near Dunvale. I 'm a co-owner of the business and know art. These guys tried to get me to put this lousy reproduction on my wall. I refused, things got out of hand just like I said. Don't know why they chose the pipe thing!"

The cop started to put his notebook away. "So, that's your story. "Suddenly he slammed the spiral down on the tray. "God damn, Magassey, you are yanking my chain. I don't believe one damn word of this!"

Adam stood his ground. "Too bad, Lieutenant, that's my story. You can choose to believe what you want."

Cavazos eyes bulged; the veins from his neck were bursting on fire. "You know before I came here some woman found this guy in a vacant lot just like you with wrist and ankle lacerations. A pipe was up his kazooed ass. A green, white and red bandana jammed down his throat and his dick was severed and placed in that pipe. I am faced with a serial killer and you are playing fucking games with me, you're such a dumb.., I don't know. You dodged a gold bullet last night. How much is it going to take for you to wake up, boy?"

Adam appeared to quit breathing as he took in the words of Lieutenant Cavazos. The moments lasted agonizing minutes as he looked at the cop who was waiting for the right answers. Finally, he managed to blurt out an agonizing question. "What did this man look like?"

The veteran cop knew he had Adam at that point wanting to give him a gut wrenching description. "6'1" around 175, light brown hair, abdominal scar, gold earring in right lobe. Oh, yeah a pretty red and blue tattoo of a heart with 'M loves A' on his right ankle."

Adam took a deep breath, leaned back in his bed and closed his eyes.

Cavazos wanted to go in for the knife cut and figuratively thrust it up Adam's intestines. "Hit a sour note, Mr. Magassey? Familiar victim, huh? He joins three others who were lying in front of the medical examiner, his golden ass on the cold metal table, the past six weeks. Ever go to an autopsy as the coroner or his assistant start cutting up a dead body?"

Murray and Sheryl were in a haze unable to understand the expanse of the cop's sharp calculating interrogation. Adam looked out the window as the sun cast it's shadows over the parking garage , choked up at the thought that Mark was on a slab, dead, never going to be in his life, yet, a nagging part pierced his thoughts that his once lover had sold him out to Kolezy silencing him from betrayal. Turning back to Lieutenant Cavazos he gained his composure. "I have nothing further to say to you, Lieutenant. You have my version." With that he turned over in his element exposing his opened gown with a heavy bandage covering his posterior.

Murray knew Adam was stunned with Lt. Cavazos' vivid description and wanting to end this inquisition. "Well, I guess that's a wrap, Lieutenant," grinning at the cop who gave it all and yet was handed a stunning defeat.

Cavazos landed back on his feet. "Not actually, Mr. Murray, as the cop flashed a challenged look, back at him. "What part do you and your wife play in this game of charades?"

Murray snapped back, "Are you calling all this a game, Lieutenant? My wife and I were driving home last night, found Adam, laying in the ditch and brought him here. That is it!"

Cavazos shook his head, sarcastically grinning, at temporarily being 'stone walled' by this. "Mr. Murray, this is not some fun game that you play. You are a total amateur. The nurses told me you camped out next to his bed in a chair. Why? The doctors and staff were capable and he was monitored."

"Just wanted to keep my eye on him in the event some....Something he needed and the nurses were not around."

"Like protecting him from those 'art experts'?"

"Well they did get out of hand and you have to be prepared."

"Sure, Mr. Murray, like what were you going to do if they came through that door? Throw the bed pan at them?"

Murray did not want to divulge that his coat pocket held a .38 special and decided to drop the conversation in favor of another way. "Guess, now, Lieutenant, you are finished with all of us for the time being."

The Lieutenant turned toward Adam who was still facing the other way. In a cold voice, the cop uttered, "Mr. Magassey, this was no art deal. Stripping someone naked, tying them up and jamming a pipe up the ass is hard to believe. No, you and this dead guy in Montrose have a connection and I will find it. When I do, you're going to wish that the pipe did its job!"

With that he turned to the couple. "If you folks had anything to do with all this, other than being a Good Samaritan, I'll hit you hard. Understand? Have a good day!"

As Cavazos strolled out the door, Murray offered a sarcastic, "Via Condios, Lieutenant!"

The cop stopped short and began to turn around to retort Murray's seemingly irreverent farewell, but thought better of it and continued on his way.

Dimas paused outside the room in anguish, tired, up all night, little sleep; he realized he came down too hard on the young injured man. Perhaps, he had enough of being a cop, as his second wife remarked to him,' living in a sewer', at times. The murder cases, especially the latest, had started to eat at him.

Murray turned his attention to Adam. "He's gone you can roll back over. You are in need of some assistance on this, my young friend."

Adam flipped over quickly from that remark, sitting up straight in his bed, he pointed his left hand punctured with the vital needles in it, "Stay out of this Murray, you've done enough just saving my life. My wicked stepfather is a son of a bitch and he will be taken out by someone soon, I hope. That is before my sister, Melanie, becomes his next victim."

Sheryl was taking all this in and suggested, "Can't you just get her from their home when Kolezy leaves in the morning?"

Adam solemnly nodded. "No way, Melanie is constantly drugged and boozed up. She is not willing to go without our mother who drains one vodka bottle after another."

"Only way then, Sheryl, continued, is to sell MABB. Adam you may be worth millions but has it been worth all the grief you and your family suffered?"

Murray stepped in to back up his wife. "You contemplated selling MABB. Now is the time to act. Then go after Kolezy and make him pay for what he has done. You know Lieutenant Cavazos said, "Four killings in serial fashion. Four young men and you KNOW the last one, don't you, Adam?"

Adam sadly acknowledged slowly shaking his head. "It's Mark... Mark Carlson, the friend or should I say, one of my 'boys'. It was supposed to be his trick. I took his place."

Murray looked over at Sheryl. "Are you positive you want to stay and hear this, hon?"

Sheryl was actually eager to hear the story. "Yes, as they say, 'Wild Horses Couldn't Drag Me Away', now."

Murray smiled at his wife acknowledging that in their years of marriage, especially the last three, she had witnessed a lot of out of the ordinary events and that even this revelation would not shock her. "Let's have it on THE BOYS part, Adam. Who are they or were they? And....ah, what did they do for you?"

"I can see you are not going away, you know that your hands may get dirty on all this. Here goes. The others, MY BOYS, Santos Gonzalez, Wyatt, David, oh David. Well he went missing. Then Eric Whitely, now Mark. They were my print models, among others. I cannot forget Derick. God, he had a future! Still have a unofficial stable including Lance, Cody, and Justin, a couple of others that I am weaning or attempting to wean off finding them regular jobs or positions with MABB. Guys I went through high school with, on the diving team or soccer team and then we went to UT in Austin and SMU in Dallas, as students who found ways to make a lot of money with older gentlemen. I struck gold myself and made seed money for MABB, lived the high good life with these near seniors. Two died on me and I picked up a lot of loot in their wills. I wanted, too, as I deserved it! Some of my boys were almost as fortunate. Officially or unofficially my friends were and are part of the company. It made it almost legitimate having them as escorts. No one was supposed to get hurt until Louis started to kill them. After David disappeared and assumed, possibly dead, I pulled the plug on most of it. Some of the BOYS had clients on the side and I could not stop that but MABB was not going to furnish any more good times for the subscribers in our magazine. You don't realize having a network of hot guys how much money is to be made. Surprisingly, we had a huge following of females. Sixty-five per cent love and enjoy looking at male porn. Louis may have caught on to this and that is the reason he wants MABB. Mark's gig was to be his last and dummy me I was going to toast it off for him! Twenty-five grand was the number from these two rich kids, supposedly, wanting to do it."

Sheryl had enough. "Look, I need to use the ladies room down the hall. You two finish up..." as she drifted out of the room.

Murray was in a quandary, not totally sure of what he heard. "So, Kolezy is murdering your employees? Is that a reason not to confide in Lieutenant Cavazos? But then, you are telling us that part is gone. Is that correct? So Kolezy has killed now four men in his quest to win MABB. Well, that is...hell, I don't know, now. He attempted to kill your sister, Melissa. Where does she fit into getting rid of her?"

"Melissa, Melanie, and Ryan were slated to take over MABB if anything happened to me. Louis by getting rid of my brother and doing the same to Melissa, leaves Melanie, who he has wrapped up at the River Oaks mansion. I have the best private detective agency in Austin and all of Texas, guarding Melissa, Alan, her husband, and their two children. It's 24/7 and they can't be bought off."

Sheryl came back in looking a little wearily. "What have I missed, guys? I've been thinking since listening to the first part that I have a different view of all this."

Murray filled her in on the last part. He then confided, "Look, I believe we can help Adam, hon."

Sheryl was more cautious. "This is getting to be past dangerous in our lives. It could spill over into our three daughters' and their families as well. We're just everyday citizens who have businesses to run, not a wanna be detective couple, hunting down murderers and other criminals on a fictitious television show. As Lieutenant Cavazos made it plain, "This is not a game for amateurs. Personally, Adam needs to change his life style, sell MABB and allow the police to go after Louis Kolezy and NOT US."

Adam concurred wholeheartedly. "Sheryl's 100 per cent right on, Murray. Louis is too much for the three of us combined."

Murray was unconvinced. "Ok, so you mentioned Kolezy has a lot of people on his side. None of them are aware he is some sort of a czar in the porn world over in Eastern Europe. If we can uncover evidence of the murders and his connection in Budapest through you, Adam, bring it to the authorities, then who would support him at that time? From there he goes to Huntsville and due justice. Right now I am very concerned on who protects you here at the hospital."

Adam looked up at Murray in an attempt to dissuade him from interceding. "Look, Anthony, I can't allow you to mix into this with Sheryl and your family. You are all at grave risk. This is totally my responsibility. Do you believe with my background that the police are going to go after my step father? I was a male porn star and stripper who has turned into a CEO of a major 400 million dollar conglomerate. Mark, Eric, Santos, Wyatt all worked for MABB. Because of that they are dead!" Then sadly, he choked up a little, "And perhaps, Derek. I just don't' know how he died...only. God, what have I done?"

Murray leapt at the chance to rebut Adam's statement. "They died on their own. Maybe Mark turned you in for the money. Right at this moment, you need protection. I have a very close friend who is well connected and his people are up to this battle."

Sheryl shook her head negatively as she interrupted. "Bill St. George's group? Rich Fedor, a former Secret Service and FBI agent. Ron Tanski, Viet Nam vet. Then the soldier of fortune, Sev Fedor, drummed out of The Secret Service and The Green Berets. Then there is Ernie Petrovich, yeah, I am positive he has a few scalps on his belt. That and the scar on his forehead."

Adam liked the 'scalps' comment. "Is he an American Indian that walks around with war paint and rides a palomino horse?"

Murray thought a while thinking of a follow up funny story of Ernie but could not. "No, Ernie is Hungarian-Russian. Sheryl knows that Ernie just talks of brandishing a knife to cut off opponent's hair since he has a receding hair line. And... the scar was from his past, well that came when his close friend, Bob Taylor, almost bought it in Chicago."

Adam was still not convinced that Murray had the power to go up against Kolezy. "So, perhaps you have this group of men that possibly could stand up to Louis, but why are you going that extra mile for someone like me that you found on the road?"

Murray looked up at the drab ceiling of the room, started to get a little emotional. "Like you, Adam, terrible things happened to me starting in the third grade of a Catholic school. A sixth grader whose name was Louie began all of it for me. We all called him Louie the Leach. He, along with two of his buddies pulled my pants down and assaulted me. He also molested our next door neighbor, Jeanne, as in my case, he got away with it. The boys in the neighborhood chased him to his house two blocks away. He got behind his big uncle who took a sledge hammer to three of the kids. After that, they moved away because they were renting. No one called the cops. The parents of the girl were embarrassed."

Adam was intrigued by the tale and wanted to hear more about Murray's trauma. "So what happened to you that day in school?"

"Sister Mary yelled at us and she told us to quit playing with the devil and get into class. Even though I was crying she slapped me for being a sissy. It did not end there for me. A family member continued to fondle me and taunt me to do things. He said it would feel good and enjoyable. In attempting to tell my parents they only thought it was horseplay until I showed them what was happening. They, too, could not handle it and said for me to keep quiet as I was violated and was shameful for it to happen. I guess, you could say I was damaged goods."

Sheryl was dumbstruck at first then rushed to her husband. "You never told me that in all the years.....I never would have called you, 'Damaged Goods. I love you so much!"

Adam started to understand the reason for Murray's intercession. "I know why you are trying to help me. Tell me, though, how long did it go on for you?"

Murray viewed this younger man who knew both the physical and more important, the psychological pain of abuse. "It was at least six, seven years and one day I had enough of his reminding me of the school rape and the groping. I was mad enough and would not take it anymore, so I kicked him in the balls, telling him I would kill him if he ever touched me again. I knew it was horrifically wrong and realized it could lead to an escalation of weirder sexual experiences. I want to get rid of the Louis' in this world and have closure for all of us, especially Jeanne."

Adam knew then that Murray was going to carry on the fight against Kolezy, but wanted to make things clear to the couple. "You probably believe that my constant allowance of Louis' lust for his step kids, including me, led to what you referred to, a higher more sexual gratification, escalating to my seemingly sleazy male adult business that I built up these past 10 years. The video shops, gay and lesbian bars in 20 cities, the upscale hotels in five other places. Yes, I sold my body to gain the vengeance on older men just like Louis. They died with a smile on their worthless faces and left me tens of millions of dollars that built MABB. My corporation has made millions for me and for a lot of charities. I am winning over the guys to go straight and placed them in management jobs. No, those old queen fags really did it. I never wanted to sniff drugs up my nose or shoot up for highs nor get drunk on Cuervo and Jell-O shots. All the money except for giving it away to worthwhile causes was invested to someday rival Louis and beat him at his own game."

Sheryl was now concerned after listening to Adam's revelation. "You need to sell MABB to get Louis away from you and your family. What will happen to your friends and the charities?"

"I have spun off a company to manage that. I knew someday I had to change my life and it has come to this. No, I want to go straight, date woman, marry, have children, and live in a vine-covered cottage with a picket fence surrounding it."

Murray was totally on Adam's side and wanted to proceed. "I know someone who will buy MABB for your price. You say it is worth $400 million? Yeah, this person has the juice for it and always looks for the opportunity to invest in a solid return. It is solid, right?"

Adam was cautiously anxious as his heart began to pump stronger. "Definitely, it is a solid business. You really have someone? Is it a man or woman?"

Murray was surprised as he cast a smiling look from Sheryl. "That is slightly amazing that you would not just ask how much does this 'guy' have? Can HE afford $400million?"

Adam was a little smug in replying. "It is a woman, right?"

"Well, there was a fifty -fifty chance it could have been Donald Thump or Warren Buffering or an old friend and early mentor from the past, Peter B. Lucas of Aggressive Insurance fame. Of course, it is a woman.

Why though do you figure a dame would like MABB?"

"As I stated before, a lot of women enjoy male porn. Stats we ran at MABB show sixty-two percent of them buy male on male videos, frequent the male strip clubs, lesbian bars, buy our magazines, even though we are not Playboy or Playgirl we run a nice third in the circulation polls. If you thought it was Robin and George in the morning. It is not. What is amazing is that most of them, another 60 plus per cent are straight. Ages run 26 to 62. They have the bucks to spend. Some are bored. Most are looking for that thrill that is different and we deliver that in the videos, in print, on the stages around our venues. Yeah, a woman who has the loot really loves MABB. I'm really cool with the $400 mil tag, Murray, trot her over."

Sheryl looked at her husband strangely. "Are you referring to Michaeleen, darling? I don't quite picture her ordering male videos and paying that amount of money for an adult business. She has an oil empire and is well thought of with her peers. She will take a lot of convincing."

Murray actually had someone who was close to Michaeleen in mind. She would be his lead in to help him sell the idea, but he did not want to explain it to his wife at the moment knowing how she might feel. Scratching the back of his head and looking at Adam. "This young gal has a lot of money and connections. I will get back to you on the details. Meanwhile, you take care; listen to the medical folks here. I lined up a guy who does THINGS for Sheryl and me, Clay Kirby. I called him early this morning, before bedding down next to your bed. He'll be here to watch over you while we are gone." With that they bid their goodbyes as Kirby came up to them.

Clay Kirby was a heavy set former deputy sheriff from West Bend County. Although in his late 60's he moved swiftly, wearing ruffled Levis and dirty brown Tony Lama boots. A bulge under a matching Levi jacket hid a .45. He was always ready for action. Murray and Clay went back into Adam's room. After introduction to Adam, Kirby excused himself stating he would be walking the halls and peering into adjacent rooms and then camping outside the injured man's door. Murray gave Adam the thumbs up sign and left.

Upon leaving the hospital in the Enclave, heading for Bill St. George's office near the Houston Galleria, Sheryl turned to her husband. "You never confided in me about the school attack or the family member who abused you."

Murray emotionally replied, "Stupidly, I was afraid YOU would consider me DAMAGED GOODS in our early dating and have you run off to that guy you liked in San Francisco. My family thought of me that way. Even after marrying you, there was not a good moment to bring that subject up as we always have had a whirlwind life even with just bringing up the kids and working together, playing together, laughing, sometimes crying together over some, who knows what deal. I just did not feel it was ever an issue after we started our lives together. Now with this episode with Adam, it has re-surfaced and the only way I can soothe my past and someway solve it without going to a shrink like Kerry around the corner from our office is to do this deal. My goal is to get Kolezy just as much as Adam wants him brought to justice and find out if he had anything to do with Troy's death."

Sheryl was now beginning to think the same as her husband. "Yes, that has struck a familiar cord even though our Troy's death did not happen the same way. Sighing, "At least, he wasn't found with...."

Murray squeezed Sheryl's hand as they both started to tear up. "NO, by god, Troy was a good kid. He wasn't like Adam or these other young men, but he was almost naked with a cord around his neck that cost him his life. I cannot believe that he was involved with Kolezy. We won't think he was selling his body for money. He had a responsible position with our holding company and made real good money, more than he made as an oil trader, we saw to that. He drove a Cadillac convertible and had an expensive condo in West University. West University?" Murray thought of a connection as Adam had a condominium in this semi affluent area. Their son was a bachelor and he had brought over girl friends from time to time but in the last six plus months before his death he was not dating. Handsome, nicely tanned, light brown hair, brown eyes like his sister, Gina, he worked out at a local gym to hone a knockout body, as one of his girlfriends's tried to encourage him to be a fashion model. "Print models are what Adam had in those magazines and videos. Oh shit, Sheryl, what if Troy was involved with Adam? After I see Bill I will check it out with Adam. We never spoke of his murder to him and the similarities of how Troy was found. It did not click in for us when Lieutenant Cavazos was listing the crime and interrogating Adam."

Sheryl had a frightful look on her face. "I hope, Murray, that Adam did not know Troy. Oh my God!"

After dropping Sheryl off at their Memorial home, Murray headed for Bill St. George's Post Oak Park office. St. George and Murray grew up together in the Hungarian neighborhood called Buckeye Road on Cleveland's eastside. St. George was an extremely talented baseball shortstop at his Benedictine High school days the major league scouts touted him as an up and coming player heading for certain stardom and a 'can't miss' induction to the Baseball Hall Of Fame in Cooperstown. Sixteen injury plagued years garnering him a couple of Most Valuable Players awards and two World Series rings from four Major League teams before being forced out by a shoulder injury, ending his baseball career with the Houston Astros. After his playing days were over, St. George cashed in on some connections he made while playing. Investments that may have been a little in the gray area of legitimacy. He was mentored by a group of Clevelanders who knew him and Murray when they were growing up in the old neighborhood before coming to Texas.

In Houston, St. George had a major investment company which controlled two mortgage companies and a title company. Sensing a turn in the housing market, he sold all three companies for nine figures in late 2007. He parlayed that into oil and gas leases that Murray and Michaeleen had touted. With even more lucrative returns, he, Murray, and friends, Rich and Sev Fedor, Ernie Petrovich along with Ron Tanski formed an unofficial vigilante group not unlike what they had accomplished eighteen months earlier when the group helped out a fellow Clevelander who got into trouble with the wrong crowd, leading to the kidnapping of his family. St. George and Rich, who had an investigative organization that was highly instrumental in the release of the family when they turned the incident over to the local Cleveland Police as they arrested the thugs.

Bill's office had a picture of himself with the New York Yankee's owner, George Steinbrenner that Murray looked at as he walked into the oak paneled den. "Hey, Bill, my good buddy", as he greeted the slightly silver-headed trim former athlete.

"Yo estate kiven", Bill asked his childhood friend as they hugged in their heritage greeting of asking 'how are you'?

Murray replied back, “Eleg yo. Yes I am fine”.

“Cafee?, feu?” Bill offered as they sat down in front of some Hungarian coffee and pastries.

Murray held up his hand turning the strong coffee and sinful desserts down, “nem kel.”

“What brings you here, Anth?”

Murray got right to the point. “Are you game on doing another venture like in Cleveland?” as he looked out the window of the 20th floor of Bill’s Post Oak office.

St. George bent over pouring a cup of the dark liquid and jamming a Hungarian leckvar pastry in his mouth. “What do you have going, Anth?”

Murray detailed Adam’s rescue with the advent of selling MABB, Kolezy’s link to all of it and adding if Troy was another unknown victim.

Bill listened intently to his buddy as he stopped eating. When Murray finished, St. George cut to the reality for his friend. “When we did the Cleveland Job, Rich and Sev had their uncle Joe, who was a captain on the Cleveland Police Department. He backed our play until it was time for CPD to come in and take over. We don’t have a Houston PD connection not even with Rich having his detective agency and security company who sometimes runs against the cops here. This Kolezy character has friends on the force it sounds like and he is an influential high powered lawyer with buccos of bucks. Now you’ve thrown in that there’s a certain someone who might buy this MABB outfit for, what, four hundred mil? I feel for you on the loss of Troy. He was a sweet kid and Betty and I was shocked over the murder as were my sons, Billy and Steve, who knew him in high school and buddied around with him until a year ago when he was dating that red headed broad.”

“Yeah, her name was Skylar Locke. Sheryl and I will deal with Troy’s death, in time. I placed a call to Michaeleen to see if she will intercede with Carol Sue Winters to buy MABB.”

St. George viewed his longtime friend with suspicion, “You don’t want to go down that road with ‘Vixey’, do you? She is one hellcat and I know Sheryl hates her. Betty doesn’t like being around her, either.

Rich's wife, Marge and she had a drag down fight last year. Anyhow, don't you want to invest in MABB? And... what makes you believe Vixey will pay four hundred million?"

Murray cocked his head back and forth and smiled. "This is right up Carol Sue's alley. She just sold another part of Miller Corp to Michaeleen's conglomerate, Ventura, Inc. for almost that amount of dough. She likes to roll it over into a definite moneymaker. MABB is the ticket for that."

St George disagreed. "Why do you think Vixey will buy an over the top adult business? Do you know for sure that she loves male sex that much?"

Murray laughed. "I was told those women, ages, 25 through 62 plus can hardly wait to get their hands on those CDs. My gut feeling is she will jump on the chance and if Adam is telling the truth on how much his sex business nets, she will be writing that check faster than a waitress going after a hot tip."

St. George, arose and went to his friend, still not convinced as he made his point by poking Murray in the chest. "Anth, I met that revolving door bitch and know you had history with her and the Millers way back. They wanted to crush you over your love for Bobbie Jean. If Vixey listens to you, figure she won't go for the four hundred mil and just jack you around. She is an emotional sex grinder of men. Type that flirts with the guys, leads them on, and fucks them, but not always physically. You gotta watch this woman. I can't get over that she and that sweet Michaeleen are related."

Murray was not going to win Bill's backing it appeared and he thought about his wife and her dislike for Carol Sue or as Bill called her by the nickname, 'Vixey'. "Will you really consider, at least, supporting an investigation into Kolezy, getting Rich's investigation organization to do it? Rich is great. He is more your friend than mine and I will pay his service company whatever. Adam is a fellow Magyar, Bill, and we don't let our people down when they are in trouble. Ok?"

St. George returned to the coffee table and picked up the leftover pastry, stuffing it in his pie hole, and chased it with the Hungarian hot brew as his eyes seemed to jump out of their sockets over the caffeine strength, catching him by surprise. "Elag Yoo, es cafee. You got me on this Anth... Damn, why not. I want to help our fellow countrymen and bring down Kolezy who is a smear against our heritage. He sounds like a bad Hunky. I know you want to find out about Troy and you will need emotional support on that. You want to smash Kolezy, Houston's prime attorney, well respected who has more connections than half of what we have combined? I just gotta believe you are thinking more with your heart than with your head."

Murray thought shaking his head in a positive manner. "It will be an element of surprise. We tell the local media Adam's story especially my client at Channel 77, Tom Zizka. We run it by him. This could be a high point for him."

St. George had a sour look as he stared at his old friend. "You're full of 'running It by's'. Michaeleen, Zizka, Me, and you still need to contact Vixey."

"What the hell are you telling me, my good old buddy?"

"Just that we are going to be up against a damn, hard-assed cock sucker in Kolezy. Cleveland was a milk run. This bastard has the backing of all of Houston. You tell me his stepdaughter, what's her name, Melanie, is a frickin' pill head. The wife is a god damn drunk, Adam, used to suck dicks for a living. Hey, I love you man, but we need character witnesses that can put this guy at the crime scene. This is a tough deal and just figure we have an uphill battle in front of us."

"Billy, I know we are facing big odds on Kolezy. It would be a great relief getting your help along with Rich and the rest. You know it would be tough for me to do this solo as this is going to be very dangerous and Kolezy is a 'saint' in the community. We can bring this son of a bitch down. I know it."

St. George surveyed the entire matter. "It could work if we got someone at HPD to come in. Rich and Sev would jump in. Ernie, shit, he doesn't want to get his hands dirty. He is writing a novel and wants to be below the radar. Damn, though, he is my close friend, too. We were neighbors on East 130th. He'll come in. You mentioned our Polak over the top, vet, Tanski."

"Ron Tanski, Nam vet, sharpshooter, killer instinct. When the time comes. Kolezy!"

St. George felt a pang. "Blowing away a dirt bag like Kolezy? Hey, I don't know about that? You may have a vendetta against him if he had something to do with Troy's death. That is what you appear in telling me. My entire family liked Troy. Of course, it is the right thing to do. Sometimes, I'm a jackass. Let's get that son of a bitch."

Murray was starting to really feel the excitement of getting deeper into the future fracas. "I can enlist Lieutenant Cavazos. He's investigating Mark Carlson's murder and the possible connection with Adam to it. He's a bulldog in the trenches and will finish off Kolezy but we have to get Carol Sue to pony up the dough to get that bastard off Adam's behind."

St. George thought that last part was funny. "Anth, that's a good one. Seems as though Kolezy is comfortable on Adam's behind."

"Jesus, you know what I meant. I'll talk with Michaeleen to help me with Carol Sue."

Back at being a little cautious, Bill disagreed slightly. "You like Michaeleen. Have you given thought that she will be a target along with Vixey, who may make it a spectacle about buying MABB? If Kolezy wants the company that bad, he will go after those two women. They have to be protected as well."

Murray paused, back at the window, looking down on the traffic and roof tops of adjoining buildings in this fast growing metropolis. Spying the huge Galleria. "When I came here, Houston was a player's town. If you had the balls, you ran with your ideas and made things happen. Michaeleen and Carol Sue are two gals that can take care of themselves. I will lay it out for them. My bet is they go head first on it. Rich has the tough guys that should be able to take care of Kolezy's gang. That is where my handy man, Clay Kirby, came from. He may be a little past his prime to roll out of cars, firing semi-automatics, but he can protect either one or both of the women."

It is early morning at #5 Remington Place, the River Oaks mansion of Louis B. Kolezy. The tall, trim man with gray at the temples, angular face, sharp nose, close cut sideburns, and a thin dark mustache, had just returned from his usual morning swim, in the heated swimming pool, situated at the beige colored, red tiled roof home in the ultra-rich section of Houston. As he came from the cabana he donned a Tommy Hilfiger silk Shorty, robe covering a swimmer's body developed over his early years of competition in college at the University of Budapest, a decade before meeting his wife, Ilona Magassey, the widow of Anthal Magassey, his former law partner in Hungary.

Kolezy and Anthal had a law firm located on Andrassey Street the main hub of the twin cities of Buda and Pest. Anthal and Ilona were raising a young family of four children, Adam, Melissa, Ryan, and Melanie. All seemed an idyllic life for them until tragedy struck on a family outing at Lake Balaton, a Black Sea resort. Louis, unmarried, had accompanied the family that week and had gone with Anthal, an experienced swimmer, in a boat then changed his mind explaining he had left his waterproof watch back at the hotel and spa where they had all been staying. Anthal drowned when his boat capsized near some rapids. The police investigated the drowning and found he had lacerations on his wrists and ankles indicating he may have been bound and murdered. There was a theory that a disgruntled former client of Anthal did the killing but the man disappeared never to be found.

Ilona, overcome with grief, on the loss of her beloved husband turned to Louis who was only too willing to eventually marry her and assist in raising her children as his own. Melissa and Adam, the oldest, did not wish to change their last name and be adopted by Kolezy. The family would move to the United States a year later, settling in Houston on the advice of a former law student who knew Kolezy at the University and now had a thriving law practice of his own in the Texas city. After arriving in Houston, Kolezy began to make his mark in the court room as an astute arbiter and a relentless cross examiner. Louis was both a brilliant defense lawyer, as well as a law suit for hire one. He won numerous cases including two large oil and asbestos awards making him a multi-millionaire and a local celebrity on the social scene. In private, Ilona, more shy, and caring for her four children, shunned the limelight. Kolezy would berate her as though she was a witness for the other side in the court room. All was not what he made it out to be in public as there were demons inside this man.

This morning, Louis came into the hall toward his study, the youngest, Melanie, 28, the most vulnerable stepchild, had just finished her breakfast in the dining room where their morning chef prepared the usual gourmet start of the day meal. She had very short hair framing a narrow face of heavy makeup and dark green eye shadow. Even though her green eyes sparkled they could not completely hide the puffiness caused by late night adventures in the Market Square bistros and restaurants, or the afterwards of a dicey meeting with a stranger at the bar for a night of splendor. Whether it be a man or a woman. Melanie was very popular with either sex at 115 pounds on her 5'7" frame. She always watched her weight, not consuming the fatty foods that others enjoyed parlayed with daily gym visits at home and away. Melanie was physically extremely attractive and available.

The young step daughter, dressed in her tight red shorts and blue halter top showing off her chiseled abs, that sported a 10 carat diamond in her navel, caught the eye of Louis who smiled broadly at his stepdaughter. Melanie was the only one of her mother's offspring who had a relationship with her stepfather; most do to his bestowing lavish gifts and money to fuel her high living style. All things have their price. For exchanging the fuel, Louis always demanded and received her presence in the bedroom where he would be granted any and all sexual deeds and fantasies from his green-eyed bed partner.

Today, eyeing the dark copper-toned young woman, he strongly desired her. She being an art major from Rice University had opened up a studio near the campus in the fashionable Kirby area which constituted her days away from him. After working out in their home gym she wanted to change her clothes and go to the studio. Louis stopped her as she planned to mount the stairs to her bedroom. "Going to the store today, my Melanie?" He gargled fallaciously at her.

Somewhat in a daze from the past early morning high life, "Yes, ah, shipment I believe is coming in from Spain. I should be there."

Panting as he peered down her halter top exposing her tight firm breast, nipples begging to break loose from their bounds. "It appears as though, you had an all-nighter that lasted into the wee hours, my dear. Do you have any energy left over to, you know, satisfy some unbridled feelings?"

Not wanting to get her dosage of her stepfather's love that moment she changed direction. "I need to talk to my mother in the dining room, as I just thought of something she suggested about the studio's inventory."

Louis was rebuffed and greatly put out with her reply. He started to reach out and grab her but Melanie pulled away quickly heading for Ilona's company at the breakfast table. His jaw tightened, "I will see you later, definitely, my lovely."

Melanie entered the dining room where Ilona had just finished her morning poached eggs and turkey bacon washed down with Stolichwa vodka camouflaged in her Hungarian coffee, greeting her daughter. "Well, Melanie, are you ready for a full day at the art studio? I heard you tell Louis there was a parcel from Spain arriving today."

Before she could reply Louis came behind the girl, groping her behind causing her eyes to widen in surprise and anger. "Louis, I told you that I was going to speak to my mother and PLEASE leave me alone!"

Unfazed, Louis bent down to kiss his wife. Smelling the strong liquid he mocked her. "Well, my dear, you appear to be your usual self."

Ilona shot back. "And you my devoted husband will go to your practice and ruin some more lives to gain more money and power, or are you content to just kill people for your personal gain, today?"

Looking admiringly at his step daughter, "I may get to all of that but need to have some recreational time this morning."

Ilona knew what he meant and hated the idea he had in mind. "To have your usual time with Melanie?"

Without hiding his feelings, Louis sighed. "Melanie likes to share her thoughts of the arts and sciences with me since you are never available, or should I say, sober."

Ilona was defending her daughter. "She shares more than that even though she does not care to. If you wanted a meaningful conversation about the arts and sciences you would take it up in our common areas not in her bedroom or yours. I have discussed Melanie living in Austin with Melissa, Alan, and their children. Her sister wants Melanie, to open an art studio near the Capitol. I want her away from your clutches. And for your information, my beloved, I drink to forget we ever married and I allowed myself to share my children with you."

Kolezy looked at his stepdaughter, breathing heavily. "I don't want Melanie to live there. Melissa is a trouble maker. But not...."Kolezy stopped before he began to divulge his intentions to rid himself of the eldest stepson. That and with Adam out of the way as he planned the other night, he could manipulate Melanie to turn over her shares of MABB to him. HE knew that Adam stipulated that in his will that the surviving sibling would be the 100 per cent recipient of the corporation.

Ilona pressed for an answer. "Louis, you are really thinking hard on this one. 'But not...' you started to say?" She began to raise her normal quieter voice, expressing her longtime pent up anger. "You have had your pleasures, flaunting them in my face these past years but it is coming to an end."

Kolezy disregarded her threat. "Go up to your room and douse yourself with vodka or is the liquor cabinet bare of that libation this morning, my lovely? Perhaps, some gin to take its place?"

Ilona slipped, as she got up, and brushed past him.

Louis sent another salvo past her. "Looks as though you already found the gin."

Melanie had enough and ran out of the room following her mother.

Kolezy wanted to grab her but she eluded him and he started to run after her when the cell phone in his robe pocket rang. It was Dimitri, his chief henchman of dirty deeds. He drifted towards the study, but stopped. "Egan", Kolezy answered as he listened intently at first then gave a large frown to his forehead. His lips pursed, eyes emulated from his face. "What! He's alive! Your men bungled this. He is at what hospital? The police are there? The man who found him is in this, too? Is he a cop? You don't know? You idiot! Dimitri, I want to see his balls on a platter. If anyone else is in the way, take them out. You understand?" as Louis' voice rang out throughout the home where Ilona and Melanie intently listened. He snapped the phone and hurried toward the study seeing both women on the stairs and for the moment forgetting that they probably overheard his end of the conversation.

As he went in to the study and locked the door the women came down the stairs to listen at the door. Ilona and Melanie wanted to know what Louis' next step was going to be. For a while only silence fell over them. The women began to move away when a call came in on the house phone. They strained to hear it.

It was more bad news as it was his oft mistreated, mistress, Carla Davis, calling from Las Vegas. Angrily, he lashed out. "I told you never to call me on the home phone, Carla. What, you want more money for you and that wimpy so-called son of mine, Brian? You have bled me for years. $10,000 a month, for the past 20 years, a $500,000 home in Henderson, and I paid for that little prick's education at UNLV. Now you are threatening to expose me, you whore! Sure, you figure I can afford to keep paying you since I fuck you. You think so, ha? Well, bitch, I intend to come out to Vegas in a week and pay you off and if you ever threaten me again, the cops won't ever find you and that poor excuse for a son in Area 51. You got me, Carla? We're through!" as he slammed the phone down.

Quickly, he reached for his cell phone and speed dialed Dimitri. "Dimitri, I want you and Drago to go to Las Vegas. NO, NO, to kill Carla and Brian. They want more money. You have to take care of that immediately, if not sooner! No, on second thought, contact Galgany and Keratezy, our men out there. Have THEM eliminate Carla and Brian. Now you are asking me how to rid myself of that bitch stepson of mine? I have an idea and you are going to do it, at the hospital. I am like Michael Corleone in Godfather One; I settle everything at the same time or close to it." He smiled at that comparison to the so-called fictitious character in the 1972 movie as he hung up.

The two women had heard more than they cared to witness. Melanie was definitely through with satisfying Louis, certainly not wanting anymore of his lust and bestowments in exchange for the murder of Adam. She always suspected that her stepfather had something to do with her younger brother, Ryan's death and now, his possible mistress and her son, possibly his own flesh and blood.

As the two women hurriedly walked away heading toward the stairs, Ilona pulled her daughter aside, "Melanie, this is getting dangerous for both of us, especially for you, it would be better that you left immediately, this home is no longer safe for you."

Before the young woman had the opportunity to reply, Louis bolted from the study, eyeing the two women, notably, his stepdaughter.

Melanie knew that look, as she turned and hurried up the stairs, as Ilona attempted to prevent her husband from pursuing her daughter and stood her ground. Kolezy ran toward her and brushed past his wife who started to grab him. "Get out of my way Ilona, you cannot stop me."

Ilona made a desperate plea to him, "Louis, don't, please stay away from my daughter!"

Grabbing her arms, pushing her force full, "Go drink your vodka or gin", as he sneered and began to chase after Melanie.

Melanie locked her bedroom door, frightened by Louis's motives. Had he found out that she and her mother knew too much and would they be on that list like Michael Corleone did in that movie? She realized all too late that playing her stepfather's games had gone too far. What would she do? In frenzy, she reached for her cell phone on the bed to phone the police.

As she started to dial 911 her bedroom door began to rock violently. "Melanie! Melanie! shouted Louis, open this door immediately or I will kick it in!"

The girl was terrified. Did he want sex or to kill her or both? Defensively she weakly sputtered out. "Please go away, Louis, I have a terrific migraine headache and wish to lie down."

"Kolezy persisted ignoring her plea. "I want you my darling. I need you now."

Gazing into her floor length mirror imaging herself seeing that she was nothing more than a toy to play with and when he grew tired of it, he would throw it down and walk away never looking back. Her stepfather's idea of sex was his bed manner likened to 'fuck her, roll out of bed to adjourn to his own bedroom, light up a Cuban cigar and have two fingers of Patron or 30 year Macallan scotch whiskey then hit the shower to wash off her Vaseline or KY jelly and Givenchy perfume that gave him hives. This time it would be much different.

Melanie begged, "Louis, leave me alone, please, our relationship is over. I don't want to continue this life with you, taking me at your will. It is wrong."

I will not taking no for an answer. "I am coming in and our relationship is over when I SAY IT IS! You conniving bitch. Now open this door!"

Melanie was even more terrified. "You are evil! I am phoning the police!" She started to dial the emergency number with her trembling hand making errors before finally getting the 911 to ring. IT rang for what appeared to her as an eternity before an operator answered, "Hold, please."

Kolezy was determined not to be prevented from her body and breached the door busting the lock and door knob offs the frame.

Melanie dropped the phone and flew back onto her bed; eyes widened the width of a demitasse saucer. Her breathing was almost heart breaking as Louis vaulted into her bedroom, dropping his robe, naked, his penis enlarging rapidly. She screamed for her mother but the cries were left unanswered. As she attempted to get up and run past Louis, he tripped her causing her to fall to the floor. He grabbed the loops of the red shorts and yanked them around throwing the terrified girl on the bed and with his strong hands tore the halter and shorts from Melanie just leaving the matching red lacy thong which he nibbled off with his teeth almost inhaling them as he continued to journey into her forbidden spot of pleasure.

She tried to plead with him as he tongued her splendidly taut body. The man was insane, pinning her hands down with his entire body, grabbing her throat, looking down, he gleefully announced, "I am going to kill your brother, you cannot prevent that and if you interfere in anyway, I will ring your beautiful neck like a Hungarian Chicken from Buda. You understand, you lovely fucked up bitch?"

Panicking, trying to save herself and another brutal attack at this maniac's hand and at the same time ask for leniency for Adam. "Look, if I sacrifice my body to you will you not harm me or Adam?"

Kolezy stopped momentarily on his mission to combine his lust with vile threats. "Will you give me your entire cooperation if I spare you? I will consider not killing Adam". He quickly had another idea, a needle in the brain leaving his stepson alive and a total vegetable. "Yes, I think we can arrange that." With that Kolezy seized Melanie and bellied her on the bed. "Your brothers use to enjoy this part." He then yanked her buttocks at the right angle and entered her. Her screams went away as they rocked together.

Hating most of it but Melanie was accustomed to doing it with another person that she enjoyed being with, the one that she really loved. Without warning Kolezy pulled out, finding his stepdaughter's hairbrush, next to her pillow. He flipped her over, Melanie lay frightened and crying, he looked down at her. "I am going to fuck you with your hairbrush if you do not do as I say, I will use this brush in your beautiful body. It will be very uncomfortably bad for you... What is your decision, my beloved Melanie?"

He began running the brush between her legs and onto her pubic hair, laughing like an uncaring maniac.

Melanie shrieked out. "Louis OH NO, please, please don't do that! I'll do whatever you want...please!"

"I will if you promise me that you will not warn your brother."

"Yes, yes, I won't. Just don't do this, please!"

With that, Kolezy put the brush down, turned her over, and re-entered with his phallus enjoying the moment of his own pleasure as they both hit their own crescendos.

Ilona, heard all of it from her bedroom and continued drinking her gin and crying not knowing what to do to help her daughter. As a mother, Ilona was a failure to Melanie. She gave solace to the fact that Melissa was safe in Austin and never touched by Louis. The white liquors clouded her logic as she felt that, at least, one of her four children escaped his clutches. Hating her own self, knowing she had no real way to support herself, depending entirely on her husband and unable to stop her drinking and pill taking.

After Kolezy finished his ravishing conduct on Melanie, picking up his robe, snarling, he looked down on his naked stepdaughter. "Remember, Melanie, if you want Adam to live we are going to have more of these sessions and you better respond differently. You need me, since you, as your brothers, are damaged goods no one else would want."

Crying, the bruised, young woman waited until he left the room, got up and limped to her bathroom where she put the shower on hoping to wash Louis' sperm out of her body. Still sobbing uncontrollably she fumbled with the hot water faucet finally getting it to warmly capture her tender, violated body.

Ilona, through her open door, saw her husband walk by like a proud gladiator. At that moment, she knew he had another conquest of her daughter. Dropping her empty glass of Beefeater, anger suddenly entered Ilona, jolting her enough to have an epiphany. She remembered her maiden aunt, Helen, in Szeged outside Budapest, known as the Queen of Paprika. The aunt always felt that Louis was untrusting and that he may have had something to do with Anthal's untimely death. The belittled, alcoholic, pill crazy woman had to get hold of herself, but needed a huge financial backing. Her aunt would be the key to it. Melissa and Alan were just beginning to make a profit with his company and Ilona knew they could only offer a token aid although her older daughter was there for her, psychologically. Melissa had given her mother the name of a Houston psychotherapist, Kerry Yanek, whose office was on Memorial Drive in Houston. She and Melanie would seek her help. For now, Ilona would need temporary additional money for that. She knew where Louis kept a stash of money in the library office. At times he left the door of the room open and she would see him take out a large roll of bills throwing them in a metal box on the right side of the desk then locking it, slipping the key under a portrait of Blue Boy that he bought in Paris years back. Yes, she must be strong and help Melanie and have them both leave the River Oaks mansion. First, she wanted to go to her daughter's aid.

Ilona entered her daughter's room and placed a chair from Melanie's dressing table, wedging it against what was left of the door knob. She then found Melanie in the shower where she opened the enclosure getting drenched and cuddled the fallen young girl. Ilona grabbed a large bath towel and dried both of them off as they began to clutch one another for comfort.

Looking up at her mother as Melanie sat on the toilet seat slowly coming down from her emotions, "Louis will pay for this. He plans to kill Adam so he can takeover MABB, even though he promised not to if I would co-operate in the bedroom. But it's over with him. Louis has lied so much."

Ilona offered hope to her daughter, "We will need money of our own to escape from Louis. I know where he hides a great deal of cash. We can use that until I contact my aunt Helen in Szegad who never liked

Louis and offered in the past enough funds to leave him. I am her only living relative and as she termed it, my early Inheritance. Adam knows that Louis wants him dead. In one of my sober moments we had dinner at his restaurant, Ryan A's over in The Montrose a month ago. He told me about the offer Louis made to him at Ryan's funeral to sell out MABB and work for him in Budapest. It was a 'do it or you may not live to see another day' ultimatum. Adam offered me a lot of money just like Helen but I was too proud to take it. Now I won't hesitate to accept his generosity. Melissa gave me the name and phone number of that psychotherapist, Kerry Yanek; together we will seek her aid."

Even though Melanie was struggling with her own demons and Louis' she was now deeply concerned with her brother's welfare. "Yes, we will go to her, but first, I have not heard from Adam and what Louis said to Dimitri makes me frightened for him. This morning before all this happened I tried to text him. He never answered."

In his bedroom suite, Kolezy prepared to go to his law offices in Downtown Houston but before he left, there was one more call to Dimitri. " My friend, when you meet up with Adam at the hospital, just inject enough insulin in his brain to make him a vegetable. I want this accomplished today. Then advise Galgany to proceed in Las Vegas to rid myself of Carla and Brian. This will pave the beginning of the takeover for MABB. It has lasted too long. Dimitri I want results!" With that he closed his cell smiling to himself. Michael Corleone would have been proud of him.

Murray and St. George headed back to Memorial City Hospital to see Adam. As they went up to his room they were met by Clay Kirby. "I think, Boss man, that someone is craw fishing around looking for your buddy in that hospital bed."

Murray's look of relaxation went away as he immediately thought of the van occupants. "What do you mean, Clay?"

"There was an orderly who told me that some heavy set man, with glasses, asking if a guy was brought in with serious body wounds. Then about five minutes ago I saw someone like that and he disappeared down that exit at the end of the hallway when I looked at him."

Murray was starting to feel the heat from all this. He was glad that Bill was with him as they now both carried their guns on them. "Bill, I figure we need some more help on this. Rich Fedor's outfit, a couple of more packing would not hurt. Can you give him a buzz and see if he can send over some backup?"

"Hell, Anth, knowing how Hungarian Rich is and with Adam, a fellow Magyar, he'll probably stand the first watch. It may take a few hours for him to set it up, though."

Murray looked at his handyman. "Clay, after we leave here, can you go another two, three hours?"

Kirby proudly exclaimed. "Boss man, I can do that standing on my head stacking be be's in the corner."

St. George did a double take looking at both men. "What, did he say?"

Murray grimaced. "Clay's a coon-assed, Cajun who likes etouffee, boudin balls, and sucking that yellow stuff out of the crawfish." With that they continued toward the room.

As Murray and St. George began to enter Adam's room, there were some tough questions that needed to be answered by this fallen victim. They witnessed a different scene as Adam had a visitor; a tall, slender, reddish haired man in his late 20's bending down, seemingly, accepting a kiss from the injured adult star. St. George began to walk out but Murray grabbed him from leaving. Adam noticed the small scuffle taking place and gently pushed away his friend. "That is just a friendly gesture that we picked up in Paris. Nothing more."

St. George sent a steely look through Adam as he remarked to Murray, "I thought this guy needed our help. Not so certain I want to get my ass in a crack over some... I don't even know how to say it, nicely. I just am not a fan of this person at the moment, ...and we're not in Paris!"

Murray went ahead to bridge the unexpected event that even he was uncomfortable with by introducing Bill to Adam. St. George was mildly surprised that Adam's handshake was firm and long lasting not the limp five fingered one he was waiting for from a supposed faggot who he felt, at the moment that his previous assault was justified.

Adam was equally on the defense and introduced his longtime friend and partner in the Montrose gallery as Jonathan DeWalt. Jonathan extended a limp wristed handshake to both visitors.

St. George finally got what he thought was a wimp's greeting and smiled as he slowly shook his head expressing the idea that he was right about him. St. George could not leave the moment. "Normally, when I greet or leave someone, kissing on the lips is not an option. I don't even allow my Lab to do it to me because he's been licking his balls and sucking on our female terrier's ass most of the day."

Jonathan defended himself. "Bill, I haven't licked my balls today and I only have cats at my condo."

St. George looked at him with disgust, "You wish to marry one another and have your company pay benefits when your so called partner has AIDS after he's been licking your cat's balls and yours."

Jonathan's eyes appeared to pop out of his head. "YOU PEOPLE are the ones that have driven us to the edge! I don't require to have benefits from my company for my lover. I will take care of him myself. YOUR kinds have us all wrong and the media has it wrong, as well!"

"I guess you are referring to a snippet from a 20/20 show or something. Our moral values have suffered in the last 25 years, kid. Everyone thinks its fine for guys to dog one another and think they won't pick up some crud. Hey, JON A THAN, AIDS might be from cats who lick their masters."

Jonathan appealed to Adam. "What are you thinking about in allowing these two fellows to, whatever, you told me about? I just don't get you at the moment, my love!" With that the redheaded guy turned on his heels like some gay Broadway actor in a off stage show and stomped out the door acting like he wanted to hear applause from the audience.

Adam then told the two men that Jonathan and his parents took him in at age 16 when he fled the River Oaks mansion of abuse. Kolezy could not do anything about it as the young man could, at the time, make it very uncomfortable for the lawyer. Adam held some damaging photos the older man shot of him and Ryan's molestation that involved both of them and another adult. Jonathan and Adam were classmates, teammates on the swim and tennis teams. After high school they each made the rounds of Texas colleges where Adam recruited with Jonathan's assistance, the core of MABB models. After attending four colleges they graduated from University of Houston, purchased the art gallery together, slept together and were lovers until he found David. A few years later, Adam opened his Montrose restaurant.

Both Bill and Murray had a little better understanding, although St. George still did not like the setup. He looked at Adam. "You know kid, my good friend, Mr. Murray, Anthony or Anth, to me, is one hell of a human being. He is in your corner 150%. I don't buy you very much. I am not into your lifestyle nor are my family, friends, associates. We're old school. My ass is used to taking a shit or just pharting up a room after downing a couple of Shiner Blonde brews. I'm on with Anth for the time being. You screw up and I'm out of here along with any of our associates." Pointing first to Murray with his thumb, jaw tightened, then turning his attention to Adam. St. George added, "And I hope his goodwill won't be compromised. If it is, I will make your life a living hell. You understand, Mr. Magassey?"

"Yes, Bill. You have made it crystal clear." Murray smiled at that ending as it was not more than last evening he echoed the same words to Dr. Abbott. This was becoming too much of a habit, he thought.

Adam took it in and gulped, "I hear you loud and clear. Believe me, I won't mess with ya'll. Really appreciate any support you can give me. I do want to change my lifestyle. Date women, marry, have children, live in a home with a pool, bar-b-queue with the neighbors, watch The Texans and Astros. Just go normal. I see it now."

St. George appeared satisfied for the moment, as he looked back at Murray. "Adam sounds like he means it. We'll see. Hey, I know you have to talk to him privately..."

Just then the man Clay saw earlier, dressed in a doctor's smock came into the room. Adam immediately recognized him. "It's Dimitri!"

Murray and St. George quickly reacted, racing toward the stoutly curly haired bespeckled Kolezy side man. Dimitri did not realize that his intended victim had visitors and knew that he would be captured if he did not run. Moving swiftly for a large man, he maneuvered past nurses wheeling patients and seasoned doctors, parading new residency shave tails hanging on every word of their experiences. The Hungarian henchman dropped a hypodermic needle in the hall, never looking back. He jumped over a gurney and headed for the exit as the pursuers momentarily were blocked by the new doctors, who stopped to hear the veteran physician spout another analogy from his clipboard.

Murray and Bill began to holler for them to get out of their way as they continued to catch up with Dimitri. Just at that time Clay immerged from the elevator. Murray yelled out, "Clay, get into Adam's room now! That guy dropped a needle back there." He pointed back over his shoulder. "Pick it up and put it in a bag!" Murray then went down the hall searching for Bill and Dimitri. He caught up with St. George.

As they got to an exit, Murray was exasperated, "Damn these halls are jammed with patients, doctors, nurses, and a lot of others in white and green smocks. I think he headed down this exit." Then they both travelled through the exit door and down the stairs jumping two at a time finding one door locked, then racing down to the next level they reached the first floor that was unlocked that lead to the lobby. Peering both ways for the heavy set suspect, Murray and St. George split up in two directions. Dimitri had already cell phoned to Drago to meet him at the side entrance. Just as Bill had the lowly henchman in sight he disappeared through the automatic doors, scampering into a waiting Mercedes with Drago at the wheel. They screeched out onto the side alley and into the busy street of Gessner weaving in and out of traffic and running two traffic lights.

St. George phoned Murray dejectedly, "Hey, Anth, our man got away in a Benz, got the first three letters of the license though. Rich maybe able to run the plate."

Murray caught up with his friend as they met in the lobby. "Yeah I saw that Mercedes tear out, looked up at the last few seconds to get the, funny, I remember the last three numbers. '345'."

Bill laughed, "I got 'MBV'. So we can give Rich the complete license, MBV 345. That should nail it."

Murray had some relief on that. "Bill, will you contact Rich and I'll see if Clay found the needle and I need to talk with Adam. "

Doing the Lone Ranger gig, St. George mocked, "Ok, Keemosabi, me check with Rich on plate. I will take it over to him now and let you know."

"Alright, Tonto!"

Murray took the elevator to the third floor and as he made his way to Adam's room he was met by Clay, who had done many jobs in his life and once was a medic in the Army. He held up the needle Dimitri dropped now, safely, in a plastic bag. "I got the orderly to give me the bag and took precautions on picking it up without leaving my finger prints on it. Can't tell if it is cyanide or a combination of some other lethal drug. When I was downstairs in the cafeteria I saw that character but lost him and that's when I was going to tell you that I thought he might be carrying a vial."

Murray was not sure if he should contact Lt. Cavazos on this attempt until he gave the needle and its contents to Rich who had a test lab and he needed Clay to stand guard until he had one of Fedor's men do it. "Clay, let's check on Adam, after that I need to discuss something important with him, privately."

Adam had heard the ruckus out there and was half dozed out over pain medicine and was now starting to come out of it. "Was I dreaming or did Dimitri attempt to come visit me?"

Murray uttered, "Visit? Sure he was bringing you some goodwill medicine." Holding up the bag with the needle in it. "We're going to have this baby tested for whatever its contents holds and the guess is not going to be pleasant."

Trying to make light of the recent encounter by Kolezy's man, Adam joked, "It seems that the hospital's favorite patient is very popular with his Hungarian Fan Club."

Feeling that Adam was attempting to shield his inner anxiety with a little humor, Murray let that remark go as he now wanted to know if Troy was a would-be model for Adam's operation.

Clay sensed that Murray had something important to say to Adam. "Appears that three might be a crowd, I better attend to things at the ranch and take that bag to Rich." With that the man shuffled out, with either Murray or Adam saying adios.

Grabbing his wallet out of his back pocket, Murray reached in for Troy's picture, thrusting it in front of Adam and waiting for his reaction to the burning question. "This is our late son, Troy, who was found murdered at a motel in The Montrose. Did you know him?"

Adam began to think about the past, taking a deep breath as he squeezed the college picture of the dead young man. "Anthony, your son, he... he. Yeah, I knew him as Derek Joseph. We met in a year or so in a bar on Fairview off Hyde Park in The Montrose."

Taking back the photo, Murray was in semi-shock as his suspicions were confirmed, that related the past events involving Troy. He knew his son was living a different life style after breaking off an engagement to Skylar Locke, a former cheerleader for one of the Houston professional teams. Wes, his son-in-law, introduced Troy to her a year earlier but the young man seemed to go through the motions of happiness with her. When she pressed for a ring he gave it to her only to call it off a month later. Two weeks after that he was found dead in that rundown motel. Murray's attitude changed toward Adam "So, Troy, was one of your guys, who lead a double life?"

Tears welled up in his eyes, "Anthony, you have to believe me, Derek or Troy, never let on he was from a family in Memorial or that they lived here in Houston. He told me he came from Laguna Beach in The O.C., moved to Lower Westheimer so he could be close to downtown where he working as an accountant at an oil company. He never talked about his job only that he was interested in print fashion modeling. He asked around and knew I liked to work with new talent. Derek or Troy, hung with two guys that were bi, not really gay and so I interviewed him at our Houston studio on Lovett Blvd. He had a very pleasing build and ..."

Murray's face reddened, "And what, Adam? Sheryl and I helped to save your life. I don't recall seeing you at his funeral. I remember a couple of un-manly young guys who came up to us and expressed their sorrows. So, they were his 'friends'? No, you did not even think to show up and throw the rose on the casket. You act as though he was just an employee. That's all he was to you, right?" Murray added, as he sat down on the bed facing a television that had Frasier on and the sound off. He did not know what to do as he committed to help this emotional meat grinder. And now, how would he explain this to Sheryl?

Adam, at this time was slightly prone in his bed. The pain medicine was wearing off; he grimaced, rising to a sitting position. "I really and truly did not have any idea who Derek was. That is, your son, Troy. When he died I was in Orange County, Newport Beach, with a couple of our execs who I meet with every quarter since we have retail outlets in Southern Cal. Wanted to go over figures on the sales and then I was headed to L.A. for interviewing some prospective models. Stayed with my best ex-friend Jake in Hollywood. He wanted to rekindle things..., well, it doesn't matter, anyway. Got back a week later, asked around about Derek, I mean, Troy. It was after the funeral. Tried to get a handle of what happened and why and where he was laid to rest. I asked around. No one seemed to know much other than he was....I'm having a tough time with this, Anthony, and now you hate me. I am so, so sorry."

Murray looked back over at the young man who was attempting to force back the emotions as the liquid ran down his cheeks. Murray felt compassion for this man who he should not have cared about at this point. Clearing his throat, he asked. "Adam, did you have a romantic interlude with our son?"

Adam's skin tanned face almost appeared ashened. "I attempted to, as I was seeking someone after Jonathan and David. Your son did not reciprocate my advances. He was special. He was not gay. I believe he was only testing out that life, peering from the outside. We never worked out the details of his modeling. MABB has a handful of straight models who, like Troy, want to show off what they look like to others, and make a ton of dough, as well. He was Straight Arrow. Maybe questioning himself. I did talk to Derek on the phone while I was in California probably the night he was found. ..."

Murray stood up and interrupted. "Hey, it is Troy, not Derek!"

"Sorry, again. Troy was deeply troubled and I asked him to hop a plane and come out to Newport. He said he had to take care of things and he might do it the next day. That's all I know, Anthony, please; forgive me, if you can?"

"I'm not certain how I should feel. Troy was not a teenager and his mother and I always gave him the right path to follow without being overbearing. All four of our kids were brought up in a good family environment, unlike what you have gone through. We came into money a few years back; I can't think it changed any of us to that extent. We were close, dad and son, but those last six months or so; Troy was tiptoeing through the tulips. Yet, here we are discussing what he did in that motel room. Did you know where he was at the time you called?"

"I got hung up on the interview..."

Murray was disgusted, "Yeah, your interviewing tactics like what Troy had to go through. Taking off his clothes and you photographing him. Then what do you do after that?"

"This is more than difficult. You want to know. Again, like I said before, it never went to the next level. He is or was a man who was tender and thoughtful. Probably how he was raised. Very respectful. He made it clear, no touching."

Murray was satisfied with an inner relief. "Leave it be for now. So the interview you had that night..."

"Like I was saying, we talked a little; Troy never told me where he was. I tried calling back after my interlude with the applicant. Again I phoned a few hours later. No answer. I went out with Jake for a round or two. Maybe it was midnight there, two AM, back here. Troy never picked up. At that point I knew from past times, when it is over it is over. We were losing contact. I never tried calling him again. It did weigh on me, though. He mattered."

Murray in a strange way had an ally in the death of Troy. Two men who loved the same person yet in vastly different ways. It was his only link to Troy's last six months on this earth.

Adam searched Murray's face attempting to see where he stood with his savior. "Can't blame you, Anthony, if you wanted to bolt out of here and turn it all over to Lieutenant Cavazos."

Murray looked down to the floor for a moment regaining his original thoughts before coming into the room. "Adam, I'm in a quandary. You really need our help, yet part of me says can I look at you and not see Troy. We are both adults and you probably did not cause our son's death. He wasn't totally honest with his mother and me. I don't know why, but I wish he could have confided in us."

"I'll try very hard to make it up to both you and Sheryl, somehow. We all will carry a heavy load."

With that Murray shook Adam's hand. He started to leave and then turned around like the detective in the old TV series. "What bothers me after all this time, though, is when we went to the motel after we were told that's where Troy was found, the desk clerk with the tats and piercings said the bill was paid by some foreigner. Maybe Eastern European, couldn't give me a name as it was cash as usual at those places. Only that the man was younger, like 20 or so, trying to be 30. Mustache, goatee, slight built, dark hair, blue eyed with a diamond ring that had a red, green, and white band."

Adam nodded "One of the guys who grabbed me fit that description. Can you get more information there? It could be one of Kolezy's men."

"I'd like to, except the following week a bull dozer/crane knocked the place down and now there are townhomes being built."

"Jonathan lent me his cell phone. I'll call around my contacts on those two guys. Derek, I mean Troy, did not mix with my guys so none of them would be able to help in this case. My place on lower Westheimer caters to certain customers who come in for dinner and the piano bar. They were more that type. I'll ask around. When he was at the Fairview bar he was uneasy, so maybe, knock that one out."

Murray was still not certain of his next move now with this latest revelation. "I'm heading for Bill's and we'll go to this person who can help you sell MABB."

Murray picked up St. George and they started over to Michaeleen's office. While in route he told his friend of Troy's involvement with Adam. Bill drew a long breath, "You have to know, Anth, that Adam is bad news. Two attempts on his life in 48 hours, now his relationship with your son. I am very sorry for yours and Sheryl's loss of Troy. So you don't feel that your son was light in the loafers? I'll only remember him as a good kid, not the one in that hotel room. Until then, you apparently want to go ahead with asking Michaeleen's help with Vixey?"

"Yes, I firmly believe that Adam was telling me the truth about Troy and our son was just mixed up at that time. He did not die like those other young men. I feel that there's more. I'll have to delve into what the police turned up. I can ask Lieutenant Cavazos if he can help and then I can confront Kolezy on Troy's death, if he had anything to do with it. Now, we have to ask Michaeleen's intercession with her aunt."

Ventura Oil Co. had its own building at the north end of Dairy Ashford in the Energy Corridor that spanned two miles on Houston's Westside and counted a dozen large named oil and gas corporations calling them, their headquarters. Murray had kept up with his benefactor almost on a daily basis, rivaling his interest in Renee, Gina, and Karen, their three devoted daughters. Michaeleen, mainly an all business person, greeted the two of them at the Texas Star oak double doors that lead to her modern modesty paneled desk. Tall, slender, blue-eyed, wound tight, she was a no nonsense business woman sporting black framed glasses that only enhanced her beauty. The mother of two she took over the company from her late husband, Robert Ventura, heir to his family's vast oil fortune, when he was killed in a parasailing accident while they were vacationing in Aruba. The five foot ten inch, svelte dynamo was thwarted by his family on the takeover until she went in to a board meeting and threatened all of them with the loss of their private parts if they did not get off her case and elect her CEO of the corporation, which they quickly did. Now raising her son and daughter, with the assistance of nannies and, sometimes with her aunt, Carol Sue Winters, Michaeleen managed to control her personal and business life on an equal footing. Michaeleen was named after her paternal great-grandfather, Mike Miller, Carol Sue's own grandfather. She was tight fisted over her vast holdings and Murray might have a problem getting her to invest in MABB.

She smiled at Murray and St. George as they were offered, yet refused refreshments, just sitting down across from her huge cherry wood desk. "What brings you boys down here this afternoon?"

Murray started by detailing the past two days and with St. George's intent to help Adam sell MABB. Knowing her straight approach for a business deal. "You have great ideas on company takeovers, Michaeleen, and from what I found out so far this company is a money maker and you do like to make money."

Michaeleen was now switching into her business mode from the friendly greeting as she leaned back in her ergomatic brown leather chair with the backdrop of the other oil company's skyscrapers outside the floor to ceiling windows. Removing her glasses to nibble on the temples, she starred at the Picasso painting across the tan paneled room. Contemplating her words as not to be misconstrued. "Anthony, you have to believe that everyone may not be interested in this adult business and investing $400 million is a considerable amount of up front funds as this Adam is wanting it in a lump sum.."

She stopped, "Actually..." she emphasized the word. "Actually, you may regret this", she continued, with one eye brow up and a slight devilish smile, "I know that my beloved aunt, Carol Sue and you are a foil. However, Auntie is in a much different lifestyle than me."

Bill looked over at Murray, knowing his longtime friend could not contain his joy over what he assumed Michaeleen would say next. "Here it comes, Anth."

Michaeleen stared at Bill. "What do you mean?"

"Oh, it doesn't matter", he muttered back.

Grabbing her composure back she looked down at her pens and stationary on her desk and started to doodle. Looking back up at Murray, "Carol Sue is your answer."

Murray was still on the other remark the young woman made, "Different life style? Are you telling us that your own, Carol Sue, 'Vixey' may actually be a buyer for MABB? I did think of her but did not want to approach her by myself as our history has been, rocky, to say the least."

"I have been around her for a longtime and we hit some places together. Yes, she is opposite of you, Murray, but.... Well, Timothy Lewis, from our Austin office dated 'Auntie" a few years back. It got around the office and he was telling everyone that she was HOT TO TROT."

Murray slid a glance to Bill as he was getting assurance that Michaeleen would be in his corner on getting Carol Sue to buy the company. "So, Michaeleen, will you help me with Vixey and sell her on the idea of a HOT TO TROT company like MABB? This is just what she needs to keep herself occupied? The asking price is $400 million but from what Adam tells me, it is a burgeoning business with a lot of profit."

"Aunt Carol Sue has just sold off another part of Miller Corp. worth in excess of that figure and always is searching for the next big deal. This could be it."

Michaeleen had always been in his corner and Murray made a direct bid. "Then you will help me convince Carol Sue on this even though she hates me and even more because you plucked almost 80% of her father's company, giving Sheryl and me over 10% of the after tax profits?"

Michaeleen was consoling. "Anthony, all females have at least two sides to them. She has even spoken about you in a positive way after the money was doled out to you."

Murray got up from his plush chair and went to the window visualizing that he would need to visit his former advisory for this favor or was it a favor?" He turned back to Michaeleen who swung her chair around following his movements. "Does she think of me as someone who may be considered as a friend? Or is it where Carol Sue may be realizing that I actually loved her sister, Bobbie Jean, years ago? Perhaps, it was that which may have made you come in and force her and The Millers to rightfully pay me with the reality that nothing could be done to change the course of events?"

As he walked back to the front of her desk, she turned around only focusing her attention on the somewhat confused man as Bill looked at them both from his position and only shook his head that he was privileged to hear some details he never heard before. "Murray, it may be a little of each from my Aunt Carol Sue, speaking from a knowledgeable manner. Let me do this, my people will research this MABB Corporation even if it is not publicly traded as you told me. I have Adam's information. It'll take 2-3 days and then I'll turn it over as you and we can revisit over all of this. If things look positive, I will make the call to Auntie Carol Sue or you can do it yourself. Don't be a worry wart, she's mellowed."

Murray drew his lips together like puffing on an imaginary cigarette. "I am banking that you're right on. Carol Sue did everything to prevent me from being with your mother just like all of their family, except Mike Miller."

Michaeleen looked up at the ceiling, "Yes, he was a great man and right now he's looking down from his spot in Heaven. As for Momma, I miss her very much. Do you believe that if you married her, would things been different?"

"Your grandfather, Tex, was like a J.R. Ewing, the character who played in the television show, Dallas. No, he would have found ways to push me out and at that time, I was a 'who yea' as what the Hungarians term, a dumb ass. Not mature enough, not worldly or street smart. Perfect ingredients for your family not to like me, but you made all of it up. I'm grateful for all you have done for our entire family, even Gina marrying into it. Wes is a great guy. Besides, in all honesty, I was not certain your mother loved me for myself or how she could antagonize her family as I was a peon in their eyes."

She listened to all he said, "Even though my momma was seemingly happy with Bret, I really think you and she would have made a great team. I really felt she may have missed out by not pairing up with you. Auntie said my mother had your Air Force picture next to her bed until Tex burned it. He pushed Bret on her or that's what Auntie claimed."

Sadly Murray replied "After leaving North Texas, I tried hard to get in touch with Bobbie Jean and found out Tex shipped her to Paris after we had our rendezvous in that two storied motel in Burkburnett. For a time I thought she and I conceived you but it wasn't the case. I wish it had been, though."

Michaeleen wanted to change the subject. "You know Murray; we both have wonderful remembrances of her. Just for now, forget the past and concentrate on my aunt. Remember Auntie lost her mother to breast cancer, Carol Sue also had it. Fact is Carol Sue had to have reconstructive surgery. It has made a difference in her life, you' see."

"Maybe that's why she has had an overnight mellowing. Does she still ride a motorcycle?"

Michaeleen laughed. "Yes, there's a picture in her office, straddling a motor cycle. It's an extended fork Harley. She tried to get me to ride with her but she doesn't like to wear a helmet to hide her exquisite hair. I'm not in for death wishes. My preference is four wheeled vehicles."

Murray wanted to probe a little deeper into Carol Sue. "At Gina and Wes's wedding, she wasn't wearing a ring and this guy she was with kept hitting on the women and young girls at the reception, so what's her story on orange blossoms and ministers? Wes has always been buttoned up when his mother is brought up and Sheryl and I are in conversation, so I don't know her history."

Michaeleen drew a deep breath, "Carol Sue divorced Rick Winters ten years after Wes and their daughter, K'Lynn, were born. About ten years ago, Auntie married Marshall Reid, the hedge fund king. He was too aggressive as she likes to be in control. The marriage did not work out as one night she found him at a Gulf Freeway motel with his secretary and they were not going over the latest market shares of the day. Auntie busted in with her pair of pink handled .38's and shot up the place. She did not hit either of them. Too bad!" Michaeleen's voice rang out in disappointment. "Aunt Carol Sue collected a hefty settlement in the divorce, mainly since Reid did not wish to have the news folks find out about it because his secretary's husband was from a prominent Dallas family that Reid was dealing with in the tens of millions. The money she settled for was enough to make up in losing the Miller Corp's cash."

Murray looked over at St. George, as they both thought it was amusing that he would actually call on this woman who he had seen at the joint family wedding of his daughter Gina, and her son, Wes. While cordial, Carol Sue kept her distance from Sheryl and him. At the baptisms of their grandchildren, she kept in the background as well.

Michaeleen broke the silence, "What's the matter? She's not going to bite you. At least not hard," laughing at his seemingly reluctance.

Murray half-heartedly nodded in agreement. "Yeah, I can do that. She does have big teeth, though. So you and Aunt Carol Sue are close?"

"We patched things up after Tex died and since I was left a lot of the controlling stock in Miller Corp., she became very endearing to me and the kids. I don't truly believe her heart was ever in it to follow her father's ruthless behavior and tactics. Funny, a lot of folks call her Vixey. I sometimes, inadvertently do. I love her play car. She has a yellow, '08 Chevy Vette with the personal license plates, 'VIXEY' on it."

Bill got into it. "Sounds like she's retired totally from Miller and is enjoying a free and easy life. . This MABB thing could work out for her."

Michaeleen clarified Carol Sue's position, "In a way, Auntie is going in, maybe two days a week for a few hours to see who may have phoned or faxed her. She has Wes handle everything now. Carol Sue does have another life in Katy where she keeps a home that's rather interesting..."

"How so?" inquired St. George, who was getting more into what Carol Sue was all about, "Go on tell us more."

Michaeleen started to laugh as she slid back in her high backed chair, "Yes, she has the mansion in East Memorial near Post Oak Drive. Then, three times a week, slides over to bowl in a league way over in Katy, or throw darts at the neighboring bar, and holds poker sessions at her Katy home. She goes by her maiden name, Miller, not Winters. Rides that cycle with other Harley people. They appear to be all very nice as she doesn't want to get involved with the wrong crowd, if you know what I mean. "

Bill interpreted as, "Like a moth to a flame but not getting burned. The thrill of mingling with the common folk from a heiress' standpoint. She likes a little adventure...Yeah, MABB is a project that will get her going."

The young girl knew her aunt and only smiled at Murray and St. George. Then broke her silence. "Murray do you look forward to hooking up with her again?"

He thought for a moment, "Well, she has this wad of cash that is burning a hole in her bank account. You can only bowl and play 'Hold "Em' so long . Yes, I believe Bill is on the right track."

Michaeleen was curious as to why Murray would involve others and not buy into MABB. "You have a lot of money, now, why don't you buy a large chunk of this Adam's company?"

Wringing his hands, "To tell the truth, while I am not a prude or believe I am better than others, that business does not do anything for me, besides, I was going to tell everyone that we invested in three boutique hotels, in Nacogdoches, Austin, and San Antonio. All historic hostels that set Sheryl and I back a good eight figures leaving maybe $50mil in our reserve fund. Plus, if Carol Sue is going to pony up $400 million, why would we need to get involved with MABB? On top of that, Sheryl, who you know, does not love or even like Vixey and would possibly kick my ass out the door, should I even hint of going in on the deal with her. Of course, all this is pure speculation. Vixey may not go for the deal."

Michaeleen persisted, "I feel strongly she will buy a controlling interest in MABB not the full amount and have other investors come in, say 10-15% each. You just told me you have $50million, put in 30 of it. You're sold on this guy and his business. What is your real reason for not investing in it?"

Murray's collar got tight, "Michaeleen, I just told you that is not my type of investment and Sheryl would kill me if we went to bed, in a manner of speaking, with your beloved aunt. That is two good reasons, alright?"

"Something tells me Murray you are not shooting straight on this. Let's leave it go. We'll run the numbers and for a favor I'll go with you to see Vixey."

Murray felt relieved.

As Murray and St. George left Michaeleen, Becky Ewing, Rich's secretary called on Bill's cell, relating that the hypodermic needle held insulin. Murray shuddered. "That character was going to shoot Adam with a lethal dose of insulin. Glad we were there. I want The Lieutenant to get it. Can Becky send it over to him at 61 Reisner?"

St. George agreed, "Yeah, your friend is living too close on the edge. I will ask Rich to do it, for now, just drop me back to my office."

As he left off Bill, St George turned to his good friend, "You know, Anth, the real reason you did not want to invest is actually you are scared that Carol Sue may have feelings for you and you..."

Murray was aghast at his old time buddy's statement interrupting , "God, Bill, you are way off on that. Hey, I don't want any part of Vixey. Can't fathom why you would even say something like that, huh?"

"You're the one that has brought her up since all that money came into your lives. At Gina and Wes's wedding and at the baptism of both of their kids, I spied her looking your way, A LOT. I really think you want a piece of the MABB action and with her."

Murray tightly griped the steering wheel staring straight ahead, "NO, NO, let's just drop it, okay? Hey, would you like to invest in MABB?"

St George stood and bent down through the open car window. "Alright, on Vixey and you, for now. Right at this time, Betty and I don't have a spare $30mil although I gotta say, if the figures come back like Adam says, maybe I can talk Rich and Sev into coming in for a 10%total."

Murray was happy over that. "You and the Fedor's can make a bundle on this and thank me for it, to boot!"

St George knew his friend was going to be caught in the middle if Vixey was going in on the deal. "I know you aren't headed for Carol Sue's place for a while. Where are you going now?"

"Back to the hospital to see Adam and check where Rich was placing his guy."

At Memorial Hospital Murray found Clay in the lobby and began to be concerned. "I hope Rich Fedor replaced you and you were heading for gumbo at the cafeteria, leaving Adam guarded?"

"Boss man, you know me better than that. I would go hungry first, then to leave him without protection. Yeah, Fedor has a security rent-a-cop patrolling the hall outside your kid's room. You gotta know, though, there's another cop by the name of Zeke Cavazos snooping around."

"Well, I'm glad Rich has a guard on Adam, and no, he is not my kid, okay? Sheryl and I found him and brought him to the hospital. Thanks for hanging in there and 'upping' me on this cop." With that they went their way.

Passing Rich's man in the hallway, Murray entered Adam's room and discovered Jonathan had returned for a visit. As he greeted the thin, reddish haired, and fair complexioned friend of Adam's their meeting was accompanied by a stranger's voice, introducing himself as he walked in the door. "My name is Zeke Cavazos, Sergeant Zeke Cavazos from HPD homicide!"

Murray and Jonathan swiftly turned to face the twenty year, former captain of the force now rifted to sergeant. He had been demoted two years before on a racial profile case involving minorities in the community. A former Texas Ranger in his younger days and a well-earned reputation of being a 'going by the book' officer. Slightly taller than his brother, and a little stouter, he packed two semi-automatic pistols in shoulder holsters. Square jawed, with amber glasses, accentuating his darting brown eyes that almost closed when he interrogated a suspect. He also carried a .425 caliber derringer in his hand tooled Dan Post boots, as a backup. Directing his words to Magassey who was fast progressing along. "Mr. Magassey, when you are released from the hospital, Lieutenant Cavazos and I would like you to come down to 61 Reisner St., Houston Police Headquarters and give a formal statement regarding the guy with the star tattoo on his right ankle who has not been identified. We can save you the trouble of coming down to headquarters by telling me who he might be. Does that make it for you, Mr. Magassey?"

Jonathan did not want to tangle with another Cavzos and remained silent on the sidelines.

Adam looked over to Jonathan who he already told of his believing of it being Mark Carlson.

The Sergeant reached in a brief case he had brought in and pulled a large manila envelope out displaying two vividly colored 8x10's. He flashed the pictures in front of Adam which almost made his stomach turn at the ghastly sight of Mark's blue, battered, bloody body. Sergeant Cavazos felt confident that he could easily corner his bed fast prey now, leering. "Know this man, Mr. Magassey?" Adam turned his head away.

Jonathan glimpsed at the shots and making a gurgling sound that Murray heard.

The policeman was losing his patience, throwing the pictures down on the hospital tray in front of Adam then tapping hard on it vibrating the sound through the injured man's chest. "Well, Mr. Magassey, do you know this dead man!"

Adam slowly shook his head. "He's Mark Carlson."

Cavazos wanted to go in for his kill. The cop reached in to his jacket for the flip top spiral notebook to jot down vital information. "What can you tell me about him? I need his address, your connection to him, next of kin, relative, friends of his to contact." Waiting for a response, he tapped relentlessly on the pad with his HPD pen.

Adam reluctantly gave his friend's address and next of kin, Louise, Mark's sister in Dallas.

"He's a friend."

The Sergeant pressed. "How long have you known The Late, Mr. Carlson?"

"We were both in high school and college together."

"What was his occupation?"

"Manager at Rascals on Fairview. Sometimes tended the bar when someone would not show up for work."

Sergeant Cavazos had a gleam in his eye, "Hmm, the gay leather bar. Well that fits like a glove."

Adam was going to give the cop a wise-ass answer but thought otherwise Instead, he started out, "That's what some people say, Sergeant.," looking the cop in the eye. "Have you ever been a patron there?"

The muscles in Zeke's neck started to stand out. His eyes went into that squint. "Not as a patron only on a murder case. Seems like the gays and lesbians have a difficult time staying alive or not being sodomized by pipes."

Adam started back knowing that the cop was trying to antagonize him. "If society would leave them alone. They are not hurting anyone by their choice of sexual partners or life style. Most of them are well educated and have higher than normal incomes."

Zeke wanted to fence with Magassey a little longer. "Maybe they're too educated and they have money because they are childless. Hey, have some kids like we did and see how much money you can accumulate. Huh! Ok! You keep referring to 'them' and 'they'. Don't you place yourself with them? You're in this bed because someone did not like your education and money. I guess, Mr. Magassey, if you and your friends would learn what your butt is for and not for pleasure, we wouldn't have to be taking statements and showing pictures of dead men on slabs with their dicks cut off and pipes jammed up their ass holes!"

Adam gave a sour look to the cop, replying, "Now where have I heard that before, hmmm?"

Zeke shot back, and then thought about what he said. 'The Before' struck him. "Mr. Magassey, we have three other victims that this happened to, same circumstances, same outcome, by some wild chance did you know them?"

Adam went silent for a moment looking over at Jonathan, who turned even more pale than usual, at the question. Feeling he had little to gain or lose, taking a deep sigh and let it out.

Zeke knew the answer before Adam replied, but was more patient, lowering his booming voice a few notches, "Okay, let's have it. Names, addresses...., Adam."

Magassey gave him the information, and then looked away.

"You know, son, that you will have to pay for all this down the road. I don't know how deep you are on this? Maybe your knowing them and not being able to prevent these heinous acts. That is enough, right?" Zeke looked at Adam for a minute not voicing anymore opinion or damnation. Was it becoming a victory in a way on a losing cause? He, like his brother, was at a saturation point in his job, the serial murders, the constant interviewing of a surviving victim; a next of kin to search out the whys and whenever's of their loved ones. Zeke knew that Dimas and he had to finish the unpleasant task and seek justice, as that was their belief.

Adam wanted to end all this and start his new life. "Sergeant Cavazos, there is nothing more I can add and it is a sad turn of events."

Zeke then turned to Murray. "I have been talking with Mr. Magassey here and never caught your name. You appear to be an interested party."

"My name is Murray, Anthony J. Murray, Sergeant. My wife and I found Adam the other night and brought him to the hospital. I wanted to see how he was doing."

Before the Sergeant could reply, another person came into the room.

Michaeleen had stood outside the door during the last five minutes of the conflict, then decided to get in the middle of the conversations. "I don't mean to barge in as ya'll appear to be in a serious discussion. I could not help it. You appear to have a mean streak in you, sir, and this man in the bed is trying to get it together. Yet, you finally pulled yourself together, as well."

The Sergeant was caught off guard as he was accustomed to male marine corp. talk. With a slight embarrassed look, he quickly wheeled around facing the comely beautiful executive, half acting mad but hiding a smug look knowing she brought him down a notch or two from his lofty perch.

"Now whom might you be, Miss?"

She extended a gracious hand, "I am Michaeleen Ventura. You're with the police?"

"Sergeant Ezekiel Cavazos, Houston Police Department, HOMECIDE division."

Murray, until this time was on the sidelines, yet, could not contain her unexpected entrance, temporarily de-railing the policeman's barrage on Adam. He raced over and gave her a hug, "Well this is a real great moment you being here."

Adam immediately sat up to welcome the person Murray may have brought in for the MABB deal. Surveying the young woman from head to her mini-skirted legs, he was already taken by her presence. He, a former gay male entertainer, for that moment became totally heterosexual. He realized at that instant, changing his life would not be that troublesome. "Well, Miss Ventura, you are a welcomed sight among us men discussing dead people, now we can change the subject."

Cavazos began to look at Magassey, but before he could comment, Jonathan worked up the courage, bristling at the last of the cop's rhetoric." Sergeant, you don't know what you are saying. It is not all black and white. Some people are pushed into a life style that other's like yourself, may not condone or approve of. You're like so many people on a pedestal, preaching fire and brimstone and not seeing the entire picture. You think what Adam went through and what happened to Mark was something they deserved? No, I don't think so nor does God."

The Sergeant looked over at Michaeleen attempting to tune out the reddish man's defense. "Ms. Ventura, I can't stand here and agree with all of you on this extremely, extremely horrendous event." He then addressed Jonathan, "Mr. whatever your name was, just look at your friend in that bed. Do you believe most people want to condone and sympathize your so-called wonderful lifestyle? I've been to a lot of crime scenes before viewing Mr. Carlson and for the life of me I will never believe God is not handing out this brand of punishment for people who like to dick one another."

Michaeleen was caught without replying, half in favor of Adam's life commitment and half agreeing with the policeman.

Sergeant Cavazos angrily grabbed the photos off the tray, stuffing them into the manila envelope then once again acknowledged Murray. "Oh, yeah, Lieutenant Cavazos, my brother, whom you met, mentioned you were the guy who found Mr. Magassey. We checked you out and your version. It appears you were there at the right time for this citizen. Can you add anything more?"

Murray shrugged. "Not anything, Sergeant Cavazos."

Knowing that he had enough of this, reaching into his breast pocket the policeman pulled out his cards for Murray and Magassey. Mr. Murray call me if you have anything more to add on this crime. And Mr. Magassey we will see you soon at 61 Reisner St., understand?"

Adam took the card and drew a deep breath. "When I get out of this place you'll be the first person I come to see, Sergeant Cavazos."

Cavazos looked at the four. "Yeah, that's why they pay me the big bucks, just to interview folks on things like this." The Sergeant then departed through the door, feeling a minor victory in all this.

Murray immediately wanted to know why Michaeleen had come unannounced. "It was a surprise seeing you here. I thought you were still researching MABB?"

The young woman looked at Adam whose oversized gown had opened enough for her to view his tight abdominals. "I just had to see what you were raving about, Murray, this Mr. Magassey. Especially, if I help you on this acquisition for my aunt. When you left my office I phoned a few well informed contacts about MABB. What they said about it clicked with your early evaluation of it."

Murray pointed to his own benefactor, as he addressed Adam, "Young man, Ms. Ventura seems to have signed on to assist on purchasing your thriving company."

Adam had his own thoughts about this young looking woman. He could not hide his glee about working with an attractive person of the opposite sex, far from what he had always done in the latest days before this near tragedy happened to him. What had he been missing? He knew if he was going to change his life around Michaeleen, would she be the start of it? "Yes, Ms. Ventura. It would be a distinct pleasure to work side by side with you on this ACQUISITION", as his eyes met hers.

The two stared at one another for ten or more seconds when Murray cleared his throat. "Sorry to break all this up, kids, but don't we want to discuss this buyout deal?"

Jonathan was shocked seeing his former lover now embracing the other side of romantic bliss and unsure where he stood with Adam, acting skeptical, like he had post menstrual syndrome he shook his head. "Well, Adam, if you insist on all this, I am leaving for now. I'll call you later." Jonathan then pranced out of the room.

Murray was overcome with this and raised his eyes toward heaven. "Alleluia, a man has been saved today!"

Michaeleen wanted to find out more about Adam. "From what Murray has told me about you, the early parts of your life living in an abused home, more or less escaping it to attend three or four colleges, being a male prostitute, a male to male gigolo, preying upon older men, getting their money when they died, rolling that all into MABB. Do you ever regret living this uncaring, wanton, selfish life?"

Magassey was blindsided by the beautiful female who had a businesslike approach to most everything in her life. Checks and balances always had to have sense and accuracy. He knew she was not going to be fooled with a smoke and mirrored approach. "In all honesty, yeah, I had some regrets too few to mention. I left with the clothes on my back and a hundred bucks in my jeans. No fancy ass car, expensive jewelry, million dollar trust fund. Go ahead, you figure I fucked a lot to start and maintain a $400 million company. I wore out a few mattresses gaining what I deserved from love starved, lecherous men. Even screwed a 70 year old widow and got a half million. They wanted it and I supplied it one way or another. You're just like the Cavazos brothers from HPD. They look down their noses at me. I can buy and sell them, anytime."

The woman was angry at that. "Hey, you tight butt head, I could buy YOU, have YOU for dinner, grind up the rest of YOU, except your penis and asshole and sell it on EBAY! For someone who wants to sell a company that is in a niche industry for some overpriced amount, you certainly can piss off someone who wanted to help you!"

Magassey's vibrant color disappeared as his mouth hung open. Regaining his composure, "Ms. Ventura, I did not want to or mean to insult you. I'm unclear about life at this point. Forgive me for being that 'tight butt head'. Let's work out a deal together, alright?"

She extended her hand at that point. "Truce?"

Adam took her hand. "Truce."

After that she pulled out some stats on his company, as Murray looked over their shoulders. "Well, Michaeleen, what do you think? And... Adam, do you believe in her figures?"

Adam managed a devilish smile. "You asked about Michaeleen's figures or did you say 'figure'?"

The young woman surprisingly did not blush and looked at Magassey. "Well, you are a surprise, Adam. Are you trying to talk me into this deal by making a move?"

"I believe we may be working close on selling MABB to whomever you think will purchase it for the price I want."

Her eyes sparkled, "Well, I, for one, am looking forward into negotiations especially when you are released from here."

Murray did not have to officiate a standoff, as he thought that with Michaeleen on their side Vixey would be easier to cage into the deal. "Michaeleen, all we have to do is convince Aunt Carol Sue to lay out four hundred big ones and if you say that she is anxious to get the Miller money into circulation, then this is a done deal."

Adam had just heard another name brought up on the deal, as his interest was even more peaked. "Who is this Aunt Carol Sue?"

Michaeleen walked away and looked out the window. "This is something that my aunt would be interested in considering if both Anthony and I were involved." Then turning back to Murray, "How did Sheryl take it when you told her about entering into this?"

Murray became a little defensive, "Actually, this has happened so suddenly that she and I have not discussed the issue."

Michaeleen was intense as she wished Murray would throw caution to the wind. "If you believe in MABB and Adam, you have to be on board or I am not pushing Vixey into laying out that huge amount of money. You have the funds as I do and I know her, she'll want you in along with me on this. You better wine and dine Sheryl to convince her that this is the next Microsoft to invest in."

Murray had never seen this side of his benefactor. "You really have blown me away on this."

"There are many things you don't know about me, but more later."

Murray retorted, "Ok, Michaeleen, so let's go with me and Sheryl, until she and I talk it over. Carol Sue is the main money mogul on this? I have to warn you, one, Sheryl strongly dislikes your aunt, and.... And two, what makes you really think that Vixey wants me in on this?"

Michaeleen, drew closer to him. "Because Anthony J. Murray, she LIKES YOU!"

"Murray was frozen for a moment, then managed to stammer, "Whaat?"

"Yes, Aunt Carol Sue has always been on your side."

"Is this some bullshit I am getting feed? When your mother and I were an item back thirty plus years ago, your beloved aunt was plotting along with their parents, Tex and Donna, to place an insurmountable wedge between us. Now you claim Vixey can't live without me? I admire and am very fond of you, Michaeleen, but c'mon. Oh, yeah, now that I have the bucks and some power she feels I belong in her world. Give me a break", as he continued not having faith in her description of Carol Sue.

"Vixey, was highly instrumental in getting the needed money that Miller Corp owed you. She advised me on where to go to and who to contact. Definitely, I had the influence because of controlling over 60 per cent of the stock, but she wanted you to have all the back proceeds for the past 30 plus years. She knew you deserved it."

Murray started to change his mind on Carol Sue. "Alright, since I trust you, it has to be right. This goes along way with convincing Sheryl to allow us to get into this deal."

Michaeleen breathed a positive sigh. "We can set up a meeting in the next two days so you can discuss all this with Sheryl. Adam, we will do our best to have my aunt buy MABB."

For the moment, Adam just watched how the extremely attractive, the young female CEO operated on Murray. "I have to believe that you will bring this all together. I am thoroughly going to enjoy being partnered with you." His eyes never left her face or her svelte-like body.

Murray was on the sidelines, viewing the couple seeing that Adam was infatuated with Michaeleen and that she started to think of him as her latest hunk.

Murray drove to their Memorial area home off Bunker Hill drive, pulling in as Sheryl was starting to leave in their late model Cadillac SRX SUV. "Hey I'm glad to catch you before you left to meet up on a shopping spree with Gina and your friends, Renate Roberts and June Brock. We need to sit down on this MABB buyout. I believe it is a good fit for us on our investment portfolio and we can kick in 10% with an almost guaranteed return on our money."

He pulled out a copy of what Michaeleen gave him on the specs. She looked them over carefully. "The numbers seem to be there and we do have an extra $30 or so million that is going stale in CD's and other avenues of little dividends. If you believe in this, we go for it even though the business is adult themed, where our friends might frown upon it."

Murray was a little hesitant on his next step in telling his wife about Vixey. "There's something more you need to know about our getting into MABB. Michaeleen feels strongly that the major player with the kind of money Adam wants is Carol Sue."

Sheryl looked at her husband for a long time without saying another word. Murray was waiting for an eruption. Finally he broke the silence, "Well, hon, I know you have an opinion."

Sheryl's normal calmness was complete opposite when it came to the topic of Carol Sue. "You are going to put our money with that WOMAN! You told me that she was everything except White and how she helped her family, the Millers, screw you out of all that money. How could you even think of lying in the same bed?"

"Sheryl, it is an investment. Carol Sue and I will probably not meet except once a quarter to review the financial end of MABB. You know, to see that the earnings are in line. We do that now with Gina's company, KnowlegeHalf. It's quite possible that she and I would not physically meet. We would correspond by email, fax, or a phone call for business, of course, nothing personal. That should work? We help Adam rid himself of MABB, invest in some more hotels, restaurants, just like we have now with the in town restaurant and the three boutique hotels."

Sheryl was a little less reluctant at that point. "You have a case, Murray. With what we could make money-wise with MABB, being with her four times a year. Wait, it is more than that, if she jams a holiday in there and we have to go to her place."

"From what I heard she has two gigantic homes and we can keep our distance from her. She'll be too busy being the homeowner to bother us."

"This is fine for now, but she better not try to get her claws in you. Vixey fits her."

Murray agreed without saying anything insightful, then realized when Michaeleen called him earlier she set up the meeting with Carol Sue at her East Memorial mansion. "One other item, my dear, Michaeleen and I are going to meet Vix...eh, Carol Sue, to show her the stats and earnings for MABB."

His good wife drew a deep breath as her eyes brightened even more than usual. Murray held up his hand in a 'Stop' manner. "I know, I know what YOU may think, but it is only this once and after that, Terry Gaiser, our attorney can handle it with his staff. No need to get close to her."

"Well, Michaeleen will be with you. I guess, it is fine, then."

Murray had plans to meet Michaeleen at Carol Sue's palatial home in East Memorial, just adjacent to the Post Oak area where the George H.W. Bushes resided. Surrounded by carefully manicured hedges, stood the two story mustard colored, Mediterranean style home with the customary red tiled roof. As he drove in with the Enclave, Michaeleen had already arrived in her BMW, just behind the yellow Corvette with the personal Texas plate emblazoned, 'VIXEY 'on it. Murray was edgy and not looking forward to his encounter with Carol Sue, whom he still considered an adversary.

Michaeleen could sense his hesitation as it was written on his face. "Don't be concerned Murray, I won't allow my aunt to bite you."

Murray attempted to make light of the young woman's' version of Carol Sue's ample ivories tearing into his skin. "You keep referring to that action like it just might happen and you will have to take a stick to her."

Michaeleen giggled. "You never know."

As they stood in front of the heavy oak double leaded glass doors Murray drew a deep breath and rang the doorbell. For a long moment, no one came to answer the bell. He thought back on how their lives changed and would have been different had Bobbie Jean's sister sided with him. Murray turned to Michaeleen, "Are you sure Carol Sue is at home?"

Before Michaeleen could respond they spotted a figure coming through the foyer and then the door swung open by an older European woman, tall, slight, in her late sixties, dressed in business attire and half glasses. She peered at the couple as though they were unwanted bible beaters, trying to preach their theological knowledge door to door. "Yes, can I assist you?"

Michaeleen piped up quickly, "I am Mrs. Winter's niece, Ms. Ventura. I called earlier to visit with her. This is Mr. Murray."

Murray began to feel uncomfortable and wondered what Carol Sue would be like as he and Sheryl had little or no contact since Wes and Gina's daughter's baptism almost a year earlier. The woman introduced herself as Eva, speaking with a heavy German accent, she then ushered the couple into a large, inviting stone fireplace accenting the formal area where the crackling of hot logs echoed through the room.

They looked for a time, at an oil portrait of two, late aged, teenage children and behind them, an older woman placing her hands on their shoulder, anchored above the massive wood burning opening. "Funny, Michaeleen, Houston is scheduled to have 65 degree weather today."

"Aunt Carol Sue is always cold."

Murray shook his head in agreement. "She does have something in common with Sheryl after all."

Michaeleen laughed, "Yes, I noticed that fact."

Murray, not seeing any of The Millers in the past thirty plus years, "The woman in the picture, is that your late grandmother, Donna, with your mother and aunt?"

"Yes, Auntie and my mom were 17."

"Bobbie Jean was a beautiful woman, and so was her twin."

"Well thank you, Anthony", a voice rang out behind them. Standing in the doorway of the living area was Carol Sue, towering at nearly six feet, tightly endowed with a narrow waist dressed in black leather pants, matching cropped jacket, western boots, the platinum medium cut hair draped her angular face highlighted by sparkling ocean blue eyes.

"This is quite a place you have here, Carol Sue", Murray complimented the matriarch of the mansion. "Again, what could anyone have expected, when you are a Miller?"

Carol Sue ignored his comment and motioned toward the well-stocked button tucked six stool bar that stood in the corner, backed by a tiffany glass back bar. "You two might want to have a toddy as we hammer out the details of, maybe, the purchase of MABB."

Michaeleen declined. "Trying to cut down on my alcohol."

Murray wanted to hit hard and leave as soon as possible, if she was or was not interested in the purchase. "You look extremely nice. Is this a prelude to your wanting to buy MABB? Anyway, it's a little early for me, too. But, thanks."

Carol Sue knew he would be nervous coming into her territory and wanted to play with him. "You are both welcome. You certainly are trim and fit, Anthony. It appears Sheryl is keeping you from those nasty carbs and calories. What else is she doing? Or should I say, not doing?"

Michaeleen stepped in. "Auntie, what do you think of the proposals and the bottom line for MABB?"

"Sweetie, you filled me in on this fantastic opportunity to own a fabulous different company. What do you think of my buying this company, Anthony?"

"You fit the bill, Vixey."

Carol Sue ran her tongue over her glistening, perfect, teeth, attempting to hide a vicious smile. "Fit the bill? What do you mean? I like to view this type of entertainment and adore men. Yes, I have this guy's video and he seems adequate. I could probably make a few dollars from owning this adult enterprise. You ARE going to come in and buy 10%?...Bet Sheryl is chomping at the bit, isn't she?"

"Yes, she feels that it is a good investment for our portfolio."

"At least you and I are on the same page on this one." Carol Sue sidled up to the bar pouring a Macallan Scotch drink. She still pushed the issue. "Are you certain that I can't interest either of you in a late morning drink?"

Michaeleen deferred. Murray waved off. "Empty stomach and not advisable to hit the booze. Lunch is more appropriate". He thought he should offer it to the ladies as he had been a part of a successful sell of a problem that caused a lot of grieve, not to mention, death to a number of people. "It's lunch time, would you two lovely ladies be interested in a great meal at Rays in Fulshear?" Michaeleen, again, chose to decline. "I have a late appointment with my attorney to draw up the papers for our part of the purchase."

Carol Sue quickly agreed to the invite. "I'm available, Anthony, and I am very, very hungry!'

Murray drew back, somewhat, wishing, in part, that he had not put out the offer, but a little hoping that she did not see his reaction and wanted to distance himself. "Actually, Rays have been growing things, locally."

Carol Sue, wanted to step it up a little, "Have you ever seen his cucumbers? They remind me of other things that you want to suck on."

Fortunately, a cell phone came in for Murray. It was from Bill and he did not wish to go through as to why he was lunching with someone he called a burr under his saddle. "I'll return the call later." Murray, had all he could muster to hold back his feelings, although he was not sure what they were. There were some odd unsorted differences in the past for someone he knew so many years back in North Texas, who was part of her family, that held him back and stole his fortune, yet he was assured that this sultry woman was a large reason he had the hundreds of millions that was rightfully his. But why did she side with him against the probable hatred of her family?

Carol Sue knew he was in deep thought about something as she was ready to head out, "What are you thinking about? I'm starved!"

Murray wanted to be blunt yet, he was in a haze, "It is nothing, let's just head over to Ray's."

Carol Sue surprised him by taking his arm, looking at Murray intently. "This is just the beginning of a new relationship, Anthony. I hope you will forget the past and go with the now?"

As they got to the cars, "Hey, Carol Sue, let's take the Enclave, more room."

She sensed his adversity to closeness in her Corvette. She teased, "We could have taken my car. Are you claustrophobic or something?"

"Yeah, something."

"Well, my group on Thursdays, like my yellow 'Vette. We often have a brewski in the parking lot after our bowling session and the guys always want to take a spin in it."

Murray had a sense of curiosity about the personalized plate. "You actually want people to call you Vixey?"

She laughed easily, "Perhaps, I want to disarm people who get to know me. Back in Wichita Falls, my mother frowned on me having an openness to people. We were always the first family there and being frivolous to the public did not set well."

"Hmm, frivolous, huh? You want people to love you for your openness?"

"Anthony, it is more than that...."

Murray opened the door for the almost blushing former Miss Wichita Falls, then walked around getting in.

As they drove away, he finished his sentence, "You do have a way with men."

She stared straight ahead without answering.

He thought the grand dame of Houston culture and arts with a palatial home were somewhat puzzling to him about her drinking Miller Lights in a parking lot of a bowling alley. Carol Sue had moved 180 degrees from what he remembered when he was vying for the affection of her twin sister. She was a debutante all over then.

At lunch, Carol Sue avoided the past and concentrated on asking about his other family members as he filled her in. He knew from Michaeleen about her devotion to Wes and Gina's young children. "So how does it feel to be a grandmother?" Murray blurted, attempting to steer clear of their past differences.

Carol Sue put down her glass of Texas merlot and started to smile broadly, "It's a blast, Anthony. I go over to Wes and Gina's home in Richmond and sit in a rocker for hours. It is heaven, holding my grandkids, especially, Noah Grant. He is just the cutest little bundle of joy. It is fabulous, just out of this world."

Murray had a new view of his former enemy. "You in a rocker, hard to conjure up that image."

She grabbed her wine glass and held it up like a shield of defense. "Why do you say that?"

He was pent up with past emotions and wanted to lash out at her. "It's not me to live in the past, with as bright as Sheryl and my current lives have changed for the better, but when I recall those times in Wichita Falls 30 plus years ago, if you want to call it somewhat, the bad times, you were steeped in hatred of me and was a big instigator in breaking up Bobbie Jean and me. It is not the picture of a gracious grandma today. I can't get past that for whatever reason, it still haunts me."

She sipped the wine putting the glass down easily, "You wound up with the money, much thanks to my niece. What more can you want from me?"

"Michaeleen was a god send to me and Sheryl. I guess from what your niece related to me was that you were a large part of our getting what was coming to us. As to what I want from you, I know you would not be here with me if I was a mere Second Lieutenant in the Air Force or even an insurance agent."

"You have a way to get it out, my almost brother-in-law", dropping her congeniality. She looked out the window and then reached for the wine; again, as to steady herself for the next line, "I can't bring back Bobbie Jean to either of us. I loved her as much as you did."

"So you admit my love for her was real." Murray at this point, acting superior as he felt a victor in this skirmish.

Her ocean blue eyes narrowed and she shook her head, "Maybe I thought you would forgive and forget my part in the breakup. It appears you won't allow me to make it up to you", as she attempted to hold back the tears, looking out the window at the traffic. "Can't you please forgive me, Anthony?" She pulled her hands up to her face, openly crying, causing the other nearby patrons to stop their conversation, eating and drinking to lean in and hear more of what was occurring at the couple's table.

Murray was caught in a cross fire as Carol Sue continued to bawl openly. He smiled at a few of the other diners. "It is joyful tears. We haven't seen one another for a long time."

She stopped the flow as he said that. "I have changed from the time you knew me. Please believe that."

Murray was unable to defend against her pleas and reached over, giving his handkerchief to her. Was it a ploy on Carol Sue's part, he was not sure. Reluctantly, "Okay, Vixey, I know you did your part on the money. I can meet you half way for now. Just why did it take so long to reach out to me after Bobbie Jean died? Why now?"

"After my breast cancer surgery and almost dying, I had time to look over my past life and wanted to mend fences and un-do the wrongs I may have caused harming people by my actions or the lack of caring. I've gone on Facebook and My Life, using Vixey Miller."

"Vixey Miller?" Why that name? You use your maiden name and nickname. Kind of cool of you. I heard you lead two lives. You have the mansion in East Memorial and the place in Katy."

Her eyes dried and began glowing once more. "Yes, I am a bowler too. Do pretty well, 175 average. Have my own ball, shoes, and bag. Got a locker over at Pin Oaks Lanes. Drink shots with everyone. Have house tequila and tonic, not uppity Patron, even drink Shiner Bock. We bowl in a high power league then head over to Wild Ride Rodeo and kick up our heels, throw darts, and shoot the shit with my fellow bowlers. I host poker nights at my Katy place, make nachos and wings for everyone. They have no idea who I was in Wichita Falls nor have they ever seen me in the society pages of Dallas, and now Houston. I ride a big Harley. Funny, isn't it, coming from being a near super model when I was nineteen? They have no idea of my wealth."

Murray tried to understand her turnaround antics. "So, isn't it self-effacing or if not that, are you wanting to be loved by everyone who was in contact or ever had a relationship with you?"

"I tried to reach out in Wichita Falls, Ft. Worth, even in Dallas. I was heavily involved with Miller Industries. I volunteered at cancer centers, chaired diabetes charities, visited assisted living folks, baked cookies for the scouts and church functions. It did not seem to work so I brought what was left of Miller Corp and moved everything to Houston. Wanted to start anew."

"You knew we lived here. Why didn't you call and go out for a drink or coffee, at least? Later when our daughter and your son got together, you still kept your distance from us at social functions and the wedding and baptisms. I cannot believe you were bashful and a wall flower."

"Pride. I thought of you every day. Wanting to pick up the phone and....You were hurt the most. The one who deserved much better. I wanted to beg your forgiveness. Even at Wes and Gina's wedding, I was so embarrassed and hid it by downing one scotch after another. Of course, at the baptisms, I could not drink. What the holy water?" She laughed, "I just made myself scarce."

"SOO , Sheryl and I considered you aloof but that was not the case, "Murray, at that moment, was feeling guilty. Maybe he was being too hard on her? Naw, he thought. Searching for the reason. "Tell me why?"

"No one wanted a former model from a well-known, affluent family that most of the common folks thought we all looked down their noses on all of Wichita Falls. Winning the Miss North Texas crown in the so-called Metro-Plex did little for me. Like I said, I wanted a new life away from everyone who ever knew me. I did not want to be an outsider. Even here, I volunteer, but people still think of me as an outsider."

Leaving Ray's and walking toward the parking lot at Wallis State Bank. Vixey started to tear up continuing to ruin her perfect makeup. He turned to her. "Maybe now, I feel that if I had reached out to you. It was a dozen years ago when I was in the Dallas area, but thought, how I would explain it to my family that someone like you was a bitter memory." For what it was worth, he touched her hand to comfort her.

Carol Sue gazed at Murray more than as a possible friend and co-owner of MABB. She saw him much differently. That being more than Gina's dad. Was she wanting a round or two at the local Ramada? "I want to discuss this with you now if you have the time?"

Murray was slightly amused as well as confused on which subject she was interested in discussing. "Carol Sue, ah, are we talking about MABB or the past?"

They each climbed into the Enclave.

"I really wish to talk about us. "She moved her leg closer to his over the console.

Murray knew it was a come on by her. "Let us head back to your home to drop you off as I have to get with Adam and his lawyer, who sent over the actual bottom line on MABB. Do the numbers make it for you?"

She changed her approach, "Only if you and Michaeleen put in 10% each and Adam stays in for the same amount. I am a little disappointed in your not wanting to make it an afternoon."

"Carol Sue, if you and I can be at least civil and friendly in a, say, ah, err, business-like or casual way, that should do well for both of us. Okay? Not sold on why it has taken so long. We had three social engagements where you basically ignored Sheryl and me. Was it just the money?"

She did not know how to respond but only offered, "I wanted to but knew that Sheryl strongly disliked me." She then pulled her hand back. "I cannot say more .. just drop me off at my Katy place. I need to get ready for tonight at Pin Oaks Lanes."

Murray did not get the answer from her and thought it was not worth pursuing. "Yes, rubbing elbows with the common man."

The well-heeled woman laughed, slightly, at that remark. "I rub a lot of things besides elbows. You need to try it sometime."

"Obviously, you're referring to bowling and rubbing your Ebonite ball", he drawled, wryly.

She batted those ocean blues at him. "Sure. I'll give you directions to my Cinco Ranch place."

With that they left and in 20 minutes his Enclave pulled up to her two story colonial with manicured lawn and curved drive where her black Escalade was parked, sporting personal Texas personal plate, WNTRS3.

As he viewed her mini estate Murray wanted to zing her again. "You know, Vixey, I think you wanted to show me you have a lot of expensive property just to let me know how much skin you have. This is just the type of move Tex would have done. I recall how he lauded it over me displaying his arrogance of wealth. How do your poker buddies view this place? Even after our kids got together for some reason I cannot bring myself to believe you. For the moment, it is business and only that."

"You want to know what my fellow bowlers think? I just tell them I am renting it from a rich uncle in Oklahoma. I sure would not want to show MY ARROGANCE to anyone. AND, that is not why I wanted you to bring me to Katy. I have to pick up the Cadillac and take it to the dealer on I-10 for service. And further, Mr. Murray, Anthony, I really wanted to see you the time I heard you were in Dallas. But my pride, once more, kept me from reaching out. I did not want to have to explain it to my family about someone who was a bitter memory, yet a part of one of my earliest best moments." She began to choke up again, then pulled herself together, "I am fine , I realize where you are coming from. It is only business..."

"I can't offer you my handkerchief. You still have it in your purse. Are you going to be alright, Carol Sue?" Now touching her hand and acting like a moon struck teenager, then finally snapping out of it as reality set in. "I have to be honest on this deal for MABB. You may be in danger because of Kolezy. While I want you in on this I don't want you to be hurt or worse. Are you still a go?"

Carol Sue reached in her Dourney and Bourke purse and dabbed her eyes and makeup with his white monogrammed 'M' hanky. Regaining her composure, "That son of a bitch is not going to screw me out of this buy. MABB is perfect. Kolezy is not going to get it. I have my duel .38's with the pink handles waiting for that cock sucker."

Murray was taken back at her reaction. "This character is bad news from what I heard from Adam. Don't be unafraid so much as he'll creep into your life."

She turned the table back on him. "What about you and Sheryl? You have committed to Adam and me on putting up a chunk of moola. What kind of artillery do you have?"

"Taurus Judge. Fires some heavy ammo. Sheryl has her trusty .22 automatic. Along with that, I am involved with a group who will help put down Kolezy."

Carol Sue laid back in her seat. "The only thing I want is to see Adam in real life. So far I have just about committed to $350 million on the strength of Michaeleen who thinks this guy is a fuckin' hunk even though he is not what I believe a man should be. I viewed a couple of his so-called movies and looking at these beautiful numbers that will 'ca-ching' in my bank account. This ass-hole Kolezy is not going to mess me over. I promise you."

She climbed out from the Enclave as he extended his hand out, she ran hers down his arm, smiling. "We'll will be in touch?"

"Yeah, Vixey, at least we can be casual friends and business partners."

"Casual?", she echoed, as she swayed out of the Enclave and got into her Escalade.

At the hospital, Dimas and Zeke were going to pay another visit to Adam before he was discharged. They still wanted to sort out the details on the serial murders. Earlier, Dimas was informed that HPD sent over an officer to take the place of Rich's operative to guard Adam.

Coming up to the room the posted, young patrolman, was asleep outside Magassey's room. Zeke felt totally disgusted from his lack of action. He kicked the chair of the slumbering cop, jarring him. Dimas yelled down to the drowsy appearing blue, "Hey, slick, you're supposed to be guarding our citizen!"

The apparent rookie cop apologized and vowed. "Sorry, Sir. I have been up the last 24 hours! It won't happen again."

With that the brothers entered the room, finding Jonathan, who was discussing their art gallery purchases with Adam as they came in.

"Who are you?" Dimas demanded of the slender, reddish young man.

"I am Adam's partner in the art gallery"

"Yeah, I remember you being part of that place that has those prissy paintings and art shit you peddle on Lower Westheimer", growled Zeke.

Dimas nudged his brother as to proceed and not make an issue of sexuality.

Adam wanted to cut out the dialogue. "What is it you want, Lieutenant Cavazos?"

"From what I am told, the doctors are ready to release you tomorrow. We need you to come down to Reisner Street and swear out a complaint on your step father. Zeke found a Hungarian immigrant on West Gray, last evening in a bar, where he was drunk and disorderly. "

Magassey was disinterested at first. "What has that have to do with my situation?"

Zeke saw that Adam was uncaring at that remark. "He mentioned a lot of Mark Carlson. Apparently, he was at the scene of the murder, so you better be interested. You get my drift?"

Jonathan grew paler than normal as he focused on what Adam was going to say, knowing his friend was with Mark, the night before he was murdered, spending the entire night with him.

Zeke caught Jonathan's reaction and before Adam could cover anything up, the Sergeant jumped on Jonathan's look. "What can you tell me about this Hungarian expatriate? You just drew a face like you know something."

Jonathan's voice dropped an octave. "You know what the man's name was?"

Zeke forcefully replied, "Yeah, Red, it was Joseph Molnar. Tell me what you think?"

Jonathan's eyes widened, "Mark mentioned he was going to see this guy at the bar that night he, ah...died."

Lieutenant Cavazos took over the grilling of the slender, gay man. At almost a shout, "HE did mention THAT name, then?"

Cowering, Jonathan, murmured, "Yes, it was Joseph Molnar."

Adam had seen enough. "Okaay, you two cops. Lay off of Jonathan. That's all he can tell you."

Lieutenant Cavazos lunged toward the bed to intimidate Adam. "I will be the judge on that, Mr. Magassey. Don't you recall that your dumb assholed-self was violated? Heh? My brother and I, with HPD want to find the killers. Do you know that we received a needle filled with insulin that was due for you? Yes sir, they missed on another attempt."

Adam put his hands up on a stop motion to the beleaguered and wound tight cop. Now believing that his departed friend assisted Louis in almost murdering him wanted to lash out. "Jonathan and I know you have a big job ahead. Murray and his friends were the ones that prevented my stepfather's stooge from using that needle. Now I will tell you about Mark. He always was borrowing money from Jonathan and me. He even stole some out of our cash register at the restaurant and what we collected in cash at the gallery, although most of that was in checks and credit card vouchers. He even forged some of the checks from our patrons at both places and did a credit card scam, I believe with Molnar. I don't know very much about that character but we always made good on Mark's lapses. I believe that Molnar may be a part of the Hungarian Mafia, too."

Zeke looked at Adam as though he was a Martian on Red Bull. "What did you say? I lost you after 'Mark's lapses'? You did not say 'Hungarian Mafia'? Whew, where are we going on this bro?" as he turned to Dimas.

The Lieutenant affirmed what he just heard from Adam's lips. "Yeah, Zeke, I heard him, too. Before you go any further, Mr. Magassey, what was the deal that night at the motel?"

"Mark wanted this $25,000 trick because he needed $17,000 to clear some gambling debts. I only had $1500 on me to give him so I told him I would do it and give him the proceeds."

Zeke was closing in on the questioning. "So, why did you go and not Mark?"

"He was lactose intolerant and had a bout of the runs."

Both of the brothers looked at one another and shook their heads in disgusted unison.

Zeke looked over to his brother. "Guess every job has consequences!"

Dimas led out a laugh, as well, "I never had to worry about that, Bro."

Zeke, flatly uttered, "Another screwed up...dumb shit."

Adam was not getting any respect from the Cavazos' duo and defended, "Mark's dead. Don't kick him around. Alright, already!"

Dimas agreed. "Fine, but what about this mafia deal, Mr. Magassey?"

"You may remember I told you about my stepfather, Louis B. Kolezy, the eminent attorney?"

Cavazos agreed, "Yeah, something about how he mistreated you and you left to become a porn star, have a fu-fu type artsy picture gallery, winding up in some sleazy motel on the Beltway."

Adam was incensed, "Damn, Lieutenant, you have proof of wrong doings by this man, who has probably been totally responsible for five killings and my near death. Thanks to good Samaritans, I was saved from being number SIX. You stand there and mock the situation. Do you really wish to stop the carnage of young men by this ruthless guy?"

"How can you show me that there is a connection? Can you implicate him in the killing of your friends?" Lieutenant Cavazos seemed to plead.

"My stepfather has to be the one who is responsible for the murders. He knows they went to school with me and were, a, ah, sort of partners, connected to me. Add to that, his overseas business with his partner, Imre Rabb. At least, my sister, Melanie, mentioned that name to me a few months back. Rabb desired Americans in his pictures and Louis wanted me to talk them into going to Prague and Budapest. If I did not do as he asked, he had Molnar, a Budapest heavy. A guy who kicks ass, if you know what I mean?"

Zeke looked at his brother, "Hey, Bro, this is what we have been looking for to break this case wide open."

Lieutenant Cavazos stiffened his jaw. "Yeah, and with Jonathan coming down to look at some mug shots at Reisner Street we can corner these slime balls. We can sweat this Joseph Molnar. Have him turn over on Kolezy."

Jonathan had a more worried face than usual at that suggestion. "I don't wish to go to a place like that."

Zeke wanted to send a volley toward the slender, deeply concerned man. "Jonathan, are you afraid that you could get your butt slapped around?"

Jonathan shot back, "Sergeant, you noticed my tight gluts? Sounds as though you might like touching them?"

Zeke blew back, "Not as much as you would, bent over with a light bulb up your ass. We got a couple of your MEN, lighting each other up with a three way GE bulb fucking one another on a downtown street a few months back. Have you ever done that, Jonathan, MY MAN?"

"If you want anything further, come by our art gallery. I am not going to Reisner Street anytime soon." With that Jonathan hugged Adam and left.

Lieutenant Cavazos wanted a little more information on this guy, Rabb and Kolezy's connection. "You said, they were partners. Partners in what?"

Male porn in Poland, even Russia, and some other parts of Europe. That is the whole reason he wants my company. We have a large market in the United States and if he got it, he could control the entire business. And, it is a very successful business. Maybe it is something you don't care about, but a lot of people in the States are followers of it especially, women. A big chunk of the sell is to women, not the perverts you think who lurk in the back alleys of a 24 hour video store. Yes, they are a part of it but not as much as those women. My company has tracked our market the last three years and due to them we ran our ads to attract the 22 to 64 female markets."

Dimas was still puzzled and could care less of the buyers of this trash. "You have a backup in case something happens to you?"

"I initially set up that my brother, Ryan, sister in Austin, Melissa, and Melanie, my sister in Houston. They would inherit MABB if something happened to me. Louis, I firmly believe, killed Ryan. He has tried twice to kill Melissa. With her out of the way and Ryan and me both dead, he has my weak sister, who he as abused continually for the past twenty plus years. Confused as she is, Melanie would do anything he asked. She might be installed as the president of the company, but like a marionette, my stepfather would be pulling her strings as he ran the company.

While Lieutenant Cavazos was scratching his head, Jonathan came in and said, "Hey, where is the guard outside the door?"

Zeke and Dimas looked at one another as they thought it was ordered for a 24 /7 on Adam's room. Before they could figure what and why, two shots rang out over Adam's head, cracking the room window, narrowing missing Jonathan, imbedding two bullets in a monitor where Adam had been moments before, as he rolled over onto the floor. A third shot broke the overhead bed light where the patient should have been. Both of the policemen dove down in front of the bed.

Zeke reached up and cut off the bed light.

Lieutenant Cavazos yelled, "Everyone get down! Stay calm, it is under control!"

Jonathan, was frozen with fear, standing by the bed. Adam got up and pulled him to the floor. They both wound up holding one other.

Zeke saw them embrace. "Do you two wish to get married by the roving hospital minister they have here?"

Adam and his friend disregarded the Sergeant's comment.

Adam spoke first, "I am very happy to get out of here. This hospital is too dangerous."

Jonathan crawled to the bathroom. "Better check a few things."

Lieutenant Cavazos ran out of the room to see why the posted HPD guard did not respond to the commotion in the room. The guard was nowhere in sight.

Zeke crouched around to see the bullet holes attempting to calculate which direction the shots came from.

A nurse came in, breathlessly asked, "What happened?"

Zeke came up. "Don't be concerned, nurse, what every you name is, just wanted to know what happened to the young policeman stationed in the hall?"

"I went by his post and Nick was gone", exclaiming the young nurse.

"Oh, you know him?" Dimas asked, as he re-entered the room. He figured she had an interest in the young stationed policeman.

"Yes, Nick was someone I knew in high school. He and I visited old times at Hastings High".

"I think he needs to tell us why he was missing from his station", questioned Lieutenant Cavazos.

The nurse explained, "About five minutes before the shots he was talking with a man who had a scar on his face."

Adam knew only too well who she was describing, "Drago! He probably is the sniper that Louis uses. Lieutenant, it has to be my stepfather's doing."

Zeke looked over the outside buildings. "My educated guess is the shots came from the parking garage across the way."

Dimas took over after listening to Adam and Zeke. "Bro, you stay here and guard the room. I'll radio for backup units."

In a matter of minutes, two Memorial Hospital armed security guards came into the room. Adam went into the bathroom to console Jonathan who fled there to escape further danger.

Zeke chided the couple. "Hey, Adam, better get dressed and checked out so you can go down to Reisner Street. We'll have a patrol car here to take you there in protective custody."

Jonathan came out and got his friend's clothes that he brought in earlier. Later as Adam emerged from the bathroom, the head nurse came in, "Mr. Magassey, Doctor Abbott wants you to stay in your room so he can dismiss you."

Adam found that amusing, on her order, "Nurse, my life has been threatened twice in this place. I'm out of here. This place is too dangerous!"

The Lieutenant came back, "Zeke, our young cop is nowhere to be found. I have a sickening feeling he is involved."

Adam was not sure he could trust the police after the Houston Police guard left his station and he knew what the Lieutenant was getting at. Questioning if the nurse's friend may have been a part of the shooting scene. A Houston cop who may have gone bad? "Lieutenant Cavazos, Jonathan and I are not heading to the police station. You have enough information on Louis Kolezy to question and bring him in. Besides, can we actually trust the Houston Police Department after this?"

"It has not been proven that our blue had any involvement in this. You're taking a chance, Mr. Magassey, it is your funeral", warned Lieutenant Cavazos.

Adam, then decided to head to Jonathan's condo in Midtown Houston, but first he phoned Murray and filled him in on the latest attempt on his life.

Murray and Bill called upon their group. Rich Fedor, Ron Tanski, Sev Fedor, and Ernie Petrovich, to again, join forces as they did in Cleveland, a year and a half ago. This time it would be to defeat Louis B. Kolezy and bring him to justice. They met over at Murray's home in Memorial, mapping out the strategy.

Rich had been a member of The Secret Service and a FBI operative for nearly 30 years, diligently acting on behalf of his country. He raised two children as a single parent. After leaving government service, he established Moonlight Investigations three years ago.

Tanski was a former Viet Nam vet who killed ten Viet Cong on a mission over in Danang with an M-1 rifle and two grenades. He still suffered from the slices of metal imbedded in his body, mostly in his legs and back from that battle. Divorced, father of two sons, he re-married to a Christian woman, Ruby Begonia, a former beauty queen from Iowa. They enjoyed an idyllic life in Colorado at their 2000 acre ranch.

Sev Fedor, Rich's cousin, was a soldier of fortune offering his services to anyone who wanted to kill or move some other king or top person, out of their position. He was always available, not caring about the face of the person who was to be eliminated. Some insiders said he found a lost gold mine in the Peruvian jungle, making him wealthy. Sev's love of danger overshadowed his bank account. His wife of over 25 years, along with their four grown children, constantly were concerned about his well-being.

Petrovich, a former on-line assembler at the local Cleveland Ford plant, put himself through law school and began as an attorney specializing in slip and fall cases. He had an early murky past, allegedly, paying off a judge in a murder case involving a stripper. He was cleared in that case. Ernie then became a specialist in divorce cases, still connecting in the legal world. He also found religion and became more charismatic and an activist in defending the people unable to defend themselves, mostly at the insistence of his wife, Lottie, a former Miss Denmark, who bore him two daughters.

The four were filled in on what Murray and Bill were involved in, explaining everything that occurred up to this point, including Adam's history. Though, still yet to meet him they attempted to be in Adam's corner. All were a little skeptical due to the young man's background and choice of sexual preference. Sev also allied with Ernie on issues and had doubts about Adam. Yet, all four agreed that Kolezy was to be brought down and Adam was the key in doing that. At that time, the doorbell rang and Sheryl let in a still shaken Adam. Murray and Bill did the introductions to others and they all shook hands, pleased that Adam had a firm grip, unlike the wimpy one most expected.

Rich started in immediately and wanted to get a rise out of Adam who was pouring himself a smoothie from Murray's non-alcohol bar. "So, are we going over to see your beloved stepdad today, slapping on the cuffs, taking him to Reisner Street? You want him behind bars before he tries to shoot you, like that hospital try. Okay, don't you, Adam?"

Adam whirled around, sensing Rich was pushing his button to see what reaction he would come up with. "Rich, I have a set of handcuffs in my car and that's a great idea. Let me down this smoothie and then the seven of us go downtown to his office and haul his worthless ass out and send him before a judge who does not like him... I like your action!"

Rich backed up a little, his glasses falling down on his nose and as he pushed them back up, "I didn't mean now or in the next hour. Like maybe tomorrow ..."

Tanski was less tactful in teasing. "Hey, Adam, I understand that male porn stars shave off the hair around their dicks so they can have a better feeling on the other guy's ass?"

Bill, who was taking a drink of beer nearly choked on the long draw. After coughing, he gasped out, "Tanski, what brought that shit up from out of nowhere?"

Tanski, defended, "Just wanted to set the mood."

"You have handcuffs in your car?" A puzzled Sev asked.

"Yes, joked Adam, they go with the whips and chains in the trunk."

Everyone was silent in the room after that.

Wanting to set Tanski straight on the hair removal, Adam was consoling. "It is more convenient, Ron, doing it that way. We use a depilatory cream to prevent an itching affect. It will still burn a little, if we don't get the hair out of our partner's ass. You wish to try it sometime?"

Tanski normally was Teflon when he was razed back but this time his face had a reddish tint to it. He decided not to comment any further. Then he shifted back as a knocked down, aggressive fighter springing back off the mat. "What the Viet Nam prostitutes did for us was shave our testicles with bamboo thread on a small rolling pin. It was a two way pleasure when we slide in and out."

Adam did not want to leave it alone. "You realize, Tanski, that you gave me a real great idea the next time I shoot a movie."

Petrovich's head backed in a violent motion."Hey, Adam, you told Murray and Bill that you were going straight!"

The young man remembered telling all, "Yeah, I forget. It is tough at times, to change habits."

Bill remarked, "Well we all got more information than we wanted and I can't believe you guys!"

Murray looked up at the ceiling, thinking what did he start? "Okay, guys, that is enough. At least Bill did not have any Chicago Cubs or Cleveland Indians group stories to tell us. Let's discuss Kolezy."

Adam related to the group that he and Jonathan relented and went to 61 Reisner St. giving a statement concerning Mark's death and his part of knowing the dead man. He mentioned the attempts on Melissa's life.

Ernie wanted to know if Kolezy was behind the murder.

Murray spoke up. "Okay. Ernie, what more proof do you require?"

Petrovich was too cautious after a duo of lawsuits filed against him. "What consequences do we face if Kolezy counter sues us?"

Adam was confident, "Not any at all, Ernie, this guy does not play by the rules. You don't need to be concerned with his bullying tactics."

Sheryl had left earlier and returned during the conversations, sipping her green tea, waving and smiling to everyone.

Suddenly the phone rang. Delores, their maid, announced to the man of the house that a Ms. Carol Sue Winters was calling, asking that Murray speak with her.

Sheryl was already a little jealous as she looked at her husband with a jaundice eye.

Reluctantly, he accepted the call knowing he was still trying to convince his wife he was not involved with Vixey. That it was only going to be business.

Carol Sue asked, "I want to go over these figures and most of all, the spreadsheet you left me as well. I need to be briefed on Adam."

"In the next few days I'll bring over Adam who can fill you in on all the particulars. He is who you actually need."

"I know you have all the facts and figures. You need to come to my East Memorial home."

Keenly observing Sheryl who acted unhappy, Murray looked over at Adam, who he wanted to bring with him and not positive what Carol Sue actually wanted. "What's up, really?"

"I have to find out about this young porn star who can fuck up a storm. Bring that hunk with you. Wes is going to be here to assist me. He is, in addition to CEO of Miller Corp., an attorney, and a whizz on legal papers."

Sheryl, hearing the one sided phone conversation, wore a worried look. They were having a good time with Bill and the group along with Adam, all having an understanding involving the events of the past and what was to come in the future. Murray's wife did not wish to have Carol Sue in on it, even though her nemesis was the key to the buyout.

Murray looked at his wife, somewhat sheepishly, "I have to take Adam over to Carol Sue's place in East Memorial. She wants to see him and go over the figures for MABB."

Sheryl still cast a untrusting eye toward her husband, "I cannot trust that bitch with you and Adam."

Murray counteracted her fears, "Sheryl, Adam is a big boy, right? Me, she could care less about. We have an early history but it is not sexual. Okay?"

As she hugged her husband, "I guess, since I trust you." Then she planted a long, deep kiss on his lips that he appeared to savor for, a record, fourteen seconds, as he gave one passionate buss back to his wife. Bill and the others stared at the couple.

Petrovich made the moment. "That's what a good marriage is all about. I can attest to that, as well."

Back at Carol Sue's palatial Memorial home, Adam and Murray arrived. She did not wish to wait long to see Adam. The siren was dressed in tight Vera Wang Jeans and an even tighter gray Gloria Vanderbilt pastel tee shirt, ladies Dan Post boots, smelling like Liz Taylor's White Diamonds. The vixen appeared that she was ready for an outdoor model shoot of years before, added to that her Christian silver cross glittered around her near perfect neckline untouched by any plastic surgeon. A Virginia Slim Long, lay smoldering in a granite ashtray situated on gold leafed coffee table next to two legal manila folders.

Murray eyed the half smoked nicotine cancer stick. "Can't figure it, Vixey, you beat breast cancer, work out daily, then inhale those god forbidden carcinogenic, white papered, deadened butts."

Carol Sue leaned over showing her cleavage to beckon Adam who had made himself comfortable on the black leather, seven foot sofa. She picked up the half lit cigarette, taking a puff and letting it out. "I'm like Clinton, don't inhale."

Adam popped up and introduced himself to Carol Sue. "I'm Adam Magassey and you are the lucky lady who is going to buy my company."

As she looked over the young executive, dressed in pressed Ralph Lauren slacks, yellow button down broadcloth shirt covered by a Bill Blass tan blazer, she held a non-descript stare, void of caring as to who he was. But that was her hard to get game. Underneath all that she was undressing him wanting to see his au natural state like she viewed in a trilogy of his latest movies. Extending her hand to his, batting her eyes at him even though that meant little as he had many a man do it to him, he felt it was a slightly comical that she was doing it. Clearing his throat as well as his thoughts, Adam figured he wanted to ask this woman where she was at that moment. "Carol Sue, are you prepared to invest the amount I am asking for my company?"

"Acting a little surprised, she offered, "You can cut to the chase pretty well, Adam, something I saw in Murray a few days ago. The thought of owning an adult entertainment, slash a hotel restaurant companion is very intriguing. My son, Wesley, feels you should stay in at 10 percent, just as my niece, Michaeleen, has agreed to do. Not to be left out, Murray should kick in the other 10 percent. Wes and I can come up with the big chunk of change. Plus you would still make those hot video movies."

Adam did not mind the stay in amount, but if he were to change his life, the movie part was going to be out and he already had his fill of those types of attractions. "Carol Sue, you are getting the very best of my players. I plan on changing my alternative life style and if you want to call it as it is, my retirement from this types of entertainment has started. I have had enough of the star role in these flicks."

"I like your ass and believe that most of my female friends definitely want to see more of your acting. My share of MABB is $230 million; I want you in the scenes."

Adam did not buy her action knowing she was horny. He wanted to gain more money from her and less from his checking account. "How about this, Carol Sue, you sweeten your offer another 50 million and I will guarantee you'll have my best studs doing their hot sweaty, sexy moves that will have you and your girlfriends clawing whomever or whatever is in their grasp. I am out of the business and don't have any desire to show my private parts on the screen any longer. I'll keep the 10 per cent in MABB and lend technical support. No more than that. Do we have a deal?"

Carol Sue wanted to eat him and knew she could get him to change his mind if he and she had a roll in the sack and at the same time keep the buy at the original price. "You and I need to have dinner tonight and discuss the possibilities. What do you say, my dear Adam?" Still pressing him to unknown boundaries she felt was limitless, running her tongue over her pouty lips.

His intention was to squeeze those additional millions of dollars from her and if it took a dinner and a night of amour he was game for it even though he was new at romancing a woman for this much money. "I would love to Ms. Winters in a few nights, although, I have other commitments."

"Other women? Or still sampling the other side?"

As she fumbled for another cigarette, Adam asked nonchalantly, by passing her cutting remark "Why did you and your last husband get a divorce? You appear to be a great combo? He is or was a hedge fund wizard. You, a hard driving business woman."

Carol Sue was confused by his request. "I am not sure why you are asking that ? What has that to do with buying your company?"

Adam felt compassion for this woman he never met but liked what he saw. " You know, Carol Sue, I am only attempting to get to know you better. Your movements are not black and white. You had breast cancer and even though you don't inhale some of that crap from the cigarettes enters your lungs. Perhaps Murray can write you a multimillion life policy so we won't get caught short on this deal. It would nice in lieu of that for you to quit smoking."

Carol Sue started to become irritated. Smashing the cigarette on the ashtray at the bar. "Oh-Kay! Satisfied? I can use a drink. Anyone else or are the two of you Quakers or First Day Adventists or Jack Olson bible beaters?"

Murray was edging to put his two cents into the fray. "Vixey, maybe Quakers drink. Just like all Jews aren't orthodox. My feeling is Jack and his wife like to have a glass of wine or even a mild cocktail now and then. Ok, I'll let you pour me a George Dickel #12, on the rocks, if it allows you to loosen up more. You're tense."

"I don't have that brand. Help yourself to the Jack Black and ice."

"No, I think I'll pass on the Jack Daniel's, since you don't carry my BRAND."

Adam declined the offer. "I think it may be too early for me. Don't want to add any pounds. I'm interested in why Murray called you 'Vixey'?"

Ignoring his question, Carol Sue gave Adam a long up and down look smiling as she did. "Actually, honey, I know you could use a little weight on your bod. Seeing you in those movies, Your tush was a little too small and those guys pummeling you had large sausages. Your eyes appeared to open wide with each thrust. Did you actually enjoy that and giving a blow job to them at the same time?"

Adam turned a deep scarlet with that 'out of left field question'. He quickly had a comeback. "What would your eyes look like in the mirror when some guy was parking your tight butt? How good are you, too, at fellacio?"

"Have you done it with a woman, Adam? Ever?"

Getting a little riled up with the banter, he lashed back, "Yes, with a woman and it was very good!"

"How much did she pay you?" Carol Sue laughingly asked as she downed her scotch on the rocks.

"Not as much as you will pay me on this transaction, baby!"

"Adam, are you telling me I'm getting fucked on buying MABB? And to answer your question, I close my eyes when someone is fucking me or I am licking their private parts."

"Someone and their," Adam mused. "Not always a man who is doing it with you? And you wanted to know why my eyes are blasted open? It is because the women who buy my videos like more animation and closed eyes do not respond to their libido when they are doing whatever to our movies. What were you doing when you viewed my movies? No answer? Maybe that is why you are called, 'Vixey'."

Carol Sue did not wish to pursue a hand to hand combat with Adam on a subject he was more knowledgeable than she. "Let's look at the figures, Anthony and Adam. That is more important so we can move on."

About that time her son, Wes, came in. Wiping his brow from the near, now early summer heat, he wanted to assist his mother on the project. "Sorry to be late, Gina and the kids needed my attention. Mom, are you sure you want to buy into this business? It is a downer type where lowlifes like to dabble with it. $400 million is a lot. So women think they like it? This maniac, Kolezy is a killer. What if he wants to pursue you and who knows, kidnap you until you give him what he wants? And... he wants this MABB. Is it worth it?"

Murray began to worry that Carol Sue was going to change her mind on buying the company. "Wes, do you think I would place your mother in danger? If and I say, If, Kolezy comes after her and that seems very unlikely. Is that good? He will have the HPD and my group to deal with. Don't believe he has the balls to go against us, not to mention the police. This is a done deal."

Wes was not sold. Turning to his mother. "Look mom, Gina's dad means well and wants you to buy this god forsaken piece of garbage. We are dealing with possible killers who may have murdered five or more people to gain access to this crummy, lifeless, business. Somehow perverts like to watch and buy things straight people would abhor. Think about what you are doing?"

Carol Sue already knew what she wanted as Adam was on her hit list for devouring him inch by inch. "Wes, I really feel that this company will pay dividends forever and ever. If for some reason things are going south I feel that we can get our money back without danger of losing the principal. I actually like the business!"

Wes was taken back. Not being a prude. "Hey, I like stag films. A bunch of us at Texas Tech, my alma mater, did some crazy things at Baptist driven Lubbock, as we watched girls and guys do it. Guess my taste is different than all of yours. Mom, if you are ok with this, let's go for it."

Murray was looking up at the heavens thanking Wes' endorsement until the next sentence came across. Looking at his father-in-law, the big guy pointed a finger. "Murray, I love you as a father and you have been good to Gina, me, and the kids, but make no bones about all this MABB shit. My mother better not be harmed because she crossed paths with this Kolezy moron. If it happens, I will hold you responsible for any danger she gets into."

"Wes, I know where you are coming from. I have a security guy on our team who runs a company stocked with former FBI and Secret Service personnel. Your mother will be protected 24 hours, seven days a week, until this deal is done and Kolezy cannot do any harm. You have my word. You can count on it."

Wes went over and gave his father-in-law a hug. "That's all I need to know. Maybe MABB can open up a good restaurant here in Katy.

Knowing the clientele at MABB's other bistros, bars, and purveyors of food, Adam nodded negatively.

"I minored in culinary arts, in addition to majoring in law at TexasTech. Anything can be changed, Adam. I've had some great food at your place in The Montrose except for being propositioned in the men's room. The place in Katy will be hands off for limp wristed customers. I'll have a big, woman loving guy in the restroom, who will double as a faucet turner on and enforcer to unsavory characters."

Adam and Wes left her home. Murray started out the front door; he then turned to Carol Sue. "On the divorce question you came unglued. Why did it not work?"

She started to look for her cigarettes as Murray cast an unapproving eye. "OK, no light up". She dropped the smoking idea. "He left me because of the breast cancer. Didn't figure I would be normal again. That's why he was fooling around with his secretary and anything in a skirt. He claimed I drove him to it by my smoking and causing the cancer."

Murray was unable to grasp her reasoning. "What is the reason that you are still smoking, Vixey?"

Carol Sue looked at him, sadly, on the verge of an eye shower, almost like the episode that occurred at the restaurant lunch he had with her. "I tried everything, clinics, acupuncture, cold turkey one weekend where I burned ten cartons of Marlboros, Camels, Pall Malls. Could not hack it. Went back to Virginia Slims Menthols. I know I need something else in my life that will combat this. Maybe a guy. Maybe, Adam. I really like his action."

Murray thought for a moment on giving her a good luck hug but thought of Sheryl and knew he would not leave her if she had cancer or some other disease. Instead, he drew a deep breath and bid her good bye. "I'll have that man at both of your places by this afternoon. Take care."

Pulling herself together, "Anthony, don't bother. I have a security company contract that checks, by the hour, each of my homes. And I carry my 'pinkies' in my purse. No thanks, anyway, I will be fine. I really appreciate your offer."

They stood looking at one another for a moment or two, and then Murray snapped out of it, turned, and started toward the Enclave.

Kolezy was in his downtown office as Dimitri timidly entered.

Kolezy looked at him knowing that the mission to kill Adam already had failed as the local television stations had broadcasted earlier in the week. "Dimitri, I just returned from Budapest to check on the operations there and I had great hope you took care of my stepson. That is why I was there, for an alibi."

The pockmarked overweight man threw up his hands. "We had a man on the inside to alert us that your stepson was in his hospital bed and a clear shot could be taken. Gabor Sziliyani, an expert marksman, attempted three shots and he saw Adam roll over as though he was hit. There were others in the room as well. The television news did not give much information other than there was a shooting at the medical facility."

Kolezy knew the outcome. "Dimitri, you come to me and cover up your incompetence. Even I know he is not dead. Luka has been watching the woman's Memorial home and saw Adam and this person who found him when you dumped him out in that ditch. He is alive, you idiot. Gabor missed him!"

"What woman, Louis? Who is she to him?"

"She is a wealthy woman who is buying MABB from what my inside source has informed me. The woman is from a family who ran Miller Corporation and was able to get control of it. Now her son is the head of it. I'm not positive why or where her interest is in Adam's company. It does not matter, I will prevent her from purchasing it by getting rid of her and Adam and anyone who stands in my way. Even if it takes my hand to do it as you are not capable of removing those in my path. At this time, Dimitri, I cannot stand the sight of you. You have failed me, again."

The heavy set man wanted to redeem himself in front of his superior. "The cop we bought, attempted to push us on the money we gave him or divulge who hired him. Tibor took him to West Bend River Turnaround and shot him, dumping his body in the marsh. It was our belief that he did know of your involvement in the planned shooting."

Kolezy was more tactful. "Well, at least something turned out right. We need to eliminate this woman"

"What is this woman's name so we can go and take care of her?"

"I am told it is Carol Sue Winters, an East Memorial socialite although she uses her maiden name, Miller, and also resides in Katy. Who can attest as to why she is in a lesser area living a different lifestyle from the richer part of Houston? She must be toying with the common people because of her wealth. It matters nothing to me, though, she can be buried anywhere her family chooses."

Dimitri was getting it. "So Adam is getting out of the business, selling to this Winters woman?"

"Yes, he must feel that once the company is out of his hands, he and his sister in Austin will be safe. Your job and Drago's is to kill them both. You will not fail me, Dimitri. IF you do, you will join the others who have met their demise in all my quest of obtaining MABB."

Dimitri was deeply concerned about his own well-being. "How do you want it done, Louis?"

Kolezy went over and embraced his old friend, "I want that bitch boy, stepson of mine, to be followed to this Winters broad's home and when they are together, you, Drago, and the Szilanyi brothers take them out. You understand how much this means to me? I feel that I will accompany all of you to be certain things are handled correctly."

Dimitri was still in a daze as to who would be involved in ridding any buyers or suitors for MABB. "There is also the man and his wife who found your stepson. His name is Murray. He appears to be a go between. Do we kill him and his wife, as well?"

Kolezy rubbed his chin slowly. "Yes, I believe that he has been the spur in getting this Winters or Miller woman to become involved in the purchase. He will be alert to any aggression we bring about him. Melanie has been my unknown mole to what Adam is doing. He has confided all of his plans to her in the anticipation of freeing her from my domination. Little does he know she is on my side."

Dimitri brought up Adam's other sister, Melissa in Austin. "Are you going to try another elimination of Melissa?"

"I have some operatives in Austin to take care of her and her husband. You take out Adam, the Winters woman and this meddler, Murray, all at the same time and we gain MABB. You cannot mess this up as you have done. Understand?"

Dimitri blew out. "Yes, my leader. We will not let you down."

What neither of them realized is that Melissa and Alan were fortified with a security force and the Austin police department was gathering information on Kolezy through their local state rep who had previous run ins with Kolezy. The noose was starting to tighten around the high flying attorney, although he was totally unaware of the downhill trend he was going to experience.

While in her spacious, semi-luxury, home she shared with her husband, Alan, and their two daughters, Melissa, tall, longhaired, brunette who was a major volunteer in their community of Westlake just northwest of the Austin City Limits, had just finished her conversation with Ilona. Those who looked down on Ilona could praise her for sheltering Melissa from the sexual abuse at Kolezy's hands. While at home in her early years, Ilona would be a constant buffer between herself and Louis in Melissa's life. Ilona always scraped the money up for the exclusive, private Catholic prep school Melissa attended in Austin. This prevented Louis from clutching his eldest stepdaughter. A constant sore point he always brought up to Ilona. After turning eighteen, Melissa attended St. Edwards University in Austin where she met Alan, a studious, computer major whose father was an executive in the industrial building material field. They fell in love and with an inheritance from a deceased uncle he founded Zippie Electronics, a go to company that searched for hard to locate computer parts. Though struggling with his company they saw daylight in an invention they purchased, at low cost, which would help revolutionize computer medical systems.

Though she loved her siblings, Melissa never went back to the River Oaks mansion unless Ilona assured her Louis was out of the country so she could visit with Melanie and go over to Ryan A's , the restaurant Adam owned. When they could, Ilona and Adam would drive to Austin and were joined by Melissa and Alan for family outings. When Ryan met his demise, Melissa threatened Louis by phone to bring him to justice for the suicide. She hated the fact that Melanie had become a whore for her stepfather's pleasure as she allowed her mother to skate as an alcoholic.

Back in Houston, Dimas and Zeke planned to see Kolezy at his downtown office unannounced.

The barrister was in his office debriefing a young, woman colleague who he promised to make a partner in the practice after evaluating her physical qualifications. The receptionist buzzed his office as to the visitors, just as Louis was beginning to grope the young, agreeable, ambitious, female attorney.

As she announced who the visitors were he slammed down the phone, "Damn, what is it, Della? Did I make it clear to not disturb me?"

"There are two Houston Police officers here to see you, sir."

Kolezy turned disheartened to his young prey. "Kim, you will have to come back so we can discuss your briefs."

The novice attorney blushed, smiling and went out the private door, as Kolezy viewed her behind.

Kolezy buzzed for the police to come in. Ever the liar and phony, known for his theatrics in the court room he welcomed the two policemen. They introduced themselves as they turned down the usual offer of coffee and Hungarian pastries or drinks. Kolezy opened the conversation. "Well, gentlemen, you're my favorite type of the Houston's finest. What brings you to my office on this Chamber of Commerce day?"

Zeke was not in the mood for his bull crap today. "Its April 26, 85 degrees, too sunny, and the city's finest 12 year old police car doesn't have air conditioning. It sucks!"

Kolezy nodded, half smiling. "Well, maybe the next mayor will have better cars for you fine people."

Dimas stepped in, "Mr. Kolezy, we're here to ask you regarding your whereabouts on March 20th?"

Kolezy was a little edgy even though he half expected a visit from the police. Flipping through his desk calendar. "Let me see the twentieth, hmmm, it was a Sunday. Most likely at home with the family. You can verify that with my wife."

The Lieutenant declared, "We can have you both come down to Reisner Street for a statement. You know to just cover the bases."

Kolezy looked at them hesitating for a moment, "Why do you require my whereabouts on that date?"

Dimas minced little words, "It's been brought to our attention that you may have been involved in the attempted murder of your step son, Adam Magassey. He was abducted, assaulted, and almost left for dead on THAT date."

Kolezy feigned utter surprise at the quasi accusation and began launching a famous court tactic. "What? You are actually saying that I would harm Adam. Who, Sir? Who would even think of believing a man of my integrity and standing in this community, a man who is at many charitable events, who raised this young man and his three siblings when their mother was a widow searching for a loving father? I have been voted Attorney Of The Year, a patron of the arts, who helped develop many of Houston's more cultural venues? I was responsible for bringing in celebrities and notables from around the world to enhance Houston's stature of being a cosmopolitan city. No, Lieutenant. Cavazos, I cannot fathom anyone who would believe that I would harm a soul, least of all, Adam."

Zeke dropped a bomb to bust Kolezy's best filibuster. "Mr. Kolezy, it was Adam who has brought this to our attention."

Kolezy got up from his desk and staggered around, holding his head, "I'm wounded, gentlemen." He then turned to the bay windows overlooking the new Discovery Green Park below.

Dimas felt that Kolezy was at a vulnerable stage and he wanted to push his buttons further. "Do you know Mark Carlson? How about Santos Gonzales? Wyatt Hart? Eric Whitely?"

Kolezy turned around semi-fast knowing he had a connection with the names. Then it dawned on him. Drago and Gabor took Mark Carlson down that night as he turned over on Adam. The others were foggy in his memory. He did not wish to betray himself by admitting the familiarity with the names. No, Lieutenant, these people are not anyone I know about."

The Cavazos brothers looked at one another wanting to kick Kolezy in the balls over this one.

Kolezy was a cool character. "Who is this Mark person?"

Zeke wanted to take the point on this one, pulling out the gruesome colored smaller pictures of Mark's dead body. "Here, do you recognize him now? We can bring over the pictures of the others for you. They all died the same way. Does this ring a bell?"

Kolezy flinched even though he had seen dead bodies in countless court cases he had defended. "No, I don't know who this Mark is or any of them? What is the connection to Adam?"

Dimas took over like a tag team wrestler from his partner. "Mark and the others all knew your stepson and Carlson was a setup man in attempting to kill Adam. Are you positive, Mr. Kolezy, that this dead man is unknown to you?"

"You're attempting to link me to this crime and to my stepson's near killing in Memorial. I love that little boy."

Sergeant Cavazos thought it was humorous. "Two items, Mr. Kolezy, Adam is almost thirty and not a little boy and how did you know he was discovered in Memorial?"

"He will always be my little boy and I read something about someone being found in Memorial in The Chronicle."

Lieutenant Cavazos thought he had Kolezy. "It never made the papers."

Kolezy rebounded quickly, "I have a police scanner and probably heard it that way."

Zeke was not finished. "Adam wants justice and we want to bring those who attempt murder to justice as well, Mr. Kolezy."

Kolezy still playing it up as though he was in summation at trial, pointing his finger at Zeke, "Justice", he shouted, filling the room with a screeching sound, "I'll tell you about justice, Sergeant Cavazos. Adam is misguided, a loose immoral person and sex driven maniac, who came on to his own sister and late brother."

The Lieutenant suggested, "Actually, Mr. Kolezy, you might reconsider those last statements as Adam described you doing all those things to him, his sister and brother."

Angrily, Kolezy stomped around his desk. "Lieutenant Cavazos, Sergeant Cavazos, we have nothing further to talk about. I am an extremely busy man. If you have nothing more than this innuendo by my lying stepson, I strongly suggest you look elsewhere for whatever murder case you working on and tell Adam he needs to stay off of those hallucinogenic drugs he ingests."

"Hallucinogenic drugs?" Zeke reached in for his notebook and flipped back to the case of Ryan's suicide. "Wasn't it what you said to the police when they found your younger stepson, Ryan, hung in the closet? In a statement, and I, let me read it...about the hallucinogenic drugs."

Kolezy's face reddened. "Yes, Sergeant, Ryan was also taking red balls or blue's or whatever and he went over the edge, killing himself. Both he and Adam are into things like that. I tried to stop Ryan but he..."

Zeke knew that avenue was fruitless but had a hook to it. ""CAN YOU explain the fact that Ryan was six foot hanging from a horizontal column that was a new piece of wood in that closet and the chair he supposedly used was three inches further from his legs?"

Louis cast his eyes down not seeing that question coming, as he thought for an answer. "Ryan. obviously, he placed that wood there to hang himself and he could have used a shoe box of sorts, kicking it as he swung from that wood."

Zeke stuck out his chest, exhaling, "Mr. Kolezy, that piece of wood was installed by a carpenter, two days before Ryan died, Your wife told the investigating officer that she thought it was strange as you requested the alteration in the closet. No shoe box was found, either."

Seemingly, as a punched out boxer, who had one more burst of energy, "My wife was mistaken. She drinks, heavily, and is not lucid, at times. In her embarrassment in finding Ryan, she probably threw the box away."

Zeke only shook his head in disbelief, at the cunningness of the attorney.

Dimas wanted to coax still another reaction from the frustrated barrister who he felt was on the ropes. "One more item before we leave, Mr. Kolezy, do you know a Mr. Joseph Molnar? He is a Hungarian expatriate from Budapest. Currently, a person of interest in the murder of Mark Carlson in The Montrose? You can depend that we will find his link to the others? Most likely, yours to Molnar."

Kolezy looked away attempting to not be concerned at Molnar's name and involvement in any crime. "Lieutenant Cavazos, because I am a Hungarian, you believe I should know him?"

The Lieutenant tongued inside his jaw, "You have a charity for funding displaced and expatriates from Hungary, here in Houston. Sure you don't know him?"

Kolezy returned to his desk to shuffle papers looking down as he was searching for some file, looking up at Dimas and Zeke, "My answer is a definitive and ending of this conversation, as a NO!"

Zeke threw out one more item for Kolezy to ponder. "The night we found that young man in The Montrose was the same night your stepson was assaulted. We strongly believe there is something relating, to the two incidents. We're sure since you are a fine citizen you would want to do your duty in apprehending killers and people who assaulted your stepson."

Kolezy took a deep breath. "I really have nothing more to add and unless you have some proof of any wrong doing on my part, please leave my office."

Zeke, stone faced, walked up to his desk causing Louis to draw back. "Mr. Hotshot lawyer, this is not over with. We don't care who you are or how much influence you have. You are going to wear this deal, sooner or later. And, Mr.K, don't leave town, we may be knocking on your door sooner than you think." With that, the two cops walked out, as Kolezy's breathing became shallow, his body trembled, heart rose, his eyes closed.

As they left the office and stepped into the elevator. Dimas turned to his younger brother. "You know, Bro., you may have gotten to that son of a bitch. I know we shook him up."

Zeke felt uplifted by that. "You're fuckin' right. We can put a tail on him. Eventually, he is going to screw up."

Back at the Murray's Memorial home, Adam drove up as Sheryl was coming out to get their mail. Their nearby street neighbor, Jenny Harrigan, who was the area busy body, was eyeing the trim young man stepping out of his black BMW. Sheryl began to wave her off as Adam came up to give his co-savior a hug. Murray, who had just come out, wanted to prevent the nosy woman from asking who and what as he did not wish to explain something that was private. Murray headed her off before she came close. "We will see you later Jenny. 'Gotta run." With that Sheryl grabbed Adam pulling him back to the house. As they reached the front door the yellow Corvette bearing 'VIXEY' on the plate blared it's horn. Sheryl looked at her husband, a little put out. "Did you invite Carol Sue and Wes over for something?"

Murray did not know what to say other than, " I wasn't positive she knew where we lived. Wes does, of course."

Adam saw that Sheryl was a little upset. "Sorry, Sheryl, I knew where you were and that you would be home at this time. "Carol Sue wanted to go over some things on MABB. Did not believe you would mind but ...."

Sheryl assured him it was fine not wanting to make a scene. She immediately embraced Wes who had pulled himself out of the low slung car. He was more accustomed to one of his SUV's or pickup trucks. Sheryl was Wes' favorite and he loved her as his mother-in-law.

Carol Sue came around her car as Sheryl managed a smile and extended a friendly handshake to her assumed mortal enemy. Wes's mother wanted more. "How about a hug for me Sheryl, after all, we may be partners in Adam's company." They gave one another the typical, sociable, a-frame hug.

Murray looked over at Adam to see how he had taken Carol Sue's remark of 'maybe partners'. Each believing it was a done deal earlier.

Adam heard it too, thinking that Carol Sue was backing down on the buy. "What do you mean, by 'maybe partners'? When last visited with you at your place you were cool with it."

Carol Sue ignored the question, as they stepped into the twelve foot ceiling home, tastefully, but expensively furnished. Carol Sue seemed pleased. "Well Anthony and Sheryl this home speaks volumes of how you definitely put the Miller money to good use."

Sheryl was taken off guard on that backhanded sentence. "We would have done it sooner had my husband not been cheated from what was rightfully his in the first place."

Sensing hostility, between the two women, Wes, stepped in, always a great buffer of possible battles. "Sheryl, it comes at a good time where you can appreciate the finer things even now, in a later life."

Coming from her son-in-law and how she viewed him as a worshipper of their daughter, Gina, and their children, Sheryl gritted her teeth and went on, offering refreshments to them. Murray wanted to cinch the deal, immediately, and led them all to the cherry wood, double doored study where they sat around a matching cherry wood table and custom chairs.

Carol Sue could not contain herself as she rubbed the surfaces of both letting out a salacious smile. "Again, very nice, Anthony." Then she began pulling out her notes from a folder she brought with her. She cast a discerning look at Adam, yet dreaming what he looked like in those movies, not dressed in the slacks and pressed button down shirt and blazer. She then switched to business with any icy stare, "Adam, we have reviewed the balance sheet and find that $400 million is not what MABB is worth. That being said, we want to offer you a total of $350 million. Wes and I will put in the $230 million and you, Michaeleen, and Anthony put in a total of $120 million. That is our offer."

Adam, who had sat back, now leaned forward, at the woman now fumbling for her cigarettes and lighter. He looked over at Wes who was flipping his pen with his fingers and wearing a placid face. Re-directing his attention to Carol Sue, "Why did you renege on the larger offer? You appeared to be firm with it and now want to back down? You have three of us at 10 per cent each. That leaves you with $280 million. You should get that back in four years. It is a great deal for you."

The platinum blond look up as she started to light the cigarette, her eyes riveted at Adam. Murray quickly responded with a rebuke and a dangerous ultimatum. . "We don't smoke in our home, Vixey, so kindly wait to smoke outside. Further, from my part in this you are late in wanting to change the terms. Stick with the original proposal or I am out."

Carol Sue looked for allegiance from Wes who surprisingly was viewing a family portrait of Murray and his family including their late son, Troy, over the glass enclosed trophy case of their sports achievements. She wanted to shake him out of his temporary trance. Wes knew, though, her tactic was to go after the younger man sitting across from them. It had nothing to do with reducing the price. This was not business, but her way to get Adam into her bed. A night or two of amour, Vixey-style, would literally bring him to his knees begging for any price she wanted.

Adam had his own thoughts but started to give alternatives of how she could re-tailor the company to suit women, straight or lesbian. "You can appeal, to a large part of women, not only here, but in the civilized world. The videos can be made in different languages. The clothing company can be, like yourself, more provocative. Sexier undergarments that would bring an angel to weep. Women novelties for playtime or individually for those private emotional moments that come into their lives. An all-female resort just like the one we have for men, in Key West or an alternate one. Guys one month, gals the next. Have some smart shops on resort property for them to spend their less, hot, love making times."

Sheryl had just wheeled in a cart of refreshments including her favorite, a pitcher of strawberry daiquiris'. Upon hearing Adam's proposal, she grabbed a glass and poured in a generous amount, taking an unannounced swig to steady her feelings.

Wes looked at his mother who now focused her thoughts on Adam's suggestions, but still wanted to make Adam her bed partner, not caring he was 20 plus years her junior. Wes was confident his mother would make the buy on her terms and over power, this former gay male escort who would surrender to her. "Yes, Mom, you can redo things. How about it Adam? What do you want to do?"

Adam smugly replied. "I believe dinner tonight at Ryan A's would be a start. Are you game, Carol Sue?"

Carol Sue now viewed him as a probable lover in the very near hours. She would get him to lower the price and still have the changes he suggested that would bring in the investment 3 or 4 times as much as she thought. Perhaps he would throw in the resorts to make the deal more attractive.

Everyone in the room knew what was occurring. Wes smiled, knowing his mother was going to give her body for a lesser price, yet he did not totally approve of her method to get what she wanted. After all, it was his mother acting like a lady of the evening. Murray thought that Adam could screw his way to the $400 million. Sheryl knew that both parties were whores, the money did not matter to her and that term Wes always gave out, MOM, yeah, sure. Mother of the Year!"

As the members of the group placed their small plates and drink glasses off to the side, Sheryl had the chance to speak with Carol Sue. Murray's wife was still at odds with her over any relationship that involved her husband and any lasting or current dealings with her. "What are your feelings for my husband?"

Carol Sue sensed hostility from Sheryl. Dropping her fork and dish off, she looked direct at Murray's wife. "Look darling; you obviously feel I want your husband. If I wanted him 25 plus years ago I would have done it after my sister, Bobbie Jean died. By that time I was already in a long lasting relationship. Anthony is a great guy, but not my type. Don't be concerned that I am after him. Whatever goes down on this MABB bull shit, it happens. Your husband is only a part of it because of the money, nothing more."

Sheryl felt a little more secure that Carol Sue was directing her affections to other avenues.

As they all fenced around one another, Michaeleen surprised everyone as she came in, unannounced. She wanted to see Adam as he was strongly on her mind as part of her quest for seeking a new man in her life. She viewed him as a probable lover as it had been quite a while since she had a meaningful relationship. The ambitious, young woman was unlike her aunt. Adam was in her feelings, ripe for the picking and not viewed as a male porn entertainer. Adam was a self-starter, as she was. Michaeleen took a small stake in Ventura Oil and grew it as he did MABB. It would be a challenge to change his sexual habits but she was up to the task.

Adam was captivated by Michaeleen as she came in dressed in her smart, upscale, yet business casual clothes. He turned his attention away from Carol Sue for the moment. "I attempted to contact you about your art collection as you wanted my opinion of the values. We just had an impromptu meeting on MABB and your aunt and I are going to iron out some issues tonight, over dinner."

Michaeleen glanced over to where Sheryl and Carol Sue were still exchanging their differences. Disappointed in the news that Adam and her aunt were going to be together that evening, thinking of not wanting to pursue him at that moment as she knew all too well he was falling into her mentor's Venus Fly Trap, coming out, minus his private parts. Seeing that he did not request her presence at dinner for now, Adam was marked off her list of suitors. At least for the time being, Michaeleen knowing her aunt did not wish to be in a love triangle although Carol Sue could not really be falling for Adam or so she thought.

Adam knew by Michaeleen's body language that she was disappointed about his dinner plans. "Michaeleen, I want to see your art collection and see you. Okay?"

The young executive thought she knew a brush off, yet Adam came off as very sincere, and for curiosity, wanted to give him another chance. "Alright, give me a call in a day or so."

Adam gave a smile that would melt any woman's cold heart. "Yes, Michaeleen I will definitely do that."

Sheryl touched Michaeleen, knowing what was happening as he disappeared with Carol Sue walking to their cars. "I am not positive Adam is worth your time. You may love your aunt, Carol Sue, but she is a man eater. He will find out about that, sooner or later."

Michaeleen defended her aunt, even though she was hurt by Carol Sue's persuasive power on the unsuspecting Adam. "My aunt is not as bad as you think."

Sheryl blurted out, "Carol Sue is not to be trusted after all the crap she put Murray through in the early days and now wants to change all the terms of the buyout."

Michaeleen poured herself a cup of coffee and raised it to her lips. "I realize how Murray was treated by the Millers and that my aunt can be a butt hole when she wants, although there is a different side to her that a lot of people are not aware."

Sheryl was interested in that aspect. "So please enlighten me. What social redeeming value does Carol Sue have which no one appears to know about?"

"Murray deserved the money that I pushed through, but Carol Sue was the driving force in guaranteeing it happened. Tex was a son of a bitch and until... he died, she was helpless in doing the correct things. "Michaeleen had that moment back in Tex's office where the scuffle between them ended his life. She felt vindicated and attempted to push that episode back in her mind as a case of self-defense and the ending of a ruthless, possible murderer of his own father years before.

" Michaeleen are you alright?"

"Sorry Sheryl, I just had a moment. Nothing special."

"I'm glad. So, you are telling me that she is a Florence Nightingale, Texas-wise. Yet, she knows you like Adam and because of this business deal, disregards your feelings for him so she can screw him."

"Auntie cannot help herself. Adam is a big boy. Well, in so many words, I have seen his movies with her and he has some real big items, so, well, she is not going to keep him and I'll get my chance."

Sheryl still had a nagging thought in her mind. "I don't fully understand why she wanted to help Murray in obtaining the money from Miller Corp? She does not appear to be totally benevolent without wanting something in return."

Michaeleen was already more concerned with her aunt's motives for that evening and appeared to brush off Sheryl's question. "I really believe you have to get over Carol Sue and the whys of what she does. At times, she isn't sure herself. You have everything you ever wanted, nice homes, travel when you want, money, cars....you name it, you have it. I have to go." With that she hugged Sheryl and headed for her Energy Corridor office.

Dimitri drove his BMW SUV, meeting up with Louis in his Mercedes AMG at a Galleria area parking garage. Without either getting out, they buttoned down their driver's side window to talk.

Kolezy wanted to know what Dimitri discovered about Carol Sue and Murray. "Well, my friend what have you found out about these two people?"

Dimitri indicated Murray's sudden wealth from three years earlier, his rescue of Adam, the doomed incident at the hospital, as well as where his residence was located. Then he began his background information on Carol Sue. "Louis, this woman is from Miller Industries, CEO until a year ago then stepped down and turned it over to her son, Wesley Winters. She owns two homes and lives two different live styles, one as an elegant woman who is around a lot of money people. Then she becomes involved with what do you call it, blue collar people, who are not wealthy and who are patrons of all things, bowling!"

Kolezy drew a heavy breath, "Dimitri, I already know about most of what you are telling me. Bowling, now, that maybe a way to get her interest in me."

His henchman shook his head, "Louis, I did not know you liked to bowl? You know, the shoes!, ugh!"

"No, you whoyea, she is alone and not guarded there. Find out what bowling lanes she frequents. "That is it.", he snapped. "Mizz Miller or whatever her name is the one we stop as her money will buy MABB. This is not rocket science. Eliminating her and this Murray person so Adam cannot depend on them is the answer to my problems. He will become vulnerable and we'll take care of things, silencing him off, as well."

Dimitri was still concerned. "But what about the police? You told me they visited with you. When we silence these people and, Adam, what will be your position?"

"You , Gabor, Tibor and Joe Molnar will take care of things. My cover will be that I had an emergency and was in Hungary when all this will occur."

Dimitri had all this in his mind and yet had a more questions. "And your eldest stepdaughter, Melissa? Is it not true that she has a twenty four hour guard? And... did you not tell me that Lieutenant Cavazos strongly advised you not to leave the city? Won't the police suspect you?"

"As far as Melissa, we planted Mischa at Alan's plant. He will eliminate her. He started six weeks ago and advises me that everyone there is trusting him as he is doing a fine job. He assured me that her demise will be shown as accidental. She is like her idealistic husband, Alan. They have been supporters of that weirdo, Sylvester Randall, out of Dallas, who is running for Governor. She has made enemies because of that. My alibi will be strong. Ilona will be with me as she told me that her aunt in Szegad, is extremely ill, and may not live another month."

"I am very unclear on all this."

"Dimitri, Dimitri, I hate to brag but who would think of a prominent attorney, a philanthropist, patron of the arts? The current Governor bestowed top honors upon me. I would not be a suspect in any of these and besides, I would have an alibi. No, Adam is a porn entertainer, an eyesore on society. Anyone ridding of him might be called a saint to whomever did the deed. A sword brandishing and stabbing a worthless piece of damaged goods no one wanted. After all, just ask my wife and stepdaughter, Melanie, I am a devoted husband and family man."

Dimitri was still flappable. "Louis, those two policeman, again. I have heard that the Cavazos brothers are relentless in their quest for justice."

Getting weary of his henchman's banter, placing his hand out to him, "My friend, these two are a pair of Hispanic rental cops who should be directing traffic at Post Oak and Westheimer or the overflow at Ninfa's parking lot on Navigation. They are just fools who are ready to meet their match, ha-ha-ha."

"What is our next step?"

"We eliminate Murray and Adam first. Maybe I won't need to kill this Winters or Miller, whatever her damn name is, if they are both out of the picture and she may be scared off from buying MABB. Actually, from pictures I received she is extremely attractive and it would be unreasonable on my part to get rid of her. Maybe I can capture her and take her to Budapest where she will be supportive to my needs after getting MABB. You take care of this Murray and my stepson immediately, while Ilona and I jet to Hungary." With that Kolezy gunned his Mercedes sedan and tore out of the garage leaving Dimitri in a sort of frenzy.

Adam was at the art gallery going over the inventory with Jonathan. They discussed the near death experience at the hospital, his business venture with Carol Sue, and his transition sexually to wanting to marry a woman, have children and live a normal life.

"Jonathan, my days are over as a male dancer and doing the mattress flopping that almost cost me my life."

His longtime friend and partner attempted to show a brave face although a little disappointed that he was leaving a life that they both shared and seem to enjoy. "I am happy for you that Sealy won't be emblazoned on your back side any more. What about this woman who is buying MABB?"

"She played me for three days, stonewalling me, now she wants to get together and says we are on for tonight. Carol Sue is unaware but tonight is the night. The time I test whether this gal turns me on, where I can truly perform as a complete man."

Jonathan was a little surprised at his friend's bold step as a hetro after being on the other side. "This gal is how much older than you? Twenty-five years? Isn't she AARP bait?"

Adam knew he would be blasted for trying to move to the other side and having his fling with a woman who was three levels of seasoning above him. "Jonathan, I won't fumble around with her and make myself look like an amateur in her bed. It is my coming out and she is very, very nice and smells of Liz Taylor's White Diamonds. I know of the scent from my sister, Melissa, who wears it. Alan, her husband, purchases it from Neimans. I am positive she will be wearing it tonight as we discuss the buying of MABB. I will work on her, in the pursuit of selling my company and she will buy it for what I know it is worth and not a penny less. Her beautiful body will be worn out."

Jonathan was really enjoying the outer limits he would probably never enjoy with a woman. "Are you going to drink champagne while making love to her?"

"Not only will that but even more, her eyes roll back. Carol Sue has never known the passion I will offer her."

Not convinced his former lover could perform like he formally did in those twenty minutes flicks from MABB. "You really feel that with your current background that a dame like her will be satisfied?"

Adam was numb as he did not expect that from his closest friend. "Damn you, Jonathan! Just because I was a male... male."

His old friend shot back, "Whore? That is what you were until... what, less than a few months ago? A shill to old fuckers who left you piles of green backs and gold. Real estate you sold when the prices were up. You want to leave the life that made you a multi-millionaire and then some. That and forget your lovers and friends you fucked saying how much you loved them. Now you are a man made in heaven."

Adam knew where Jonathan was coming from. He knew that the person, who initially asked his family to take him in to their home, at sixteen, was now cutting himself loose and becoming what men do. Love and live in a man and woman's world, conceiving offspring and having families and vine covered cottages with two cars in the drive working together to raise their children as they grow up before their eyes.

"You know she is not a Rock Hudson and will demand an all-nighter. This Miller or Winters gal is expecting a night of ecstasy. If I had a glass of that 1995 vintage merlot we drank a month or so ago, I would hoist it for you on your night as a lothario."

As Murray and Sheryl were at their Memorial home that afternoon he saw a van pull into their cul -de-sac. The markings showed Acme Plumbing as it slowly made the circle past their home. Out stepped two uniformed men. One tall and thin, slightly dark complexted with a small mustache, the other was stocky, large boned, menacing looking, with long sideburns sporting dark glasses. The tall, thin man was coming up to their front door while the stocky, large man headed for the locked gate that led to the rear of the home and detached garage, carrying a large, long, package.

Murray called out to his wife, "Sheryl, did you order a plumber to check out anything here?"

Sheryl yelled back, "No, hon, everything is fine with the plumbing. Should not have any problem as the house is only three years old, don't you think? Why did you ask?"

"There's a couple of guys wandering around with Acme Plumbing Co., emblazoned on their uniforms."

"Yes, Sheryl, I saw them but thought they were in the wrong place."

She went back to her recipe book that she was thumbing through before he asked. "They must have the wrong area or home. Just tell them all is fine."

"Yeah, only why did one of them go to the back and not leave. This joker doesn't look like he would take 'No for an answer'. We are not going to answer the door bell. Murray was starting to get edgy as the bell rang and rang. Then the thin man started to push on the door, pursued by a heavy knock followed by more pushing on the door. The sound was hard and ominous like as the "Big Bad Wolf" was at their stoop trying to break in'. Murray thought quickly and moved to his study where he opened the drawer of their oak desk and removed his Taurus Judge revolver. He made sure it was fully loaded. Quickly, he cut through the family room to the kitchen where his wife was still engrossed in planning dinner that night.

"Sheryl, this is not a up and up company. It is not Bill More Plumbing Co making a no cost call to us. I feel it may be something from what has been going on with Adam."

She acknowledged a deep concern and felt petrified that someone was going to do harm to them for helping and saving a human life.

She reached for the landline phone and started to dial 911 for the police. Panic oozed from her as the line was dead. "Anthony, I can't dial out. What is happening?"

"Sheryl use your cell phone."

Her throat tightened. "It's in our bedroom, forgot to bring it out to the kitchen. Where is yours?"

"It's in bathroom from this morning."

"What can we do?" She beseeched.

He handed her the gun, "If either of those jokers come through the back door or window, blast the son of a bitches while I go back and get your cell. Is your .22 still in your underwear drawer?"

She acknowledged with a slight shrug, "Yes, not a great place for it, right?"

"At least you and I can locate it and no grandkid is going to look in a bikini and black bra drawer for a gun."

He raced down the hall to their bedroom and grabbed the gun from her lingerie drawer and his cell phone from their bathroom. He double timed it back to the open area to the kitchen where his trembling wife was pointing the large revolver at the floor. "I don't know where they are? I am afraid to look out and yet feel they are close to us."

Murray started to dial the cell to summon the Village Police where they had an officer's station less than two miles away off Memorial Drive. He quickly was connected to a dispatcher and explained that intruders were prowling their property. They assured him that a patrol car would be sent over to investigate. Feeling more confident, he hugged Sheryl. "The police are coming, we just have to hang in there. I am calling Bill and the guys to come over here."

"You have the police coming, why get Bill into this?"

"He is close and has bigger guns than we do," as he hit speed dial for his old buddy. "Hey Bill, if you are in the neighborhood. We have some guys masquerading as plumbers snooping around and they seemed to have cut the land lines. I just placed an emergency call to the Village cops and they are coming, but in the event they are arresting some old lady at a tea party playing strip poker at the Fifth Baptist Church.

Yes, Sheryl and I have our weapons ready but they may have bigger fire power, you know what I'm saying?"

"Anth, you're in luck, Rich, Sev, Ron Tanski, and Ernie are over playing dominoes for 50 bucks a shot. We'll be right over with our artillery."

Murray felt more at ease, "Yeah, bring over that automatic rifle of yours, which should do the trick."

That lasted only a minute as he hung up with Bill, Sheryl exclaimed, "Murray, look the big one is coming around the back and has a large 16 gauge pump shot gun in his tattooed arms, ready to blast our back door."

They closed the curtains to the huge family room, but not until they saw the thin man with an AK 15 around the cabana pool, with a crazed look of not giving in until he accomplished what he thought he was going to do.

Murray turned to his wife. "That guy looks like a 'Looney' with a purpose except we are not going to be in that category."

Sheryl was carefully peering out , "Oh, hell!"

"Whaat, Sheryl? Is the big guy coming to the back door?"

They stood froze for several minutes listening for which way the intruders were coming at them.

Suddenly, they heard a crash in the back. Murray's heart began to pound as though it was going to explode out of his chest. The Taurus was in his left hand as he started toward the hall where the sound came from. Sheryl was behind him, holding the .22 in both of her hands. Turning back to face his wife, his mouth dry, as he breathed irregularly as though a heart attack was on its way. Even though he had a regular shooting ritual at the indoor target range where it was easy to fire at a stationary target, this was for all the marbles and now he was being called upon to protect his wife and property from intruders. He surmised that they were acting on orders from Kolezy, an evil person; he still was yet to meet. This was all lunacy as he could not fathom how all this was coming down. Saving a stranger, getting fired upon, now being stalked by two goons hunting Sheryl and him. All because of being a Good Samaritan. No, he was ready to blast those assholes. Enough was enough. He glanced at his watch. Ten minutes had gone by. Where were the police? As the couple carefully walked down their hall, backs to the wall, both sweating, guns cocked, suddenly, they heard a loud pop, pop, pop, coming from somewhere, outside.

Sheryl knew the familiar sound. "Those are gunshots. The Village police probably have shown up and are battling those thugs." She remained behind the comforting of her husband in the event she was being overly optimistic.

Murray acknowledged the sound as he turned toward his wife. "Yeah, I think you're right, but I believe it is must be Bill and his group, not The Village People!"

Sheryl thought that was funny, even though they were in the midst of being hunted down in their own home by misguided foes. 'The Village People'? They were more into YMCA and that heavy set guy was not a workout fanatic.

Murray's mouth opened. His heart pounded as though it was coming out of his body when a shadow appeared in the hallway in front of them. Murray cocked his revolver, holding it with two hands, waiting for the assailant to appear. Could he use the Judge to dole out the righteousness that these invaders deserved? Take a life? He knew that was the only way. Trading their lives for these hell bent intruders against dying.

Attempting to catch his breath, Murray raised The Judge, then lowered it, as it was Bill. Murray and Sheryl were mentally exhausted; dripping with perspiration they began to feel normal once more.

Bill looked at his old buddy, "Glad you didn't empty the .410 slugs from that cannon you have in your hand."

"I am, too, as you were not the bad guy coming in. What was that out there?

"We had what you would term a 'disagreement'. I fired over the big guy's head and he took off after coming out your bedroom door."

Murray wanted more, "What about the thinner guy?"

"Ernie and Tanski were in the front. I am not positive what happened. There was a siren."

Murray dryly responded, "That is most likely our Village cops, unfortunately, coming after the fact." As they all walked back to the living room, he placed the gun on the table and walked out the front door.

As Bill related, Ernie and Tanski were mingling around Ron Tanski's Hummer.

Murray wanted more, "What happened to our two plumbers?"

Tanski, a Viet Nam vet and top sharp shooter gave his version. "I had this guy in my sights, just like Dang Po San, an off the beaten path Nam village. Back then, three of us were pinned downed. I checked my M-1. A bush moved and I whipped around, nailed two gooks, one, and right between the eyes. His pupils bulged out, red all over his tan uniform. Today brought back those great memories. I blasted your plumber or what the hell he was, who was coming from behind your home. Shot him enough that his skinny buddy dragged his fat ass into their truck. As they drove by Sev blew out the back window of the truck with his 410. We attempted to block them but they did a '90' and flipped away. Then the local police came up. And here they are..."

The two local Village cops departed from their patrol car, guns drawn.

Murray recognized the lead policeman. "Hello, Sergeant Paige. Glad you did make it, though we almost had a close moment ...."

Paige, a fourteen year veteran of the local enforcement, strode up to them, as he holstered his 357 magnum. Murray figured he never used it much, as things like this don't occur in their jurisdiction. "What is going on here, Mr. Murray? We heard shots as we entered the neighborhood and saw that the plumber's van had a broken back window." Paige noticed the hardware that Sev and Tanski brandished. "Do you two have permits for those arms?"

Murray came to their aid, "Forget that crap, Sergeant, they all saved our lives. Where were you when we needed your protection?"

Paige defended his position, "We are undermanned, Mr. Murray, and responded as soon as we could. What happened here?"

Murray went and detailed the events leading up to the shooting.

Paige took out that all too familiar spiral notebooks like all police use as though there was a sale of them at Wal-Mart and began to earnestly add the comments that were given him. Sergeant Paige and his deputy went around the home, made a few notes, and came back to Murray and Sheryl. "Well, if these varmints come back, let us know, and we will take care of them."

Murray thanked the Village Police, waved to them as they left in their police cruiser.

Bill shook his head, "It is a good thing we came along. Those good cops are stretched to the max and could not have saved you and Sheryl. I believe those two gunsels were hired killers and The Village police would be under gunned and not in their league. I will get Rich to post two of his men, 24/7 on your home."

Sheryl felt more comfortable at that suggestion. "I don't want to go through that again, anytime soon."

Murray placed his arm around his wife, "Most of all, my honey, I want you to be 100 per cent safe in our own home as well as when we head out somewhere."

Adam arrived at Carol Sue's Memorial home to pick her up for dinner at his Montrose restaurant, Ryan A's. She personally answered the door, letting her servant off for the evening as a prelude to bringing down the young man she considered a dessert. It was to see his reaction without anyone seemingly supporting her in the background, wearing her Donna Karen NY baby blue outfit accenting her copper toned skin and those ocean blues batting at him. He was captivated. She undressed his dressy casual wear, Armani, Gucci's, with Lagerfeld, irresistible male cologne, slapped on in a huge dose. They were a match made only in their own worlds.

Carol Sue beckoned him in as she put her arm around him, knowing her escort for the evening was in for her brand of schooling in the ways of man-woman relations. Or would she? He was an experienced sex machine, albeit men, but he had the basics, even with the notches on his condoms. She definitely had heavy romance in mind seeing him with nicely broad shoulders complimenting, her remembrance of his movies, sporting a hard set of muscled abs, hidden by a tight satin shirt, down to a narrow waist. Even with slacks on her memory of his tight glutes and honed muscled legs brought back his trio of movies that made her tremble and now she had the real thing before her. Carol Sue wanted this young man, even though her junior of over twenty years. She was a 'cougar', going for the hunt.

Adam recalled how her early swim suit edition for a sports magazine showcased her long, beautiful legs up to her twenty inch waist, with a minimal top barely holding in her size 36c's. This former Paige Putnam model kept herself up with daily aerobics, weight training, and running at least three miles daily while supplementing 30 minutes of swimming in her heart-shaped pool installed at both of her homes. He was beginning to feel her heat. Were they both there to conclude a business deal or was it a prelude in negotiating that would have them test out one of their mattresses? Adam drove his BMW convertible to show he was in charge. Next, was the seven course dinner at Ryan A's, where they would fence one another for the next two hours. As they progressed to the lobster and steak with stuffed crabs and asparagus, she threw out a comment from nowhere. "Hmm, crabs, are you ever worried, Adam, about getting any?" as she wanted to get a rise out of him.

He froze for a moment and sat back in his chair, "You need not be concerned unless...."

"I would like to talk about your movies."

"It doesn't surprise me that you know about my star performances", as he scooped out the meat of his lobster tail dipping it in a secret concoction they served at the restaurant and thoughtfully savoring it. "Lobster served this way is a lot like enjoying sex."

"I am not positive there's that much connection but your movies are first class. Good story lines, well casted, well-acted, good lighting. Those twenty minute flicks don't do you justice, at least not in your sports coat, pressed, body tight shirt and form fitting slacks."

"It's all in the genes, I imagine."

"Yes, Levis or Cremeaux."

"I like what Cremeaux puts out but what interests me is your website. 'Vixey@GoodTimes.com'."

Slightly shocked, "You have viewed my site? Did not think you would be able to since...."

"Since you play games on it. Do you worry that the executives with the companies you deal with will find out that you lead a double life?"

"Not anyone knows it. Not even Wes and K'Lynn, my daughter. You really are coming after me, aren't you?"

" I find it different, to say the least, that you are so self-effacing, embracing humility, asking viewers to comment whether you are a real or plastic, when you shoot a picture of your long beautiful legs, in a bathtub circled with lit candles as you drink of all things, cheap wine by the half gallon bottle. Or the pics at the bowling alley downing jell-o shots and vodka and riding the motorcycle. Then hosting a benefit for breast cancer survivors. Yes, you are two people. Which one are you tonight?"

Carol Sue took a long sip of the expensive wine. "At times, Adam, I am not sure. Maybe the right person needs to show me the way."

Each proclaimed their enjoyment at dinner with two bottles of $100.00 wines. Afterward, they sped off in the Beemer, down Westheimer and over to Katy Freeway heading west. Carol Sue nudged her hand on Adam's leg, moving quickly inside his loin, stroking it slowly until it began breaching his private parts and causing a bulge in his slacks.

He had prepared Plan B just in the event Carol Sue started to come on to him. "You realize your place is another fifteen miles and I had a little more wine than you. Let's take it easy and I'll get us a room at the Merriam Hotel."

She smiled at the offer of sorts, as it was more a pre-planned event in her mind. "Well, if you don't believe you can make it to Katy, it is probably wise on your part."

Adam knew that he could please her as he had a so called, dry run, forty-eight hours earlier, with Kitty, a Montrose prostitute, who normally commanded a minimum $5000 a night, where he performed for two hours on her terms. He triumphed with Kitty and had a load of confidence in being able to take Carol Sue to the level she would expect of him and that he would win her over and easily convince her that MABB was worth the extra $50 million. Kitty knew him and declined the $5000 as a mutual professional courtesy in his quest to change his life style preference.

Carol Sue's heart began skipping a beat as he swung the dark blue convertible in a turnaround under the freeway and sped up to the Merriam.

Going in as he often did to register with the night clerk, but not always with a woman. He wanted to perform for Vixey where she would be bound up in his passionate endeavors never forgetting it. The female desk clerk somewhat recognized Adam as two of his movies were on their pay for sex channels. "Have a great night, Mr. Anthony?" She smiled broadly at a now nervous Magassey who greatly felt pressure to give this older woman something she has never had before.

Carol Sue waited in the car for her young lover by sprucing herself up and slapping on more lipstick, a little more makeup and spraying another dose of White Diamonds that would have made Liz Taylor happy enough to get married again.

Adam opened her door. "It's all set", as he flashed the card keys to the room. They went to the side door bypassing the front clerk accessing the back elevators, journeying to the fifth floor.

All along Carol Sue was reliving, seeing her suitor for the evening in those three movies. She remembered him as Ryan Anthony who was totally into his craft, noticing how his eyes remained open as he climaxed into his partner's body with his nipples hardened. She wished to have her nipples hardened by his unceasing penetration into her waiting cavity. This was from someone who was twenty plus years her junior and never experiencing someone that young as her lover. Carol Sue wanted Adam more than ever and could hardly contain herself as she surveyed his tight butt ahead of her, wanting to feel what he does as he climaxes and how she would experience it at the same time.

They arrived at room 515. Adam was nervous and fumbled on the key insertion as the light continually registered red instead of green. Carol Sue wanted to get into the room and softened his momentary clumsiness.

"Maybe, sweet, you should put some pussy hair around that slit."

They both laughed as he finally turned the key card around with the green light registering and the couple stepped into the dark room. He reached on the wall for the lights turning, on both the desk and bed lamps.

Adam thought about the condom trick where his partner would have the rolled up latex shield in their mouth and he would penetrate it past the lips driving his phallus down his lover's throat, giving in this instance, the woman, much pleasure on both ends. His question was, would Carol Sue be game for this? He figured looking at her observing him, that it might not be ladylike for her, sober or not, to swallow his ribbed, jellied protection.

Carol Sue was getting anxious waiting for his move on her and her libido was ticking. Adam, are you doing alright?"

He looked at the king size bed and flat screen 55 inch TV. While searching through the honor bar and mini frig for sodas finding some Jack Daniels on the top shelve of the cabinet. He thought they might need a little loosening up and spotted the ice bucket. "Yeah, I'm good, let me get some ice down the hall and we can relax. Maybe find some glasses in the bathroom, ok?"

She looked a little disappointed. Reluctantly she agreed. "Don't be very long, I....."

Without her finishing the sentence, he darted out the door and searched for the ice machine. He quickly loaded up the fiberglass bucket with the cheap plastic liner, then raced back to the room and this time had no problems with the key card turning the light green as an early indication he was on GO.

Entering the room Adam found it darkened except for the cracked door of the bathroom light. His saliva thickened and he drew deep breaths. Noticing a strong smell of White Diamonds that Carol Sue was wearing as they strode down the hall earlier. Things were beginning to happen. Evidentially getting with the program, searching for her in the room, "Carol Sue, where are you?" There were no sounds, she couldn't have left as it was only less than five minutes to find and load up on the ice. OR was she tired of his uncertainty? Again, he asked, as he became more accustomed to the semi-darkened environment, "Carol Sue, are you jacking me around or what?" Then he spotted the covers turned back. He placed the ice bucket next to a pair of ready glasses and the Jack Black pint bottle.

From behind, her sultry voice cut the silence of the moment. "What are you waiting for, my young and tight-assed Romeo? I am hot to trot, all over you!"

He turned quickly as he peeled off his shirt, flipped off his Gucci's in the corner, unzipped and rolled off his slacks wearing only a light blue thong. Even in the dim light, standing in front of her his nipples pierced by one inch pins, her ocean blue eyes lit up like the sunset over Galveston. She wanted him to rip her clothes off with reckless abandon and devour her. His heart began beating as he thought his ears would pop. Without hesitation he went toward her, awkwardly waiting for her next move.

Admiring his frontal view, "You still wearing your whale tail?", as she opened her blouse displaying a mini black bra barely holding her red, cherried 36 c's. He proceeded to take off her bra and skirt, leaving only a gold and white lacy thong. She already removed her three inch heeled shoes.

They both stood motionless for a few seconds, Adam went up and gently pulled down the lacy restriction to his avenue of pleasure. She grabbed his behind almost tearing off the whale tail. They each stepped out of their mini materialed undergear.

She whispered in his ear, "I'm going to treat you to some amazing sex that has been banned in fifty countries." With that she proceeded to suck on his nipples while massaging his testicles. Then she moved upward, their lips met as he felt her tongue in his mouth. He managed to push her down on the bed, momentarily in a pushup position then lowering himself on her as they sated in eternal ecstasy. He began to suck on her amble red breast working his way down between her well-toned, tight middle body stopping at her clitoris, which begged for comfort and forgiveness. Placing his tongue into the wet, juicy never ending joy, he heard her groan happily and beseeched for even greater deepness and tolerance, almost screaming for an unending continual pleasant attack on her hot body. He wanted to love and show her how much a man he was. She was more than a matronly, wealthy female, unlike any woman he had met as a paid gigolo. He was positive she felt he was a worthy lover, at least for this night.

After Adam had his early pleasures, he wanted to explore Carol Sue's inner body both front and back as he knew he could pound each street and pour out his juicy liquid into her gorgeous, beautiful, tight figure. Carol Sue was totally captivated with her suitor in this unknown fifth floor room, not caring who she was in any circles only that her world was with Adam who acted like smooth oil rig pumping into her love erogenous zone. With precision like swiftness, he began pulling out and attempted to place a ribbed sheath on his pulsating penis but she slapped his hand wanting to accept his total fluid into her cavity. She did not care whether he was clean of any social malfunction that a government branch designated as dangerous, if not protected. Only that she wanted to be his for that moment. Their eyes met as she fell back writhing in total pleasure. Carol Sue screamed out, "Adam, you are the one! I am yours, forever! Fuck my pussey until it oozes out with my female cum juice. Then take it in your mouth and share it with me."

They both enjoyed that time which felt like an eternity.

Adam was overwhelmed with his performance and fell back next to his lover, who was soaked in both her White Diamonds sweat and the large amounts of his pent up juicy fluid pouring down her splayed limbs to her red tipped toes. Her eyes rolling back with fun filled moments from the experience.

Digging into his back with her strawberry colored fingernails, she writhed, "Oh, Adam, you are so wonderful!"

Rolling back to her, he decided to tongue his way down her avenue of sinewy flesh. Each spot accompanied by her pleasure reaction, as the woman began her hand journey over Adam's anatomy, stopping to playfully pinch both of his pinned pectorals while slipping her hand between his open ended, taut legs encouraging his pleasure but stopping his flow, as she wished to enjoy more of it for near future times.

He hesitated as she swung around throwing the covers off the bed. "Oh, Adam, I have never felt this much love from a man" as she bucked upward, writhing as her eyes gently closed. He was on his knees grasping her surprisingly narrow hips in his hands, placing her body at a ninety degree angle, flipping his joy stick into her anal cavity throwing a curve into her expectations with her only smiling as though she had previously experienced this position with others before this night. He pummeled her for what passed for the twenty minute flick he normally performed in. It was just like old days except he had a feline on the front line not a Bob or Mike and it made his night for the future of change.

Carol Sue and Adam both reached their crescendos together as they each fell onto the king size placard of the field of their sexual journey.

Lying on her side, Carol Sue beckoned her horny partner. "Oh, Adam, you are so wonderful! Never did I ever believe, that I would ever experience such great sex again."

He had other things in mind. Turning his lover over, as his mouth went to work on licking each part of her x zones as she moaned in a slow, erotic way to the moving action. Each spot accompanied steamy action as she began her hand journey on her lover's anatomy pinching his left pec, sliding her hands south between his legs as she found his hard organ. He seized the willing and excited beauty pulling her onto him, bucking the wanting woman, gripping her buttock with both hands and releasing his love into her as she did to him. "Oh, my fantastic Adam, I am coming, it is sooo beyond words. Thank you, my love."

Carol Sue began to shiver. Adam quickly retrieved a nearby blanket placing and tucking it around her, then cuddling her body into his arms for warmth.

After a brief interlude, he once again removed the blanket and started to excite the somewhat love lost female. She had been without a serious love interest in almost a year and was more than willing to make another round with this almost Adonis even though of his past sexual ways. He hit all the erogenous zones once more and when they were sated he placed the blanket over the matronly beauty. "We probably can use a drink to warm us up." He nakedly got up, opened the Jack Black and poured it into the glasses with ice, topping their drinks off with Diet Coke. Her eyes followed, heart beating. They sat propped up together, sans clothes, in bed toasting their after dinner love making, although he thought it was not champagne.

Carol Sue opened up first, "For what it is worth, when I saw you in that male movie, little did I realize how fabulous you are as a man to woman lover. You certainly exceeded my love meter by at least, fifty points."

He laughed looking up at the half lit ceiling from the television's multi lights, at the meter's comparison. There was an uplifting feeling he had for this older, wiser, well-conditioned, worldly woman, he shared the past hour with in a foreign environment that perhaps another couple had done the same hours before in this same bed. He felt more than lust for Carol Sue in the attempt to sweeten the deal for MABB. It was a real love. He genuinely liked her for herself. Out of left field he remembered something. "Tell me, how does it feel to be a grandmother?"

Taking a sip of her drink, she almost choked on his off the wall question. "Adam, we just spent an out of this world time together, banging one another, and you asked me that? Being a grandmother is not the same anymore. I am not old and ready for assisted living, you know!"

"You just don't appear to be old enough to have a son or daughter at an age that they would bore an offspring, that's all. Your movements in bed certainly showed that. Wes is a real standup guy who loves and is protective of his mother. Believe me, you are a solid '10' in my book and then some."

She reached over after putting her drink down and planted a tongue filled kiss between his lips. "Are you doing all this to make me ante up the bid for your company?"

"You would figure that and I am not blaming you and, yes, it really crossed my mind to ply you with sex and alcohol. You are really not what I thought you were."

"Not a bitch, you mean? At least not a female one?" She tenderly placed her hand on his thigh running up to his shoulder. "I don't know what it means to be 'misused' by an adult. My family, were mostly supportive and did not abuse me. You have been burned by this step father."

"From what I heard about your father, Tex Miller, he was not the supportive one. Overbearing, hatefully aggressive, cruel, ruthless, uncaring, self-opinionated."

"Yes, Tex was all that and more. Successful, a family provider, people looked up to him even though he was an asshole. He never did hurt his family. He wanted me to marry into a wealthy oil family to double our family's assets. There was this guy who was a hunk of sorts, whose family was almost as rich as we were but he really was a boy in man's body."

"And what do you think of me? Just another boy toy in a man's body?"

She picked up her drink and slowly started to drain the glass as she carefully chose her words, "You're a very mature man who has experienced some tough times but managed to overcome a lot of that adversity."

"I am not a guy who's trying to overcome our differences. I can really go for you, Carol Sue." With that he reached around and removed her glass and kissed her passionately. She scooted down onto the bed as he embraced her for another segment of lovemaking by sucking her tanned and toned thighs working his way up to the golden area of her heavenly being. After the mutual love ended in exhaustion they drifted off to blissful sleep in one another's arms.

The couple began a late nighter and siesta afterwards. Down below in the parking lot, a white panel truck pulled up next to Adam's Beemer. Unbeknown to Adam a tracking device was placed under his front fender when he and Carol Sue were dinning at Ryan A's. Inside the van were Kolezy's men, Tibor and Gabor, and they had mayhem in mind for our lovers. The duo had been unsuccessful at Murray's home but wanted to get Adam to make up for their inabilities. Gabor stood watch, still favoring the grazed bullet he suffered at the botched attempt at the Murrays. His brother, Tibor, a foreign car mechanic, came out with a device that contained three sticks of dynamite and a trigger which when placed beneath the vehicle would detonate when the ignition was engaged. Tibor rolled out from underneath the BMW and scampered into the truck. The two brothers 'high-fived' their effort and the visualization that Adam and his lover for the night would be eliminated when they started the BMW in the morning. Then Kolezy's two Hungarian operatives drove their truck out of the parking lot, scheduling to return in the morning and watch as the dark blue convertible would be shot up to the heavens with body parts strewn over the Merriam's property.

A few hours later, two Asian young wanna be hoods slowly drove through the lot in their Toyota Camry pulling next to Adam's car. The lead, a 19 year old, thin, spectacle wearing, spiked black haired, youth, got out to place a 'Slim Jim' through the window. As he popped the lock, he slid in and cut the motion alarm off then tying the ignition wires together to start the car, using his car-jacking skills, as the vehicle started up ....it just vaporized. The driver, Beemer, as well his Asian buddy in their Camry, all blew up, sending them to their maker. Another driver, who was an early checkout, also became a bystander victim, as he loaded his car.

The blast caused alarms of at least a dozen vehicles to go off in the hotel's parking lot, sending the security guard out to try to save the young misguided men but, to no avail as the men were beyond help. The only job he had left was crowd control of dozens of guests who came out to see if their cars were damaged and to rubber neck at the violence.

Up in their room, Adam and Carol Sue were jolted from their bed, naked, holding on to each other, standing in front of the openly draped window surveying the burning hulk of the BMW, numbed and speechless, by the incident. Down in the parking lot some of the guests drifted out to see what the explosion was about. When they saw the devastation some began clutching one another. Others could see that lives were lost as they turned away in horror. The frenzy began.

Carol Sue, woozy, from a deep sleep could not put the actual from the previous encounter though more pleasant, than what she thought she was witnessing down below. "Adam, what is happening?"

Knowing in the back of his mind that his car was the target, Adam was trying to piece it all together. Perhaps Kolezy had perpetrated the horrendous act, injuring innocent bystanders or even worse, someone may have been killed all because of him. "God, this is not good. My car is no more. When will he stop?"

Carol Sue was still unaware that the incident was possibly an act of violence against her young lover. Holding her hands to her face. "How could anyone even commit this...this terrible crime?"

Adam knew he had to find out more and being five stories up would not help. "We have to get dressed and go down. Second thought, you may not want to get involved. It could be more dangerous if it was not a random act of car bombing the wrong person."

Carol Sue wanted it to be a random act, not directed toward them. "You really believe that this was meant for you?"

The couple, from their vantage point, could see that his BMW was a burned out hulk. Vehicles on both sides of his car were still ablaze.

"Carol Sue, my love, this is the fourth attempt on my life. If I am not mistaken, Louis is not going to stop until he believes we are both dead."

The woman, who had started to put on her thong, fishing for her bra, had a jolted moment. "Maybe I need to call Wes and have him come here. This is something I am totally unprepared to deal with now."

He looked over at her in the faded light of the desk lamp. "Yes, if it is more comforting to have your son here, then do it. Carol Sue, please don't allow this to stop our relationship that has just begun."

Carol Sue stared at Adam, taking in his words. She hit the speed dial to her son. When he answered, she was extremely calm, asking him to come to the hotel, detailing as much as she knew about the car bombing and assuring him that she was in no danger. Adam knew Wes was asking more questions on the phone but Carol Sue did not want to go into any more detail. He agreed and was on his way to the hotel.

Surprised at her steadiness in relating the incident to Wes, Adam was okay with her getting additional support for her fears as he finished dressing. He waited for her to slip on her clothes. They departed the room and headed for the elevators. Upon getting off the elevator, the couple clawed their way through the now clogged lobby. Many of the bewildered hotel guests where asking questions from the challenged hotel staff. No one appeared to have the answers.

Adam and Carol Sue finally pushed their way out into the parking lot. Sirens filled the air as the fire department trucks, a dozen Houston police squad cars and Harris County Sheriff's cars congregated, followed by three ambulances. The law enforcement held back the hotel guests, now swelling the scene. The people variously, omitting out screams, acting shocked, questioning the police. The ambulances pulled up as the EMS personnel quickly hauled out body bags and gurneys, standing by for whether they should attend to the injured or retrieve one or more victims. All first responders seemed helpless as a hush finally fell over the brightly lit parking facility matching what fire was left from the devastation. The fireman put out the holocaust as many of the onlookers knew no one would be saved.

A police sergeant was questioning the night manager as Adam cut his way through the crowd. "Officer, my BMW was one of the vehicles that suffered the explosion."

After obtaining Adam's information, the cop turned to him. "A witness told another officer that she saw two Asian men break into your vehicle. Apparently, someone else may have booby-trapped it before they got to it. What can you tell me about who may have wanted to take you out? Like who did this horrific thing? What we can tell there are two victims, maybe three? Someone, sir, does not like you. Did you by any chance rig this for anyone who might steal your car?"

Carol Sue came up, catching the last remarks. With anger in her normal placid eyes, contrasting the remnants of the inferno across the way, "You have your nerve, Mr. Policeman. My boyfriend would never perpetrate such a terrible thing or endanger anyone, especially me while riding in his car. You sir, have no reason to question him that way!"

The somewhat youngish cop was flustered. "Ma'am didn't mean to imply....I've never seen anything like this. You know what I mean?"

Carol Sue was in no mood, "You have to be a rookie. No one in their right mind would plant a bomb in their own car."

Adam was caught off guard, not as to the officer's accusations but Carol Sue's defense of her 'boyfriend'. He felt he was elevated to a new status. Due to the last few hours he went from seller of his company, to friend, to lover, to boyfriend. Hmm, he figured that the extra bucks were a guarantee for MABB. Yet, was he just in it for the money? Carol Sue appeared genuinely wanting him, not the partner in the business but a probable longtime partner in life.

The policeman jarred him "Sir, we still require all the information on your car and anything you may add as to why your vehicle was targeted for the incident."

After declaring what was necessary, Adam and Carol Sue headed back to the room, showered, dressed, and waited for Wes to arrive. The clock struck 4:30 AM. Adam wanted to have Murray in his corner, so he called waking him from a sound sleep. Half awake, Murray was upset and not thinking clearly. "What's going on at what, 4:30, in the morning?"

Adam did not want to delay the call, "Someone car bombed the Beemer at the Merriam on Katy Freeway. Killed two or three people."

Murray rubbed his face and ran his hand threw his mop of short hair, "Oh shit, Adam, are you okay?"

"We're fine, Murray."

Murray quickly questioned, "We? Who in the hell else is with you?"

Adam wanted to clarify his companion to Murray. "It is Carol Sue."

Even though it was the early morning Murray attempted to stabilize the moment. "Is Carol Sue alright?"

"She is doing fine. We spent the night together and it was a damn fine time, even under the tragic circumstances."

There was a long pause. Murray caught the moment coming to grips to Adam's move. "Just a little surprised that the two of you hit the sheets together. Could you use some support?"

"I can really use it, big time, as Carol Sue already has Wes coming to her aid. You know what he told you about sheltering his mother. "

"Yeah, I was totally hoping that no one was going to screw her over. I was definitely wrong. Kolezy is not going to stop until he kills everyone connected to MABB. Hell, I will be there in 45 minutes. How about meeting in the front of the motor inn?"

Murray double timed it, arriving to witness the vast amount of activity occurring at The Merriam, as the fire and police milled around, not even attempting to prevent the onlookers from coming in and fouling up the scene. He spied Adam and Carol Sue coming out of the hotel, as Wes was going in to meet and comfort his mother. The trio moved back into the hotel's lobby and found an alcove, away from the bustling crowd, to discuss the serious event.

Her son was semi emotional. "God bless, Mom that you are alright. Hell, what happened? Why were you here?"

Carol Sue turned to Adam knowing she had more explaining to do and thought her new lover would be more apt to tell a story that would not go deeply into their lovemaking, a few hours before. "Why don't you fill in Wes with our, our, ah, meeting to iron out the final figures? On MABB, that is."

"Well, you see Wes; we thought a neutral site to finalize the sale would be easier than my place or your mothers."

"Do you really believe I am buying that double talk? Yeah, especially since you still have lipstick on the back of your neck? Mom, how could you wind up in bed with this guy?" He vented in disgust. "Can't conceive he could get it up for you."

This time Carol Sue was appalled, "Are you telling me I can't get a hard dick going because I'm a little past 39?"

Murray found the three assessing the intense occurrence, and upon hearing that last remark. "Whew, a little family spat, Vixey?"

She shot back. "Surprised to see me here, Anthony? Yes, Adam and I fucked our brains out. You will like that Mr. Murray and, even more, he is getting the price he wants."

Wes was shocked. "Mother, I thought we agreed that was too much!"

"It is done, Wes, I am signing the papers tomorrow morning."

Murray corrected her. "Vixey, it IS the morning. Actually, my dear, Adam called me about forty-five minutes ago and told me about the two of you. It is none of anyone's business. At least until someone may have wanted the two of you eliminated. I am certain you both enjoyed yourselves."

She proclaimed, "I plan on standing by Adam and going with the deal."

Adam was totally into Carol Sue and did not wish any harm to come to her. "Look Wes, I know this may look bad to you, but I will get your mother total protection even after the sale of MABB is completed."

Wes was staggering around the lobby, now empty, as most of the guests had either gone back to their rooms or were still gawking at the burned out hulks of vehicles surrounded by an armada of fire and police personnel. "Gosh, Mom, I wanted you to do what you wanted and Murray said you would be safe from these goons. Here we have three cars incinerated with their owners inside. You were lucky thanks to your new, gentleman friend. I initially thought this was a good buy but now have my doubts."

Carol Sue touched her son's face, compassionately. "It is something, Wes, I intend to do and no one is going to stop me."

Wes knew that tone from his mother. "Alright, you win for now, Mom, but I will be monitoring everything until the MABB sale is completed."

"Don't worry about me, I have my trusty twin pink handled, .38's around and without any hesitation they will be used on anyone trying any crap!"

"Even though you have the artillery, I have been at our ranch in Columbus shooting my Bushmaster 223 caliber rifle when it comes time to protect the people I love. You, Mom, Gina, my wife and the two kids mean so much to me. Anyone who crosses my path to get to my family will pay. Pay, dearly."

Murray never knew his son-in-law's other side, yet agreed. "WE will use our weapons, if threatened; same as the day those two gunsels came to break in at our home. Had it not been for Bill and his group I would have shot the son of a bitches dead! DEAD!" he emphasized to the three of them. "You have to make that decision to protect your family, regardless of the consequences."

For no apparent reason, Carol Sue came over and hugged Murray. It lasted a long moment and for some unexplained reason he did not wish to let go. They both looked at each other, into each other's eyes without any embarrassment. Murray cleared his throat, "Well, Carol Sue, you take care, alright?"

She continued to stare at him for a few seconds, "Yes, I will and you as well." Then she glanced at Adam and Wes, who both sported surprised looks. Nothing was said as Wes took his mother to his home. He did not wish to leave her at one of her residences after this near fatal attempt on her life. Murray offered to bring Adam to his place for the same reason. As Murray drove the two men were silent. Each were thinking of Carol Sue, avoiding the event which occurred hours before.

Murray was still thinking about the embrace not knowing what the reason was, but traveled back in time when he had Bobbie Jean in his arms. Strangely familiar, that it felt almost like that in that Burkburnett motel over thirty three years before. Whatever he thought there were more important things he needed to focus on as three more innocent people died due to Adam's involvement in MABB. Thinking back to Carol Sue, was she really up to dealing with Kolezy? Unknown to him, Adam had given her a hedge to use in the event Kolezy would threaten her. She was assured by the former adult star that his stepfather would not do her harm if the Magyar Duna was used.

Murray pulled into his home at 6:00 in the morning to see Sheryl waiting at the door, wearing an extremely concerned look. He had awakened her before leaving for the Merriam Hotel on I-10, giving only his destination and that Adam was involved.

She was relieved that her husband was back. "I turned on Channel 77 and they were on the scene telling about the car bombings and apparent deaths of three people. I was hoping that it was not Adam." Then she saw Adam and ran to the young man, squeezing him uncontrollably.

Murray had another mind blowing episode, besides explaining what happened in less than two hours before. Now he was faced with whether to tell his wife about Carol Sue's being at the hotel.

"You were at the Merriam at this time of the morning for what reason? And your BMW was blown up?" Sheryl questioned Adam.

Adam looked over at Murray as he knew Sheryl loathed Vixey. "Well I was entertaining, so to speak."

"Oh? And who were you with?" she chided devilishly. Thinking he was still mattress testing with another man. Now teasing the red faced, young guy. "I thought you were done doing tricks?"

Adam was attempting to think fast as Carol Sue in conversation was not a pleasant option when discussing the long legged, former Miss Texas runner-up turned model with Murray's wife. "Actually, Sher, I was with a woman."

"Really?" Sheryl acted out of a combination of bewilderment and suppressed joy. "Why not at your place or hers?"

Adam shrugged his shoulders hoping Murray would step in on this difficult moment. Murray did not want to, knowing that an upcoming A-Bomb blast Sheryl would put them through, once she found out who it was. Adam finally piped up. "She lives in far west Katy and a ..."

Sheryl's eyes started to dart around having figured who it might be. "Oh, far West Katy, hmmm. Just how did you meet this gal?"

Murray finally had an in to end the interrogation. "Adam, not to change the subject, but did you see this Eastern European guy with a Hitler type mustache looking pretty intent at the scene?"

Adam became relaxed on the subject change. "No, cannot say I did. Why?"

Murray gestured with his hands. "The man did not appear to belong at the hotel, not as a guest, at least. He had this scar on the right side of his face, wore dark glasses and a gimme cap pulled down. He looked familiar."

Adam's light bulb went off. "It's Drago! He was one of the guys that night at the motor inn on the Beltway. Yeah, most likely sent by Louis to make sure things went well. And ....the possible sniper that day at the hospital."

"What's Drago's story? now a concerned Sheryl asked. Was he the one that may have planted the bomb?"

"Drago was a former porn actor in Budapest and from my sister's story about him; he was a braggart on his many conquests as told to her by Louis."

Murray continued, "He left the scene when I looked at him and disappeared into the crowd even though I wanted to follow him. It was better to lie back since I did not have any weaponry."

Adam agreed, "It was wise, Murray, as he always carries a stiletto in his boot, as told to Melanie, again. Drago is a piece of work. Better at eliminating what has to be done than Dimitri? I'm afraid that he... well, let's not go there."

Sheryl was curious, "Not go where?"

Adam did not want to bring up that Drago saw both he and Carol Sue and now she would be in great danger. For now he was not willing to tell Sheryl that she was with him at the Merriam. "I don't know, Sheryl. Just a passing thought."

Womanly intuition got the best of her. "You're worried about the gal who was with you. Correct? Oh, that's what you said that she lived in far West Katy...Geez, it was Carol Sue and you did not want to tell me, either of you. God, she is someone who will cut you up, eat what she wants, and spit the rest out."

"You are too good at figuring things out, Sheryl," Adam conceded. "It is my life and if she wants to eat me, I will gladly allow that to happen."

Sheryl was about to pour herself some hot tea and put the kettle down. "I believe Carol Sue has already done that to you."

Murray just began drinking some decaf, almost coughing the brown liquid through his nostrils on that remark.

Adam was deeply concerned, "I better call Carol Sue over at Wes and Gina's, to warn her about Drago." He then departed the kitchen for the living room.

Murray tried to defend Carol Sue. "Sheryl, she has changed."

"A ha, just like her 'Love Me or Hate Me' site along, painting herself up like, who knows what. Not an angel in white. Michaeleen also defended her Auntie Carol Sue, but I am not buying any of it. I really think she likes you."

He retorted, "Remember, she was a major force in getting our money."

"Oh, the money thing, again. Maybe we would have been better off without it. We never would have been on the road to our home and found Adam. Not been a target for Kolezy. Certainly, not buying into MABB. What do we tell our friends who ask what investments we made? A porn business!"

"Adam's alive because of our discovering him that night. Most of the work on our being here in this two million dollar palace is because of Michaeleen with her aunt's support. Can't you leave it alone? The woman is not into me at all. So what about our investment into an honest adult business? Adam has been cleaning it up and there are people out there who we can never change, anyway."

"Yes, you are right on with all this. I am just hung up on Carol Sue being in the middle of our lives."

He gave his wife a long, deserved kiss and embrace. They both started to journey toward their bedroom past Adam who was in a serious conversation on his cell. Murray stopped. "Better check on our guards out there, first".

Adam finished his conversation and headed to the guestroom for a well-deserved sleep.

Sheryl was still concerned, as her vivid memory of what happened with the so called 'plumbers' earlier. "What about the Village Police? They come by on the hour don't they?"

Murray scoffed at that. "If we are so lucky, maybe two, three times a day in 24 hours. Cannot depend on, what, five sweeps at the most, for our protection. Remember Sergeant Paige related to us that there is a manpower shortage and our own Harris County deputies are strained to the max. HPD is not in our jurisdiction. The Constable has only so many cars for this part of Cannon Village boundaries. No, kiddo, we are on our own with what fire power we have and those rent-a-cops from Moonlight Investigations outside our place."

She peered out the window to the rent-a-cops vehicle. "There were two patrolmen if I recall."

"Yeah. Why?'

"One man is lying back in the driver's seat and the other guy was not visible. They haven't used the bathroom at the garage apartment, have they?"

"That is how we set it up and if they needed snacks, sandwiches, coffee, no alcohol, although the one guy Rich sent over smelled like he fell in a vat of Jim Beam."

"What, not your favorite bourbon, George Dickel, #12?" she asked casually.

"That guy would drink $8.00 bourbon. Kind of feel uneasy about this." With that he went over to the desk in the study and pulled out the Taurus Judge and handed her a Smith and Wesson .38. "Keep this close." He placed the .410 in the back of his slacks and prepared to walk out to the security guard's vehicle.

Sheryl pulled him aside, "I think Adam was going to lie down in the guest bedroom, should we wake him?"

"Naw, when we came in an hour ago the guys both waved. Probably the boozer is getting some shut eye and the other one is most likely zipping up his fly. I'm over reacting I guess, but after that hotel deal we can't be too careful."

Murray opened their front door and peered around. Seeing no other person leering around, he headed for the patrol car looking directly at one guard who was still visible lying back on the headrest. As he got to within five feet he saw blood on the seat, running down the still form. Murray's heart was beginning to beat rapidly as he observed that the man's eyes were wide open as blood dripped out of his mouth. Knowing he was dead, Murray pulled The Judge from his slacks, cocking it, as he strained to hear a rattle of a branch or seeing a glimpse of metal from a weapon now in the early sunlight of day. With it being near 7:00 in the morning the Spring Branch School busses started to run as he heard their faint stop and go screeching brakes and the whiff of their diesel spewing through the air. Where was his partner? Would he find him dead, as well?

The Brocks, David and June, their closest neighbor in the cul-de-sac, were off to Europe on their usual jaunt to see their wayward daughter and her live-in freeloading boyfriend. Bob and Sharon Powell, whose home was at the entrance of their section, were getting their grandkids ready for school. Sharon came out and waved to him. He was not even aware as to whether she saw the gun in his hand. She started toward him. He frantically waved her back. It was then that she saw the big revolver in his left hand. Her face resembled, a fright only remembered by the victims of the Texas Chainsaw Massacre cast. Her eyes riveted on the dead man in the car. "Go back, Sharon, you don't wish to be here. Keep the kids in the house. Lock your door! Call The Village Police!"

Without looking further, Murray swiftly ran back to the house. Running in, and bolting the front door behind him, he yelled, "Sheryl, where are you?" As he headed for the kitchen, she appeared. He grabbed her tightly as she almost had the air sucked from her body. He spotted the .38 on the counter. "Oh, sweetheart, I am glad you are safe. One of Rich's men is dead. Don't know where the other one is. We have to get the cops here. Lock all the doors."

Sheryl stood there frozen not hearing what her husband was telling her. He shook her. "Lock the doors, hon!"

She went to the kitchen door and verified that it was secure. Murray gasped, "I'm dialing 911 for the Village police to get here as soon as possible." His heart started to pound like it did when the intruding plumbers were attempting to breach their doorstep. Only this time Bill and his group were not available. They were all in a fishing tournament north of Houston. As he began dialing on the cell he heard sirens in the near area. Hoping it was the authorities, this time and not a fire truck. Just as he was putting the cell down, Sheryl gave out a cold shriek. "Murray, there's a man at the kitchen window!"

He quickly pulled the Judge, without thinking of any consequences, ran past their maid's quarters and laundry room, which was to the rear of the massive country kitchen leading to the back door. He slowly unlocked the door and stepped out the back, cautiously surveyed the outside searching for the would-be killers wandering around their back yard waiting for their prey to emerge. It did not take long, suddenly a large man darted past the garage that was 60 or so feet away. Murray froze for that second then got the courage and hollered. "Hey, hold on or I will shoot!" He wanted to pull the trigger but suddenly, recalled the instructor in the family gun class. He made the students think that using their weapon and taking a life was a huge responsibility. His mind flashed back to the past when he was in Cleveland with Bill and the guys bailing out their Hungarian buddy, Les Monostory. There, again, recalled a .38 thrust in his hand by Rich in the event a bad guy came running his way and wanted to kill him. He did not use the revolver back then. Would he use it now?

This was totally different, these past months, where killers lurked. It was all different from the self-defense classes and Cleveland where he was little more than a card board cutout with a gun. Murray knew little about what to do, other than to squeeze a trigger. The gun class instructor offered friendly advice that the assailant must be coming toward you and is armed. That was a qualified YES and he would empty out his weapon on this creature who was obviously attempting to kill him and his wife. But the large man was not in sight. Sheryl called out to him. "Someone is at the front ringing the bell. Maybe it is The Village Police!"

Murray looked out toward the garage, not seeing anyone, closed the door, locked it and headed to the front of the home to join his wife. He peeked out through the drapes and saw Sergeant Paige of the Village Police. They unbolted the front door.

"Your neighbor reported the doings here", as the slightly bald, towering, officer pointed towards the victim in the Moonlight Agency's vehicle where the dead man was being investigated by another Village police officer. A third police officer came back from the rear of their home. "Sergeant Paige, I chased a large man in the back, but he went through the bushes and I lost him."

As they stood there, Adam made an appearance, joining them. "What the hell is going on, now?"

Murray gestured toward the crime scene. "Everything happened as fast as you headed for the guest room for your siesta. I don't believe you and Sheryl would wish to see Rich's guard in the car."

Sheryl deferred. "I am going back to the kitchen."

Murray touched his wife. "Hon, it will be okay. Brew some tea for yourself and I will come back in when we finish."

Adam only shook his head in a negative manner. "No, only fill me in on the last hour."

Murray began relating the circumstances to both Paige and Magassey in discovering the Rent-A-Cop's murder and another attempt of someone breaching their home.

Adam remorsed, "This is all my fault. I am so sorry that you and your wife got into all this. Now Carol Sue and her family...but, I am not giving in to Kolezy."

Sergeant Paige began to ask what Adam meant, but was called over by the other officers, stating that the man in the car met his demise at the hand of another. Paige had his patrolman call the Harris County coroner. The Sergeant knew he had more paperwork than he wanted as he came back to the men. Not recalling Adam's comment and wishing to leave for the station. "I heard enough Mister Murray and will file the report. We will get this scene cleaned up for ya'll as soon as we can. I am sorry that you and your wife had to face another crisis. I will ask a patrolman to stand guard for the next few days.

"I appreciate that Sergeant Paige." With that he and Adam bid the Sergeant a good day and went back in, locked the door and joined Sheryl in the kitchen.

At the River Oaks home of Kolezy, the man of the house had finished his morning workout preparing to shower when he spied Melanie who came down to breakfast after a long night. She had partied with her very close friend, Alicia Gonzalez, at her town home. Louis salivated, as usual, at his sensual stepdaughter. Their houseboy, Joska, announced that Dimitri and Drago were in the library. Kolezy was not expecting them until later. He realized something was up. Where they successful in eliminating Adam and Murray?

Joska, disappeared down the hall as Louis' eyes followed his young servant and sometimes lover until he disappeared into the kitchen. Kolezy had visions of getting Joska, Melanie and himself in a ménage troi. For now he had to put it off until his men would leave the mansion.

"Well gentlemen, you have good news for me?" Kolezy asked, hopefully. "I viewed the early morning news on Channel 48 where three people perished in a car bomb at the Katy Merriam along with a non-related murder of a man in Memorial whose throat was cut. Tell me that you took care of both Adam and this Murray character? It appears that the two of you were extremely busy the past three, four hours. I am jubilant of your exploits. Thank you. It appears I should toast the two of you with Dom Peroigne. Better, I will ask Joska to go to the wine room and get that bottle now." He offered his two trusty sidemen Hungarian Kava and pastries ironically bought at Murray's Buckeye Road Hungarian Bakery on Rice Boulevard, just in the shadows of Rice University.

Drago and Dimitri did not wish to tell their leader about the bungled attempts and remained eating.

Kolezy continued munching on the delicacies and laughing, "Well, that Hungarian won't be purveying anymore of these delicious pastries. Too bad, they are extremely to die for as someone said once upon a time. Ha, ha."

Dimitri knew he had to end the festivities even at the cost of great emotional upheaval that was forthcoming from his employer. "Louis, actually, we found that someone broke into Adam's car after Tibor and Gabor placed the bomb. How would anyone in their right mind, at that time of the morning want to steal a car? The Asians were the ones who perished. Not Adam or that woman."

Kolezy had enough pastry, placing it on his plate and sat down holding his head. "You missed another opportunity to rid me of my damn stepson? How can this happen all the time? He was spared, again? Is this man a cat with nine lives? Oh tell me that the Memorial incident was the end of this Murray?"

Drago, stepped in. "Louis, actually, I saw this Murray at The Merriam after the car bombings. Afterwards, Gabor and Tibor went to the Murray's residence. They had to remove a private detective that the Murray's had guarding their home. Before they had the opportunity to kill him, the Cannon Village police interceded our intentions of doing him in." Kolezy should have known but still became enraged. Arising, with his English china coffee cup in hand, dropped it on the tile floor spilling the dark liquid all over his glistening white workout shoes. He turned, disappointedly, to Drago. "Dimitri, I figure may not get things correct but you, my top line of offense failed me. Drago, I had it all laid out, we obtained a valet key to Adam's BMW that you gave to Gabor and Tibor so they could plant the bomb. We had a homing device to follow him and that lady friend of his.... What more could I do.? And the take down of this Murray was screwed up, again!"

"At least your step son's woman was not harmed. You did not want her killed. That is what you said. So, at least she was spared." Then Drago looked down at the spilled contents of the broken plate, ever obedient to his master, Louis, totally disgusted at their inability to rid himself of the Murrays.

Kolezy placed his hand on Drago's shoulders. "I made you from a cheap hustler living in Szeged performing for 200 forint per scene in porn movies. Brought you to Budapest, made you a man, then you were sent back to me. After that, I sent you back to learn English and star in my European adult movies. You were adored. I loved you. I protected you from being misused and abused by the cockroaches in our business, those fucking casting producers. You have had a good life here and when you return to Budapest or Brno, in The Czech Republic, there is money, nice clothes, jewelry. You enjoy a high rise condo, here, in Midtown. You travel. You are paid handsomely. You have never let me down.....until now. Drago, Drago, what happened?"

His eyes choking back the uncharacteristic tears for his mentor, "Louis, yes, three people perished but they were two Asian thieves. I was not able to prevent them from stealing the car and some woman saw them attempting the theft. She is the one who related to the police that they were of Asian descent. I heard her. The car blew up and they vanished. Another person getting something from their car also died. I do not know who he or she was. I witnessed that blond woman with your stepson and later two men, one older and another younger, large man, were talking among themselves."

Kolezy took his hands away and slowly moved to his desk placing his palms down to steady himself. Finally speaking in a hushed tone. I continually miss opportunities to eliminate Adam and others who ally with him. Drago, Dimitri, we must move quickly on this. We just returned from Szeged early this morning. That will be my alibi if they choose to question me. This has become so personal. It is my will to kill Adam myself and still make it appear that it was someone else.. He will continue to see this woman, I am certain. When they are together they will die in each other's arms. I will accomplish it my way."

Dimitri was concerned about his leader's legal position when the authorities would interrogate him. "Are you worried about the repercussions on this, Louis, and when the police might come to see where you were during this incident?"

"My friend, I have an inside person who alerts me when the police are coming my way. I am like that Italian fellow from New Jersey or wherever, the Teflon man, John what's his name. No one will take me down including The Cavazos' brothers."

Drago and Dimitri left, knowing that the road to eliminating Adam, Murray, and Carol Sue was becoming less approachable, yet not revealing it to Louis.

Murray and Sheryl were at their dining room table counting their blessings from all the crunching events they had encountered. He was deeply concerned for the welfare of his wife. Sheryl was fighting the tears, in her blue eyes, as he placed his arm around her in an attempt to comfort her fears.

His wife could not contain herself as her emotions erupted. "When are they going to leave us alone?"

He cradled her with tenderness attempting to hide his own dark thoughts of when this latest episode would end. "Honey, listen to me, as long as I am here to protect you, nothing will happen to you. I believe, though, that it would be safer for you if you were not here. The Roberts have been asking you to come down to their Clear Lake home, especially Renate, who is a shopping guru. Some time with her might be the best cure for all you have been through. In a week her husband, C. W. is planning a return to Budapest, as a staff attaché, to clear up last minute details he had been working on before his retirement back to Texas. I will get Clay Kirby to watch over all of you. He has been itching to get into this fracas since the hospital incidents. He has a place near there but can camp out at their NASA area home. If I am not mistaken, Marshan, the Robert's eldest daughter is in for a visit from Germany. I believe it is the best, now, for you. I will lock up the house here and stay with Bill and Betty in their guest cottage or at Adam's place."

Sheryl was alright in her situation but wanted more answers. "Are you going to see Carol Sue?" as her tears subsided.

"I'm not sure what you're driving at? Adam is heading over to her place as we stand here fencing the subject."

"She may be playing Adam. He is naïve when it comes to women. She has eyes for you and with me fifty miles away in Clear Lake and her being at Cinco Ranch or East Memorial..."

He leaned his head on her head patting her brown hair easily. "When are you going to realize she doesn't want me as her lover and I am only interested in you, so come and let's go down the hall to our bedroom."

Sheryl's mood quickly went 180, ripping his Stephen F. Austin purple shirt off. He grabbed her Sam Houston State jersey pulling it off as they raced down the hall to the master suite. Both of them peeled off their jeans and under garments revealing their many times at the clothes optional spa and that late February trip to Bali, cementing a darker brown to their bodies, reaching their master suite he viewed his blushing wife he met and married over thirty years before. She was a fitness fanatic, at 5 foot, 10 inches, maintaining her slender weight of their earlier days of marriage. He was almost at his early 20's weight. They now revisited their love for one another placing behind the recent ordeals they shared. He had no intention of connecting with Carol Sue and he was ready to show that to his lovely, comely wife. Gently pulling her to the bed, caressing her, aroused, looking at her tightly, shapely figure. Kicking the bed covers off onto the floor, she was appreciative of his near 'six pack'. She screamed with joy, which he only happily obliged. In the next hour, the occurrence was repeated ending in their steamy bodies exhausting one another. He seized the moments continually making love to her as she tore into his back moaning, allowing their emotions to steer uncontrollably to the zenith. Their passion and devotion for one another continued for an insurmountable time as they climaxed together in a cascade of perspiration and bodily secretions. They were sated, out of breath, lying on their backs, savoring the past steamy affectionate moments.

As they tried for another round of romance, the phone rang next to their bed. It was Lieutenant Cavazos who wanted to see them as soon as they were able to roll out. Half disgusted at being interrupted on a happy matter, he tried to disguise it as he wanted the cop to continue being in his and Adam's corner in bringing Kolezy to justice. "Hey, Lieutenant Cavazos, what's going on?" He then unhappily viewed Sheryl grabbing the bed sheets around her beautiful body which sported a love heart with an arrow above her right shoulder. Just as in the movies, he watched his lovely wife traipse into the bathroom dropping the sheets as he was forced to talk with the cop. Continuing with his conversation with Dimas Cavazos, "What do you have in mind?"

The Lieutenant asked, "I would like you both to come down to Reisner St. for a lineup."

"We will do it if you can protect a gal who is a part of Adam's life and wants to buy his company. She is in danger because of it. She lives in both Harris County and in Katy. There has been an attempt on her life."

Lieutenant Cavazos wanted to know if she was involved with the car bombing and was she there as the police report showed that it was

Adam's car that was enveloped. Murray filled him in on the Merriam mayhem the evening before. Cavazos felt that meeting at Carol Sue's Katy home may have been better than police headquarters. Murray concurred and gave the policeman her address. "Lieutenant, I will meet you out at Carol Sue's home in Cinco Ranch as soon as I shower."

With that he looked up and saw Sheryl's leg exposed behind the bathroom door, beseeching him to enter and shower with her. He leapt from the bed and raced into their bathroom for another round of skin to skin rubbing.

An hour later Murray left their home, dialing Adam, to be certain he knew that the police were on their way.

Adam advised him that Carol Sue had already called the Fort Bend Sheriff after being warned of the murder, at Murray's own home. The vixen still believed that she was in grave danger and the next target for Kolezy.

Adam arrived, at Carol Sue's Katy home, well ahead of the Lieutenant. Carol Sue greeted him with a screw driver cocktail, and a wink. The former model pulled him in, wearing tight sliced, rolled up, hot shorts and denim shirt. Her heart was beating rapidly seeing her Adonis. She wanted his flesh in her recalling the shorten fling at The Merriam. Here the street-wise broad, acted like an adolescent girl.

Adam felt the same. He quickly placed his drink down. Without any further thought, he kicked off his flip flops and pulled off his t-shirt. The cougar drooled at his six pack abs, savagely pulling off his Levis and Calvin Klein briefs. He tore off her shirt, revealing her unprotected breast. Sucking on her cherry tits, he removed her shorts, only to find she had sans any panties. The young man could not get enough of this cougar as he tongued her clitoris making it wet enough to penetrate her hot love zone. Clearing off the dining room table, they both hopped upon it. He entered her, plunging his love stick to her delight. He drew her body to him, banging hip to hip.

Carol Sue moaned, "Oh, Adam, you are such a love machine. Pleeeze fuck the daylights out me." He reared up like a hydraulic machine, seemingly pushing his entire body through her. With that she vibrated so much that the left over silverware on the table fell off onto the tile floor.

After coming like a 1000 barrel a day, West Texas oil jack, she glanced at her lady Rolex diamond encrusted watch. "Well, I better get ready and take a shower, the cops are coming." With that she pulled out and rolled off the table, grabbing her scanty clothes and wanting a shower and a make ready. The young man smiled to himself as his eyes followed Carol Sue heading to her bedroom. He thought she was his lady. Adam was in heaven, even though, doing it on a Ethan Allen dining room table.

Adam climbed off the table found his briefs, jeans and t-shirt. He believed that he made a one hundred per cent conquest of this older woman. Unquestionably, he was her number one man. But was he? He retrieved his flip flops and journeyed to the bathroom off the kitchen and wiped himself off, beaming in the vanity mirror. He was on top, so to speak. Taking a huge gulp of the screw driver, he thought to himself, what an appropriate drink after that table event. All that was to end soon as both Cavazos and Murray were almost at the Cinco Ranch home. Louis and his henchman were a few miles away in Kolezy's 700 Series BMW. The car was outfitted with heavy metal sheets under the car to prevent a car bomb from penetrating the passenger compartment. Luka liked to drive this car, making him feel more superior instead of being a gopher boy. Inside the attorney was making vial threats. "We must silence this woman, now, my men!" With that they turned onto Carol Sue's street and parked two homes down from hers. They spied her yellow Corvette parked in the circular drive. Then he ordered Luka to drive in front of the home next to Carol Sue's.

Dimitri volunteered, "The tall woman is here. I see another parked car, a BMW SUV. Wait, here comes another vehicle. It appears to be an undercover police car. One additional, a Buick Enclave....it pulled into the circular circle drive, behind the police car."

Kolezy saw for himself, it was what he thought Dimitri witnessed. Lieutenant Cavazos got out as Murray alighted from the Enclave, and shook hands with the cop. Kolezy never knew what Murray actually looked like. He quickly asked Drago. "Do you know that man?"

Drago confirmed. "The man without the western boots is Murray. The other man looks very menacing and his jacket is hiding a gun. I can almost trust my feeling on that. He is a policeman."

Kolezy stared at the boot clad man. "Yes, that is Lieutenant Cavazos. He and his brother came to my office and questioned me about Adam and Joe Molnar, attempting to implicate me in all this."

Murray rang the doorbell, Adam answered the door and as he greeted the two men, he viewed the large black 700 BMW, next door, at the curb. "Look, Murray and Lieutenant Cavazos it is like a car my stepfather would drive. I think it might be him."

Cavazos was intrigued and wanted to confront Kolezy, again. "I want that man's ass. He is a killer." With that he started to unloosen his holster to draw his gun and head toward the black luxury car.

Louis did not want to tangle, for the moment, with the policeman. "Luka set the car in gear and let's get out of here. NOW!"

The young houseboy, obeyed, smashing the accelerator as the BMW screeched out.

As Kolezy's car swerved around the corner it was almost met by Sergeant Zeke Cavazos' cruiser. Zeke had been summoned by his brother to help on questioning Carol Sue.

Dimas held up as the large black car took off. He saw the license plate and wrote it down, 'Atrny 1'. Smiling to himself, now thinking that Kolezy was such a dumb fuck trolling the neighborhood with probable intentions to do more mischief, yet sporting personalized license plates.

Zeke pulled into the circular drive. "Hey, Bro, what the hell is going on? Don't these uppity Anglos know how to drive?"

Dimas holstered the .45. "That my Bro was Louis B. Kolezy. The slime ball who was going to do some heavy shit here. With that the brothers wandered back toward the house where Murray and Adam were waiting outside the door.

Dimas verified Adam's suspicion "Well, your guess was correct, Mr. Magassey, it looks as though Kolezy was here to look up Ms. Winters."

"Lieutenant, my stepfather will not stop until he tries to rid everyone who has anything to do with my selling of MABB. That includes Carol Sue."

As almost on cue, the lady of the house came from her bedroom to greet Murray, Zeke, and Dimas. Earlier, she wore her sliced shorts when Adam arrived and they made passionate love. Now she donned a tight pair of designer jeans and a spangled, pink t-shirt emblazoned with, 'I Love All Men'.

Cavazos' interest in interrogating her was peaked, to say the least. Smiling at her, while looking at the two, braless, ample mounds. There was a moment of silence from the four; Adam was still thinking of his latest roll on a hard oak table with her. Murray was biting his tongue flashing back to how much Carol Sue resembled her late sister and what it could have been. Cavazos wanted to start the questioning or was it some fluff bull shit he would come up with as he was very aroused. He started, "Since the other gentlemen won't introduce me to you, I am Lieutenant Cavazos of Houston Police Homicide Division. You have to be Mrs. Winters?"

Her eyes wandered over the broad shouldered, roughly handsome, boot-clad, cop. She extended her hand to him. "Actually, Lt. Cavazos of

Houston Police Homicide Division, I am just plain Carol Sue Winters." As their hands met, their eyes were riveted to each other. For the moment neither of them wanted to let go and eventually the wily woman slowly, did her sensual, pull-away. Her immediate opinion of him was that of a Mexican enchilada ready to eat.

Adam was stunned. He sensed her magnetic energy extending to the cop and felt he was just a sideshow to this main event. It was all a cruel joke. The former adult star had a hot time on her dining room table less than an hour ago and now it appeared he might as well go back to the prostitute who had pre-trained him in the ways of making a woman want a man. Adam knew, at least, he was going to get his price for MABB. Carol Sue only had eyes for the big cop, wanting him to protect her. She kept smiling at the Lieutenant.

Zeke sized up the duo. "I am Sergeant Zeke Cavazo's, HPD and Ma'am, ur, Ms. whatever your name is? Sorry, that I don't know what it is. You just introduced yourself as Carol Sue Winters, yet on your answer bell it shows 'Miller'. Whatever you go by, I am here, with my brother, to help sort out the problem you are involved in."

Carol Sue approached him extending her hand. It is both Miller and Winters. I am very glad you have come to my home. I can really use your support."

"Could I get you gentlemen something to drink? Ice tea, mineral water, scotch, some good ole Mexican beer. Ha-ha", continuing to bat her eyes, flashing her stunning white teeth and acting overall, play full.

The Lieutenant, was a little apprehensive. Even for a seasoned woman's man, he was going to meet his match if there was to be a serious relationship in the future. "Yes, ah, Ms., ah, Carol Sue. Yeah, I really like Mexican beer, Carta Blanca is a favorite. What's yours? Favorite, that is?"

Zeke piped up. "Don't forget me, Ms., ah, Miller? I am into Chivas Regal scotch. No water. Two fingers."

She laughed throwing her head back. "You Cavazos brothers ... well I am going to treat you two right. Will get that two fingers of scotch for you in a jiffy."

Murray gave out his order, George Dickel, White Label, Number 12."

Carol Sue looked over at him, uncaringly, "I don't think I have it. Go see if there is some Jack Black in the bar."

Murray could care less on the choice of drink but wanted to steer the conversation away from Carol Sue's and Cavazos' budding romance to be and spare Adam the embarrassment she was laying out. "Lieutenant Cavazos, don't forget why you came here, Okay?"

The Lieutenant gave Murray a strange look at first and then reality set in. "Yeah, Ms. Winters...I noticed your car license has 'Vixey' on it. What made you do it? You know, to have that on your car?"

She smiled as she passed the Carta Blanca into his hand. She purred, "Care for a glass, Lieutenant?" My friends call me that, well, I will tell you that later.... Hell, it has to do with being a vixen."

The Lieutenant wanted to make a comeback remark but thought better. Somewhat struck for an answer, still looking at her body. "No, Miss Winters, I like to drink out of the bottle. Well, at least today. As for a vixen, I, a, a, yeah, I think I know what that is."

Adam was getting jealous after all he gave up his other life style to dedicate himself to women, starting with Carol Sue. Even though he thought that she only loved him for the moment and to get the price she wanted. Yet, she did give him the price or would she change her mind? All this raced across his mind as she and the cop were cozying up for a future date of whatever she had planned. He blurted out, "Carol Sue, do you have a DosEquis in the frig?"

Murray was also trying to pry her off of Dimas. "Hey, Vixey, how about a George Dickel, White Label and Diet Coke for me?"

Somewhat put out at the bar requests, "You both know where the bar is in this house? No, Anthony, I said get the Jack."

"Actually, Vixey, I don't. That is, where the bar is. Do you, Adam?"

Magassey indicated, "Yeah, let me show you. I guess our hostess is too wrapped up in giving statements to Lieutenant Cavazos to be hospitable."

As she began to retort the comments, the front door buzzer rang.

Both Zeke and Dimas volunteered to answer the door as the Lieutenant laid his hand on his .45. "Just want to make sure it is not the wrong kind of people" looking through the sentry peep hole, he could see that a police officer was standing there. Quickly he opened the door. There stood The West Bend Sheriff, Ed Lachowski. They exchanged officer courtesies. Lachowski, 6'2" early fifties, in top shape, with two silver and pearled handled, 357's strapped in a holstered on his hip, loud voiced dressed in a traditional brown and gold uniform with the word 'Sheriff' emblazoned on his shoulders. He appeared to just bolt into the room like a bull in a china shop. "So what is going on here? Are you Ms. Carol Sue Miller?" As he pointed to the ex-model dressed in her casual outfit.

She extended her hand, looking at his name tag, "Sheriff Lachowski."

"Yes, that's me, Sheriff Lachowski." The lawman looked at his name badge.

"It is nice meeting the number one protector in all of West Bend for Cinco Ranch. My last name is actually Winters."

"Well, Ms. Miller, uh, Ms. Winters, our department handles over 200 square miles, not only Cinco Ranch." He bellowed out, then turned his attention to Lieutenant Cavazos. "Just what is a Houston police Lieutenant doing in my jurisdiction?" He demanded.

Cavazos was in no mood for another police officer from neighboring area to screw up his investigation. "Sheriff, four innocent people have been murdered, all possibly linked to Louis B. Kolezy, the attorney."

Lachowski roared back, "You mean that high priced Houston lawyer?"

"That's correct, Sheriff, and he may be responsible for an additional five murders." Cavazos flipped his pocket spiral notebook running off names and dates of their demise. "That and two cases of attempted murder at Memorial Hospital. We believe a HPD officer may even be linked to that, unfortunately, a blue going bad."

The Sheriff's response was typical, "Looks like we have a bad dude, here. There was a young Houston PD found a few weeks back at the turnaround off 59. We get three or four bodies a year being dumped down there."

Cavazos acknowledged that fact as he related to Adam and Murray. "Remember that new, young policeman, at the hospital, that the nurse talked about? The one that left his post as the sniper tried to take us all down? Well, he's the one the Sheriff is talking about."

Murray and Adam each had the same reaction. He was the one many thought, Kolezy was paying to keep the attorney abreast of what was going on.

The Sheriff was curious as to why the two men were there with Cavazos. "I sort of know why the Lieutenant is here. What are you two guy's stories?" Are you just friends of Ms. Miller?" Without a response from either of them, Lachowski pulled out his note book. "Anyone have a pen?"

Zeke, who was silent to this point was enjoying the West Bend Sheriff who he thought belonged on the old television series 'Dukes of Hazzard'.The Sergeant handed him a gold pen he carried. "Sheriff, here's what we use at HPD. Only, make sure I get it back. Guess your department has a shortage of writing utensils, eh?"

Gruffly clearing his raspy throat, most likely from drinking bourbon the night before, "Those folks at the station like to play games with me and my note book, sometimes hiding my BIC pen from me." With that he began scribbling names and addresses like a middle school monitor reprimanding students for chewing gum in class.

As he began questioning Carol Sue, "A-ha, Ms. Miller or do you go by Winters? Hell, I'll put both your names down and we'll sort it out later. You say that these people allegedly are after you to do you in?"

Carol Sue laid her hand on the Sheriff's, "I was almost involved the other evening in that horrible bombing at The Merriam on I-10. If it were not for Mr. Magassey, here, I would have been a victim, too. Then, before you arrived today, there were suspicious people in front of my home, most likely the same ones who carried out that tragic deed at the hotel."

He looked at the casually, fashionable dressed woman with perfect platinum hair staring at him with those beautiful, ocean blue eyes, somewhat memorized by her. "A-ha, Ms. Miller, you believe this Kolezy is going to do you harm?"

Again, she rubbed and touched the Sheriff, softly murmuring, "As I told you, the hotel tragedy, and the innocent people dying. Those people are going to break into my home and violate me. Yes, going to harm me. What are you doing about all this?"

Lachowski looked at all of them in the room. "No, I did not see anyone in front of your home. Yes, I was running late and missed them. They may have been realtors looking at your home for all I know. I got here as soon as possible, Ms. Miller or Winters or whatever, look I did not catch any description of these people in a car."

A voice from the rear of the room, echoed, "I did, Sheriff."

Everyone looked back to see her son, Wes standing in the back of the room. "It was a black BMW with license number, 'Atrny 1'. I came back and saw them before they screeched off."

Dimas butted in, It was Kolezy's car and presumably, with him and his gang waiting to harm Mrs. Winters."

The 6'2 Sheriff looked up at the nearly 6'4" young adult who was protective of his mother, "Don't worry, son, we will get an all-points bulletin out on these characters. There is no evidence, though, that this Kolezy person was even in the car."

Lieutenant Cavazos was totally disappointed in Lachowski's response. "Hey, jefe, I will get HPD to take care of it."

The Sheriff was put out to say the least, "Well, Mr. HPD, I am positive you will single handedly wrap these hombres without our intervention. You can do whatever pleases you. I am out of here, if you need me you know where I am at."

Carol Sue was deeply concerned. "I need protection, Sheriff. What can you do to guard me?"

He looked at the ex-model with a lustful thought. "I will personally see that you have around the clock protection." He finished writing in his notebook and stuck the gold pen into his breast pocket. "Well, I surely hope that you will be satisfied with this, Ms. Miller, slash, Winters?"

Carol Sue smiled. "'Slash'. Wasn't he in some rock band back in the eighties?"

Lachowski was beyond that and shut his eyes, "I don't know, ma' am. Best be on my way. We have some real problems in Rosenberg with some undocumented folks."

Dimas started to say something about that term but Zeke held him back. "Well, treat those folks real good, jefe. They may be cutting your lawn or cooking those enchiladas over at Gary's or that great seafood place, Dock 90 on Highway 36. Oh, by the way before you leave, I need my gold pen back."

Lachowski begrudgingly fished the pen out of his shirt pocket and handed it back to Zeke. "Ah, thanks for the pen, Sergeant." The West Bend officer then strolled out the front door.

Zeke was in a hurry to get out and left. The conversation with Adam, about Troy, nagged at Murray. He thought that Lieutenant Cavazos may have been involved with Troy's investigation so he found him in the kitchen munching on a chicken salad sandwich. "Lieutenant, my son, Troy, was murdered nine months ago in The Montrose. I never received any satisfaction on his case that the HPD was tracking down any leads. My wife and I cannot bring it to ourselves that he was....."

Cavazos put the sandwich down, "Gay? When I looked up you and your wife after all this Adam deal came into play, I found out Troy was the one Zeke and I investigated. For what it is worth. I actually believe he was killed by a woman. The scent of perfume still filled the room, along with lipstick on the pillow cases and bed sheets. It just stacked up that your son and this person, a woman, and not a guy dressed as a broad, were playing kinky games. It got out of hand, maybe. We still have the case open and after this deal with Kolezy, I promise to check into it. This business with Mizz Winters has us stretched. I have a son, too, a little younger than Troy was and I feel for you. I really believe your son was not a part of these Montrose murders. The M. O. does not match."

Murray was a little more convinced that he and Sheryl had a straight son who was trapped that night in the 'No Tell Motel'. He thanked the cop and started to leave when he ran into Magassey. Adam wanted to linger and see where he stood with Carol Sue. Dimas was staying put and had other ideas.

Murray was walking out, dialing Sheryl to be certain she made it over to their friends, the Roberts. He hit the speed dial for her, suddenly; Wes grabbed his arm, pulling him aside before the connection was made. "I know you are not fully responsible for my mother's predicament but you came back into her life and all this talk of having her protected is beyond me. It began with you getting into this MABB deal. She is headstrong and you pushed her buttons on this. She better not be harmed."

Murray defended his actions. "I offered this business to your mother. She could have walked. I know you love her. Just don't blame me if she enjoys danger and living on the edge. You know as well as I do she likes to take the hard way in life. Carol Sue has always been that way ever since I knew her in Wichita Falls. You take care of our daughter and the grand kids and not 'mother' your mother. She's able to take care of herself."

Wes looked at the sky for a while as Murray began to re-dial Sheryl. "I know you are right. Better head back to give my 'goodbyes' to my mother and take Gina and the kids in my arms."

Murray agreed. "Yeah, Son-in-law. Take it easy." Sheryl answered an instant later. She was safe and secure with C.W. and Renate Roberts. They were all on their way to Austin to see their youngest daughter.

In the house, a triangle situation was developing. Adam started to ask Carol Sue about Dimas, who appeared to have similar ambitions toward the woman. "Carol Sue, I really do not want you in danger as I have been selfish trying to get you to buy MABB. This damn company has caused a lot of trouble and hurt."

Carol Sue had just made herself a Nigerian Cabdriver cocktail. "Look, Adam, I'm a big girl and if your stepfather tries anything, he will be looking down the barrel of these." Just then she pulled from her purse, a twin pair of Smith and Wesson silver with pink handled six shot .38 Specials. "I don't need any man to cuddle up to make me warm, cozy and safe. I will be waiting for him or anyone who he sends my way." She confided in a staunch way. "It's like the pink ribbon of my cancer survivorship. I think pink will take over the world."

Dimas had used the bathroom, off the kitchen, and came in as she waved her two .38's around. He stood there admiring this former beauty queen recalling a Virginia Slims cigarette commercial that he thought fitted Carol Sue, "You Have Come A Long Way, Baby!"

She looked at the cop with her golden smile. "Yes, Lieutenant, I definitely have!"

Seeing the guns in her hands, he pushed to see where she was heading, "Ms. Miller, by chance do you have permits for those guns?"

"Lieutenant, do you want to slap the cuffs on me? To answer your question, yes, I do."

Adam was feeling threatened by Dimas' coming on to Carol Sue. "Lieutenant, don't you have to go and arrest some people or check if Shipley's Donuts on Mason has a batch of freshly made Czech sausage kolaches?"

Cavazos sensed the hostility in Adam's voice. Looking at Carol Sue's long legs wanting to explore her womanly aspects. "Look, Ms. Winters, I may want to ask you more questions in the next few days. Are you going to be available, maybe for lunch?"

Checking out his broad shoulders and flat, muscled chest, she beamed up, "How about tomorrow? I just know I'll be full of answers to your questions."

Adam squinted at that response. "You don't even know what he is going to ask?"

"It doesn't matter. I am certain I will enjoy the questions." She smiled in the way a woman anticipates a future, probable romantic interlude with someone she barely knows but wants to find out in bed.

Dimas laughed at her retort to the perturbed, younger man. "Adam, at least, I won't have to ask you anymore questions. You're not the type I like to interrogate, anyway. Ms. Winters, I will call you in the morning and pick you up for lunch of your choice." The cop began to walk toward the front of the home, then pulled a 'Columbo', stopping and turning around gesturing with his index, right finger. "Yes, Ms. Winters, I do have a question now. You never answered it earlier, why did Mr. Murray refer to you as Vixey?"

She came up to the cop, rubbing the lapels of his coat. Murray likes to call me by my nickname. "You do know what a vixen is, don't you, Lieutenant? I will be waiting for your call. And it is not Ms. Winters. It is Carol Sue."

Dimas was stunned and caught, momentarily, speechless. He came back to his senses. "Ah, I believe so, ah, Carol Sue."

Adam saw the hotel love nest, and the table sex that occurred earlier, as just a fleeting notch on Carol Sue's bedpost. He thought, based on his demeanor, that Cavazos was between women and was available. He could not believe this woman was openly flirting in front of him after he thought they had something going. "Well you two, I have to head back to my restaurant to check out some booked parties".

Cavazos also needed to get back to headquarters. "Me, too. Looking forward to lunch tomorrow, Carol Sue."

Her look belayed more than that. "I will be waiting on pins and needles."

Adam, deeply dejected and hurting inside, left the house, not caring what was in his way when he met up with Murray who had just finished talking with Sheryl on his cell. "Well, you look like death warmed over, my lad. What's going on?"

"Oh, not a lot. Just got screwed over by a woman. A first for me as I am accustomed to being screwed by a man. My balls ache where she literally kicked them to death as our friend and protector, the Lieutenant, came on to her. Loyalty is not her virtue."

Murray befriended him by laying an easy hand on his back. "You are not the only one who has experienced her whims. Carol Sue is not a one man's woman. You might wish to approach Michaeleen. She appeared to take an interest in you."

Adam looked down, desperately seeking to find answers to alternative love of a woman. He began to perk up, somewhat. "You may have something there. I kind of sloughed her off a little with the thought of going after an older, mature, street-wise, broad."

Murray concurred. "Yeah, 'Broad', does fit Carol Sue."

Adam knew what he meant as he 'high-fived' Murray and got into his car.

As Lieutenant Cavazos was beginning to leave after tearing himself away from Carol Sue, Murray went up to him. "You mentioned my son may have been murdered by a woman last year. It was..."

Dimas waved him off, "Yeah, like I told you before. It was not like these others, though. Your son was, well... actually, Zeke, was the investigator on it. He did tell me that, for what it is worth, and I should not reveal things as it was my brother's case. Zeke would tell you that it was a strange case. Your son was not expecting what happened to him. It strongly appeared to have been a woman who was involved in the murder. That is all we know. I will check into it, I promise, Murray."

Murray thought out loud, "He was straight and murdered by a woman."

"Like I said earlier, it may have been a red head, maybe a natural one. Then there is the lipstick and perfume. Not some guy pretending... Do you know any gal like that he was dating or knew him at the time he was killed?

"Yes, he was engaged to a young lady my wife and I liked, but we had a sense that he was going through the motions. Perhaps to please us. Her name was Skylar Locke, a natural red head."

Cavazos could tell that Murray was still troubled by their son's murder. "I know we are on different sides. Skylar Locke? Again, I will check into it and see if she comes up. Okay? I realize you are on Adam's side, although I am not convinced that he is a born again and totally a changed woman loving guy."

"Well, Lieutenant, my wife and I started to back him and he is of my Hungarian heritage. We stick together just like if you found him and he was Luis or Lupe or Pedro, you would want to see it through because of being a fellow Latino."

Cavazos knew that as well.

With that they left getting into their own cars.

Murray went over to Bill's office where he found the group, The Fedors, Tanski, and Ernie Petrovich. They began to plot the capture and conviction of Kolezy and his Hungarian Mafia.

Rich Fedor, though casual appearance in Ralph Lauren blazer and slacks, had FBI written all over him. Today, he sported sunglasses which made him a little mysterious, drawing away from his small mustache and a slight built. His cousin, Sev, a former soldier of fortune, enjoyed being an operative for Rich's Moonlight Investigations, when it called for extreme danger or thorough interrogating. Ernie Petrovich, the legal expert of the group, enjoyed his jaunts with this group, away from his law firm. He had a passion for writing novels When he sold a trilogy of best sellers and became well off, using his pen name, Dicky Hudak, he cut back on his law cases, only to handle needy cases and referrals. Ernie harnessed the money and partnered with St. George on a few local ventures. Ernie was the least likely of the group to draw a weapon, becoming a strict conservative and activist. Ron Tanski was the other member of St. George's group. Tanski was a former Special Forces agent and shared many harrowing experiences with Sev. Ron savored danger and intrigue that he left behind as a government specialist. He did not share Ernie's views. When the economic woes occurred in Cleveland, Bill looked up Murray, down in Houston and they encouraged the other four to relocate to the Gulf Coast.

Murray started it. "Guys, this Kolezy is one tough son of a bitch and has to be brought down. We got to have someone on him 24/7"

Rich conceded. "He may even be too much for my Moonlight Investigations. I already lost Benny when the Village Police found his throat cut outside your home."

"Where was his partner? He should have had a backup. Right?" pursued Murray as he gesticulated around the room.

Rich could not deny it, "Benny's sidekick, Henry Lynn, was taking a piss next to your tennis courts in the back. He never heard anything."

"Christ, Rich, how long does it take to spring a leak and walk back to the car?"

Rich defended his operative, "Someone cold cocked him between the pool and the garage. The police found him unconscious after they investigated the premises."

Murray was still unconvinced. "They slash Benny and blackjack this Henry Lynn? Why not do him in, too? Gotta say this, Rich, it does not smell right? Does it? And where is Mister Lynn today?"

Rich fell silent on the question. Slowly he began to explain. "Henry always had money problems. I would have Becky Ewing, our secretary; give him an advance until the next paycheck. His wife Lillie was a spender and he always wanted to please her. Then she had a kid with him. Henry had two other children with Dulce. Anyway, he called in the other day after Becky attempted to get hold of him to see how he was and to send him out on another surveillance case. Lynn said he had to go to his other job in Rosenberg, working at an appliance store there on the side to make extra dough. He really wants to get out of the detective business for now and send his check to his home off 1960 and Copperfield."

Murray sat down in a chair and looked at Bill and the others who were thinking the same thing. "Yeah, it sounds as though Kolezy bought him." He blew out his breath and continued, "Whatever he was paid, my bet is he won't be around long to spend it. Look at that cop from the hospital, Eh?"

Rich pondered the thought. "Maybe you are right as you have had more dealings with this Kolezy person. Everything in public, indicates that this attorney is pure white, no blemishes. He has to have a lot of people in his pocket." He then pointed to his cousin, Sev. "Sevrin, you and Ernie want to take a trip over to Rosenberg and see how Lynn is doing? Maybe ask what is going on with him?"

"Yes, there's a great Mexican place, Larry's, which serves shrimp enchiladas down there", piped up Ernie.

Sev looked at Petrovich with disgust. "You're as skinny as a rail. Hell, I look at a taco or chimichanga and gain 5 pounds."

Tanski threw in his two cents, "Sev, it ain't the Tex-Mex that causes you to bloat out, it is the three Tecate's you down with the chow."

Murray snapped his fingers, "I know this crazy guy from Lubbock, we were in the Air Force together. His name is George Igo. He was CIA after we split from the Service. He moved to San Antonio to work in the new industry, hi tech computers and listening devices. He lives in The Woodlands. He can probably plant some bugs for us so we can figure Kolezy's next moves? We can do a 'Watergate' and go on what

Kolezy says before he has the chance to screw up someone else's life."

Rich agreed with bringing in another wrinkle for getting rid of Kolezy. "Yes, I know George, he can do it. We've done some minor work with him. He's worked Desert Storm and early Afghanistan before all hell broke loose. One of the State Department biggies used him there, even though he was older, like us."

Murray had a temporary solution on keeping Kolezy in view. His go to guy for emergencies, "Clay Kirby can follow the attorney around."

Rich had the experience in items like this and did not feel that Kirby was up to it. "Look, I'll get another of my men to shadow Kolezy, at a safe distance. Until then Cuz and Ernie can go to where Henry works."

Sev and Ernie started to head out the door for Rosenberg, about 25 miles southwest of Houston, to get Henry Lynn's version of the happenings the night his partner, Benny, was murdered. Rich cautioned his cousin. "Sev, don't overdo it? Okay? Remember that you were removed from the Green Berets for some heavy handedness on those prisoners at Guantanamo."

Although Sev was his cousin, he liked the chain of command with Rich being in charge. Sev, was a year younger, had added about 25 pounds since his active military time, getting less in the hair department , yet he still carried himself extremely well enough that women would still take positive notice of him. "I will get the information out of him. There won't be any bull shit on this", he vowed. Lighting up a Camel and taking it in, Sev wanted to assure his cousin, who was giving him a second chance. "Cuz, don't be a worry wart, Lynn will be treated with kid gloves. I feel like Murray that our former operative has a lot of explaining to do about that night."

Rich peered over his glasses. "Cuz Sev, I know you don't need the money but take it easy on Henry. Alright?"

Sev let out a relaxed laugh. "Sure, Cuz."

Ernie bumped hand to hand with the two Fedors, "I'll be there, Rich, to be the buffer. I am not a rough and tumble guy like Sev. My part in this is to get Lynn to tell us about his part in all this. If he refuses to listen, Sev can kick the dickens out of him."

Dickens? That is what Rich was concerned with. He had to be a go between with the law and the citizens after his cousin pushed a little too much. Perhaps, it was time to open it all up and damn the consequences as Kolezy needs to be stopped.

Ernie pleaded, "I really can't see you taking on this high profile attorney. Maybe we need to let the police handle it. That is what they get the money for. They can bring him in and question his whereabouts. If he is clean, let him go."

St. George could not take that from Ernie. "You're my oldest friend, next to Murray here, but Ernie you are so full of sud. Kolezy is a murderer."

Murray laughed, "You're talking Hungarian, Bill. Just say shit. Yes, he is full of it. Knowing what I do of this man, he is a killer."

Bill looked at Petrovich, "You are too liberal."

Ernie defended "Yeah, Bill, sometimes, my views have changed over the years defending the innocent who cannot stand up for themselves. You are most likely correct on Kolezy."

Adam walked in and heard the group. "Drago and Dimitri have to be brought down first. At that point, my step father will be lost for the time, but like a two headed monster he will bounce back and recruit some other dip sticks to do his dirty work, for his Hungarian Mafia. Cut the legs off of the dragon and do it quickly. Louis told me his father was a 1956 Freedom Fighter over in Hungary. They almost beat the Russians except our government had given them some equipment back in WW2 and that helped crush our countrymen."

Rich wanted to know more about Kolezy's gang. "Who else is connected to your beloved step dad?"

Adam looked at Rich. "He has the Szilyani brothers, Gabor and Tibor. They are the second string to Drago and Dimitri. There's also the young guy who he replaced me, as a part time lover and who was in on the first attempt on my life at the motel. Kid's name is Luka. Joe Molnar is out on bail. He may have done in my buddy, Mark Carlson, the night Murray and Sheryl rescued me from the clutches of death!"

Just at that moment, the television news from Fox began about a car bombing in Las Vegas. The television reporter was interviewing a hysterical, slightly injured, cocktail waitress, who only an hour before, had her car bombed. She appeared frazzled. The woman's name was Carla Davis. She and her son, Brian, narrowly escaped their end as the device was poorly installed by unknown culprits. Everyone was talking in the room at Bill's, creating a mass confusion. Adam yelled out, "Hey, quiet, I think I know who that person is!"

Murray and St. George threw down their hands to quiet the others. especially, Petrovich and Sev, who were the loudest. The story continued that the woman was leaving her shift at the Four Fountains Hotel, along with her son, Brian, a valet parking attendant, who worked there.

Bill asked, "Adam, What's your connection to this woman and her son?"

"Melanie, my sister, heard that Louis had this dirty leg in Vegas and he may have fathered a son, Brian. The woman's name was Carla. She worked as a cocktail waitress at one of the hotel's casino. She overheard him mention the name Carla, at Ryan's funeral. He had connections in Las Vegas. From my experience he always went out there every month. I now know why. He was fucking her and she had this kid. Now Louis wants to get rid of excess baggage that ties him down. My guess, she is bleeding his worthless ass and he has had enough. My stepfather is like that. Kick it to the side in the gutter and let the trash people throw it away. From what I experienced, the car bombing is a standard way to rid your problems. Of course, it is zero to two. He has to be livid that this gal and her son survived the bombing."

Murray thought for an instant. "Hey, Bill, how about hitting the Strip tomorrow? We can contact Lieutenant Cavazos to see if he has a local contact with Las Vegas PD. I really believe we can nail Kolezy on this. Let's fly out there and interview Carla and I bet she will roll over on that bastard."

St. George was hyped up with that off the wall suggestion. "How about fueling up the jet for tonight? I'm itching to roll the dice at The Golden Nugget or Horseshoe. Probably both. Stay up for the next 24 hours; drink some doubles of Chivas Regal...? Anth, you are right on involving Carla Davis? She looked petrified at her near death experience."

Adam was thrown into the hysteria of jetting to Vegas at the spur of the moment. "Can we invite Carol Sue?"

Murray looked at Magassey. "Maybe you need to rethink that request. How about some other gal? Better yet, there's a lot of female flesh at those strip clubs, or maybe Michaeleen?"

Adam became enlightened with that suggestion but backed off. "Well, Carol Sue is wrapped up and I have not approached Michaeleen. Best to go solo, yes?"

St. George agreed. "Yes, The Wild Horse on Industrial Road may be what you need."

Adam, acted a little concerned, "Are we going in without any police backing? Can we just contact Lieutenant Cavazos and his brother, Zeke?"

Bill assured everyone. "We don't need either of them. I know Chief Sam Hamond of the Las Vegas Police Dept. We can leave a message with Cavazo's office that we are heading to Vegas on this Carla Davis 'incident'."

Murray was for it. "Great, Bill. I will call Jon and Arnie, our pilots and have Nikki, the stewardess, on board for drinks and food. We have a micro wave and she is a whizz on whipping up some great snacks. Did not know you had Vegas cop connections. I am impressed."

St. George smugly replied, "Never had to mention about my 'In'. Sam and I played baseball together at Triple A in Tucson when I was a shortstop and he played second base. I was called up to the 'Bigs' with the Cleveland Indians and as they say the rest is history. Sam lingered in the minors for a couple of years then gave it up for law enforcement in his hometown. We always kept up, though and he did some favors when one of my sons went over the edge at the Flamingo one night after losing about twenty grand."

Murray was stunned by all that. "Gosh damn, Billy, I never knew about your kid and this connection you had in so-called, Sin City. At times, you don't let everything out. But, you're playing 16 years in the majors and you have this high power old buddy in Las Vegas who can help. Hell, you are such a hero! You could have been a baseball hall of famer. You had a World Series ring or two, one with the Yankees. You were a marvel at shortstop and later second base, my good bud."

St. George agreed. "Damn straight, my Hungarian friend. Hell, though, in thinking of what could've been for my career, I did real well. You know, Betty and I have had 36 wonderful years of marriage. No money can touch that. It is worth a lot!"

Murray looked out the window of Bill's office as the others were discussing the upcoming trip to Las Vegas among themselves. "Yeah, us too, Sheryl and I can thank our angel, Michaeleen, who came to us out of the blue yonder. Still cannot figure it though. Coming from the Miller clan and how they despised me. Bret's and Bobbie Jean's kid. She has never totally opened up and it is a little vague but, damn, maybe I am over analyzing it. I am like that Frasier character on TV..."

Bill agreed, "You do have the tendency to take the high road on a lot of things."

Murray could not let go of the subject. "Michaeleen has been somewhat unclear on things. I attempted to probe, after the shock of our huge windfall wore off, but a bevy of Miller's and other attorneys just threw Sheryl and me all that money, tax-free, and I let it slide. We just began to enjoy the trappings of being ultra-rich three years ago. She came into our office in '05, by herself, no attorney, to act on her behalf. A super rich young woman. Maybe, to look us over?" Murray began to recall the original turn of events those years back. He continued as he looked at the floor at first then to his friend, "Michaeleen was different then."

St. George was still puzzled. "How so? Not money or power crazy?"

"Yes, just like that. She was dressed in an average way. Today, you see her in expensive women's wear, whatever that is, but you it jumps out at you and along with expensive perfume fragrance, even after she leaves you. The scent is there. She made a mark. No, that day in the office in 2005, it was almost like a young woman in search of knowing Sheryl and me, who were going to be wealthy and what kind of life changing it would mean to everyone including her. I don't know, Bill. Just some still unanswered questions going through my mind at times."

St. George wanted to get on with the plans for Las Vegas. "WE really have to get going on this, Anth, Michaeleen is a great gal and she is in her own world. I wouldn't dwell on the whys and whatever of becoming another Donald Thrump, just roll with it. You said you needed to talk to your pilots of the Gulfstream. I'll contact Sam in Vegas; Have my secretary get a suite or two at Caesars."

Waiting for all this to settle, Murray wanted an alternative hotel to stay at. "Actually, Bill, Clay Kirby has a relative that runs the Mohave Hotel. It is close to everything."

Bill gave a dejected look and agreed. "Caesars would have been better for my crap winning streak but I can always go there when we have some down time."

Adam still wanted to have Carol Sue accompany them on the trip as he dialed her cell phone. She answered amid to a clatter of loud and boisterous conversation in the background. "Hey, gal, a group of us are heading to Vegas in a charter plane. It would be great fun there and I would like to have you go. We can rekindle a night like the Merriam and your place."

Suddenly, there was a strange silence as she had the speaker on and was hosting a 'Texas Hold Em' poker tournament at her place in Katy for the gang at the bowling center 'including a number of her bowling buddies, Mandi and Doug Fought, Sam and Delia Silva, along with the Mirshaks,Jim Sands and Chip and Wendy, all in the room heard the invite as she turned around to face the ten or so players at the two tables she set up in the pool room of the home. Smiling casually at everyone, she clicked off the speaker. "Hey guys and gals, I need to take this call and will be back in a few minutes, just drop me out on this hand." With that she confidently strode to the living room. "Adam, honey, what is it you said? I couldn't hear you. Got a bunch from our bowling league, playing cards, throwing darts, and drinking whatever is not milk or ice tea that gives you a buzz!"

He repeated the offer for Las Vegas. She thought for a long moment then realized she had a date with Dee Cavazos tomorrow. "Oh, baby, I can't. I would really, really like to but the kids are planning something and asked me to be there. Sorry, Sugar, another time, okay? I have to run and keep those bowling friends of mine in the game. For some reason I am a lady gambler and a hell of a dart thrower. I feel terrible, at times, in taking their money. Damn, who am I kidding? I like to beat them. I am just a good ole gal that everyone in Katy loves." She felt secure and in her mind dared Kolezy or any of his henchmen to screw with her. Those twin, pink handled, silver .38 Specials in her bag and a derringer in her boot insulating those tight jeans made her the force to be reckoned with.

Adam had enough. "Well, Carol Sue, go back and do what you like to do and we can connect another time. See you." He realized that a couple of rolls on the Sealy did not guarantee her love and affection. He thought of Michaeleen but knew she was going to be in a series of business meetings in San Antonio where the Ventura Hispanic Service Station dealers were lobbying for an extra two cents a gallon. Maybe this former adult star would need to choose another female in his life just as soon as he returned from this junket to Capital of Gaming and Debauchery.

Murray could see from Adam's face that Carol Sue had let him down. He attempted to console the crestfallen youth. "Looks like we are all bachelors this trip. Like Bill told you earlier, The Wild Horse Club on Industrial next to the Strip will give you all you can handle and then some."

Rich and Sev came up to Murray. "WE are itching to take on the tables in the desert," Sev anxiously said, with Rich smiling in agreement.

Murray was torn with this and having Sev and Ernie check on Henry Lynn. Rich had left the room and tried to phone Lynn to see where he was. He walked back in. "Murray, looks as though Henry has flown the coop and quit his job at the store and with me. His sister told me that her brother has moved to Casselberry, Florida, just outside Orlando, to work at Disney. He left no forwarding address and may contact her later. Sounds as though he was bought off. Maybe if he was, Lynn will live long enough to spend the blood money I believe he got."

Murray was disappointed at the news but thought they had a better lead in Las Vegas. "I have already alerted the first officer, Jon Irion, to fuel up the Gulfstream and get his second in command, Arnie Kaplan, to put in the flight plan to Las Vegas. "We leave at dawn", as he shouted and high fived all who were in the room. "Get your gear and meet at The Sugar Land Airport in a couple of hours. Don't forget to pack your favorite weapon."

Rich interrupted, once again. "I tried to contact George Igo to plant those bugs but he is in Guam with his wife for the next month. They own a melon farm and the harvest is in. Let's skip the listening devices for now and concentrate on this Carla Davis woman. I'd forget about Clay, too. He is up there in age and may wind up like Benny."

Murray and Bill agreed with Rich. Then St. George reinforced the favorite weapon idea. "Guys remember, we are dealing with hardened murderers, so make positive you have enough fire power and clips."

Tanski joked. "We never even thought of that part just enough underwear and socks along with the full metal jackets."

The good part of their being able to 'pack' was most of the time TSA would not stop them as they alighted from the plane at the charter terminal. Generally, the security guards at the terminal did not bother them since the vast number of 'whales' or big money gamblers came in that way. They have body guards who watched their bosses rake in the money and needed the protection to leave the casino at the hotel without being taken down by the elements that lurked around the corners of the casino cage, waiting for those gamblers to make the big scores.

They all met at hangar 21. St. George, dryly looked up at the number, "Very appropriate for most of you guys who lose at the blackjack tables. I'll stick to craps and treat all of you to that midnight steak dinner for three bucks they serve at The Frisco Coast, because you will be in between getting your markers at the casino cage asking for more credit."

Tanski barked, "St. George, I took in twenty grand from Bally's last time, playing 21. You just gotta know how to count the cards."

Bill thought that was amusing, "Bet you lose your underwear this time, Amarillo Slim!"

Rich piped up, "Even I know, Bill, Amarillo Slim is the champion Texas Holdem' player. He would probably blow all his winnings at blackjack."

Adam was enthused that they were heading for the fabulous city in the desert West. "Where are we going to bed down tonight, Anthony?"

Sev could not miss the opportunity as he had returned from Las Vegas four months earlier. "Adam, you most likely would want us to stay at the Rio."

Adam did a double take, "Why there, Sev?"

"The Chippendales are doing their show and I bet you would like to see them strip."

Adam held back his anger and wanted to physically confront this wise ass remark but he looked at the group who were waiting for him to stand up for the change he proclaimed in his life. "If any of you worked out at a gym and have witnessed men working out. Have any of you looked a little longer at a guy with a nice bode?"

There was silence.

Murray stepped in to break up a possible meltdown by his group."Hey fellows, we are staying at the Mohave. We have to do a job and we can't be sniping at one another."

Bill backed up his friend. "We signed on to stop this dickhead, Kolezy. Adam is not the enemy. We are flying out to Vegas. Everyone get your act together. We are a team."

Sev knew he was out of line and held up his hands, directing his feelings toward Adam, "Sorry, kid, I am from the old school and can't buy into your life. ... Cannot get over you like to do things that are not manly."

Murray and St. George both started toward Sev. He just said, "That's me, okay?"

Ernie wanted to join in a positive way, "Who wants to go to The Venetian and see the Blue Man Group? They are tremendous and worth the bucks to see."

Arnie Kaplan, the co-pilot, came into the hangar office. Almost in a high pitch scream, "We're ready to take off for Lost Wages!"

The Gulfstream took off from Sugar Land, heading west with the group's quest for putting the skids to Kolezy. They partied a little, played cards, and slept a few minutes knowing what happens in Vegas won't stay there this time.

Landing at the charter terminal, there was a Cadillac limo waiting to whisk them to The Mohave Hotel, one of the oldest properties in the new Las Vegas. A city where old is an implode of a resort even if revered. Change is the way for this town that The Rat Pack put this town on the map nearly fifty years ago.

The Mohave stood at the north end of the Strip. Only three other hotels were older. Murray's go to guy, Clay Kirby, referred him to the hotel as his brother-in-law who was the general manager. Murray also wanted to be inconspicuous while seeking the whereabouts of Carla Davis and her son, Brian.

Rich and Tanski grumbled at the dark Moroccan interior of the hotel. Tanski looked up at the unappealing walls and ceiling, oblivious of the clang and chatter of the slot machines and yelling at the crap tables. In the corner slightly away from all the gambling, 70's music filtered from the downtrodden lounge. It was where former stars whose careers nose-dived years before attempting to restart their somewhat fame in this dingy arena, playing to a handful of half-drunk patrons and small time gamblers, trying to remember who these people were when they were quasi-famous.

Tanski could not resist the setting. "You know what would help this entire place the most?"

All of them waited for the answer to his question as they stood in the VIP line waiting to get their suite. Bill glanced at his watch as the time ticked by finally falling for the trick question but not caring that he was part of the joke. "Alright, Ron, I am waiting with baited breath for the answer."

Tanski enjoyed the limelight of his quirks. "Dynamite The Place!!"

Murray clapped, "Forget that. Now, we can get on with our lives."

They arrived at the penthouse suite and moved toward the elevators to the 16th floor with the bell hop directing the way. St. George sidled up to Murray. He was normally in his friend's corner except in this case. "Anth, we could have stayed at least at the Tropicana or Flamingo, Even the Rivera. I know you wanted to be incognito while searching for the Davis'. That and being we are on the north end instead of mid or south strip, we have less congestion, but it cries out 'OLD'!" I guess it is close to Sam Hamond's office, away from that traffic from the mid-strip and below which is hellacious and time consuming. I realize we want to talk with Carla and her kid to see what they can tell us about Kolezy. Can't help it, Anth, this place smells 1960!"

Smiling at his old and trusted friend, I knew we could count on you to go with all this. Adam really does appreciate all of you."

Knowing Murray had taken on a responsibility many others would have left go down the road for the authorities to sort out, "Anth, I know this will all work out and don't worry, we are all here for the duration of bringing Kolezy to justice."

The bell hop took them to the top floor of the dated hotel where fresh paint permeated their nostrils. Ernie gasped, "Smells like we are in Home Depot's paint department. I would not care to light a match in the hallway. This place might go up like the MGM did in 1981. Murray, did you see any fire extinguishers anywhere?"

Murray was tired of the flak in defending his friend's historic hotel that hosted Sinatra, Dean Martin, Sammy Davis and Joey Bishop many years before. "This place speaks volume in fame and fortune. Ya'll don't appreciate the way old Las Vegas was. Don't care what Wynn is doing to his hotels or Fertitta and the Golden Nugget downtown. This is the place for us. It is clean and comfortable and under the radar, so no one will suspect our plans. That, and Bill can clean up at the crap tables."

They entered the double door suite, termed 'Presidential Suite'.

Sev could not pass up the opportunity. "'Presidential Suite'. Yes, I believe that, George Washington probably slept here."

The large suite offered six bedrooms for the taking. A fantastic view of The Strip awaited them. As the evening started to set in, everyone began to search for their private room in the suite. The issue was seven in the party and only six bedrooms with each of the party wanting their own privacy. Ernie, Sev, Rich, and Tanski headed for individual rooms almost like Oklahoma Sooners. That left Murray, Bill, and Adam standing in the main room over a blue felted pool table, to figure out who was to get the remaining two bedrooms.

Adam sensed that both of the surviving members were hesitant on bunking with him. Murray was a step ahead and suggested that they cut high card draw for the living room couch. "We can gamble for the pullout in the living room."

Adam was resigned with his being the odd man out. "Look guys, I will go for the couch and you two have your privacy."

Murray felt bad. St. George did not, as he wanted to head for one of the unoccupied bedrooms. Murray, halfheartedly, uttered, "Okay, Adam I will bunk with you if you promise to not roll over on me. "

Bill scanned The Strip as evening started to set in. "That is a relief for me as I am semi-sleep apnea person and if Betty, my wife, is not next to me, I can't get a good night's sleep, plus I saw Adam in a dream wearing a lacy, black, jock strap. You know how it is..."

Adam felt the brush off, a stigma he had to learn to live with as long as he was marked as a gentleman who preferred men over women. He managed a quick retort , " Yes, now I know what to tell your wife to get you for Christmas. We have them in stock." Actually, Adam had packed some lacy, light blue thongs for bedtime. Normally, he was au natural but with a hetro sharing the king size mattress he was uncertain whether Murray would go for that. For now they all wanted was to hit the buffet line, then the tables and take Vegas for a ride!

Murray and their group met just outside of the Oasis Coffee shop of the hotel. One person was missing. Murray declared, " Damn, Bill has deserted us and has headed for the crap tables to bust their walnuts!'

Rich looked at Murray. " Whaat? Bust their walnuts?"

Murray responded, " Yeah, Rich, you know him as well as anyone. If he is not in Lake Charles or in Kinder, Louisiana at Coushatta, throwing the dice, he goes into a deep freeze when you sit and talk trash, right?"

Just then St. George appeared stuffing a wad of Franklins in his pocket and wearing a huge smile.

Sev knew the look. "Bill is all set. He has won a bundle and is good to go on to the next casino."

All of them hung together that night in semi-preparation of meeting with Sam Hamond in the late afternoon as the next day they would not be in any condition for a morning meeting. After all, "Hey, this is Las Vegas!"

They all went grazing at the Mandalay Bay Buffet at $25.00, each with all the trappings and then hit the show at the MGM Grand to see the fabulous magician, David Copperfield. After that, a round of gambling downtown at Binions where St. George rolled his way to nearly thirty grand in an hour. Cool as any high rolling gambler, he remarked, "Fellas, it is all in the wrist and balls."

Tanski lamented, "I lost five 'g's at the 21 table." Ernie was hunting for nickel slots and lost an estimated ten dollars the entire night. Most of the others broke even as they downed the complimentary drinks in the casino for gamblers only. It was nearly 3:30 in the morning when Adam glanced at his watch. "Wow, I haven't been up this late, in who knows, when and it must be the casino oxygen as I am barely tired."

The guys, other than St. George, were trolling the downtown casinos, hitting Binion's, The Fremont, Four Queens, and The Golden Nugget, not feeling any pain and having a little lighter wallets.

Sev was still aching for a rub on their young friend, conveniently forgetting his earlier ribbing of the former porn artist. "Adam, there is an all-night male strip joint off Ogden and Main that you can still catch."

Magassey had been downing Bacardi and Cokes all night while laying bets at all the hotels for roulette. He looked a little bleary eyed at Sev. "Maybe I don't have to go to Ogden and Main, you look pretty appetizing in those leather jeans and muscled shirt. Have you been there, since you know where it is, Sev? Besides, MABB has a male club on South Industrial. I don't need to go there, but if anyone of you is interested in going there, I can make certain you get in on the front row, in the VIP section. Just have five dollar bills ready to stick in their jocks."

The guys, smiled, thinking it was a good comeback, except Sev. Adam raised his eye brows in a sexy motion toward the soldier of fortune. "Ok, kid, Sev muttered, half embarrassed, "You win this round. I think I will grab a cab and head back to the Mohave and lock my door!"

Rich grabbed his cousin. "Sev, we came downtown together, we are going back together."

Bill reappeared, a little bent out of shape, counting a small denomination of bills. "Damn, they changed dealers at The Four Queens when I was up fifteen grand and I almost lost it all. It was time to 'hook em' and quit until daybreak."

All of them became quiet and walked on. Murray had a rental Ford Excursion that was parked at The Fremont's parking garage as the hotel offered four free hours of parking. They left from there and drove to the valet section at The Mohave piled out and forged through the half full casino toward the Penthouse elevator to their suite. A lady of the evening stopped Ernie as he patiently and soberly waited for his turn at the elevator.

Sensing some quick money, knowing they were penthouse bound she thought one of them would be an easy mark for $300 and an easy lay.

Dressed in a short mini sequined dress and four inch high heels, make-up piled on like concrete to a wall, the fortyish hooker grabbed the somewhat stoic Petrovich, "Hey, sweetie, don't go into the elevator I can take you higher than that!" She batted her phony eyelashes that could cut a steak in half, covering a purplish eye shadow, desperately trying to conceal her last twenty plus years of mattress flapping, "I think you are the cutest thing around."

Ernie's Adam's apple fluttered up and down in his throat. Actually he was in a Sodom and Gomorrah setting. This was Las Vegas and what happens here, stays here. Could he really gamble on a night with this devil from the deep who wanted to whisk him into her lair and make compassionate, forbidden wonderment, even though he was happy with his wife and their marriage?

Bill looked at his longtime friend seeing that he was actually weighing the possibility of spending money he never thought before of letting go. St. George looked at the bold mistress of the evening. "Honey, my friend is happily married and his wife is up in the room waiting for him in a see through negligee ready to clasp the hand cuffs on him after she rips off his clothes. You can't compete with that. Check the service elevator for the night security guard who may want a little nookie."

She turned in a huff and trotted off to the service entrance. They all got into the supersonic glass elevator that swiftly catapulted them to the top floor. As the doors opened they stumbled out wandering into the suite to their rooms. Murray was behind Adam when he started to regret the invitation to sleep in the king size bed with the former adult star.

Adam saw the hesitation on his bed companion's face as Murray surveyed the bed choice. "Yes, Anthony, I know what you done to show the others that there is nothing wrong with sharing a bed with me. You are uneasy with this situation. I really appreciate your stepping in and showing the other fellows. I prefer being naked when I sleep. Free and easy. No bindings. Can you live with that?"

Murray stammered, "Sure, the bed is large and I won't peek."

Adam was okay with that, stripping off his clothes right in the middle of Murray's last word. Though Murray was momentarily shocked, at the nudity, as the young man raced into the bathroom, flipped on the light and urinated in the toilet. Then after flushing it, turned to the double sink, brushed his teeth while bending over the basin. Murray last saw that at the 24Hour Fitness Center minus, of course, the tooth brushing, not being bothered by naked, sweaty workout enthusiasts like himself and not thinking that all of the workout warriors were just cleansing their bodies in search of hygiene enhancement. Here, though, he was cast in a situation far from being in a fitness center's locker room where he could shower quickly, dry himself, put on his clothes and leave the others behind not thinking about the nakedness of his mostly unknown fellow gym rats. Murray, himself also enjoyed au natural in bed, as he and Sheryl loved to touch one another, romantically. Would he keep on his briefs or sans them?

Murray stood for a moment with his slacks on, bare-chested, as Adam came back full frontal on the other side of the large bed. The elder man attempted to look directly at his young bed partner's face, mostly avoiding something he never thought of when volunteering to share the accommodations. The air in the room was thick with consternation. Adam smiled broadly, "You really did not think this through when you jumped in to be a Good Samaritan, did you? Why I cannot understand from you, Anthony, is that you and Sheryl found me naked and now you are hesitant on sharing a mattress with me. You still have that issue you confided me about? Are you afraid you might like....?"

"Murray was both tired and exasperated with the situation. "Wait..I don't wish to..."

Adam cut him off "What, have sex with me?"

Murray looked up abruptly to the slow moving fan above the bed. "No, I thought after a round or two of George Dickel #12 and Diet Cokes, I could handle it. That is not happening. What I will do is bed on the pullout couch."

Adam was an expert on getting guys in bed. "You don't need to worry, I will be very gentle. Oh, only joking! Let's turn out the light and you can remove off your clothes and slip into bed. I am totally beat and won't do anything to you. Please we are adults and I know you are tired."

Murray agreed, flipping off the lights, climbing into his side of the bed... with his slacks still on...

The Hungarian group met at 11:00 in the morning in the hotel's Oasis Coffee Shop where Sev and Tanski appeared with hangovers from their carousing The Strip. Rich was his prominent self. Bill wore a professional gambler's smile still counting his Franklin's. Ernie eased back dictating in a pocket recorder on another chapter for his novel. Murray and Adam looked refreshed as the other five surveyed if Murray was any different from the time they all rambled into their respective suite rooms six hours earlier. Each wondered how he managed to get any rest, sharing the same king size bed with the former number one adult star. No one, surprisingly, asked about the other's early morning doings. As the orders came and everyone ate and drank some strong black coffee, Murray turned to Bill. "When and where are we meeting Sam Hamond?"

"We're going over to the main police station downtown. It is not far from what Sam told me. He's waiting for us." Murray, Bill, and Adam left and headed down that way. As the three entered the chief's large office, adorned with pictures of famous movie and sport stars, as well as Las Vegas headliners, St. George introduced Murray and Adam to the city's top lawman Sam Hamond. Murray was immediately thrown for a loop. Hamond appeared to be almost a dead ringer for the late Dean Martin who played in the first Ocean's Eleven movie shot in Las Vegas in 1960. The original movie about the eleven holding up five Vegas casinos for millions of dollars came back from the past. "Where's Frank and Sammy?" asked a joking Murray as Hamond was accustomed to a similar greeting based on his looks of the former crooner and being in this popular city where Elvis was on every corner. The veteran cop ignored the comment and wanted to visit with his old friend St. George, even though Murray and Adam were a big part of the equation.

Bill congratulated Sam's progress to chief of police in the nation's fasted growing city in 2008. Sam reciprocated, detailing their start in the minor leagues to Bill's long career in the majors. Both appeared to chuckle over some inside joke over that and got down to business.

St. George asked the chief, "Sam, has Lieutenant Cavazos from the Houston Police Department Homicide investigation contacted you involving the recent bombing incident at The Four Fountains involving a Carla Davis and her son, Brian?"

Hamond was a good ole boy born in Turkey, Texas, home of Texas swing country and western legend, Bob Wills. He leaned back in his chair, "He knew you were coming and we visited briefly on the phone yesterday. I gotta tell you ole buddy, his department, not him, mind you, does not believe there is a connection to this Carla Davis car bombing deal. You are asking about a very popular gal who dispensed some very likeable libations. I even, sort of know her. She is a very luscious woman."

Murray immediately felt "I can't believe that no one is going to the assistance of Carla. Has anyone been implicated in an attempt on her life?"

Hamond bent down from his high top chair, directly looking at Murray. "I have to figure there is a connection, otherwise my good buddy, Bill St. George would not be involved with this damn bombing. It is not good for the visitors, either. This Lieutenant Cavazos, from your hometown is the only one who believes a connection exists between you, our local gal, Carla, Adam, and an attorney, Louis B. Kolezy. Of course, a lot of my department figured Carla may have done some extra things that may have gotten her in hot water. This Kolezy guy is a regular at The Four Fountains and the Pirate's Chest Hotel. He's pretty close to being a whale. We have not had any problem with him and can't say I ever met him. For some reason, we don't frequent the same church. By the way Bill, Carla Davis and her son had to leave The Four Fountains for the Pirate's Chest or as we call it the P.C. She is doing her cocktail waitressing thing there."

Adam still thought that they were being stalled by the chief. "I overheard my step father, as well as my sister, Melanie, mention Carla's name, and that she worked at The Four Fountains. He has been paying her off for twenty plus years after she gave birth to her son, Brian. Louis states that they have bled him for millions by what my sister and I have gleaned on his phone conversations."

Murray felt he needed to add his own near death involment. "They attempted to kill Adam, and now, Carla Davis, because she knows too much about Kolezy's bad connections and possible involvement in illegal activities, including murder. My wife and I have been targeted by Kolezy's men. We had a near brush with death and thanks to Bill and his men it was thwarted. Added to all this, HPD is stonewalling the case of five young men who have been murdered, that are linked to Adam. Kolezy has to be behind it. This should be enough to conduct a further investigation?"

Hamond drew a deep breath, folded his hands across his desk and looked at St. George and Murray. "Can you actually prove that Kolezy was behind you and your wives' near death targeting? Now to The Four Fountain's incident. There was a bomb planted in a car. Mizz Davis had a car, from the report, that was like a dozen others in the parking lot. My investigator wrote it off as a case of misidentification. Basically, the wrong car was bombed. She just had the misfortune of having the same color, model, make that the thug or thugs, who planted it, thought it was for the mark who was supposed to blow up. It was a coincidence; unfortunately, she was at the wrong time and place. As I mentioned before, she and her son are now working at The P.C. In getting back though, I have no idea what you are referring to on those five murders. Adam, what is your connection to them?"

"Chief, these men were friends of mine, who also worked for me."

Hamond began to piece the picture together. "So your little business, we will say involves escorts? You figure he is killing your employees to take over since they are your main source of income?"

Adam was beginning to lose his patience. "Chief Hamond, those young men were my friends. Maybe they did a little moonlighting to those who were lonely? My corporation is not dependent upon that segment of income. It is, at most, discretionary. The company has resorts, restaurants, clothing, and other ancillary aspects."

Hamond relaxed in his chair as he drank the dark liquid, that may have been spiked with Old Grand Dad., "Definitely, ancillary, huh? Well, well."

Murray's composure fell. "What is it going to take, another car bomb going off? Three people are dead in Houston from being at the wrong time and place. Well, at least we know where Carla works. We need your help in locating her at the P.C. and seeing if she is being pursued the wrong way by Kolezy and his gang."

Hamond had another coffee sip, as he leaned in toward the requester, attempting to choose his words carefully. "Mr. Murray, Anthony, we frown upon citizens who are not in law enforcement from infringing on our territory trying to solve crimes. You may very well have evidence substantiating a connection between the Las Vegas bombing and Houston's. While we would appreciate your not involving yourselves with the Davis incident, you have the right to see them on your own. Keep this in mind, my department nor is the City of Las Vegas sanctioning any private investigation you may conduct. Bill is my dear friend and the only reason we are having this conversation. "

Bill stepped in, "Sam, I believe that Louis B. Kolezy is the person behind both bombings. Adam has been targeted four times in a little over two months because he won't sell his company to his step father."

Hamond was slightly interested, and directed his question to Magassey. "Just how much does your company make that would interest your step father to want it?"

Adam looked over at Murray and St. George. "Actually, chief, it is a multi-entertainment and habitation combination corporation, making hundreds of millions of dollars in sales. Almost Fortune 500. It is very lucrative."

Bill and Murray both were impressed by Adam's description, as they always knew it was sex on a stick with some rooms being sold for the night and food dished up by scantily clad waiters and waitresses.

Hamond smiled a little as he thought it was just bull shit. "Yeah, I bet. Well, everyone bets, right?"

Bill wanted to get on with the reason they were there. "Sam, can we, as a huge favor, as we are not policemen or legal authority, FBI, or Secret Service type, see the report on Carla Davis' address and the times she is on at The P.C.?"

Drawing a deep breath as the Chief closed his eyes, momentarily. "You know Bill, I really think highly of you and these two men you brought in are probably fine folks. Normally, I'd have to say get out and no possible way to view the report but since it is you and you gave me those tickets to the World Series when you played for the Yankees. Oh, screw it, I'll get you a copy but don't tell anyone where you got it from or who gave it to ya'll. There's a lot of other folks who would want me out of this job to get in one of their cronies. The mayor and I are tight and he's not seeking re-election the next time around so I have to be careful." Hamond gave them a copy complete with pictures of Carla and Brian Davis along with address and phone numbers, with the approximate times when each would be working their new jobs at the Pirate's Chest Hotel.

While Sev, Tanski, and Ernie played would be gamblers, they left The Mohave for the mid Strip hotel, The Flamingo, Bugsy Segal's fabled place built in the late 1940's. The three would wait for Murray or Bill's call if they were needed. Rich joined Adam, Bill and Murray as they set out to The Pirate's Chest to talk with Carla and her son. From the report they knew their shifts as the harried woman gladly gave up the information since Carla felt she was in danger. While she suspected Kolezy had wanted her dead and would enjoy his time with Brian before eliminating him as well. Carla, for whatever reason, did not implicate the attorney to the police.

The four went over to a 21 table in her area, looking around to be positive no one else was watching them, other than the casino personnel, or that Carla was being trailed.

Carla was a striking, combination red head, brunette with nice legs, an ample breast, though slightly chunky, possibly from some real fine times. Her makeup was heavy, most likely to hide the past seventy-two plus hours of her harrowing experience and bruises.

She noticed the four, approaching them. "Would you gentlemen care for some of our best drinks that we serve here at the P C? Or a domestic or foreign beer? How about cigarettes?" she continued in a slightly Louisiana accent. Her name plate dangling off her left breast.

Murray recognized her dialect immediately, though, as Cajun, the backwater area in Southwest Louisiana. "Are you from Lake Charles or Lafayette, Carla?"

The woman normally took customers in stride as Louisiana was over 1400 miles from where they were sitting and was moderately interested in being asked about her Bayou Country. "Actually, I am from New Iberia, down from Lafayette. You're good, ah, Mr.?"

"The name is Murray. I knew a woman sometime back from Lourieville, a long time ago. Her name was Breaux, Janice Breaux. She lived in Houston, worked at Texaco in the credit department. She was homesick and would go back with her Corvair to Louisiana on the weekends. She was a fine person. We dated on and off for six months. Nothing came of it. Later she married some good Cajun and I found the woman of my dreams."

Carla was an expert in delving through relationships even though hers was a disaster at times. "The way you said Janice's name just made me think you really liked her."

Murray was not there to discuss old girl friends and was caught off guard. "It was a lot of years ago, Carla. I just recall what a good dancer she was. Actually, if you have it, I would like my favorite, George Dickel,#12, White Label. Janice was an early advocate, should I say, of that brand. Of course, that is not the reason I drink it today."

Carla looked at him with skepticism. "Ok, whatever you say. How about you other guys? "They all ordered their favorite drinks as she left to check on the other patrons. The four stood by making sure no one else was interested in her, other than as a cocktail waitress.

They returned to blackjack as Rich, Murray and Adam started to win a few hands. Bill was itching to hit the crap table. "Are the three of you going to keep winning? I am having a hell of a losing streak and want to move on but know we have to get this woman to open up."

Carla came back and set the drinks down in front of the players. Murray wanted to dig deeper into her past and why the attempt on her life. He started back on the Bayou Country. "Talking about your part of the world, Carla, that Acadia Country is very nice and things seemed to be looking up for everyone there, economically speaking. Why did you move to Las Vegas?"

Murray had her relaxed enough to push the conversation, so Carla drifted back to her earlier days. "My momma died when I was 15 and Daddy had to take a job in Houston as things in Houma were really souring. I met my ex when they both worked together on the docks at the Ship Channel. As they say, one thing leads to another and I got pregnant at 18 with my first son, Cletus. We divorced shortly after that and I met a guy in Houston. Did not want to raise a boy and when Daddy re-married he took Cletus to live with him in Pasadena, just outside of Houston. Anyway, this guy was a hot shot lawyer and always came to Vegas so I came out with him. He adored me early on and convinced me that I should start a new life here. He set me up in Henderson in a big home, nice and everything. Then I got pregnant again, and he wanted me to get an abortion but I did not want to. I missed raising Cletus and figured I screwed up by letting Daddy raise him because that damn woman he married mistreated my son. Well, my hotshot lawyer friend tried to force me into being a prostitute.

I did not like that and I also found out he was married to a woman in Houston. I threatened him that if he did not leave me be on the prostitute bit, his wife would find out about me and the kid."

Murray took a bold approach. "You blackmailed him!"

The woman did not know how to respond to someone she thought was somewhat trust worthy although a complete stranger guessing her current status. Trying to defend what may have appeared obvious, "You know a woman has to take care of herself and when there's a boy to raise....it costs money and Vegas is not a cheap place to live."

The others were listening and waited for Murray to lower the question they all knew was forthcoming. "So that is why Louis Kolezy wants to kill you and your son, Brian?"

Before she could answer, Adam rolled off his seat, going to her, extending out his hand in friendship, "Carla, we saw the news on your car bombing three days ago. You are in grave danger. I know what this man is capable of doing to you and your son. We came here to protect you as friends, not to hurt you."

Rich tossed his losing hand in and followed Adam, offering further assurances, yet wanted to ask for information in his former FBI type voice. "Hi, Carla, my name is Rich Fedor, someone who has the experience in taking down people who try to ruin other folk's lives. We strongly believe you are a target for Kolezy and have to find out from you how much you know of his current and former business dealing outside of his law practice?"

Carla's large green eyes darted out like miniature beach balls under the barrage of questions prefaced with care for her well-being. "How did you find me? Why do you want to be involved with all this? Yes, Louis wants me and Brian dead. I don't know how to answer if it has been blackmail or out of necessity that he caused me to be the mother of his son and my anger out of his pushing me for the abortion and the prostitution thing. I will tell you this, I don't know if you can bring him down, but if you are the cops, it may be tough to do. He is connected and has these wretched men he refers as his Hungarian Mafia."

Bill found the trio discussing the problem Carla was in and heard the last part. "Oh, oh, that Hungarian Mafia thing has bitten us, once again."

Carla shook her head. "You came from where? You four want to cross Louis. What is in it for you?"

Murray broke in, making the introductions of Bill and himself then grabbing Adam's back, "This is Adam Magassey, the stepson of Louis Kolezy. Louis has attempted to murder him a number of times. My wife and I found this young guy sometime back close to death by the hands of his Hungarian Mafia. Kolezy is a blight on our heritage. We are all Hungarians and our goal is to bring him to justice and you can be the key to it. Will you help us?"

Carla was confused. "I really need this job. The hotel people have been very nice to me after that incident the other day. They took me in when my old boss was edgy about keeping me at The Four Fountains. You know the image and things like that. The floor man and pit boss both made it clear here, 'no more incidents in our hotel'. I am on 90 day probation with the corporation. And... Yes, Louis mentioned Adam to me." The woman gave a smile as she looked at him up and down in an almost fantasizing fashion. "You're a very handsome young man."

Magassey thought she belonged in that 62% who liked his videos but did not want to go in that direction and only offered a 'thank you'.

Wanting to move it along, Murray advised, "Carla, don't be worried about your job. Your life and Brian's are more important. You can always find another work place."

As a former FBI agent, Rich was more accustomed to questioning and getting a person of interest or suspect to act normal in a more near hostile setting, as he gently touched her hand. "Carla, we have to take down Kolezy. We are quite aware that you are a god-fearing, hardworking woman who does not wish any additional trouble in you and your son's life. You know that Louis will continue to make attempts on people he feels are in his way. Both you and Brian are part of it. Is there a place you can go where he won't find you?"

At that moment her supervisor, wearing a name tag of Carlo De Desenzo, came up to them. He was a cross between Alec Baldwin and Al Pacino. "What can we do for you gentlemen?"

Bill improvised to the delight of Murray, "Just some conversation about old times in Louisiana. We're all kind of from that part of the country."

After giving them a steely look for a moment, he relaxed, "Well you gentlemen are very welcome here and hope all of you will order some libations so this young lady can make some money."

Murray did not wish to push it further, "Mr. De Desenzo, Ms. Carla, is quite a joy to behold and happy we met up with her."

De Desenzo shifted his glance to Carla and then to the four men as he was measuring them up. "Well guys, okay, enjoy our trappings at the hotel and casino while you are on our property." With that he walked away.

To instill confidence in the deeply concerned woman, Rich gently uttered, "We'll protect you. We need to speak to Brian as well."

Adam was anxious to get more information and felt Brian would be more approachable as he was a guy that had been used by Kolezy. "I know, Carla that Brian is a valet here. What shift is he on?"

Carla, unsure, looked at Adam. "He's here and just finished his break. Brian is extremely fragile from this so please don't push him. He is really delicate, and a little, the uptight person. I have to protect him, you understand? Please?"

Adam thought all this through, 'delicate', 'fragile'. In the past, the same things, he would have gone for in a man. He then emotionally slapped his mind. He was not going back to that life even with a novice ready to be carved on his plate, if he so chose."

Murray knew enough of Adam's appetite for an easy prey. "We won't get Brian into any trouble. Two of us will be guarding you and we will protect your son."

Carla appeared relieved. She would be safe on the casino floor and converse later on with the four concerning her lover, Kolezy.

Bill and the rest of the group were all very attentive to what she had to offer. Most of her so called testimony, off the record, had all the men nearly mesmerized from when she was a young naïve girl to the present, more street wise woman. Murray and Adam had enough as Rich and Bill shorthanded the details that Carla was all too anxious to relate. The two headed for the valet area of the hotel with a recent picture of Brian, as Rich and Bill gave her assurances that her son would be in capable hands. With all the floor personnel in the casino and the two of them doing surveillance, Carla was relatively safe.

Murray and Adam found Brian parking cars and SUV'S. A Lexus was waiting for his call. He was, as his mother described, as delicate, bewildered appearing, tall, slender, light brown hair and fair features, making him a perfect game for Kolezy. He was outfitted in Pirate's Chest garb, hands in the pockets of his loose above the knee shorts as he continued to look down, acting passively.

Murray stayed slightly behind Adam as he zeroed into Brian. Adam attempted to introduce himself after the young man parked the Lexus, but Brian ran toward the next vehicle. Adam stepped in his path. Brian was surprised at Adam, dressed in pullover, sleeveless light weight sweater and tan shorts, simple leather flip flops, seemingly not a threat to him as he acted easy and unarmed.

Adam was ready to dole out why he was there. "Your mother told me where to find you."

His fair complexion started to turn whiter as he quickly recalled the earlier car bombing, acting extremely guarded, his blue eyes darting for help if he needed it. "Who are you? What has my mother have to do with you?"

Adam looked back, as Murray; leaving his secluded position next to the racks of incoming luggage began to move towards the duo. Adam continued, "Can we talk? It is about Louis B. Kolezy."

Panic took over at the sound of Kolezy's name. "I, I, I can't talk about him. You can plainly see that I am working! What is this all about, anyway?"

Murray began to come forward as he viewed the slight confrontation between the two, hearing the last sentence of Brian. "Son, we are here to protect you and your mother. It is extremely important that we can talk. You want your mother and yourself saved from the dangerous clutches of this man. Right?"

Brian sized up the two men who were vying for his undivided attention on saving his butt. He chose Adam who was younger, tighter, and wore his choice of clothing. Looking at the younger man he asked, "My guess is you are not with the police. Just who are you?"

Adam half smiled again, reaching out to Brian to comfort him, "We are not the police but we are very interested in making you safer. I am Louis' stepson, Adam Magassey."

Brian was riveted to Adam and almost speechless trying to come to his senses, he spit out, "Yes, I really want to talk with you. My break is in thirty minutes. Louis has spoken about you quite often. We may need to compare notes, for now, let me finish my shift."

Back at the casino, Bill and Rich were keeping a close watch on Carla and on those who were offering close looks at the skimpy clad cocktail waitress. Rich decided it was time for Sev, Tanski, and Ernie to come over to the P C, so he called them and related where to find him and Bill.

Rich surveyed a more than interested slot player who kept looking at Carla while pretending to pour dollar after dollar into the one armed bandit even hitting a small jackpot after jackpot and not caring about the payouts. The man, late fifties, dark complexioned, sported a thin sideburn to chin beard with an equally thin mustache, medium build, wearing some foreign cut clothes. The man continually followed the whereabouts of the cocktail waitress without approaching her for a drink order. His name was Alex Galgany, another Kolezy Hungarian Mafia operative.

Rich cell phoned Bill who was at the opposite end of the pit area. St. George slowly wandered in the direction of where the man was keeping track of Carla. Galgany moved from the dollar carousel to the quarter machines, slowly feeding a fifty dollar bill into a 'Wheel of Fortune' jackpot four reeler, hitting a big amount, disregarding the large payout. He caught the glimpse of St. George who was pretending to push in a series of Lincolns into a machine across from him. Bill hit a small jackpot a few times to throw off a possible shadow. He would get up and take the voucher winnings, wandering to the casino cage. His next step was pretending to leave the gaming area only to return and head to another bank of silver and red whirling machines screaming out to be played.

The bearded man returned to a Super Dollar group of machines. He feed a twenty into the slot and slowly pulled down the lever, all the while retaining an eye toward St. George and another following Carla. He hit a large amount as the siren went off signaling an ultimate payout. Still unfazed on collecting hundreds of dollars, spotting Carla by herself, he was hailed by the slot manager advising him that he was leaving a huge amount of winnings in his machine.

"Sir, you have won the largest jackpot today on this machine, you need to wait and we will pay you the money."

Galgany was startled, attempting to half listen to the slot supervisor and watching where Carla went realizing that he was being followed by a stranger.

Rich came closer on the other side to head off the man if he began to pursue the cocktail waitress.

The slot floor man advised Galgany, "Since you will be paid off on this machine you will need to move to another one as we are shutting this one down for maintenance."

Galgany was still befuddled, not expecting the winnings yet having a mission to go after Carla who disappeared for another round of drinks for the players. Coming back with the slot winnings on the machine, the floor man counted out the money to the man. Galgany gave some of it to the payer not carrying about the amount as he looked for the woman, getting up, going towards the bar area where she worked.

Bill followed him parallel so not to be noticed. The man looked around but did not see St. George surveying him. He then pulled out his cell phone and headed toward the restaurant area where he met a tall man, Keratczy, who walked with a limp, wearing a blue blazer and reflective sun glasses. St. George called back to Rich who was losing heavily at the 21 table where he decided to gamble on a whim while waiting for the next chapter of Carla's life story and at the same time keeping a close eye on her.

Bill called over Murray. "Hey, this squirrel who fell into winning a big jackpot has just hooked up with another guy at the coffee shop. They saw me looking at them so I am heading back figuring they won't think I am tailing 'em. He definitely is not here to gamble because it looks like he hit the red, white, and blue slots for a thou and did not give a damn on playing for a killer shot at the tables, the dumb son of a bitch. You know if it was me, I'd hit the dice tables and roll the bones."

Murray laughed it off, then Rich cell phone from his vantage point as he was watching the two guys leave the coffee shop. Rich thought they were starting toward the valet's direction, away from the casino.

Murray mentally took down the description of the two men, a European and a guy in a blue blazer wearing sun glasses, "Okay Rich, we are talking to Brian right now on this."

Brian was edgy as he looked at the two men, "Hey, Louis will not like this, once he discovers that you guys are getting in the middle of all this, as he is very volatile when it comes to his property."

Murray re-introduced himself, "You trust Adam, somewhat. He is a friend of mine and listen we would not be here if we thought Louis was a dove of peace. Get it? You were on the edge of death the other day. You have to trust us."

Adam looked directly into Brian's eyes and held up a thumb and forefinger a half inch apart. "Brian, you and Carla are this much away from being history in the desert. I know from what I overheard on a telephone conversation that the two of you are on Louis's payroll and maybe blackmailing him. He is through with that."

Brian started to stutter, "A, a, ah, my, my mother and I are owed that money. She and I deserved it these past 22 and one half years. Blackmail is a very harsh word."

Murray was there for a purpose but Brian's behavior on the word 'blackmail' stuck in his mind. "What do you mean 'owed'? From what we can decipher, he may or not be related to you and your mother. Kolezy supposedly has been giving the two of you a fucking bunch of money, what, these past, as you say, twenty-two and one half years?"

"I cannot totally answer that, only he got my mother pregnant some twenty-two years ago and I am 22. So go figure. He screwed her. Had a son. Me."

Murray started to comment to Adam when Magassey's phone rang. He flipped it open. "Hello, oh, it's you." It was a complete surprise that Murray's head lurched backwards.

Adam smiled broadly after thirty seconds of one sided conversation. It was Carol Sue stroking him twelve hundred miles away. Adam continued to listen for another minute then cut it short. "I am real happy you called except we are in the middle of a major, you can say, meeting with ah, well, a person of interest. I plan on getting back to Houston real soon and when I do, let's pick up where we left off. Great! Yes, I cannot wait." He hung up with Murray raising his hands in a 'what's going on?' motion.

Looking at Brian for a split second, Magassey felt a reprieve from losing this older, gorgeous, worldly woman that he wanted to continue having a relationship with. Maybe it was a realization on her part that he could offer her what riches she was accustomed to as well as his physical persona. He blurted out, "She wants me, Murray!"

Murray was wise as he looked at his young partner in this endeavor. "Adam, we can't get into this for now, but let's discuss this a little down the road. We have a lot of work here."

They returned to Brian's problem. Adam wanted to make a vital point to the young valet former student at the University of Las Vegas. "So you are Louis' illegitimate son. You are looking at your sort of half-brother. Both of us share the same problem. Louis B. Kolezy. Brian, I have been there before and each of us can say we have had enough."

Brian was not positive he wanted to tell the dark parts of being Louis' pet. "What are you getting at?"

"Isn't Louis giving you a lot of things besides the money in turn for sexual favors? How long has the physical abuse gone on? Mine was twelve years starting at age 4. When did yours begin?"

Murray could write a chapter on what Brian was going to confirm to Adam.

Brian turned away to face the wall, head down, he began to sob quietly, as he hit his head continuously against the brick wall of the valet shed. Turning back and staggering toward Adam, almost falling into his arms. Stopping his tears, he blurted out, "Nineteen years! Age 3. I remember he came into my room surrounded by Care Bears, Dr. Seuss, G.I. Joe dolls and pulled my shorts down and when I began to cry he placed his hand over my mouth and whispered that boys are supposed to do this as it was a beginning of their lives. It was a natural way to be a good boy and bad boys did not do this. It would feel good."

Adam looked away. Murray, again, was forced to relive his own time at age nine, shortly after the encounter at school; a family member fondled him time and again. How it hurt. He would live with the horrid memory for many years before being released from his mental and physical bondage finally ending the abuse at age 17.

Brian continued, "I thought at 21 that it was over. Then six months ago, he sent over Alex Galgany and another man arrived over to the home I was sharing with another guy. They dragged me out, handcuffed me, threw me into a van, and drove to my mother's home in Henderson, where she, Louis, and I performed a threesome. She only did it to get more money out of him. He refused. Laughed at both of us and zipped up his pants and left."

Adam was puzzled at all this. "What about the police? Certainly he can't do all this without the knowing about his wonton behavior?"

"She called and threatened Louis after that. He returned and he grabbed her, threw her down and warned that he would eliminate both of us if we did not co-operate when he had his desires. Then told us he was cutting the money in half."

Rich phoned Murray at that instant, warning them that the two men were coming and their descriptions. Murray looked at Brian, "There are two men coming. One has a limp and wears sunglasses the other a medium build man with a narrow beard, small mustache, dark European features. Know them?"

Brian had a pained look, knowing who they were, "Alex Galgany is the medium build man and his partner is Miklos Keratezy. They were the two who strong armed me that day for Louis' plaything. Is this nightmare ever going to end?"

Murray put on a brave front, not actually knowing how this was going to go down. "Today, this is all going to go away for you and Carla."

Adam looked at Murray wishing he would be right as Brian was melting, like the Las Vegas sun, at the challenge facing him.

Murray, remembered, he was told that Carla received a call the day before the car bombing. "Hey before we get these two goons, didn't your mother speak to Kolezy prior to the bombing?"

"Yes, she knows a cop on the Henderson police force who likes her and my mother was braver because of it. He advised my mother to phone Louis and tell him she did not need his money any longer. My mother phoned Louis and told him that she was through. If he pursued her, she threatened with going to the police on some things he did here in Vegas. She told Kolezy that she had a close friend on the force."

Adam was concerned with Brian's welfare perhaps even more than Carla's as he laid his hand on the young man's shoulder massaging it and looked deep into his eyes. "Brian, can your mother trust this policeman? I have always been leery with Sin City's brand of protection. My company has an adult club here on South Industrial. You might know it, Rascals West?"

Brian's eyes lit up. "Yeah, that is one of my favorite meeting places! Wow! Your place, huh?"

Murray was getting antsy. "Okay, you two, we have these guys to deal with, but when did Kolezy come here last?"

"Why do you ask?"

"It only seems that Carla made threats before and all suddenly, her car is bombed and now these two schmucks are heading to take you out."

"Well, three weeks ago, when I was at UNLV, my mother tipped me off to stay away from our home. I went to Mt. Charleston for a few days with my friend. Louis was mad because she would not tell him where I was. He finally left and when I returned she was bruised all over, most likely by Galgany and his side kicks." Then he thought, "My mom should be coming off her shift any minute."

Murray pulled out his Taurus Judge and spun the chamber to be sure that it was fully loaded. Brian was impressed. "Well, I know that these two guys will be very surprised. I feel wholly safe with the two of you."

Adam backed up Murray. "And we have five others who are on their way here."

Kolezy was having dinner at the River Oaks home with Ilona, who was stone-cold sober, as she was secretly going to therapy for her alcohol and drug abuse. On the additional side, unbeknown to her lecherous husband, she had been having an affair with Dr. Gregor Ladveck, an eminent Houston heart surgeon. She and Gregor knew one another as children, he from Transylvania and she from Szeged. They saw one another from time to time in Houston although he was married with a family. He was now divorced and free but with the problems, Ilona had only offered a gentle support and a roll in the sack. He had a brief affair with Carol Sue a few years back, when he was attempting to get a divorce. The doctor met her at a charity ball that she hosted at her East Memorial swankienda. Carol Sue had gone to a psychotherapist, Kerry Yanek, a close friend, and whose husband, John, was Murray's chief pilot. Carol Sue apparently overcame a lot of her past problems. Gregor knew this and quickly recommended Kerry to Ilona.

Melanie accompanied her mother for sessions as the dark aspects of her behavior were torturing the girl's normal life with blatant sex of lesbian lovers as well as the constant pain of Kolezy's gluttony for her well defined body. Mostly, Melanie wanted out of Louis's clutches as she was deeply involved with Alicia, a systems analyst, for an Energy Corridor corporation in the Eldridge area of West Houston. Melanie and her lover mingled in the club scene in this city's revived and exciting swinging midtown. Her life was changing, yet half empty.

Louis was turned on by a new model look from Ilona. Having some sexual thoughts for his wife after the filet mignon and crème bruile settled, he wanted to have a roll in the sack with a now more attractive Ilona. "Well, my dear, you are looking very ravishing and is that a new outfit? The style suits you well, my love." His eyes darting up and down a new slimmed down wife.

Ilona was only too happy to bust his bubble. "Yes, Louis, I have begun a new life. One, without you. I have been in therapy with a psychologist and stopped drinking, going to a spa daily after my two hour workout at The Memorial Athletic Club. My mind is made-up; the only way to defeat you is to be clean and sober."

Kolezy listened to his wife and contemplated her words, almost laughing in her face, as he leaned back in his leather arm chair. He leered, challenging her. "Oh, trying hard to get. Just like in Buda when your beloved husband died and you were left with four wailing children, loss of his money, and no place to go, as your own parents were dependent on Anthal's money to support all of you. Here you are, twenty or so years and doing the same thing. Dependent on my money to make you what you want to do in life. Without me you are NOTHING. A NO BODY!" His eyes bugged out like a magnified horse fly.

She laughed. "You really think you know me after these twenty plus years!"

"You sound as though you are not ready to move back into my bedroom, my love?"

"Louis, don't flatter yourself." Ilona was simmering at his remarks. "Never again will you see me in your bed, especially, the one where you and Melanie stained the sheets. I have many avenues of opportunity to make me happy and forget you!'

Kolezy still wanted to turn the knife. "Curious as to your intentions, my love, do you then think you can whore around with that male hairdresser, Edwin?"

Her love was not the semi gay hairdresser at her favorite Galleria, $250 a throw beauty salon, she has frequented for the past 15 years. The reality was Gregor and Louis apparently did not know that. She wanted to lead him away and make Edwin as the man in her life. "Oh, so you found out. How did you?"

"I know everything, my love. Anything you have done or have seen is under my microscope. I am advised that your therapist has beautiful, long legs, to accent her short blond hair. Her name is Kerry Yanek. I think she would like to be in my bed", as he bragged, reaching for a Cuban cigar from a nearby humidor he stashed next to his chair in the dining room.

The way he described her made Ilona concerned. "She is not your type. Leave Kerry out of this!"

"Kerry's legs intrigue me. Yes, you see her on Tuesday and Thursdays, spending one to one and a half hours with her. Does she do anything physically to you? Then Melanie has her session after that. Three women in a close room. What really goes on in there for all that time, my love?"

His accusations caught her by surprise, somewhat, as she knew he was always snooping around. She spoke up with unbridled authority toward her husband. "Louis, it is none of your business about my life. You have been unfaithful to say the least. What I do is my business as you have chosen in the past not to include me in your life. You have had affairs with both men and women, which is normal for you, only if you can call anything in your life, normal. I have not felt this way since my Ryan left this earth, very likely at your hands."

"Your weakling son hung himself on his own. Is that why you threw yourself into falling into that bottomless pit drinking that vodka?"

"He was through trying to please you and wanted to leave and you could not bring yourself to let go of him. Yes, he was weak and I am at fault in not protecting him from scum like you. Louis, you will eventually pay for his death here on earth or at the hand of God. He will punish you in total damnation. I am sorry that my downfall was the bottle and a vial of pills."

Kolezy threw his head back mocking her dialogue. "Whew, Ilona, punish me in 'total damnation'. Where did you ever come up with that? Kerry Yanek? I think she requires a visit from me. We can get to know one another. Maybe she likes a foot massage or a toe sucking?"

At this point, Ilona was at full bore toward her unfaithful husband. "You are totally despicable. Fucking my daughter, sodomizing both my sons, having that puke, bitch, tramp, Carla, in Las Vegas harboring and screwing most likely her son as you are the worse than a sick bastard. I know you killed my husband and I will see to it that you die in Huntsville, if that is the last thing I do."

Even after all that, Kolezy was unfazed and puffed on his Cuban. "Well, Melanie sure has loose lips. That and you took the household money and hired a private detective. Just have to cut your allowance down to eliminate that part of your search, my lovely."

Riled up at his unconcerned attitude and total arrogance. "You need not bother, MY LOVE. My maiden aunt in Hungary, the Baroness of Szeged, the heiress of the paprika corporation her father founded, and she ran. Well, she passed away a few days ago and left me her entire fortune."

A conceited, relieved smile came over Kolezy. "Well, my dear, this means my hold over you is a lot less. I am looking forward to not giving you any more money. You will, I assume, my love, be moving out?"

Waiting to lower the shock on him, "Yes, Louis, along with Melanie. So you will know it, Terry Gaiser, my attorney, will be handling the divorce."

Kolezy appeared surprised at that statement, "Divorce? You are the unfit mother of my children. No, you will be separated from me. Never will I grant you one, AS LONG AS YOU LIVE!"

The last five words echoed from him as she felt an inward shutter.

He continued as he got up and stood over her, picking up a sharp steak knife, wielding it in his hand as his lower jaw locked in anger, "You will never see another dollar of my money. Melanie is not, NOT, leaving my mansion. If you persist in that, you will definitely regret the consequences."

Ilona, an average size woman, rolled her chair back and at her 5 foot, 7 inches jumped up with a determined, unafraid look, staring at her husband, "I am not going to be beaten down with the likes of you. Not even brandishing that knife. NEVER is not in my dictionary. We will get that divorce and the sooner the better. You are not going to prevent me from telling the authorities in Houston and Budapest. I am letting them know of your past and present sordid and criminal life. If you try stopping me, Louis, my unfaithful husband, wretched, and corrupt person, you are deeply mistaken and will sorely regret your action. I will seek out your involvement in my husband's death twenty-four years ago. Your brandishing that knife does not terrify me."

Louis was stunned by her pent up outburst, attempting to ascertain whether she was on a binge brought on by pills and vodka or was stone cold sober. If the latter was the case, he was in for a major conflict, even knowing he had to silence her before going to the police. Quickly he reacted, "Ilona, I will stop you from ever turning me into the authorities, here or in Hungary."

"No you won't DADDY DEAR," came an unusual, but determined voice behind him. It was Melanie. She held a 9 mm automatic with two hands, coming into the dining room.

Kolezy turned around; still clutching the steak knife, wanting to confront and settle her down from what he thought was a childish move on her part. As he looked into her eyes, filled with hate, he realized her intense distain and dropped the cutlery. Coming to his senses immediately after the shock, "You are both making a very serious poor judgment."

Ilona moved over close to her daughter for further safety. "WE do not wish to be further pummeled by your own poor judgment, Louis."

Kolezy found humor in this new found epiphany from the two women. "I can live without you Ilona but Melanie, my beloved piece of ass, you are going to miss my crown jewels to massage and eat as you rub yourself with that vibrator."

Melanie 's face reddened, "I'd like to stick that vibrator up your damn asshole and then blast those balls off your son of a bastard body so no one else gets contaminated by your filthy, disgusting way. You kept me drugged up all these years. My mother, Adam, Melissa, and I will see you get what's coming to you. So take one step toward us and you'll go from a rooster to a hen!"

Enraged by her statement, Kolezy started to pick up two steak knives from the table, Melanie reacted to his overt confrontation as she squeezed off two rounds barely missing him and imbedding the bullets through a china cabinet, scattering prize remnants of their upscale, expensive dinner wear. Kolezy dropped the knifes and dived for the floor. The women scurried out of the home as Jeeves, their butler, and Gloria, the cook, came in to see what the clatter was all about. They viewed their employer almost glued to the ground. He looked up and grabbed the edge of a chair to steady himself and arose, embarrassed from all the mess as they surveyed Kolezy's fall from grace status. They always knew what was actually happening in that River Oaks mansion off Kirby Drive. Secretly, they felt relief for Ilona and Melanie.

Weaving around the table, Kolezy's face wrought with anger, "Don't just stand there. Clean up this crap, be useful for once!" He then cautiously went to the front room to see if the women were still there. He did not find them and peered out the front drapes where the tail lights of Ilona's and Melanie's, Mercedes 300 SL's were stirring up the dust in their flight to leave River Oaks for a safer haven.

Kolezy scoffed at their departure. “Good riddance to both of those bitches!” He bellowed out raising his hands upward toward the Italian crystal chandelier in the foyer which hung 2 ½ stories from the ceiling. Slowly, and somewhat dejected, he walked to the study, closed the door and poured a half glass of Gran Patron, straight up. Looking at the large glass of expensive liquor he thought of calling Dimitri and Drago for some planned foul deeds to the women but only downed the drink and sat alone, looking at the fire place attempting to find out what had just went down. Was this the time? Where did the two women go? He would begin early the following morning after downing a half dozen Patrons, starting with that damn psychotherapist. She’d tell him where to find them. He’d take his two men and persuade this Kerry person to reveal their whereabouts or encounter cruel physical consequences that he would only be too willing to administer.

Kolezy pulled into the parking lot on Memorial at 9:00 AM the following morning. It was a black glassed building near a busy intersection. Dimitri and Drago accompanied him. The trio stepped out of the BMW and surveyed the building.

"Drago, you check out the back. Dimitri and I will go in the front way." Upon entering the small two story lobby, Dimitri spotted the directory next to the silver and glass elevator. Kerry Yanek's office was located on the second floor in suite 220. The two went up on the slow elevator and stepped out looking for her suite. After turning a few corners they found it. The suite was empty, as the floor to ceiling window was dark. Peering through a window next to an oak door with 'Kerry Yanek, Psychologist" on the door, they spotted a dark waiting area of couches and chairs. Dimitri was ambitious and knocked even though it appeared that the office was empty. There was no answer, of course, as he turned sheepishly to his mentor who had a less than satisfied look on his face.

The slightly, stocky man recalling the comic strip character, 'Lucy from Peanuts', he offered, "I guess Lucy is out. She must charge more than five cents for each visit."

Kolezy was in a daze as to what he was referring to, "What the fuck are you talking about, Dimitri?"

Dimitri's head hung down, attempting to make light of the situation, "I guess you don't read the comics?"

Louis was a surprising John Wayne follower, who always had his one line in countless movies and uttered, "Not hardly, Pilgrim."

As they began to depart the area, Drago came up the rear steps. "What does this woman look like?"

Kolezy remembered what Gabor told him when he came by one day and found her. "Gabor said she is tall, very tall and slender, with short blond hair and may drive a late model Buick Regal."

Drago had a sinister smile. "She's coming into the building now, Louis."

Kolezy's eyes glistened, waiting to see the woman. "Drago, wait downstairs in the lobby, just in the event she bolts and attempts to run away."

Drago became eager at the instructions. "It will be my pleasure to prevent her from, as you say, bolting? I sincerely hope she tries. I will gladly stop her."

Kolezy was a little concerned with that. "I want her in one piece, alive!"

As Drago moved along the dimly lit and worn, stained carpeted hall and down the steps, the elevator opened, and out stepped, a long legged slightly freckled face, upper class looking woman, dressed smartly in designer, gray slacks and an expensive looking white blouse, matching fringed jacket with Gucci half boots. As the woman came around the corner she was met by Louis and Dimitri. Somewhat startled by their appearance as she was expecting a woman client and it was unusual to find strangers in that part of the building, although they were dressed in business attire. Her normal, large saucer eyes almost jumped out of their opits. "Are you gentlemen looking for anyone in particular?" she inquired, hoping that they were not there for her as she sensed trouble in their body language and appearance, wanting to disarm their hidden agenda.

Louis looked up and down the psychologist. "We are seeking a Ms. Kerry Yanek, would that be you?"

Thinking about his Eastern European accent and appearance, she quickly thought about the fact it could be Ilona's husband and Melanie's step-father. Kerry had remembered the text message from Ilona late last night to call her but did not have the chance to return it. Was it a warning? Hesitating for what appeared to be minutes as the two men, at first, wore off to an anxious concern look of an answer. She had mace in her purse, would she be able to pull it out and use it if they were bent on kidnapping her or worse? Or was it the blue belt she earned at the Westside Gym that would save her?

As she began to answer, a neighboring tenant, Don Purser, an architect, came out of his office. Don, a white haired, white whiskered, red faced, short, former Texas Tech Raider fullback who could now be taken for a fit, Macy Department Store Santa Claus. He was interested in the two men, "Are you two gentlemen here to see me on that commercial building we are working on?"

That is all the diversion Kerry required as she hurriedly ran off down the hall to the stairs, mumbling, "I forgot something in my car...."

Drago, already down in the lobby, was at his strategic position as he saw her running down the stairs, toward him. He attempted to block her escape and, once again, luck was in her corner as Bob and Rita Dumaine, tenants, who ran Sam Houston Philatelics, on the first floor, came into the building at that moment. Kerry was able to wedge herself between Bob and Rita, as she physically lunged Bob into the harried path of the henchman. Rita was confused at first, and then realized Kerry was being threatened by the scar faced man, yelling out, "Hey, what are you doing? I am going to call the police!"

Drago disregarded Rita, as he pushed off Bob. Kerry eluded his grasp as she ran through the front doors, car keys in hand, hitting the button to unlock the car, quickly climbing in and keying the starter and screeching out of the parking lot leaving a breathless, pissed off, Drago in a wake of exhaust fumes.

Kolezy and Dimitri, who finally caught up, reached a spent Drago, his hands on his knees, bent over as he raised his head to take a mental beating from his boss. "You allowed her to escape" Kolezy shook his usual reliable operative in a violent manner showing grave disappointment in the outcome.

Drago started to alibi his way out of his inability to prevent the woman from leaving, "Louis, she came between me and a couple who came into the lobby. It is almost like they were running interference for her. I really attempted to grab her. Perhaps, they knew I was going to harm her as they held me up before I was able to break loose. I know I failed you, Louis. I will try double to find her and bring her to you.

Kolezy did not want to hear any more excuses as he was totally rebuffed by women, last night and now by Kerry. "I am at a loss for what to do. This whole fucking crap has to end. It is unbelievable, Adam is going to sell MABB to some high society bitch, my wife and step daughter are on the loose, and now this blond broad gives us the slip and leaves us hanging out here in a parking lot!"

Dimitri wished to ease his boss's current circumstance. "We still know where Carol Sue Miller resides. Let's go after her. We snatch her; eliminate the problem and the sale falls through. She is the key to all this."

Kolezy took his squatty body guard-lackey by the shoulders of his well-worn, Budapest tailored made, sharkskin suit. "Dimitri, you have given me a new life. Yes, we should go after that Miller woman and stop the purchase of MABB. "Then Louis gave a slightly disgusted look at the coat. "Don't I pay you enough to buy better clothes than this?"

Dimitri shrugged his shoulders, but half agreed. "They use to do better in Pest, maybe it is made out of Chinese cloth."

Carla was coming off her shift, and had a concerned look as she checked out Rich and Bill who were joined by Tanski, Sev, and Ernie. "What about Brian? I am deeply worried that he is in danger outside."

Bill sputtered out, "We are going right now to intercept two guys who have been following you through the casino. Brian is being guarded by two of our group. Are you aware of these men?"

Surprisingly, Carla told him, "There was man who limped and wore sunglasses, even in this casino lighting. He was at the slots and I know he was watching me. That guy's a creep and one of Louis' men who brought Brian back to our home for fun and games with Kolezy. I was not worried about him now since you were here guarding me, so to speak. When I was at The Four Fountains he would come in and play blackjack at my section. Once he grabbed my leg and ran his hand up to my laces while laughing at me, as he looked down my halter top cocktail outfit. "

Rich was waiting for the catch. "Did you tell your boss about it and have him thrown out of The Four Fountains?"

"My leader saw it and smiled, turning his head away, believing that the players came first. He termed them 'suckers' and wanted us to take whatever they handed out to us. He could have cared less as long as we did not sell ourselves on the floor and just kept them at the tables. Most of the people there were great, but my leader was an ass hole!"

Bill added to the conversation. "That's my favorite description of an ass hole, A, JackASS!"

Tanski was searching around the floor. "We better get to the valet and take out those two dip sticks.

St. George cut in. "Just what I was thinking, Ron,"

Carla then blurted out, "Look, there's the gimpy guy and Galgany moving to the front. They look as though that they are splitting up from the Garden Terrace Coffee Shop and maybe heading to where Brian is at the valet station! Galgany is heading in another direction."

Rich ordered, "Sev, follow the gimp to see where he is headed. I'll alert Murray to see if they are still with Brian at the valet section."

Sev took off in pursuit of the gimp while Rich cell phoned Murray, where he and Adam were in discussion at the front of the P C's entrance with Brian. Murray was in agreement that he and Adam should stay with Brian as Galgany and his cohort were on the loose and probably going after the young man, in two different directions.

Murray confirmed their where about. "Rich, we'll stay put. Brian has only another five minutes left on his shift, but hell, he needs to get off now! Have Ernie and Bill stick with Carla in case Galgany and Mr. Shades double back. You, Sev and Tanski back us up."

Rich wanted to know, "Are you ready?"

Murray assured him of that. "We'll just need you and the guys help to take on the duo. I know they want to finish what they missed before."

At that moment Galgany and Mr. Shades walked by, not knowing of Murray's implications in their quest to silence Brian. Murray hurriedly dialed Adam who was guarding Brian. "Adam, those two lofus' are heading your way. Take Brian to the other door and I will meet you back at the casino cashier's cage."

Adam acknowledged the warning and grabbed Brian, pushing him past the key boards and outdoor Patron's umbrellas used by hotel guests waiting for their vehicles. Adam and Brian vaulted into the casino, calling for the graveness of the situation. Murray met up with Adam and Brian as they sped through the throng of husband arguing with wife on why he lost a bundle of money at the crap table or the girlfriend of the young, barely 21, boyfriend, who attempted to pinch a cocktail waitress and she caught him at it wanting to kick him in the groin, or a major jackpot was signaled with a loud siren and flashing lights of a dollar mega buckeros machine. All this was sublime as Murray pushed Adam, who was behind a streaking, panicking Brian, as they attempted to keep their distance from Kolezy's men and the danger they might encounter if they stopped.

They reached the cashier's cage; Bill was waiting with a plan. "We need to take these two jackasses out the back way. Running through the casino might injure or kill some innocent person. Then we will have our hands full explaining the entire shit. I called Sam Hamond. He has a couple of their black and whites coming. My idea is to set up Carla and Brian as bait. They won't have to go through with it. The

Vegas police will step in way before that and we will catch these two dumb fucks in the act."

Murray was skeptical about the way it would go down. "That is asking a lot, for these two to place their lives into our hands,"

Bill agreed in part., "Here they come now, let's ask them. "Hey Darlin' these two hunkies want to get rid of you and your son. Now is the time to take them down for good, then both of you can go to the local police, telling them everything about Kolezy. They'll extradite Kolezy to Nevada for attempted murder. This is much better than the Houston cops who are not able to get the goods on him in Texas."

Carla looked hesitantly at Murray, "What do you think?"

"Carla, we don't have time on this, Bill's been there and he and Rich are exceptionally good at devising a plan that works. We are seven and there are only two of them. Go to the parking lot and we will surround them."

Carla was spent between what has happened and the future. "As long as this damn nightmare comes to an end, I am game for anything!"

Ernie, who was posted as a lookout, exclaimed. "They are coming!"

Bill pushed Carla and Brian toward the parking lot. "Go ahead, we will protect you."

The seven scattered as Carla and Brian were to become targets for Galgany and Shades who thought they had their potential victims in their sights. The woman and her son ran through the rear doors of the casino past the throng of hopeful gamblers dreaming of making thousands on their pennies. As Carla played along, acting as a decoy, occasionally looking back as the two would be killers appeared to be closing in; little did they realize that they were falling into a no return trap.

Bill phoned Sam pinpointing their location so his men could intervene and haul off Galgany and Keratezy. They needed time to stall for the police to close in but that was not in the plans.

Carla and Brian did their part and arrived at the spot outside as they were instructed by Bill and Rich. In less than a minute Keratezy limped up, pulled off the sunglasses showing a sunken, almost dead look, in his eyes glaring at the two seemingly helpless soon to be sacrificial lambs. He reached around his slightly bulging waist and pulled out his automatic. He pulled back on the gun, clicking it as it made a heavy metal sound.

Galgany followed, as they secretly searched around for anyone witnessing what each thought would be a clean cut assassination of these two.

Unknown to the duo, Bill, Rich, Tanski, and Murray drew their weapons, strategically surrounding Galgany and Keratezy, waiting for the Las Vegas police to break in and take over in the arrest.

Murray whispered to St. George, "When is Hamond getting here? It is getting too close for us to back off. These dumb shits mean business!"

Bill replied,"It has been twenty minutes and you know the traffic on The Strip. Rich are you ready to roll on this? Sev and Ron, we are going in and can't wait any more. Let's take on these two hunkies!"

Rich was back at being in charge as he commanded in a deep voice, "Okay, Galgany, and Mr. Shades, drop the guns!" The group moved in and started to disarm the two surprised men. Sev, swiftly moved and stuck his .45 in the back of Keratezy. Tanski drew up and did the same to Galgany, except the bigger Hungarian whirled back and kicked Ron in the groin, disabling the veteran who doubled up releasing his Glock as it discharged a round striking a P C trash receptacle.

Keratezy took full advantage of the discord and he being a third degree black belt whirled around with a karate knee block disabling Sev as he lost his .45 on the ground making a hollow sound on the concrete. With renewed energy, Galgany laughed, pulling a hidden .38 from his ankle taking a bead on Tanski who was bewildered by the sudden thrust of these two Hungarians, looking with his good eye as his life passed over him.

Murray was blown away in the less than a minute of the turn of events. Shouting to the others, "Dive to the ground !" Only he had presence of mind and pulled out The Judge Taurus revolver sending a message toward Keratezy missing him by inches and imbedding that round into the side of the parking garage.

Galgany looked back as Rich came forward with a forearm to his face, forcing the Glock he picked up to be dropped in its place. Ernie swiftly picked up the gun, actually not knowing what to do with it as he pledged a non-violence life, thinking even Manson was almost a good guy, had he not been abused at an early age.

Keratezy had a bigger trump as he grabbed Carla, terrified and screaming, thinking he had it made until St. George slugged him in the side of the head, releasing the frightened woman from his grip and at the same moment Tanski came to his senses, kicking Keratezy in the scrotum, and following it up with two fists in the face toppling the gimpy man slamming his face in the pavement.

Galgany, groggy, was attempting to right himself when St. George leg kicked him, upsetting his stand. Carla cried in Brian's arms and an official voice rang out as Sam Hamond, himself, led the charge of the Las Vegas Police. "Okay, all of you stand down", as he viewed the two alleged hit men sprawled on the concrete. "We're in charge now, Bill!"

St. George snickered, "Yeah, Sam, we were just subduing these clowns until you and your finest came to the rescue."

A Las Vegas police lieutenant read the two gunsels their rights as two other officers cuffed them and hauled them away.

Sam turned his attention to Carla and Brian. "I'll need your statements, Miss and you, son, by coming over to headquarters, downtown, to swear out the complaints. After that, we will put these two away for a long time. We do not cotton to people like this in our good city," he assured her, stroking Carla's arm.

Murray added. "The real culprit in all this is Louis B. Kolezy, in Houston, Texas, Chief."

Sam reared back in confidence. "We will sweat them out. This is Las Vegas justice, Mr. Murray. Ya'll, can put your hardware away when you are here. I'll be in touch Bill, on all this. Meantime, sample our hospitality, enjoy yourselves, and bust their walnuts at the tables. Take in a show. There are some real good ones, a hypnotist, Anthony Cools, at the Paris. Then if you like Bon Jovi, he's at the MGM Grand, or if you like a lounge show, Caesars has a great one or if you like comedy, head to The Trop."

Tanski thought out loud as they were loading Galgany and "Mr. Shades" into the squad car, whisking them to a Las Vegas metro cell. "Actually, I already busted those 'walnuts' when we took down those two dip shits that are heading for Las Vegas justice. Sam seemed to be a PR man for Las Vegas entertainment."

"I'm positive all this will stay in Vegas, along with my cash," snorted a disenchanted Ernie, not known for parting with his money.

With Carla and Brian totally co-operating and opening up to the Las Vegas police about the car bombing and the positive involvement of Kolezy, in all of it appeared a spike was driven into the Houston barrister.

At the hotel, St. George turned to Murray, "Anth, you appear to be uneasy with all this", as they sat in the Mohave's lounge listening to a group who was on the down swing of their career, sipping a double on the rocks, George Dickel#12, white label straight up. "This should be a great celebration for getting that bastard, Kolezy."

Murray leaned back and downed the 90 proof and sprang from his chair. Bill, do you really believe Sam will make sure that those two 'moo mocks' will roll over on that bastard? I really want Kolezy bad. He is a blight on our Hungarian heritage. He needs the maximum thrown at him, not a 10 or 20 year sentence. I want him to admit that he had something to do with Troy's death." The father who, before, voiced it to the Las Vegas cop, but in the back of his mind, a little of him had doubts of who was really responsible.

At that time Hamond strolled in to the lounge and heard Murray's remarks.

Sam Hamond was ready. "These two characters have a long sheet and the judge will throw the book at them. I don't know who this Troy is to you but the strong look on your face told me he was close to you."

"He was our only son and was a great kid. He had his entire life ahead of him until someone murdered him and with the way Kolezy was involved with the other deaths similar to our son's, he has to have been behind Troy's."

Sam sat next to Murray and offered a friendly nudge. "I will do everything and then some to have our two current felons implicate Kolezy; you can rest assured of that."

Murray shook Sam's hand, got up, and walked out of the bar. Bill ordered another round for him and Sam as they talked about more of the old times in baseball.

The next afternoon, after a full night and morning of gambling, waiting around for Hamond's word that he was successful in breaking Galgany and Keratezy, Murray, St. George and their group waited anxiously for the successful outcome.

Sam dejectedly walked in. Speaking candidly to all of them, "We received word that the two men were sprung by a high powered lawyer who had handled some former Las Vegas crime bosses thirty years earlier. We believe that through some almost untraceable contacts that Kolezy concocted he was able to free his men. We were unsuccessful in getting them to talk. "Mr. Murray, Anthony, I am very sorry that we had to let these two scum balls lose but when we came upon the scene at the P. C. You had already subdued them. Mizz Davis and her son could only give their version and it did not connect Galgany and Keratezy to the car bombing. We did not have enough proof even with the Pirate's Chest action, yesterday. They claimed that ya'll sprang it on them and they reacted to protect themselves. Had to let 'em go. You don't know how bad I feel about all this. We are going to put a tail on them. If they spit on the sidewalk we'll get 'em, you can count on that, I promise. Okay?"

Murray was trying to bite his tongue and somehow hid his true feelings at the disappointing news. "Okay, Sam, appreciate whatever you can do."

Sam hugged Bill and headed back to his office.

St. George was forlorn. "Anth, can't figure it. You were 100 correct that somehow those two jackasses were going to beat the pinch. At least Sam is putting a tail on them."

Murray began to let go his frustration even, after Hamond promised more pressure on the two bad asses. "Fuckin' creeps. They're walking. After all this shit we have been placed through. What did Sam want, both Carla and Brian on a slab before they threw these bastards in the Metro Jail?"

Bill tried to defend Harmon, "Sam is doing his best. Kolezy has people here doing his bidding. We will get both Galgany and 'Mr. Shades', okay?"

"Sounds like you have been around your old baseball buddy a lot, but we don't have any other choice."

Adam wandered in. "My sister and mother left the River Oaks mansion yesterday. They could really help put Louis away." Throwing his hands up, "Nothing is happening here; we can all go back to Houston and have them give testimony, sealing my step father's fate."

Everyone wanted to leave Sin City and be in on hunting down Kolezy and his Hungarian mafia. Murray and his group knew that Adam's sister and mother may be in danger as they fled from the clutches of Louis.

Rich thought that getting some of his operatives to protect the women might be a better solution to their safety. "Adam, I will contact Becky Ewing my secretary to set up around the clock protection for Melanie and your mother, Ilona."

"Rich, how can I thank you? That would be great!"

Murray wanted in as well. "After we land in Houston, let's head to Kolezy's office with the Cavazos' brothers who I figure are ready to issue warrants for Louis' arrest and his scummy bunch."

St. George thought that was a funny word. "Hey, Anth, can't you come up with a better description of our Hungarian friend?"

Murray gave the shrug and palms up, "Bill, that is the best I could come up with, okay?"

Louis sat alone in his 735 BMW, on his cell, wondering what his next move might be. Then the Las Vegas call. It was Galgany, reporting their release from the interrogation by the police.

The leader griped the soft leather steering wheel until there appeared a large groove in it. "I cannot get over how all of you are mindless loffases, Yes, that is dumb shits in English. Stupid Asses. Sheggy Lukes! Now you are requesting a third try at that bitch and her faggot son, Alex. How?"

Galgany attempted to reason with his boss, "Everything we tried seemed to wind up in the toilet. The Vegas cops know of your link with Carla and her son. We could not help that."

Kolezy thought quickly, "Carla and Brian have implicated me in the attempt on their lives. That bitch has sucked me for over two and one half million dollars. You must stay there until I think of another way to rid myself of that cancer." With that, Kolezy leaned back in his leather air conditioned seat as he reached over in the glove box and pulled out Gran Patron flask he kept in the car, drawing a deep sip. He thought out loud, "I need to take down Carol Sue Miller or Winters, whatever, with the hope of using Dimitri and Drago who as most of my men, lately, failed to complete their tasks. I will use the Szilagyi brothers, Tibor and Gabor to capture this woman and bring her to her senses in allowing me to takeover MABB and not her."

While Kolezy was dreaming of bringing in Carol Sue, at the home of Dr. Gregor Ladveck, an old friend of Ilona, she, along with Melanie, were invited to stay at his high rise until they could formulate their future plans. The fashionable high rise overlooked the famed Buffalo Bayou area of East Memorial. Growing up in Hungary in neighboring towns, he and Ilona had met up, again, when she and the children came from Budapest, twenty plus years ago. Gregor was fond of Ilona but like her, was in a marriage. Gregor's wife divorced him, finding him in the arms of his surgical nurse. His wife had borne three children, two of whom had become doctors in the Houston area. After the split, the doctor buried himself into his work, eventually breaking it off with his nurse. Ilona found out through a common friend of Gregor's. Now that he was free, Ilona let it be known to that person she would like to have the famed doctor call her. Gregor, wistfully, thought of Ilona many times, although he was not going to break up her marriage, even though she had told him of her unrest in the relationship. They began seeing one another, secretly, as Louis was not aware of their relationship. She confided to him about the problems in the River Oaks mansion and he began to encourage her to seek the ultimate alternative which she and Melanie finally did, that is to leave Kolezy. Gregor recommended the psychologist, Kerry Yanek.

Kerry Yanek, boldly, told Ilona to seek solace in the company of others and leave Kolezy, which she finally wound up doing the night before, leaving her pills and booze. Ilona had called Gregor that day and told him of her plan to leave her husband. The doctor was elated that they could now be together without Kolezy's interference. She and Melanie each pulled up to the palatial high rise in their cars. The valet parked their cars in a secure area in the event Kolezy followed the women.

The high rise pent house on the 21st floor overlooked the nearby bayous and parks that made up the Memorial Park vastness, rolling from the downtown towering, glass buildings that threw an inordinate abundance of light which ricocheted from them to passing vehicles, swiftly going from here to there in this thriving, alive city. Ilona loved the height and sight distance that the concrete and glass palace offered after living in a two story mausoleum for the past twenty years. Gregor loved having her there along with Melanie in this sanctuary. He was as powerful as Kolezy, although they each travelled in different circles. The Doctor was legitimate and the top of prominence in Houston's quality and world respected medical community.

Gregor was extremely intense although he patiently listened, once again to the latest atrocity that both women were subjected to with Kolezy. When they were through, he finally spoke, "Ilona, since our rekindling meeting a few months ago, I researched Louis behavior and background that he had hoped to hide from many, not only in the Houston high power society he sought, but in our own heritage, the Hungarian community. They concurred with your stories of his evil behavior and the second life he lives here and over in Budapest. You and Melanie have done the correct thing in coming here. You will be safe from his Hungarian Mafia. Louis must be brought to justice."

Melanie was enlightened by Gregor's involvement and agreeing that Kolezy was a menace. "Dr. Ladveck, my brother, Adam, let me know of his friend, a Mr. Murray, who has considerable wealth and power in Houston. He is also a Hungarian."

The doctor smiled, "Is that Anthony J. Murray, the CEO of Insurance

Executives, the largest independent insurance agency in town? He also has an outstanding bistro and bakery in the Village."

Melanie agreed, "Yes, that is what Adam told me."

Gregor was pleasantly surprised at the mutual knowledge of Murray. "We met last year at a Christmas function for the Hungarian American Society dinner and dance. His agency has taken over my vast insurance holdings."

Ilona was troubled as he spoke, not for the Murray connection but her once seeing the doctor with an extremely attractive brunette socializing at the Rainbow Lodge, a famous and old inn off Memorial Drive. "Gregor, will you be seeing anyone else?"

Sensing the time she witnessed the meeting at the inn. "Ilona, the lady you saw me with was a former fiancé. It was not a fit, and we mutually broke it off over a month ago. In case you were, ah, thinking there was more to it at the time."

Ilona looked at him with sudden admiration. "Why Gregor, it was your business then, that is about that other woman, your fiancée. That was entirely your time with her and now it is over?"

"My wonderful woman...., he hesitated as he looked over at Melanie who appeared to like what she thought could blossom into a new life for her mother.

She knew he wanted privacy. "Dr. Gregor, I have to phone someone and you need some time with my mother." With that she slowly walked out as he had ideas looking at Melanie's beautiful figure.

Melanie cell phoned her close friend and lover, Alicia Gonzalez. Melanie wanted to be with her, already planning a party for the two, tomorrow night, that included one of her brother's films, 'Hot Nights in Hawaii'. That, along with a bag of highly cut heroin would send them in their own world. Alicia had always been there for her and now Melanie missed being with her very much. She excused herself from the devoted couple preparing for her evening with her lover.

As her lingering scent left the room, Gregor turned to Ilona. "I welcome your return into my life. I can thank Kerry Yanek for you and your daughter's turn around now that you are totally away from that evil and deceitful, Louis. I wish that we would become a couple, except for your daughter."

Ilona knew what he meant. "Melanie could occupy the lower level of your gigantic, fabulous, condominium. Most of the time she would probably be over at her very closes friend's townhome, near the Energy Corridor."

Gregor listened at the suggestion, "Yes, my love, we would live in the upper level, looking out at the million stars in the darkened sky and viewing the brightly lit skyscrapers of downtown Houston."

Ilona's heart beat even faster at his words. "Such beauty from a man of the heart. "Gregor", as she and he grew closer on his seven foot Corinthian leather couch, "I would not wish to intrude, nor would Melanie. As you may be acutely aware, my maiden aunt from Szeged, as Louis always referred to her, 'The Paprika Queen of Hungary', left her entire fortune to me, since I was her favorite niece."

Gregor was thankful, in his mind that this woman would be independently wealthy and not be only interested in him for his money. "Now my darling, Ilona, you are my favorite," as he handed her a glass of expensive tokay wine, he lifted his glass and touched hers, "We are drinking from the font of love, a new beginning for each of us." Suddenly as planned, the lights dimmed and a Hungarian waltz came on.

Gregor arose, and he offered his hand to Ilona, pulling her up and they danced to the music and toward the bedroom.

Louis had kept tabs on Carol Sue's itinerary and fondness for bowling at the Katy area lanes where she was on a league team. Kolezy's plan was to kidnap her after the bowling session late that night. He intended to send Gabor and Tibor later that night, planting Luka at the lanes to observe and steer the Szelanyi brothers to her. Kolezy's ulterior motive was to strongly persuade the tall, platinum blond to drop the claim to MABB or get rid of her, permanently. What he did not count on was that she had a new suitor in her life. That someone had the power of the law.

Luka had a picture of Carol Sue which had been given him by Dimitri. While still in a quandary, himself, regarding his sexual prowess, he kept a vigil on her as she began her scoring on the approach to knocking the down the identical ten, white and red trimmed, somewhat pear-shaped figures obediently waiting for the blast of a round plastic sphere, thrown by a league bowler, hurdling them into a dark pit only to be swept up by a conveyer belted machine waiting for another team member to do their utmost in knocking them over, once again. Carol Sue had the same intent, wearing ultra-tight spangled jeans and even tighter sparkling, pink shirt, she had flawless form as her bowling ball did magic on the lanes.

Luka had not been with a woman of any value since his high school graduation and that was set up by a mutual friend. At twenty-one, he was an afterthought plaything for Louis. He was put up at a downtown condominium near Minute Maid Baseball Park, the home of the hapless Houston Astros. All that was thrown out as he was totally mesmerized by Carol Sue. Even though she could have been his mother's age, it did not matter to him. The woman strolled around the lanes like a queen at a ball as most of the men, near her, had a difficult time retaining their minds on strikes and spares. All the league members were unaware of her wealth, only that she was a fun-loving, dart throwing, poker playing, kegler who hosted Texas Holdem tournaments in her Cinco Ranch home. Even her fellow members of the lanes did not know of her East Memorial mansion and the sleek, black, Mercedes or Escalade parked in the rose covered circular drive that led to the home where many doctors, astronauts and other professionals from Houston's and Texas' upper crust met. She hardly portrayed the former CEO of Miller Corp or that of investing in the very near future, in a near half billion dollar adult/hospitality empire, drinking bar scotch in lieu of single malt brands. Just a good ole gal nicknamed, 'Vixey'. She really likes the so-called suburban lifestyle of Katy knowing that her upbringing and being the head of a large corporation with all the money and entitlements made this style possible. Luka day dreamed as he was the man who would finger her for the kidnapping arranged by Louis and handled by Gabor and Tibor. He had mixed feelings thinking she might be harmed and that he was the one who would do it. As Luka tossed his mangled thoughts back and forth, his cell phone beeped. It was Louis.

"Luka, are you ready to inject that substance into her and make her easily vulnerable so Gabor and Tibor will be able to capture her?"

"I, I, I think so, Louis" he stuttered, unsure of himself. Kolezy immediately sensed a problem.

"Look, kid, you better be ready with your gun and those restraints so the others can handle her. Do not fuck this up or so help me you will pay for it."

Luka realized what his fate would be as he had been on the wrong end in more ways than one before. He shuddered at the realization of being stripped naked, thrown in a pit, and having two predators corner him for a bare back session. "Yes, Louis, I will not fail you."

Little did they know, though, that Gabor and Tibor were involved in a chain reaction accident, three miles away on Highway 99, on the outskirts of Katy, and would not be there to abduct the tall, platinum blond, blue-eyed former model, turned grandmother.

After reveling in jello shots and several Scoresby scotch on the rocks, Carol Sue excused herself from the celebration as her team won First Place. She bowled the high woman's score of the evening. Unbeknown to her, she would face a crisis of sorts, not associated with bowling.

Gabor called Louis from the scene of the multi-car pile-up. "My leader, Tibor and I are being delayed indefinitely by the police due to this car accident. They feel we were at fault and are now taking statements. Our car is disabled; can you send Luka to pick us up?"

Kolezy wrung his hands together as he paced around his library. "I did not need this tonight. You idiots! Luka will have to take her as Dimitri, Drago, and Molnar are at the Sugarland airport readying the Falcon jet for our trip. I will call him as he is armed and can force her into his truck." With that he cell phoned his young, naïve prodigy.

"Luka, the Szilanyi's have been in an accident. You will take her but don't harm her. I want that pleasure all to myself."

"Luka obeyed, "Yes, sir, I have those police plastic strips to tie her hands and a roll of duct tape to silence any emotions she may offer."

"Good boy, er, Luka. I will be waiting here in River Oaks for the two of you." He closed the phone with a contended smile on his face "Finally, I will have that tall, blond, bitch to honor my bed."

Carol Sue bid good night to her team members and other friends as she started toward her Corvette, knowing she was going to meet someone she really liked.

Luka came up behind her, brandishing an almost replica of a child's cap pistol .22 automatic, which he never fired in his life, Sticking it in her ribs. "Miss Miller, do not cry out or I will kill you. Come with me. I do not wish to hurt you, please."

Not knowing what the reason was initially, or who the gunman was, she attempted to turn around slowly, dropping her bowling ball bag in the drive. "I don't think you want to do this and I don't know why or who you are. You can leave now and we will call it a draw." Now she was facing a nervous, pockmarked face of a barely out of his teens look.

"I have to take you with me now. I will shoot you if you don't come." Now shaking the .22, trying to hold the gun with both hands to control the level of action if need be. Please turn back around or I will kill you, right here!"

Carol Sue had been through many close scraps with roustabouts at her drilling locations, a past jilted boyfriend, and an aborted attempt to hold her up at a Houston eastside, Mexican restaurant, where she shot mace at the would be thief, thus getting away. Now this kid was getting on her nerves. "I have friends coming to meet me here in the next minute or so. You need to get the fuck out of my face, euro trash."

"No it is my duty to take you, now!' he bellowed almost alerting some open bowlers coming to the lanes and the next door dance hall to do a double take. As he pressed forward to his intended prey, a .45 Glock clicked in his ear.

"You're the one, Gringo, who has made a major mistake Kid. Put the gun down, NOW! If you don't I will blow your ass away faster than you can squeeze the trigger of your gun!" It was Dimas, Carol Sue's latest boyfriend.

Under the pale lights of the parking lot center, Carol Sue felt safe, once again, with her new hero there. Luka dejectedly dropped his weapon causing it to sound like a plastic toy. Cavazos pushed the boy away and picked up the smallish arm. Laughing, "You know, kid, you could shoot your eye out with this cap gun."

Louis did not matter at this point and his failure to tackle the job only made the young Eastern European man, inexperienced in all aspects of life, concerned with losing his life and being imprisoned. He realized that his slight features would make him an easy target for the inmates. "What are you going to do with me, kill me? It might be better than what I would be faced with..."

Not listening to his plea, Cavazos ordered him to place his hands behind him. "You asshole, from what I can tell killing would be too good for you. I know some of those love-starved men in orange jumpsuits will enjoy seeing you occupy a shower." With that he cuffed the even more frightened young tool of Louis, and pushed him down on the ground next to Carol Sue's car. Then he turned his attention to his new lady friend, "Are you alright, Carol Sue?"

Her eyes were bit misty from his sweeping in like a knight on a white horse to save her, "Yes, Dee, thank you so much! For a moment I thought this guy was going to take me away, rape me, shoot me and leave me in the bayou somewhere." She threw her arms around her new lover and savior, landing a long and sensuous kiss on his lips.

Just as Dimas was ready to follow up on that, some bowlers, including Mandi and Doug Fought, along with Sam and Delia Silva wondered what all the dealings were about, observing Luka handcuffed on the ground and the long, post bowling passion by Carol Sue. Doug, a constable, yelled over to them. "Hey, Vixey, what's going on? Need any help?"

Carol Sue responded quickly," No, ya'll, we got it handled"

Doug shook his head as he looked at his wife, Mandi, "Vixey always has some stuff going on. Never a dull moment."

"Mandi and Doug, along with the Silva's, felt that Carol Sue could handle any situation as they knew her from not only on the lanes, but at her Katy home where they enjoyed and partied, feeling she was a tough and sustaining woman.

Doug just left it and he waved back to Carol Sue. "Okay, great bowling tonight, Vixey." The others figured that everything was under control, as they continued walking to their vehicles.

Carol Sue looked at Dee. "Yeah, bowling. Just want to be one of the guys. Maybe I should have stuck to the ballet tonight at Jones Hall except I enjoy rubbing elbows with these great folks. They are not pretentious. I get a rush on competing with the best of them, bowling, darts, Texas Hold'Em. Yes, in Vegas, I ran up against Amarillo Slim at Binion's for the chance at The World Series of Poker."

Cavazos was almost floored, "Can't figure you to be sitting in with a bunch of sharpies at The River. You ever win against those big boys?"

"I held my own. I can bluff when it calls for it."

The cop looked at the dejected Luka on the ground, head bowed, sobbing. "Could you have bluffed your way past, even, this kid?"

"I was prepared to launch my karate kick in his groin before you interceded."

As Cavazos started to dial the West Bend Sheriff for assistance, he acknowledged her long limbs as a weapon. "Those nice legs of yours could have done the trick unless he panicked and still managed to pull the trigger. The kid is on a mission and if I recall he was the driver who wheeled Kolezy's car away from your Katy place. This job was his intro for the next level of evil spun by our high powered attorney foe." Just then the West Bend Sheriff's dispatcher answered. He held up his hand to her for no response. "This is Lt. Cavazos, HPD. I have a suspect involved with a case Sheriff Lachowski is working on. Person is cuffed at the Pin Oaks Bowling Center's parking lot, send units. May be more of this suspect's partners who are armed and extremely dangerous coming to his rescue."

Surveying Luka to be positive he was not going anywhere, Cavazos once more turned his attention to Carol Sue. "Rubbing elbows? You did more than that awhile back. Wasn't it rubbing some guys behind?"

She offered a Cheshire grin, "Well, Lieutenant it appears you may be a little jealous."

Wishing to make his point, "It's that we may have a good thing going here and I want it to be exclusive."

"You're not bothered by my wealth?"

Grabbing her by the waist, "I can definitely work through that. I don't require a woman to keep me. It's too much being on a leash."

With that she caressed him, unzipping his slacks and reaching in for his throbbing penis, wanting him to shove it into her trembling pussey "You're my hero, Dimas!"

Just as he started to pull her zipper down, the sirens and lights of the Sheriff's car came into the parking lot. Coincidently, it was Sheriff Lachowski's unit with two of his officers.

Both Dimas and Carol Sue restored their clothes, now looking angelic to the waiting officers.

With Luka sitting on the ground acting confused, alone and abandoned, Cavazos filled in the Sheriff who had his men take the boy into custody as they read him his rights. Lachowski, uttered, "You must really like our county. Maybe, I can find you a spot on our short-handed force."

Cavazos shot back, "Sheriff, you always seem to be on the call so you really are short-handed."

The Sheriff agreed. "West Bend is growing faster than we can get bond issues on the ballots for more law enforcement. That, and there was a big wreck on the 99. Couple of guys in a SUV Benz, caused a chain reaction and with ambulances and the wrecker driver's waiting for the action you have to get in everyone's face. One of our guys was on it moments after it happened. He spotted some weapons, duct tape, ropes, and a taser in their vehicle. They were up to no good but our guys had a hard time with their language. They said it was a couple of Hungarians. Whatever, though, they were going to do some bad things. They barely understood their rights as we hauled off their asses to the lockup."

It dawned on Cavazos that the inept Luka was a last minute

replacement for the two Hungarians on their way to kidnap Carol Sue. "Sheriff, what were the names of those two Hungarians?"

Lachowski pulled out the flip top spiral, "Tee-bar Szully and Gaybar Szully or some gypsy, fuckin' name. Probably brothers. Why?"

Cavazos was putting it together, "They are part of this douche bag in a conspiracy to do harm to Ms. Winters. It all goes back to the murders in Houston, Louis B. Kolezy, the attempt on Adam Magassey's life, the Murray involvement and their near fatal demise by unknowns. It all fits. She is the key because of her intentions of purchasing Magassey's company and Kolezy connections to his stepchildren."

The Sheriff, finally acknowledged Carol Sue. "Ma'am, good to see you again, and hope you were not really bothered by this character?"

Carol Sue started to recall the earlier evening. "Sheriff, thanks for your thoughts, I did see this kid look at me in the Center as I went back into the bar area. He followed me around and I could tell he had that Eastern European accent and trying to dial his cell and not having much luck at it. I just blew it off, bowled, and drank. He probably was getting reinforcements since he knew I could take him." She then leaned back running her hands down her lean figure, laughing, "I could have kicked his little behind all night!"

Lachowski was impressed. "Yeah, Ms. Winters I sure bet you could."

Carol Sue thought even more, "Sheriff, we need this boy to implicate those two Hungarians so they can do the same to Kolezy. I would bet a Mexican dinner for you to do this."

Lachowski's eyes lit up. "We have got a great Tex-Mex on 90, in Rosenberg, called Larry's. Fantastic cervazas and 'ritas. Maybe I'll see you over there, sometime, Miss Miller, er, Winters?"

"You never know, Sheriff", grinned Carol Sue.

Murray and Bill were joined by Ernie, Rich, and Tanski at The Flamingo Hotel's breakfast buffet. Ernie was anxious about how Murray and Adam's sleeping arrangement was turning out.

"So how is Adam doing this morning as he must have had a long, long, night and morning and could not get up for this fantastic spread?," Petrovich eagerly probed as he looked over at Rich and Tanski to see how they would respond.

Murray was nonchalant about the question. "I am sure Adam is doing fine."

Ernie felt a little rebuffed. "You don't know? Well, the two of you were in bed together."

Murray still was playing it cool. "Well, Ern, remember the city's tourist slogan? 'What Happens In Vegas, Stays In Vegas'. You need to ask Adam when he comes in this morning from... well, we'll allow him to give ya'll the' blow by blow' details. Actually, the last three nights he has spent the night with someone. Guess all of you are sound sleepers or kept missing Adam who hasn't been in the suite. The first night, when we arrived, I slipped down to the casino and gambled on one of my hunches which did not pan out, until 5:30 in the morning. Adam was up and I grabbed a couple of hours of sleep. Next night, he stayed up with Rich and Tanski, when he returned I was up and anxious to roll the dice, with Bill, at Harrah's, next to The Flamingo. So to answer your question, we missed that opportunity to lay naked together waiting for that mystical moment of bliss. We also have a pullout couch in our room, if needed. If you were hoping to hear from me that we are or were an item, sorry to disappoint you. Sheryl and I found him that night and, yes, he is what he is, or was. I'm only here to carry out this MABB deal like the rest of us coming to the rescue of a fellow Hungarian. I haven't dialed Sheryl to see if she would mind my sleeping with him and having a mutual ass rub."

Tanski, Rich and Bill roared in their bagels and cream cheese. Ernie was taken back and continued to finish his ham and eggs.

Bill broke in, "Ernie, while we are cooling our heels in Vegas, I am losing my retirement money at the crap tables. The shooters are weird, the dice is cold, something is not happening. I am ready to shove off from here but we came, as Anth said, to take care of things and seek justice. If Adam wants to fuck somebody, it is his business. You know, I have been friends with both of you for forty years, since playing Little League on Buckeye Road in our now non-existent, Hungarian neighborhood. My good buddy is loyal to his wife and would not be involved in some adult shit that everyone would be sorry for in the end. So, my other good buddy, Ernie, let it go, okay? We have to round up Sev and Adam. They were both over at Flamingo munching on Chicago Sausages. Bill texted to meet them over at the Pirate Chest and they were to hook up with Carla and Brian. Of course, Adam already had a part of that duo earlier and left Brian in a maze of sheets and pillows.

Tanski was a little under the weather at breakfast. He just opened up without any asking. Now, wearing a worried look, "Ruby, my wife, would shoot me with my over and under if she knew I lost over ten grand at Keno last four days. I better join in on this so I won't lose more."

Murray winced in disgust, "Keno! Ron, we came to Las Vegas to play 21, craps, even roulette and slots and you lose that much at Keno? Yeah, Sheryl and I come here, maybe in a five day span play one hour of Keno, hitting for some good money as she has this system of numbers and damn if it doesn't work every time. We may make a couple of hundred then go to play blackjack and roulette which is an even bet, at best. It is a system we both came up with on slots, bringing back 83 per cent on that. But, what the hell, Ron, how do you blow that much on a glorified bingo game?"

"Easy, I guess, but I have a system to double down at blackjack and get back all the money I lost at Keno."

Murray, Bill, and Rich only nodded in unison.

Bill uttered, "Good luck, Ron."

Ernie was still insistent on quizzing Murray on Adam. "So, you and Adam have not slept together?"

Murray was still amicable toward the subject but losing patience. "Ernie, I would like to relate some sordid detail so you can be satisfied that Adam is every bit the adult star everyone loves to see on the grainy porn screen in some slimy movie theatre over in Montrose but nothing happened since I was not interested and he was not either.

Can you just lose this shit or are you infatuated with his tight ass and hard pectorals?"

Ernie got up and went to pour himself some more regular coffee, picking over another two Jewish blintzes.

The valet brought up the SUV, after breakfast.

Ernie stopped Murray at the valet. "That first night, I don't recall a pull out couch. "

Murray in front of everyone wanted to give Ernie a jolt. "Adam came in as I was getting up. He looked hot. I was naked in bed. He flung off his clothes; we each peeled on a Trojan. Adam was every bit what he shows on the screen. I just laid in a rumble of sheets begging for more. Then pop, I woke up. It was all a dream!"

Everyone broke up except Ernie, finally getting the point. "Okay, let's don't go there anymore."

The black Chevrolet Suburban rolled up from valet. The five got in, and went to pick up Sev and Adam. As Murray and the guys pulled up to the P.C. drive thru only Sev was waiting. Rich yelled out at his cousin, "Where's Adam?

Sev did the arms up and shrug, "He phoned me early this morning and told me he was not available and would meet us at Carla's place."

With that he climbed in and the six took off down I-215 to Henderson, Las Vegas' bedroom community where the boom in the area was the largest. The estimated new population was over 5,000 per month. Many of the masses, fled from the Southern California area flooding The Valley. The great majority, getting in on the cheap interest rates that would soon turn sour on the entire country. A lot of the newcomers were in the hotel and casino industry. Carla and Brian were there well before any hint of the pot of gold at the end of the rainbow was even thought up by the politicians and greedy developers.

Carla and her son, thanks to Louis's indulgence, had a large, two story, 3000 square foot, stucco and stone home, with a red, tiled roof tucked away from all the hype and newness of south Las Vegas area and northern Henderson. It contrasted with similar cookie cutter homes of less area and prestige. She wanted this protection far away from The Strip's reputation, in order to raise her son in a better environment.

As the six pulled up into the horseshoe drive cut, through the landscaping of yuccas and miniature palms that were embedded into the rock fill that surrounded the front of the home, they saw a new BMW730 CLS sports convertible with a temp plated 2008 Ford Mustang fast back in front of it.

Bill commented, " A real nice place for a bar maid."

Rich, added being the former government man and always looking for the possibility of a wrong doing. "Guess she isn't concerned about leaving her cars out. Carla must think that her problems are over and doesn't worry about turning over her ignition", he added, nonchalantly.

Murray's forehead and eyebrows arched, "That's a point, Rich, there are two attempts on her life, and then she goes out and buys a Beemer and a Mustang."

Sev got out and looked under each car, feeling along the sides to see if a bomb was attached anywhere beneath the chassis. He was aware that BMW dealers installed thick armor plating to protect the occupants if a bomb would go off. Many dignitaries, he oftened protected over in South America, as well as in The States, when he was a Soldier of Fortune, had large BMW's where the vehicles were fitted with that protection. After going through the rituals, Sev rolled out from beneath the Beemer and dusted himself off from the sandy winds that whirled outside the area this sunny day. "Looks as though Carla has another day to live. Nothing here. She is living on the edge or has lost her mind and doesn't give a rat's ass about herself and the kid."

Bill gave his opinion, "Hey, This is Vegas, Roll the frickin'dice!"

The group moved toward the sego palmed shaded entry way and Murray rang the bell. A sentry camera hung overhead to the left of the front doors. Bill gave his stamp of approval. "Well, at least she has that going for protection."

Carla viewed the visitors from a monitor in the kitchen and moved toward the front doors to allow their entry. "Well, guys, what brings you all out here? "She asked in a cheerful, although guarded manner.

Murray wanted to get things going, "Carla, we are here to discuss the next move on taking down Kolezy."

Bill wanted to emphasize the urgency to place Kolezy where he belonged. "You know those two heavy weights he sent are out of police custody. It is not safe for you to be alone or go back to work". He advised more as a father to a daughter as St. George had one of his own.

Carla was unconcerned as she led them into the morning room by the kitchen. "Can I offer you all some coffee and Danish. I bought some fabulous pastries from this new great kitshy place that just opened in Henderson?"

Tanski and Ernie looked at the others having the same thought go through their heads. Was this woman for real and why were they risking their lives and time in Las Vegas while she does not care about her own well-being?

Carla moved toward the large open kitchen from the marble tiled great room. Rich was first to take her to task. "Carla, your demeanor has changed or are we getting desert loco being out her too long? Did you hear that the man who limped and his friend are out and may be on their way here as we stand? The police are not guarding you or are we missing the police car in front?"

Before she could respond, Sev started up. "No cop cars, your Beemer does not have armor plates underneath to thwart another bomb going off and blowing your butt into Lake Mead. You then go traipsing around town buying fu-fu pastries and acting as though nothing has happened. I recall your crying in that P C restaurant with all of us just a few days ago, expressing grave concerns that you were going to be murdered by these men. Now, hell, Carla, answer me this, are you on valium or some weird blue thunder balls that you down with vodka and sail into some la la land?"

Carla dressed in a matching outfit of shorts and a tight sequined top, no bra look, that accentuated her ample nipples, jacked up on four inch heels with a diamond studded anklet on her right ankle. She sipped a coffee laced with Bailey's Irish Cream, gazing at the men, offering a small smile, blinking her green eyes especially at Sev. "You really checked under my new car? How thoughtful. Actually, Louis called me early this morning and assured me that all of this was a dumb mistake by some men who had the wrong person. They were trying to collect a marker from someone at the Four Fountains."

All her would be protectors were speechless as Sev looked for something to drink that was stronger than a Starbucks latte she had perking in the brewer. Murray's theory of getting Carla to take down Kolezy was a near bust. The Houston attorney got into this dimwit's head and he was all for hauling his ass out and letting the Henderson police sort out her motives. He wanted badly to lash out at this bosomed lass. After all, they had all placed themselves in danger of protecting this woman and her son. Most felt taken but held back from kicking her beautiful ass. The others stared at Carla with piercing looks as they fumed at her careless attitude. Murray had all he could take, "Carla, what the god damn fuck are you about? Galgany and Keratezy had you in their sights, just before we caught them. Huh?"

The woman stood alone, placing her coffee cup on the gold specked granite counter top, stuttering, "I, I, can't, can't explain that. Maybe those men, they ...ahh. I don't know, so sorry."

Rich in all his experience as an FBI interrogator, Secret Service surveillance operative, then in private practice was totally astonished at her ignorance. "Damn, they were there to blow you away along with your son. Don't bet against that, Carla," attempting to hold back his anger, he dropped the gold lipped, china coffee cup in the sink breaking it into a dozen pieces, "I need to head to the bathroom."

Ernie had downed two cups already, concurred. " Yeah, me too."

Sev knew they wanted to clear the room, "Okay make that three for the run."

Carla piped up," You can use the hall bathroom and there is a guest bathroom two doors past the hall bath.

Sev looked at his cousin, "You want to flip for the first flush, cuz?"

Rich calmed down. "No you first, cuz."

Ernie brushed past the two Fedors, as he went the two doors down the hall. Carla giggled, "Opps, I forgot, he shouldn't go in there. Oh well, Ernie may get a charge out of it."

Murray and the others looked at the beaming woman, wondering what she meant.

Ernie turned the knob and started to enter the mid-morning lit bedroom, going past the king size bed. From the corner of his eye, he spotted two figures under the sheets. The top cover blanket kicked off. "Excuse me."Ernie offered half apologetically, until he realized the two heads popping from under the white satins were Adam and Brian.

"Well, hello, Ernie," smiled a tasseled hair, Adam. "How are you doing?" Brian, surprised by the intrusion, only smiled.

Ernie was dumb founded as to what to say. Standing in the semi sunny lit bedroom, he was speechless. Even though a moderate liberal, at times, he could not buy into Adam's life style.

Brian did not waste any time and emerged from the covers, naked, bending down to retrieve his black satin shorts that were thrown down next to the bed during his time of apparent love and passion for Adam. He looked at Ernie at the same time as both stood within feet of one another unable to speak.

Adam seized the moment, "Ernie, did you need to use the bathroom?"

Petrovich came to his senses, "Yeah, yeah, I... I have to use the toilet." He proceeded to the bathroom and clicked the door. The sound reverberated across the bedroom to the delight of Adam and Brian.

Adam suggested, "Let's use the hall bathroom together, okay? We can get a rise out of everyone."

Adam got up and grabbed a set of cutoffs, pulling them on, and then he threw Brian his Levi's as they both slipped out the door down toward the hall bathroom, walking together.

Sev was just adjoining from the hall bathroom, zipping up his slacks. He spotted the two would be lovers. He looked at them in dismay, "You guys are something else. Can't figure all this in or out in Vegas. Brian, you almost get your cock blown off and the next minute you are blowing a cock. Adam, is he that good?"

Adam placed an imaginary survey on all of this, "Absolutely, and with a certified gold star." The two young men then proceeded to the bathroom together.

Sev stood there for a minute as Tanski came looking for the louver. "I imagine, there is someone in there?"

Sev nodded, "You can say that. Actually, two people, Adam and Brian."

Tanski was taken back, "You mean, as he pointed toward the closed door, they are in the bathroom together? So Murray DID NOT have dibbs on Adam, after all?"

Sev was losing it, "Ron, baby, those two are probably douching one another, I suspect." Sev headed back to the kitchen to search for something to drink stronger than coffee.

Rich, who began all of this, hightailed it to the master bathroom, without caring what, or who or why this was about. Just then he met a blown away Ernie.

"Rich, hey, do you know what I saw a few minutes ago?"

"Yeah, Ern, but I have to go. See you back in the kitchen."

Ernie came down the hall, viewing Tanski, who wore a glazed look. "Still need to use the bathroom, Ron? Where are Adam and Brian?"

Tanski pointed to the hall bathroom. "You can really say it is occupied. Otherwise, I guess I should go to the master bedroom's bathroom and use it."

Ernie looked at the light under the hall bathroom and at the others, "Guess, Ron, you definitely are going down the hall, to head to the head, except Rich is in there. Take a number, as you won't believe what's going on!"

In the kitchen, Murray was wrapping it up with Carla. "So what do you wish for us to do?"

Carla was confused, the reddish brunette confessed "Louis says he loves me and cannot wait to take me into his arms and make unconditional love to me. Yet, my instinct tells me he wants me out of his life." Her eyes began to tear.

Bill knew she was not together. "Yeah, for good, Carla." He viewed her as fragile and felt, unsupportive and not to be trusted. "My Hungarian feeling, Anth, that Carla is going to pull everyone one in and get us killed. She is screwed up."

Murray wanted to cut to the chase. "Carla, why did you even consider him as your lover? After the car bomb and then these two Hungarian Mafia pricks. They were not going to take you for a joy ride in the desert. Las Vegas police related that they had plastic body bags, duct tape, rope, and shovels in their trunk."

Carla defended her actions, "The police phoned me and said they left those two men go as they had no evidence that they were going to do me and Brian in."

Rich returned and was ready to head out, "I can't see how we can protect you if you believe that Kolezy is your savior."

Carla countered, "Our local police assured me that those men are under surveillance. If they come near me, the police will protect me."

Rich probed further, The Henderson police cannot protect you as the latest incident at the P.C., occurred in a jurisdiction in the Las Vegas area. The cops won't arrest them for spitting on the sidewalk."

Bill wanted to emphasize what Rich was trying to get over to Carla, "Look, Sweetie, just for your info, I spoke to the Vegas' Chief of police. He has alerted the police, especially in Henderson, but they cannot guarantee to respond if these two ass holes come after you and Brian. The description and plates of their car has been sent to all of the different police in the area, but I know for a fact that if they use another vehicle or vehicles, they may not be able to track them."

Carla was beginning to see more to her predicament. "You know, you are so very right. I am not thinking straight. Louis has had his way with me for 23 years. He made me have two abortions and if it was not for my stubbornness, Brian would not be here."

Sev heard that, he could not resist the opportunity to jab her and included Murray as well. "You should be proud that you saved him", as he poured some more coffee for himself. "You know, Honey Bee, your son is doing Adam as we speak, in the hall bathroom. As long as you are happy how he turned out... You really have a sexy boy there."

Murray defended Adam, "You do not know what Adam's life has been. He has been taken advantage of by that low life, step father."

Ernie thought it over, "Well, Murray, I believe you are right."

Adam had heard some of Sev's and Ernie's remarks as he alighted from the bathroom starting to go back to the bedroom but turned around to defend the situation. He had enough and wanted to set the record straight. "Ernie, you and Sev are totally off base. I enjoy Brian's company but he is not my type. I could not do it. Right now, he needs me to steer him to the straight life, after all this. My stepfather has made him a virtual vegetable. Believe me; we did not do anything these past nights together. I thought of my old life when I was with him, but the way Murray and Sheryl have stepped up in helping me change my lifestyle. I cannot disappoint them. We wanted to get a rise out of everyone but it backfired a little with your thinking we were an item. Far from it, guys."

Sev and Ernie looked at one another, finally getting it. Sev spoke up for both of them. "Yeah, you cannot judge a book by its cover. None of us have ever gone through what the two of you have endured at the hands of Kolezy. "

Murray had to restore normality to the group and place it back on track, "Alright, you guys; we have had enough tom foolery here about Adam and me, now Ernie. We have a task to do here in this town and I want to get home to my family. So pull your head out of your butt!"

Bill looked at Murray "Tom Foolery?"

Murray looked up at the popcorn ceiling, "Well, that is the first thing that popped into my mind. Anyway, we have to take care of Galgany and that other Hunkie now. Carla, you told us that you have a cop friend at the Henderson PD? Can you get him now or take us to him? We all want to take care of you and need to get back to Houston and finish off Kolezy by putting him behind bars, at the very least. "

Adam stood there in his state of near undress and laid his arm on Carla. "I have a stake in all this, Mizz Davis. We know that Louis can be convincing, but take it from me he is an evil, calculating man and does not want to leave loose ends behind. You and Brian are that. My stepfather cannot be trusted no matter what he promises."

The woman knew he was right. "I'll call Dennie at the police station and we'll go to see him."

Carla had phoned ahead to assure that Dennis McGough, the captain of the force, also her very close friend, was in his office. That day, his desk was cluttered with files and an empty donut carton, barely visible was his name plate, 'Dennis C. McGough, Captain'. She led Bill, Murray, Rich and Adam into his office introducing each of them to him as he offered a weak handshake to say they were not welcome in his town. He was a frequent visitor when she worked at The Four Fountains. McGough was a short, fairly fit, close hair cropped, pulled down tie, sort of a cop. He was a former college wrestler and attempted to maintain his weight in his later years despite irregular eating habits attributed to his job. Dennis had served as a detective out of the Houston PD. He left there tired of the regime's constant politics that had always appeared to surface with the mayor's office and the department. Before that he was a former Orlando, Florida patrolman. Dennis was divorced, fought for and winning the custody of his two sons. He was raising them with the assistance of his sister, in Green Valley, outside of Las Vegas. Dennis liked Carla but could never figure out Brian.

His only focus was Carla. When she came in, he unashamedly grabbed her, holding the woman tightly, wanting her and seemingly ignoring the four out-of-towners.

Dennis in a graveled voice, "Hi Babe, you finally came in I was so worried about you. Who are these guys?"

"It is alright, they are trying to keep me from being killed by Louis B. Kolezy."

McGough was puzzled but came to his senses, "Actually, after the car bombing, I was ready for you to move in with me."

"Dennie, I have a home and a son to protect. I am worried because once these angels leave Las Vegas I may not be able to defend myself against Louis. The two men who tried to harm me were released yesterday."

McGough sat down in his chair and leaned back, looking at Murray, Bill and the rest. "Yeah, I got it off the wire from Sam Hamond's department. Galgany and Keratezy are not your average hit men."

St. George broke in, "Captain, Sam has advised us that these two are under surveillance wherever they go. He promised if they even look at Celine Dion's sign on The Strip the wrong way, he will throw them in jail."

McGough knew the drill, "Sure, as long as they stay in the city limits, but we are so fractured in this town and surrounding suburbs, if you want to call them that. Who knows even if they commit a crime, what will come of it? And they know it. Hell, Vegas is made up of Paradise, Henderson, North Vegas, Green Valley and a lot of nook and crannies. Each municipality tries to help, but don't count on it, Carla."

She looked at McGough, lost in her thoughts, "Dennie, what should I do?"

"As much as I care for you, Babe, have you given any thought about leaving Nevada? Sell the house before the bust happens. Start over, maybe in Orange County, California. I have a cousin in Tustin, just east of Huntington Beach and she could take you in. Change your name, ditch the kid. Hell, he is old enough to fend for himself, even though he is not a 'he' man. Sorry, Carla, but it is true. He gets a nose bleed every twenty eight days."

Adam winced at the Captain's harsh remarks about Brian. "Captain, Brian, is a lovely young man who has had some tough times and is coming of age."

McGough took a swig of his over brewed Folgers java, "You apparently have an eye for this kid, er, your name, again, is what?"

"It is Adam. Adam Magassey."

"Okay, Adam Majesty." Then he looked at Carla. "I really want you here. Maybe I am wrong about your son."

Adam believed he may have won the cop over.

It was Rich's turn. He was used to interrogating and getting on, "Look Captain McGough, Can you help us?"

McGough leaned back in his rickety chair, "Sam Hamond told me he has a handle on these two Russians and I will follow up on it."

Rich looked at everyone, "Slight difference, Captain, these hoods are Hungarians, not Russians."

The copy was used to blowing off out-of-towners as well as Las Vegans, "Alright, so they are from that area in Europe. Hey, don't even think about it. We will put them away in Carson City in a snap."

Rich countered, "How? We already attempted to put them down and they walked?'

The cop tried to assure everyone, "Carla, will go back to her job at the P C. I'll get Sam Hamond to give us their addresses and we will put the two guys, 24/7. They make their move---Bang! They're history!"

Murray injected, "Captain, we need Galgany and the limping shade guy to implicate Kolezy, so don't have your men rub them out if you can avoid it."

"Well, Mr. Murray, when I was on the Houston PD, Louis Kolezy defended a guy we collared on an attempted kidnapping and murder. He was a clever and aggressive litigator. We lost the case. He got the guy off."

Murray searched his past, "I lived in Houston, but cannot recall the case. What was the defendant's name?"

McGough looked up at the roof of his dingy, ill lit, office, rubbing his neck thinking then burst with an answer, "It was Dorat or Drago. Yes, it was Drago, something."

All of the fearsome four looked at one another. "Drago, again!" shouted Bill in haste. "He's part of Kolezy's crew along with the Szilanyi brothers and Dimitri."

That name jogged McGough's memory a little. "Yeah, Dimitri was the other low life who was Drago's accomplice in the case but we could not hold him and only Drago was indicted. Don't remember this Dimitri's last name."

Adam volunteered, "It is Peckoch, Dimitri Peckoch."

The captain snapped his fingers in the air. Yeah, that's it! What are he and this Drago character? Polaks?"

Adam thought it was funny. "No, like all of us here on this side of your desk, except Carla, of course, it is Hungarian. My stepfather recruits them since he has his Mafia of the old world. They are his cronies. Doing his dirty work behind the scenes, just like Galgany and his lame legged friend, here in Vegas."

Just then Murray's cell rang. It was Sheryl. "What's up, my honey?"

She told him the Lieutenant Cavazos called about the incident with Carol Sue at the bowling center and he was trying to contact him.

Murray asked if all was safe for her and the Roberts at their place. She assured all was fine, as Clay Kirby was diligently acting as a guardian angel. That left one another with their 'love you, mores'.

Rich thought that was very cute. "Still love birds. That's great."

Murray blushed a little then changed the subject to Cavazos' call and the dangerous incident involving Carol Sue. He added, "Lieutenant Cavazos nipped which quite prevented Carol Sue from losing her life."

Adam was disturbed over it. "Is she alright?"

Murray was nonchalant, "Sheryl said she thought so. Knowing Carol Sue is so resilient for a former beauty queen, a pretty tough ole gal..."

Adam knew he wanted to be with this almost unreachable woman. He had to be with her. She made him whole.

Seemingly all that Captain McGough could assist at this time, Murray and his group thanked the cop with the assurances that he would have a patrolman outside Carla's home for the time it took to bring Kolezy's two hoods to justice. After Carla said her personal 'good-by' to the Captain they all left and drove back to her place letting her off but not before checking out her home and cars in case Galgany and Kerestezy were lurking there. Neither or both were not around, so she hugged and deeply thanked Murray and his crew. The group went back to Las Vegas and the Mohave. Their job was seemingly done, Carla had given a statement to the Las Vegas police about Kolezy's alleged wrong doing and they would follow up on it. His two Las Vegas operatives were under surveillance.

Carla planned were to live in Henderson, team up with McGough and work at The Pirate's Chest. Brian would continue to be a mystery to the cop even though he would be making future plans to leave the state and be with Adam.

Carol Sue, naked, only clothed in her satin sheet, lounging in bed, had just awoken. Her bowling clothes were scattered on the floor. As she sat up in bed she could smell the aroma of cooked bacon emanating from the kitchen. A soft knock on the bedroom door ensured a sultry response from a disheveled hair, platinum blond. "Come in, whoever you are? "

It was her god send from the night before, Dimas, carrying a tray of fresh breakfast with coffee. He laughed at the almost nun liked appearance, as she looked, innocently at her suitor. "It was quite a night you experienced. I sure wanted to keep you company."

She was speechless at first, then in her normal try to blow off someone, "Dimas, it was a wonderful night and probably this morning. Oh! You are such a body guard....and a lover."

He could see her bull shit coming as he frowned, placing the tray down in front of her.

She picked up on that and decided a little thinking was in order from her normal brush off that did not make it with the cop. "I really meant that, Dee, actually you, oh, my savior. Where have you been all my romantic, broken, and unfulfilled life?"

Cavazos wanted more, he grabbed a cup and poured the coffee, giving it to her, "Unfulfilled life? You have done a great amount of things. A son, like Wes, who is your CEO in a gigantic oil company. A wonderful and beautiful daughter starring on Broadway. You are still active as a successful business woman, not to mention your heading Miller Corporation. Do you really want MABB? It has cost lives and others who almost have lost theirs. Car bombing, hospital shootings and the death of a cop. If it was me, 'Darlin', forget this shit and let me be your lifelong protector."

Sitting up now, sipping her coffee, with the bed covers wrapped around her, not revealing her deep, tanned naked body, exposing only a simple gold and green cross around her neck. She pushed the tray away. "I have to go with it. No one is going to prevent me. Not Kolezy, not anyone! My mind is made up. I am going to require a strong man in my life." Cavazos was being pulled in on this, "When this bastard, Kolezy is thrown in jail for life or killed, I want to be with you, totally. Join me for life!"

The Lieutenant sat on the edge of the bed, his cup of joe, in hand, looking into her ocean blue eyes, "Sounds as though you are proposing, Carol Sue. Isn't the guy supposed to do that..?"

She placed the coffee cup on the night stand and dropped the covers to her ample breast. "Okay, Mr. Policeman, let's begin all over."

He placed his cup on the bed stand and unwrapped the covers all the way to her red polished, toes. "I really believe there are a lot of possibilities in that direction as he leaned over and started to lick her muscled thighs and up to her clitoris, continuing on to the ruby red nipples giving them a thorough tongue lashing and finally landing on her flaming lips. As he was getting aroused and began to unzip his slacks, when his cell phone rang.

She looked at him and he back to her, grunted, "Damn, I bet it is that Sheriff Ed Lachowski."

Carol Sue beseeched, "Don't answer it. This is our moment!"

He apologized to her, "Sorry, Carol Sue, this could be vital."

She started to cover up once more as she was getting chilled waiting for him.

The call WAS from Lachowski, "Hey, my good Mexican fellow cop, I hope your day will get better after I tell you this. This Kolezy guy, well, he sprung these two Szelanyi brothers this morning. The Luka kid, is still being sweated out. He's a damn, fucked up kid and I know he will crack on Kolezy. Wait, I am getting a text. The boys at the station beat down Luka and he is rolling over on our low life attorney guy. You need to pick Kolezy up, Lieutenant Cavazos. Wait, more, Luka has implicated Kolezy on the Vegas bombings and the threat to kill a Carla Davis. Over and out."

Cavazos looked over at Carol Sue. "This will all have to wait. We are going to get Kolezy."

She looked at her Spanish man of the hour, "I want you to cream inside me like you danced so beautiful in hours before. That prick head, Kolezy can wait, I have needs..."

Cavazos glanced over at the digital clock next to the bed, and then to Carol Sue, whose luscious lips pursed waiting to swallow his endowed manhood, and then placed it in her hot bed of desire. "I want you so very, very much." She begged.

His heart beat told him to venture into her steamy and waiting body as she flipped back all the covers and opened her legs beckoning his passionate desires. He could no longer contain himself and stripped down to his socks burying his flesh into hers. Kolezy was me n'ana.

Back in Las Vegas, as Galgany and Kerastezy were packing to leave their Paradise Road apartment, off The Strip. A heavy knock, followed by a loud commanding voice of the police requesting entry and wanting more questioning.

The two reached for their automatic weapons.

Kerastezy whispered, to his partner, desperately, "Let's go out the back. We are going to have to fight our way out of this, Galgany. Let's make our getaway and head out to the desert, to this cabin my brother has."

They readied their AK-45's. Kerastezy started to jump out the bedroom window as the Las Vegas police broke down the door. The limpy man turned around and squeezed off 30 rounds of ammo shooting one patrolman in the shoulder and side, narrowly missing another uniformed badge. A third officer emptied his Glock striking the streaking Hungarian, in the neck and chest, mortally wounding him, as he reeled back still firing his weapon into the ceiling. Galgany leapt out the bathroom window. His automatic rifle jammed. He then pulled out a .357 magnum, unbeknown to him on the fatality of his partner; he landed on his feet somewhat like a seasoned paratrooper. His gun ready, firing indiscriminately only to come face to face with a young street detective, armed with a shotgun.

Galgany's gun was empty and seeing the intensity of the near novice with a larger caliber, he decided to give in and take his chances legally down the road. It would be another nail in Kolezy's coffin, greasing the skid for his boss's future in the legal world but on the defendant side.

When McMahon found out from Hamond about the shoot out and custody of Galgany, he called Murray with the news who then relayed the good tidings to the others at their Mohave Hotel suite. He shouted, somewhat relieved and happy that their job here was practically over, "WE got that shit head, Kolezy. Mr. Limpy, Kerastezy is dead and Galgany is uncontrollably blabbing everything on his boss. Ha, Hungarian Mafia, my ass!"

Tanski wanted to order champagne to toast the occasion. Rich and Sev just wanted to head back to Houston before they lost more money at the tables. While St. George was disappointed to leave so soon as he hit big dollars at Caesar's the night before shooting dice. Ernie viewed everyone, jotting notes in his spiral and putting the venture on his micro recorder. Adam wore a disappointed look as he tried unsuccessfully to reach Carol Sue but her phone was only answered by the deep voice of the Mexican cop. He knew she was heading away from him and he was just looking at falling back into his old haunts and maybe Brian. He was in a state of confusion for the first time in all this, as it vexed his insides. Their job in Sin City was complete. Carla would be joining McMahon in a better relationship that would not include her son, as he now hoped, likely selling her home and settling with a man who would treat her respectfully. With that move, Brian could be available, although Adam was not interested in pursuing the young man.

As Adam packed in silence, a knock was heard at their suite's door. It was Brian. Ernie answered, I imagine, you are here to see Adam. He ushered the young man in and pointed to the area where Adam was packing. As he entered, he touched Magassey. "I guess this is good-by, Adam, he sadly uttered, looking away. Your work is through here and now you are heading back to Texas."

Adam confronted Brian, "It doesn't need to be. Houston has plenty of opportunity. I was thinking that the time we spent together would make you change your plans on staying in Vegas. I have to be honest, though, while it meant a great deal to me, like I confessed to you, I want to go on the straight path, settle down with a woman, have children, and do normal things... I could introduce you to a lot of folks and you can work at the gallery or in the restaurant office until you find your niche."

The young man thought it over. "I could learn to like Houston, even though my memories of past times there were filled with physical abuse when Louis took me to a downtown hotel, never to his home, to fulfill his fantasies with me. I realize you are attempting to just comfort me, turning me to a non-gay life. That is fine and, hey, Vegas is full of hot desert and bad insects that I won't miss."

Adam smiled as he did not have the heart to tell Brian about the king size roaches and mosquitoes that hovered around the Big H, instead Adam looked into his eyes with assurance. "You never have to worry about your father; he's on his way out and will be behind bars very soon. He may also get the death sentence for all the murders that he created in Houston and my own father in Budapest. The Houston Police are closing in on him from all sides. Lieutenant Cavazos and his brother, Zeke, are behind it to bring Louis and his Hungarian Mafia to justice. I hope he gets what he deserves in Huntsville and I want to witness it. Maybe they will allow me to shove it into his low life, despicable veins."

Brian, surprisingly manned up, "I want to be with you there, Adam, only as a friend, as you are determined to change your life. Maybe I can do the same. It will be difficult. Louis has hurt me and my mother too long!"

Adam was much relieved at Brian's turn around. "It is settled. You can pack a bag and come back to Texas. The big stuff you can get later. I sold my townhome and now have a large home in Houston, in the Memorial area, with a nice heated pool and Jacuzzi. I'll have people over for you to meet and who knows what will happen?"

Brian wore a troubled look on his face, "I won't have a job and only have a couple of thousand in the bank, with me quitting at Pirate's Chest and all."

Adam grabbed Brian's arm, "If that is the only concern you have for now, like I mentioned before, I can put you to work as my assistant at the restaurant in The Montrose or the art gallery I co-own with my friend."

Brian was relieved on that saga of his life, as he stumbled out the door.

Just then Murray came in. He was half listening to their conversation with great enthusiasm to Adam's view on his new, promised life of being straight." Adam, I was eves dropping on your conversation and am very happy you discussed this with Brian. I firmly believe you will pull it off. Brian's new outlook on it, too. That is blowing me away. I thought that when you were out here, in Las Vegas, you were fucking some cocktail waitress I saw you with that first night. And you screwed Carol Sue to boot. You didn't like her pussey? Then to find out you really were with Brian and trying to convert him to a straight life. Until then I wanted to bet the farm that you were heading back to your old self. Somehow, after this go around with him, you decided to make the move to being a normal, red blooded, I want to be with a woman, loving type guy',.. It appears that you won't be playing grab ass in your heated pool. What about Carol Sue? I realize you had a fling with her. She flirts with all men but I was hoping that you and she would keep seeing one another."

Adam wanted to make his point. "Murray, it is tough to change courses, just like a ship. It takes time. Besides, I phoned Carol Sue and Lieutenant Cavazos answered, twice. He told me he she was in the shower, He chuckled at that as though he was taunting me. I tried to call her back and she won't call me. She screwed me for MABB, that beautiful bitch."

Murray was almost laughing, "What the hell were you up to that night? Huh? You wanted to explore her hot patch to get your money for MABB. You both succeeded. She's buying it for the price you wanted, as long you both make it to the final table to sign." He then got serious for what could be another tragedy in Adam's life." I got a call from Zeke just a few minutes before your play on Brian. There was another murder of a young guy, dumped a block from where your buddy, Mark, was found. This kid's name was Cody Black. Know him?"

Adam turned pale at the news. "Are you sure of the name?"

Murray knew what Adam was asking,"Ya, Zeke was very specific and even described a birthmark above his right buttocks. By your reaction, it is in the affirmative. Was he one of your 'boys'?'

"Oh, Anthony, I just did not need to hear that kind of news, he...he , I cannot believe he would be that dumb and after I warned him and the others ...Christ, why in the hell did he do it? Cody promised me he would keep going to University of Houston to finish up his degree in hotel management. Was he cut like, ah, like, Mark was?"

"Zeke did mention his state of that. Yeah, Cody's private parts were ....missing. Not pushed anywhere. Maybe they for some bizarre reason, well possibly kept as a ...."

Adam choked up, "Souvenir. A prize to hang over their mantel or ship to me to let me know that my bastard stepfather is in control and wants me to surrender MABB or he will continue on killing the rest."

Murray wanted to give Adam some friendly advice, but his and Sheryl's life had been dealt the crushing blow losing their one and only son to the same possible serial murderer. He was not even listening to his own words he sputtered out, "At least you considered the welfare of Brian and turned him around. Yet he is going to be with you even knowing those around you either die, are threatened, or just missed on being killed. You may want to tell Brian that until Kolezy is in jail with his mafia that he may be in danger. You can always teach him to use a gun. I am not preaching to you but it may be in your interest and his to sever the relationship now. As far as Vixey, she has had her fun with you and now has Dimas Cavazos as her knight to protect her. She's like that. When the danger passes, she will drop the cop like it happened to you. Carol Sue has never changed as far as I have known her."

Adam appeared to agree with Murray's logic. "Maybe I ought to let Brian stay in Las Vegas. He needs Carla now and should not get in the middle of what is coming down the road. He could be in grave danger and if he wants to testify against Louis, then he can come to Houston. Well, Vixey, as you call her, or Carol Sue, is a man eater all right. You know, though, I saw a picture of her daughter, K'Lynn. She did mention at her Katy place, that her daughter was not seeing anyone. If she is as good as her mother in bed, I'd like to sample it. Yet, I did tell Brian to come to Houston. I have an obligation to allow him to stay with me." He sighed, "Brian is my responsibility...for now."

Murray had a mischievous grin, "You really want to lay K'Lynn to revenge being dropped by our flirtatious Carol Sue Miller, slash, Winters, don't you?"

"It would satisfy me to fuck her, to gain partial revenge, but I have to take on other things."

Murray winced at that statement. "Whatever floats your boat."

"You would not approve of that. Well her mother did it to me. Besides, Vixey, ah, Carol Sue, has another guy in her life now. You're correct; I need to stay the course. I would still like to see what K'Lynn is like and I'll screw her in the conventional way. Of course, she may like it the other way, too. I was about to do it to Vixey, once more, but she was worn out from my screwing her. We fell asleep, and then the bomb went off. In any case, I realize we have a job to do in bringing down Louis. That and what to do with Brian." With that Adam walked out of the suite and down the hall for privacy, flipping on his cell, telling Carla's son he needed to stay in Las Vegas. Brian's life with the former adult star was becoming too dangerous with Louis still being on the loose.

Murray peered out the suite door looking for the bell hop to pick up all the luggage when he spotted Adam gesturing on the phone presumably telling Brain to stay in Las Vegas, but from Adam's body language, he was not getting his point over. He finished his call and staggered back toward the suite where Murray greeted him.

"Adam, since we're in Las Vegas and I am a betting man, would the term 'all in' apply to your not getting Brian to stay here and his wanting to take you up on your Houston deal?"

"Yeah, you would win all the money on that", he replied dejectedly. "Guess, I am not much of a salesman like you. You're successful in your insurance business and I would bust out after three months."

"Well, my friend, does that mean we have to make room on the plane for Brian?"

"Do you mind?"

"No, I will just have to update the rest of the guys. They won't believe right away that you and Brian have decided to go the straightway. Well, not as first. After all, you and he went into the bathroom together."

"We did that as a joke, to get back at everyone, not you, of course, just to tease everyone. You and Sheryl are supportive of me and my life style, not the others. Sure Bill may raise an eyebrow but he is quiet about his comments. Rich is more reserved, but I can tell he is against my past and now this thing with Brian. Ernie, Sev, and Tanski don't mince words, so I will get an earful when we drive to the airport and on the flight back home."

Trying to encourage Adam, "If he doesn't change his way, you can always hook him up with another guy in Houston. Your black book has to be filled with possible candidates. You know that he can stay here. Las Vegas has an abundance of production shows like the one we saw at Monte Carlo the other night. Brian has that dancer's build. Hell, he could get in that show or half dozen others. Cher is at Caesar's; maybe she has those certain type dancers. Elton John is coming in. Hey, right combination."

Half dejected, yet hopeful at Murray's suggestion, "You're probably right. Really, Brian has some bed hang-ups. Yes, I think he would be better with a couple of other 'candidates', as you call them. He has tried to go to auditions as a chorus boy but he has two left feet. Nice try, Anthony. Will you tell the guys about Brian? Of course, I can? I know how tough it is to support me in all this. Now it is this supposed thing with Brian."

"I know where you are coming from, as I was a target like you. Somehow, I beat the odds. You, too, have a chance. It won't be easy. Of course, what could you do with Louis constantly threatening to harm your mother and Melanie? He held it over your head. I'll square it with the guys and our pilots, Jon and Arnie. Meantime, work hard on getting K'lynn's number from Carol Sue. She might turn out different from Vixey. After all, she is a newer model with less miles on her."

Bill walked in at that time. "Ok, are you ready to blow this Sin City?"

Murray looked at Adam, then turned to Bill, "We have an extra passenger and luggage coming with us. Brian wants a change of scenery and Houston is the cure. He is staying with Adam until he decides where and what in his hectic life."

"Oh... kay, whatever," St. George's jaw locked down, looking at Adam with an unsurprising assurance. "Well, um, yeah I guess if that is what the two of you want to do. I am okay with it. Sev, Ernie, and Tanski may not be overjoyed with it, but hell, it is only a two hour and what? , a fifty minute trip not including landing and taxiing off, and not having to be with the bathroom and bedroom deal we had at Carla's."

Murray hugged his old friend, "Good, I know you'd be fine with it. At least, for the time it takes."

Bill looked back at him, "For you, Anth, I will do anything that makes sense and even if it doesn't, somehow you are on target for things. I will break the news to the others. If you hear a howl just disregard it."

Murray thought it was hilarious as he ribbed St. George.

What lies ahead for Louis B. Kolezy, the attorney of the year in 2007? Unaware, at his River Oaks mansion of the net closing in on him. Galgany would turn states evidence. Luka was both afraid of Kolezy and being sent to prison but knew he would somehow survive with a shorter sentence by testifying against his mentor. He hoped that the judge would send him to a more protective custody, away from older, violent inmates desiring his fragile features. Though not wanting to go to prison, the wimpy boy-man, would not give any details of how Dimitri, Drago, and the Szilagyi Brothers carried out the cruel and unusual violence in the name of Kolezy's Hungarian Mafia plan. Murders and random acts of unspeakable, vicious acts, that he could not bring himself to discuss, hoping that Louis, somehow would free him before he turned the attorney in for those crimes.

Kolezy thought he knew where Melanie was. She had left the River Oaks mansion to join her very close friend, Alicia Gonzalez. Alicia, age 26, part Hispanic, part Anglo, was accustomed to wearing tight jeans and sporting long, cascading black hair running down her back. She drove a late model, black, Cheverolet Camero convertible, top down, allowing her mane of hair to blow in the wind. She and Melanie met at a Houston downtown bar, two years back and were on and off lovers. Alicia had attempted relations with men, actually having a fiancé before meeting up with Melanie. All of that went out into outer space upon her attraction and hot moments with Adam's younger and eager to please sister. Alicia was the dominant one in their relationship as Melanie was more accustomed to a passive role in a sexual relationship.

Alicia worked as an analyst at a major oil company in the Energy Corridor of Houston, not far from her luxury townhome. She made large amounts of money and enjoyed a high life style. Her late parents, had land and retail interests in Nuevo Laredo, near the Texas-Mexican border, as well as extensive property locations in the Houston area. They were worth tens of millions of dollars. One evening they were shot to death in their Southwest Texas hacienda by a drug cartel. Alicia and her two siblings were left with over a five million dollar trust fund. An uncle, she suspected, was connected to part of the underworld. He watched over her, sometimes being more than a protective relative in her private life.

Melanie fit in with that high life style as she kept a tidy sum that Louis gave her along with the trappings of jewelry and other pawnable baubles he bestowed upon her for his sexual favors. That and now that her mother, Ilona, had inherited the paprika queen's vast fortune which allowed her daughter, an unbridled amount of money, some of it going to recreational drugs, excesses of liquor, and picking up women in Houston and Galveston's social trolling venues. Ilona could afford to bestow upon Melanie whatever she needed to survive, live, shop, party, and do low risk party drugs, although she assured her mother that it was only some grass, now and then. Melanie had new found freedom. This day at Alicia's was no different. A wild weekend ensued as the two awoke with a duo of pickups from a long night of reveling in downtown Houston's newest playground. The night before, Melanie was totally unaware that her taking Alicia to Ryan A's, Adam's Montrose bistro and restaurant, was all being watched by Tibor Szelegyi, freshly out of jail. Upon orders from Louis, Tibor had followed the unknowing women from Ryan A's to Adam's, MABB's run, gay/lesbian lounge, Runners, in near downtown Houston.

Runners, was a two story club, women on first floor and men on the second floor with very few exceptions. Both clubs had d.j.'s laying mood music and rock. The booze flowed. Adam had a 'No Nonsense' drug rule that was mandated and thoroughly enforced. If anyone was caught smoking, sniffing, or shooting up, they would be asked to leave immediately, photographed, and never allowed to come back into any of MABB's clubs. Adam fondly called the blackballed former patrons, his gray book people.

Melanie and Alicia patrolled the first floor, while above, the men, could survey the women below as the lighting shined down on the female's couches and cocktail tables, slightly gaudy, yet subdued lighting that enhanced each part of the venue. Melanie enjoyed her freedom often after seeking another woman by herself and boldly inviting either both her and Alicia or just soloing it to an empty seat in an attempt to pick up one of the many, slender, early, late 20's to 30's female of any origin or color. At times, she and Alicia would take turns dancing with their new, found friend, touching, groping, each other's bodies much to the delight of the same persuasion. Tibor watched from a distance. His mouth savored the lust that the two prey seeking women poured out. This night, both Melanie and Alicia were clicking on all cylinders. Melanie was walking out with a white, reddish, tall, late twenties female dressed in high heels, fishnet hosiery, and tight, barely ass covering leather shorts. Alicia jackpotted with an Eva Lorenzo look alike type, Hispanic, dresser in a micro mini butt revealing mesh skirt and a bare appearing, halter top. The four walked to Alicia's valet parked convertible and sped back to her Eldridge townhome for after hour high jinks.

Tibor, followed the car. He was anxious to cut into the long, black haired, Alicia, dressed in her black, ultra-tight leather jeans. He reported to Kolezy that the women seemed secure for the night, at the Eldridge townhome. He laid in wait almost like a viper desiring the time with his victim.

Kolezy was uncontainable, knowing in a few hours he would have Melanie down, stripped naked. As told by Tibor, that the two women had company that early morning and just waiting for them to depart. Louis had devised a sure plan for letting himself into the townhome. `

Early the next morning, Louis drove over to the townhome in his personalized, dark blue BMW 730i. Louis had mayhem in mind and a fresh box of long stemmed Texas, yellow roses which Melanie fondly loved.

He pulled up next to Tibor's old, Jaguar XKE, getting out of the Beemer and into Tibor's car, Louis remarked, arrogantly, "We just need to wait for those two whores to leave. I know my Melanie; she will get tired of fucking her dirty legged, broad, sending her home in a cab."

Tibor, was unsure of Melanie's previous method of operation, "Louis, they may be in there for the entire day how do you know when it will occur?"

Kolezy drew back and looked up at the dingy ceiling of the XKE, "You know, my friend, you should have this inside top cleaned. It looks like you jacked off onto it. No, my naïve man, the taxi or car will be here. I have been outside this place before, often, as you did, following her from those downtown places, and seeing what happens. Been there, done this, more times than I can remember. My hardness manifesting the fantasy of sheer joy as to what was taking place in that abode."

As he finished his sentence a yellow and a red cab, each pulled up. Melanie's date piled into the yellow cab while the red taxi pulled away with the Eva Lorenzo look alike in the backseat. In an almost horizontal state, a sleepy eyed Tibor warily spoke, "What do you want to do my Master?"

Kolezy had a sinister, lustful look on his face, "WE will go in my hot blooded friend. You may have the black manned lass. I will covet my stepdaughter's browned, tight body with her loose and easily accessed openings. She will enjoy the scent and beauty of the bouquet I bought for her as she offers me the pleasure of her succulent body."

Tibor grew wide eyed, "Louis, I cannot wait, let us be there, quickly and enjoy the spoils of their heated selfs."

Melanie was totally unaware that her stepfather knew her where about as she strolled, barefoot with denim, cutoff shorts, and black halter top that bulged with her ample bust and cherried nipples, ripened by Alicia's intervention moments before. Melanie was in the kitchen searching for a set of clean coffee cups and plates for the left over sausage quiche the four women baked and ate earlier.

The doorbell rang. Alicia, who was in the upper loft overlooking the living area, yelled down to her lover, "Hey, Mel, will you get the door, my squeeze may have left her earrings on the nightstand. It is likely that it's her."

Melanie could not leave that request alone. "Or maybe, Lecia, she wants a threesome, ha, ha."

Peering through the sentry peephole, she saw a flower box. Knowing that both of them enjoyed the fragrance of flowers, the young woman thought they were for Alicia. Although she had an uneasy feeling that someone would send a messenger at 8:00 in the morning, all caution was thrown into the wind. Perhaps, it was a former ex-partner of her lover that wanted to reconcile. As she began to unloosen the door locks, Alicia looked over the railing at her partner, "Mel, what is it?"

Turning back and looking up in a reply, "It looks like flowers, Lecia..."

Something gave Alicia a shivered warning, "Don't open the door!"

It was too late as the last lock was unbolted and Melanie turned the handle...Louis barged into the room, pushing her down, landing and pinning her to the floor. The box of flowers broke open strewing the yellow roses in a cascade of stems and peddles raining down upon them and the highly polished hardwood floor. As she began to warn Alicia, Louis cupped her mouth with his free hand. She was unable to move under his weight. Tibor followed. A wild, dreamily expression broke his normal pasty demeanor, anticipating the acceptance of his advances upon Alicia. "Where is that black haired bitch?" He asked Louis.

Kolezy did not care where she was, "Damn, if I know, Tibor, go find her and screw the shit out of her like I am going to do to my lovely bitch stepdaughter."

Uncupping his grip on her mouth, Melanie saw what was going on as she shrieked in horror, "Please, do not hurt Alicia and me!"

Tibor saw his black haired lass and started up the steps.

Melanie was overcome with terror as she negatively attempted to shake her rumpled, brown locks, murmuring , "No, No, Louis!"

Holding her down even more, his cognac breath spewed in her face, almost drooling on it. Laughing, playfully like a pocked marked teenage boy behind the football stands to an adolescent cheerleader, "You did not mind my doing that all those years. Why not now?" He wanted her to feel inferior and unable to seek aid. "You will regret your decision to see that damned, therapist, who caused you this discord between us. I've done nothing else but think of how you and I will go back to enjoying these moments of amour. I will take care of that woman so she never comes between us ever, again." His breathing almost sprinkled with sound bites of palpitations.

Tibor, meanwhile, started his long, awaited journey toward Alicia. He began to attack her in a savage, clumsy way, awkwardly using a John Wayne type walk toward the apprehensive but street-wised, black haired beauty. A desperate warning from her enhanced lips, cried out.

Kolezy, amusingly, heard her screams as he enjoyed his victims when they wished to fight back, making the sexual moments more fulfilling. Knowing that there was little hope in their finding refuge from the abuse, he began to encourage Tibor to strike Alicia and assault her. He eased his body enough for Melanie to thrust a strong leg into his scrotum, causing the attorney to fall back and away, "Ughoughed", as he bellowed in unanticipated, excruciating pain.

She had enough leverage to push him off and scamper up, past her writhing stepfather. He made an attempt to reach up onto the nearby black, leather couch. Melanie grabbed an expensive, tiffany lamp, releasing her pent up emotions of years of his uncaring feelings of raping her, she pummeled him on the head and face, resulting in a scarlet trauma.

Knowing that her partner was in danger, she called out, "Lecia, I'm coming", frantically two stepping up the stairs and onto the loft where she witnessed Tibor unzipping his slacks, dropping them to his knees and then flicking his Fruit Of the Looms further down over the Hungarian made gabardines. She saw that Alicia's Houston Texans jersey night shirt had been ripped off. Grunting toward her, as he was trying to remove his clothes and pursue at the same time, reaching to remove Alicia's purple, silk tong from her shivering body. Frantically, Melanie ran to the bedroom and located two guns that were stashed in the nightstand, a .38 special and a 9mm. She grabbed both and vaulted down the hall to take care of the intrusion. Fear left her body having those fully loaded weapons clutched securely in her hands. Fury erupted.

"Hey, asshole!" she rang out at Tibor, who upon hearing her voice, relaxed himself from clutching Alicia.

That enabled the naked girl to squirm from his grip with a now free right hand and thumb jamming it into his left eye, making the dumb Hungarian to wince painfully at the unknown move.

As he looked toward Melanie, she took aim, squeezing both triggers simultaneously, 'zat, zat, zat, zat, zat', catching Tibor in the face, neck, and chest. Splinters of his skull flew out. The big man's mouth filled with blood. He wheezed for the last breath he would ever take, staggering as he fell backwards from a couch bed, over the loft railing, dropping onto a glass coffee table below in the living room, crushing it to splinters and chards.

Kolezy stood motionless for seconds as he looked up to see his now emancipated young step daughter drawing a bead on him. Instantly, he knew she held all the cards in a win or lose poker game. Melanie screamed, "You fucker, you're next, cock sucker, bastard, child molester, mother fucker, murderer!" She dashed around the banister of the loft firing at Kolezy's head. With a second one hitting his left arm with a .38 shell. She emptied one more round from her silver six shot revolver. Scampering down the stairs, in blind rage, triggered off four more shots from the 9 mms hitting its mark in Kolezy's lower left side. He fled out the door limping and in a semi-shock, bleeding profusely, ran to his Beemer, piled in and gunned it out the driveway.

Melanie, in hot pursuit, took final aim. With a shooters stance and two hands, Melanie emptied the automatic into the rear of the getaway car. Bewildered neighbors, who heard the commotion in the townhome and later the shots, stood in awe, unable to speak at the moment.

Melanie muttered to an older lady walking her Corgi, "That sonofa bitch got away, this time, but he is going to face the facts. Kolezy is going down for all he's done!"

"Whaat Sweetie? That sure was a fancy shootin' deal you did to that no good son of a god damn asshole who apparently jilted you for another woman. Was that old guy a lost lover or an ex-hubby cheatin' on you?"

Melanie was standing there with a smoking automatic and did not want to act like a post menstrual broad having a hot flash. "Ma'am, go walk your little dog!"

After that she turned on her barefooted heel, stomping back toward the townhome wanting to review the carnage and tend to her partner...

As Melanie entered the now crime scene, Alicia, naked, was staggering down the stairs, crying. The empty .38 was lying on the floor beneath the stairs. Melanie instantly dropped the automatic and ran over, tightly embracing an almost now hysterical, Alicia, kissing her, all over, as they sat at the foot of the stairs. Both were silently sobbing onto one another, oblivious of the dead Tibor lying no more than a dozen feet from them, half naked, eyes wide open, staring up at the ceiling, oozing with the crimson flow pouring out of his mouth, eye, and chest.

The two women heard a noise from a dark figure by the door not knowing who it actually was; they were at first, terrified that it might be Kolezy. It turned out to be Alicia's next door neighbor, Good Samaritan, Jerry Koch, who ran in to see if he could be of assistance. Seeing the dead body and the two women apparently requiring consoling, he wished to defuse the situation the best way he knew as a doctor of chiropractic medicine, "Ladies, I wish to help you. Before that, do you have any Mogan David? I called 911 and I believe a number of our neighbors did the same."

Soon the sound of sirens filled the air as it appeared that the police were almost at the scene.

Lieutenant Cavazos was returning from Carol Sue's home in Katy, journeying down Interstate 10, when he heard the bulletin from headquarters of the shooting on Eldridge and Memorial. He knew that Murray had an office near the location and curiosity overcame him. He placed the police emergency bubble on top of his car to cut to the chase, while flipping the siren on and pushing the cars on the six lane freeway out of his way. It created an aura no one else could ever know unless they were in his boots, feeling free and easy, blaring the red and blue light, going on a call for whatever may come up. The vehicles parted the freeway, for Cavazos, just like the River Nile for Moses, determining, jutting his chin forward, liking the cars parting out of his way.

At Hobby airport, Murray's plane had just landed from their Las Vegas venture. As they disembarked coming into the waiting area, the television news from Channel 77 was broadcasting the shooting and bloody mess that had taken place at the Eldridge townhome. The name Alicia Gonzalez and an unknown friend, filled the news broadcast of the killing of Tibor Szelanyi.

Murray, Bill, Rich, and the rest, with Adam and Brian all turned to one another as Adam; asked, knowing it might be Melanie, "My sister was staying at a place on Eldridge. What was that girl's name? "

Rich volunteered, "It was Alicia Gonzalez."

Adam's mouth dropped, "Hell, that may be my sister and her good friend."

Murray wanted to support the problem that Adam would know in a few minutes.

The news bulletin continuing the blaring message, "On Channel 77, from the on the spot area, a shooting took place in a townhome on Eldridge and near Memorial where one person has been killed and another may be on the loose..."

Adam wiped his face with his hand, "Oh, my god, my sister lives with this ...I just hope it was not... Murray I have to go to her...."

Murray knew a situation when he saw it, "I'm with you, Adam."

Bill looked over at his good friend, "I'm on board, too, Anth, and Adam."

Rich felt that it had to do with Kolezy, deciding for the rest, "Murray, Bill, Adam, we all have to go, too!"

As Murray and his cohorts were ready to go to the murder scene, Brian wanted to know where he stood. Adam was caught off guard, "Brian, I cannot assess what we are doing at this moment as my sister may have been involved in a murder. You know we have to table our lives for the time being, okay?"

Brian was thinking only of himself. "Yes, I know, but I thought I had a new life here?"

Sev spoke up in defense of Adam's statement. "Look, Brian, we helped rescue you and Carla in Vegas, spent more than a week losing our shirts at the tables, while those two shit wipes were trying to blow both your butts into Reno. This deal with his sister is much hotter than your wanting to cut Adam in bed. Even he is pushing your skinny ass aside for his sister. Good for him! You want to stay behind as we take care of things? He can get you later."

Brian, at that point, knew his place." No, I will go with all of you."

With that said, Sev and the rest piled into the large Chevy Suburban, glued to the newscast that was on their car television. The group had followed the newscast and went to the Eldridge site where a bevy of the local television stations already had set up their onsite broadcasts. As they alighted from the Suburban, Lieutenant Cavazo's cruiser screeched to a halt next to them.

Channel 48's helicopter was whirling above, relaying a feed back to the station broadcast. Meantime, the Lieutenant knifed his way to the front. He located his brother, Zeke, who had just completed a television interview with Channel 77's, highly respected reporter, Tom Zizka.

"Hey, Bro, got you in on this one", Zeke gleefully, acknowledged to his older brother. "Guess who did the shooting?" Zeke asked in a half comical way.

Dimas was not in the mood for question and answers. "Don't know, Zeke. Are you trying to piss me off? Who are you referring to?"

Zeke laughed, "You sound like a Mexican owl on that one, Dee. It is Adam's sister, Melanie Magassey. She fuckin' blew away one of the Hungarian Mafia, Tibor Szelanyi. He looks like reddish Swiss cheese. Are you up to looking at him before lunch, Bro?"

The Lieutenant looked at his brother, "As President Reagan once said to the peanut farmer who was in the White House, 'There you go again'. Zeke you are always trying to get the best of your older brother. I can handle it even if he is covered in whale shit. Lead the way, Sergeant."

Zeke winced at the demoting remark of rank. "Yeah, Bro, I will get my bars back as captain real soon, after we crack this case and put the Hungarian Mafia or whatever they are away for good."

Dimas agreed as they walked through the door to view the carnage that Kolezy and Tibor started only to have Melanie finish it up.

The Lieutenant looked at his brother, "God damn, Zeke this looks like our days at University Of Houston at our frat house, except for a dead body. Although, remember that time after the...let's not go there."

Dr. Nelson, the Medical Examiner, who had already autopsied six young men, including his own son, in Montrose, now was on the spot where the covered Tibor's corpse lay. He grimly looked at Dimas. "You are always on top of these crappy scenes aren't you, Lieutenant?"

Dimas thought for a moment, "Yeah, Doc, this can be a drain, but, they pay me the big money for all this fun." The cop then bent down and uncovered the bullet riddled body of the Hungarian. The Lieutenant took a deep breath and looked up at the coroner, "Yep, Doctor, he seems to be dead."

He then turned his attention to Melanie and her lover, now clad in her torn shorts and wearing a button down expensive shirt, as they clutched one another, both sobbing quietly, sitting off in the living room on their loveseat. A Harris County Constable Sergeant was nearby and spotted the Cavazos brothers. He looked at them, recognizing Zeke from another homicide a few months ago. "Well, Zeke, are we going on this one or HPD?"

Zeke wanted in on this as it involved Adam's sister and surely was part of the Kolezy investigation. "Yeah, Sarge, this probably is a segment of a case my brother and I are working on."

Dimas stepped in as the ranking officer on the scene, "Yes, we can work with your findings but this is definitely our job. Have the two women said anything?"

The Constable negatively shook his head, "They have been bawling since I arrived and the other officers haven't talked to them. They pretty much have buttoned up and are waiting for a lawyer or some family person. I thought I heard the shooter, cell phone someone and when I went up to ask her something, she began to cry."

As the Constable left to talk with his fellow deputies, Zeke whispered to Dimas," For what we already know about Kolezy and his crew, this gal would get off with a group of Hungarian jurors supporting her."

The Lieutenant agreed in part, "Don't really need Hungarians to acquit her, she's white and pretty with a nice bod. Take a Lakeesha or Lupe and they get the book thrown at them. Yeah, Melanie could get a Rusty Harden or Terry Gaiser or that George, what's his name, attorney that defended that gal who drowned her five kids in the bathtub from Clear Lake, 6-7 years back. Well, let's see what we can get from the duo love birds. You know her dark haired girlfriend looks like......"

Zeke completed the view, "... A ha, yeah, part Latino; part Anglo, nice tight ass, name's Alicia Gonzalez."

Just then, a constable sergeant came in and announced, "There's a next door neighbor who saw and heard the entire episode. His name is Jerry Koch, a self-proclaimed Jewish Orthodox guy. He's an older, bearded type with a cap on. Smiles a lot.

Lt. Cavazos was interested in this witness. "Thank you, Sergeant. We will see what our Jewish friend has to say. By the way, that cap is called a yamika.

Zeke brought Jerry Koch to the kitchen where Dimas was looking around seeing some uneaten pizza and empty Shiner beer bottles. "Hi, I am Jerry Koch. I am like the football type of coach, my name pronunciation, that is, Captain err..."

Dimas, smiled faintly, peered down on the shorter, white bearded man, "IT is Lieutenant Cavazos. I haven't been promoted as far as I know, although I could use the extra money", as he pulled out the spiral notebook. "The Constable and Sergeant Cavazos gave me your name. Is it spelled C-O-A-C-H?"

"No, Lieutenant, it is K-O-C-H. That is alright though; my name can be pronounced three or four ways. Take for instance..."

Dimas was not hearing anymore, "Look, Mr. Koch, I need to know what you saw and heard. Give me the entire story on what happened in this unit."

The neighbor knew that his wit was wearing thin with the Lieutenant. "Yes, I was the witness. These girls were accosted. It is my civic duty to tell you all about it. The one lady, Alicia, has lived next to me for two years. I know she has other women come over and they spend the night, sometimes the entire weekend. I hear them moan and groan. I am not really a busy body, Mr. Cavazos?"

Dimas looked dryly at the bent over Jewish man, who knows what he was, merchant, rabbi, jeweler? "Mr. Koch, please stick to what you actually saw."

Koch drew a deep breath and stroked his six inch, white and gray beard, "The two men caused a lot of commotion as one banged on the door of Alicia's townhouse. Usually I do not pay much attention, but who knows what goes on!"

Dimas was ready to head towards the two women who now were entangled in a life and death hold. He knew he had to get as much out of this man. "Mr. Koch, what else did you see?"

"I was walking my dog, Seth, and the one man had flowers in his hand, and the other was behind him. Alicia or her friend answered the door and the two forced themselves in. I went back to my home and phoned 911 then went back to Alicia's home. The door was not closed and I saw the entire episode. I saw the one man force Alicia's friend down on the ground. She attempted to struggle but could not as the man was larger than her. The other man went up the stairs to the loft after Alicia. The girl down below kneed the man who was ripping her clothes and forcing himself on her until, she broke free and ran up the stairs. I clearly viewed the other man tearing Alicia's jersey from her as she screamed for help. Are you getting all this, Mr. Cavazos?"

The Lieutenant was busy writing and looked up, "Mr. Koch, I never had it so good... go on sir,' as he encouraged the neighbor.

"I wanted to help, but ...my hip, you know, I am not that well of a man and as I was talking to my doctor, Doctor Soloman the other day... Oh well you want to know more. Anyway, the hip, I once went on a pilgrimage to Lourdes, maybe to convert, I don't know. Who does? I thought of converting but a Jew to a Catholic, my family would be turning in their graves, much like Elvis when his daughter was married that whomever singer or were they?"

The Lieutenant had enough, "Look Mr. Koch, I don't give a fuck if Lisa Marie liked to get it on from that whomever, cut to the chase, what else can you tell me before I turn another year older!"

"Well, I had a glass of Mogen David this morning and was feeling good and thought of running in there and hitting the man downstairs with a karate chop I saw in a Bruce Lee movie and practiced it on a mannequin I bought from this haberdasher downtown off Main street where some of the homeless hang out. I knew, Lieutenant that I would not be a match for them. I don't own a gun and would only hit them on the head like; Alicia's friend did to this ugly man. She raced up the stairs in a minute to protect Alicia and shot this real ugly bigger man. He fell over the loft rail onto the coffee table. The man downstairs looked up and started to climb the stairs but Alicia's friend yelled at him and I saw such hatred in her eyes as she shot at the man, hitting him in the arm and side. He ran past me not even noticing me. The girl ran down using such profane language with her weapons raised to use them, which she did. I came around, following her as he raced for his car. I think it was a BMW of sorts. Anyway, I was not a match for those two tough ones. I figured that I should wait for the police. Alicia's friend saved everyone. She was magnificent! Her killing that wretched man who wanted to ravish her lovely partner was in her right!"

That hit Cavazos, 'partner'? But then, who cared. He was there to mop up the scene or was it the Harris County constable who was responsible? He then countered, and he told the sergeant that he was taking over the case. He looked at Melanie's lover, barefoot, hot-shorted, wearing a button down shirt. She was inviting, younger than Carol Sue and vulnerable. Why did he feel that way?

Zeke could tell his brother was bothered by the moment? "Hey, Mejo, focus on the crime not on the flesh. Okay?"

The Lieutenant went back to the Jewish neighbor, "So Mr. Koch what else can you add to this?"

Recounting his previous story, "The bad guy went up the stairs and was shot. I was in the back of this other guy and at the shooting I ran out and hid in the bushes. The man who I was behind came running out holding his right arm. I could see he was bleeding. The girl came out with her gun and shot at him as he got into his BMW. I did get his license number. Here it is." At that the man gave the cop a crumbled piece of paper. It was 'Atrny 1' "That is all I know. Alicia and that very nice looking girl, I realize are lesbians but they are both very seductive and I can only wish I was thirty years younger ..."

Dimas tried to close his mouth on the older man's fantasy. "Well thank you, Mr. Koch, if we need anything further, someone will contact you."

Dimas went over to Zeke and in a low tone, "Let's do the prelim on this, these girls are going scott free, thanks to the next door neighbor's story."

Zeke knew his brother's level of potential love affection, "Hey, Dee, you want to make time with Alicia? She is one hot tamale. In her state of condition, she would welcome an older, hot blooded, Hispanic in her bed.

Attempting to fend off the obvious as he felt very well that Zeke knew his sexual temperature, pushed it off, "Zeke, I got a squeeze in someone."

'Who, that broad in East Memorial?"

"Now you are the one that sounds like a Mexican owl", laughing and slapping his brother on the back.

"My gut is that your honey is that tall, platinum blond, blue-eyed, hunk of tanned drink of water."

"You got that 'Z', she is the one. I have waited for such a long time for someone like that to come into my life."

"Not wanting to bust your lovesick bubble, do you want to go arrest Kolezy, or have HPD get all the credit?"

The Lieutenant came back to earth for that moment, "Let's put that bastard, son of a bitch, behind bars until he gets the needle. Luka, his house boy, and Galgany in Vegas have turned over on him. So much for being Mr. Attorney of the Year! We'll round up his friends, Dimitri and Drago to help him cope with the life of a con."

Zeke concurred and said, "We need to get the girls' statement to seal the whole thing."

Adam at that time, brushed past the yellow tape.

The men in blue yelled to stop, but he disregarded it as he was only concerned with the well-being of Melanie.

Rich flashed his CIA badge at the same policeman and rushed into the carnage before the blue had the chance to find out that the credentials were marked 'retired'. As the cop thought of it, Tanski and the rest skinned through and joined the scene. Although being a Viet Nam vet and being in the middle of a lot of death, he gasped at the sight of the immense amount of blood smeared around the living area. "Oh damn, look at all this shit. It reminds me of olden times over in Nam."

Murray shuddered at the sickening setting. Flashing back to Cleveland, almost two years ago, where he and his fellow Hungarians rescued their friend, Les and his family. Murray was not subjected to seeing the men he helped get killed, in that bloody battle. Tanski and Sev did the shooting. The police came in and wrapped up what was left of the bad guys. He was the cardboard cutout with a gun he did not fire. Everything was tied up neatly and they all flew back on the Gulfstream, celebrating their victory and congratulating one another on their bravado. Looking at the medical examiner now, shooting a series of photos on the bullet riddled Tibor, made him wish he was back in the arms of Sheryl, in his button down, uncomplicated world. He knew he had to move on with his promise to Adam and the involvement of Bill, Rich, and the others. He could not quit now.

Bill was at a loss, serving in the U.S. Army, in Viet Nam, knowing what death meant. He was reminded, once again, of something he wished to forget.

Sev and Ernie only looked, lustfully, in their own ways, both Melanie and Alicia, totally ignoring Tibor's dead body only twenty feet away.

Brian's stomach began to turn at the ghastly sight. He attempted to close his eyes and pretend to the others that all this did not bother him. He could not take more and bolted from the crime scene joining the onlookers and curious who were trampling the lawn.

In each of their minds they were there for support. It was Adam's show with his sister and her lover.

Bill knew what he was thinking. "Anth, are you going to be okay?"

Murray looked at his longtime friend, softly, answering, "Yeah, Billy, I will be."

They found the Cavazos brothers taking statements from Melanie and Alicia. Adam was starting to cuddle his sister attempting to relief her stress.

Adam tenderly asked her, "Mel, are you okay?"

Still in total shock, bleary eyed, "Oh, Adam, this is an unbelievable nightmare, but if I had to do it over again, I would shoot that cocksucker, again and again. It was all due to Louis. Tibor deserved to die and I tried to kill our stepfather. I don't wish to go to jail. It was self-defense."

Lieutenant Cavazos was listening from afar and decided to step in, "Yeah, 'Darlin', you are right on, self-defense all the way AND you have a neighbor, Mr. Koch, who can back that up. He will testify to what happened," as Dimas looked her over head to toe and internally wanted a piece of her, himself. "Can't see you wearing jail orange. Let me get some brief information from both you and your girlfriend."

Melanie was caught off guard on his calling Alicia her 'girlfriend', yet it fit. Was it that obvious to the police that she was living the life of a lesbian? It did not matter; she loved Alicia and even envisioned Adam joining in.

Adam asked the cop, "Dimas, do you feel we need a lawyer?"

Zeke strolled up, and wanted to get into the action, "Bro. I cannot see these nice gals needing an attorney. Let's get the usual statements of self-defense, file it and let them be to themselves." It took all of ten minutes for the Sergeant to write down what happened and with the neighbor's version it all coincided. "These gals are innocent. It's a 'No Bill'. You can bring some legal person down to Reisner Street when you are able." The two brothers left to go after Kolezy.

Dimas turned to Zeke as they were passing the throng of lookers and news people, "Let's head over to our legal eagle after obtaining an arrest warrant and see what hospital he went to take care of his wounds."

As the scene was being wrapped up, Murray and others started to disperse, allowing privacy for the two women, along with Adam.

Bill spoke up. "There's nothing we can do here, guys, let's head back to my office.

Adam thanked each of them for their presence support, as they walked out.

Turning to his sister, "Mel, this place is a mess for now, until everything is cleaned up how about my place in Memorial for you and Alicia."

Alicia was ready, eyeing a tight butt. "Adam, that sounds so, so great, maybe you and I and Melanie can get together for a ménage troi. We only would require one bedroom." Tonguing her lips.

Adam knew better, "Alicia, I have known for a long time that my sister and you are, as one would say, an 'item'?"

Alicia was up to the task, "Yes, Melanie and I are deeply involved and in love. That probably is not news to you, as you have thought for a while that your sexy sister is extremely a burning bush in bed. Have you had a taste of that, my hard dicked, brother-in-law to be?"

Adam wanted to counter, "That is wonderful, Alicia. You should meet Brian. He flew back with us from Las Vegas. Brian is unsure on what he wants to do and until then he will be sharing some time with me. Brian is available. He is a 'hard dick'. For your information, Melanie and I have not shared anything more than a plate of nachos at Ninfa's. Sorry to disappoint you."

Alicia, lovingly cast her dark eyes at Melanie, seeing that they would continue to have their close relationship. She was still curious about Melanie's brother. "You mean, Adam, we may not be catching you and this Brian in your own relationship sharing the same sock drawer?"

Looking at the long, dark haired, young woman, Adam tried to refrain from blushing but returned a volley toward her. "Alicia, it is not like you and my sister sharing the same bra and panty drawer.

Brian needed a change of climate and is really not my type. I have chosen a new avenue to go, leaving the old one behind. I believe he had enough of this and went outside. You can go out and judge for yourselves."

Alicia let one more shot over his bow, like she did as a former Navy WAVE. "Adam, I bet you would look good in one of my black satin thongs that has a zipper in the right spot or do you already have one of those?"

Adam laughed a little, "What do you think? After all, I have a company that sells nice items that even women like to purchase. I used to try on all of the naughties, but that got old and it is a new way for me now. Would you like a new set of them?"

Melanie elbowed her brother, "Okay, you two love birds, cut it out or I may become jealous. How is this Brian, in the sack, Adam?"

"Maybe the two of you should ask Brian, and see where that leads. I am going for the straight life, not with Brian as he needs to make friends here and circulate. The two of you would be perfect to introduce him around, as I will. "

Melanie persisted, "You never answered me. How good is he?"

Raising his hands as in a fend off, "Whew, gentlemen don't gossip about it. Would I ask how is it for each of you after a roll on The Sealy Posturepedic? Let's head to my place after you gather up your satin thongs in the bra and panty drawer, and meet Brian."

Murray, along with his trusted crew, began formulating the plans to finish off Kolezy and The Hungarian Mafia, in the event that they slipped through the HPD net that was starting to tighten around the motley bunch.

As they began to lay out the details, Murray's cell phone rang. He knew it was not Sheryl as he had spoken earlier to her upon returning from Hobby Airport, and later on the murder scene in the Energy Corridor. Sheryl, with their friend, Renate Roberts, were on their way to Austin where the Robert's daughter, Julie, and son-in-law, Warner, were attending The University of Texas. Sheryl had planned on being up there for almost a week which was a blessing for Murray, knowing that his wife was in safe hands and away from all the commotion of their continuing adventure.

The call was from Michaeleen Ventura. "Hey, Michaeleen, this is a nice surprise. What's up?"

She wanted to meet with Murray that afternoon for lunch.

"Well certainly, I can meet you at Rudi Lechner's at 1:00. Sheryl is going to be in Austin, seeing our youngest, Karen. I can make it for a late lunch. Is it good news?"

She whispered, "It is something very personal which requires a detailed explanation. It might be better if Sheryl was not there."

That last part stunned Murray, thinking why not have his wife there? "Okay, Michaeleen I will make the reservations." As he hung up the phone, something told him it was going to be involving Carol Sue.

Louis, bleeding from the gunshot wounds, needed to seek immediate medical attention. He could not chance going to a hospital, knowing the police would be checking for him. He had a long forgotten childhood friend from Hungary, Doctor Anton Horvath, who would help him. Unable to reach his friend at his office, he sought safe refuge at his secret midtown apartment that Luka shared with his friend, Janos. There he would get temporary self-medical bindings until seeing Horvath. He would be able to get another gun at the apartment.

After self-administering his wounds, he left and drove to Horvath's home now, in the early evening. Kolezy was driving furiously to get there as his wounds were bleeding again. Doctor Anton Horvath, who was also friends with Ilona and her late husband, immigrated to America first to Boston and then to Houston. He became a noted internist with a successful practice in the city's famed medical center. Louis pointed the Beemer in the direction of the doctor's home in the upscale, Rice University area of Houston, home to many professors, doctors, and would be millionaires. Upon arriving at the two story, ivy covered, Victorian home, he knocked heavily on the solid oak door.

The doctor was in. "Yo estate, kevon, Kolezy, Litchie," greeted a surprised Dr. Horvath. "Welcome to my humble home, my good friend, who I have not heard from in, how long, ten years?" He spotted the red stained wounds, on his arm and side.

Losing blood and starting a woozie state, he stammered, "Anton, you must help me", looking up at the large, gray bearded man standing 6'5" and weighing nearly 250 pounds.

Upon viewing hundreds of similar wounds in emergency stopovers in Boston and surrounding cities as well as in Texas, Horvath knew they were from a gunshot. "Who shot you, Louis?" as he ushered in the unexpected patient, peering out to see if anyone had seen him arrive at the home. "Come to my private office where I can tend to your injuries."

Kolezy, in a rare moment, started to confess to his friend from those youthful days in and around Budapest as the doctor looked at his wounds.

Horvath started to go back to those early days, "Yes, I recall, as a young boy, we swam in the Tesareas, not as large as the Danube but much cleaner."

Kolezy, remembered his excursion back in 2006. "My friend, it has become much polluted, as I went back there two years ago."

Horvath was curious, "Why did you go back there? I recall, all your family was gone. I believe you did not have any reason or is it your way to close your youthful days with Vargo and Nagy?"

"Yes, Anton, I went to see our fun spot and tried to see if Vargo and Nagy were still in the area. Vargo lived in Mackrunsh in the north section. I did not follow him and Nagy relocated to Bavaria, Germany with a frulein named, Martha."

Horvath, wistfully recalled the early days, "Vargo, Nagy, you and I, swam naked in those clean clear waters, when our minds were uncluttered and pure. Then he viewed the wounds, "Well the bullets are superficial and only a tissue wounds. Cleaning and bandaging them will take care of it. I will swab out the impurities adding the medicine to make positive you will not be infected and there will be healing."

Kolezy was very appreciative to his old and trusted friend. "What can I say, thanking you is not enough," acting somewhat ashamed and looking down.

Horvath felt the official part of the law. "You wish to tell me about all this? You, surely being a friend of the court, definitely know what I am compelled to do by law. I must report the gunshot to the authorities."

"Anton, I did not know where to turn. Nem tu tem. You will see the nightly news and know what all this is about."

Horvath probed as he would in his profession, seeking the reason why someone was ill or had a disease. He felt that his old friend had a disease. "Our deep friendship precludes any news at five or ten o'clock."

"Well, Anton, back in our childhood at the River. You and Vargo."

"Louis, I pushed that back in my memory. We were adolescents at the time. Innocence prevailed. Boyish pranks. My life and mind became different after leaving our homeland. You, as well, my friend. Did you really leave that chapter of your life behind?"

Kolezy for an instant had a guilty moment sweep across his mind, sparked by anxiety as to how his life turned to those numerous dark chapters over the years. Not having a comeback, only a feign moment, "I recall the time you were in that house near Andrassy Street with Vargo after an afternoon of swimming with him. He had that brief swimsuit on and you..."

"Louis, what is past is another forgotten chapter in our young life. I did not have those feelings. Since you insist on recalling those insignificant moments, I cannot understand why? Perhaps, your thoughts are actually of your own guilt. Not mine of a distant time where we frolicked. What is all this leading to? You appear to want to unburden yourself on some issues." With that Anton finished with the two dressings.

Kolezy thought he had the upper hand, "Anton, you need not be concerned, I will not contact your family or the medical community of your early indiscretions. For that, you will not turn me in to the police."

Horvath began to think that Louis was using him and bluffing his past knowledge of a useless, youthful, painless past they both encountered. "Just what have you done, Louis, which caused all this?" The doctor's temples bulged, breathing heavily.

Looking serenely at the doctor, "My life has not been exemplary as yours. The innocence of my own youthful indiscretions escalated after we departed Budapest. This requires the unburdening of my conscience to someone from the early years. Why I made these decisions, I can somehow, cleanse, as my colleagues say, 'Wipe the slate clean'."

Horvath could not put the current issue and the one in the past in the right category. Shaking his head and wanting to know more, "Louis, why now?"

Kolezy touched his left bandaged arm, "It could be the end for me. Yet, I will not go down easy. There have been many atrocities committed."

Horvath was not totally convinced of any major crimes even with the wounding of his childhood friend. "All can be rectified, correct? As The Lord has told us, 'There is no sin committed that cannot be forgiven'."

Louis began to smile and nod as though his friend had given him absolution. He then came back to reality. "If the sins were mere mortal and a priest wanted to hear my confession, it would be impossible to have me enter the gates of heaven." He peered downward and closed his eyes." I have raped, embezzled from my own firm, committed murder, and failed to render services to my clients, who are now in prison. I ruined my competitors, attempted to kill my eldest stepson, and did murder his brother," now spouting out without any prompting.

Dr. Horvath stirred uneasily, as he fell back in a chair listening intently to Kolezy. What if he was planning on confessing all this guilty life then decided to murder him in some fiendish ritual, after all, no one was aware that Kolezy was even there. His housekeeper was gone for the evening. His wife was in France visiting their daughter and her fiancé. Troubled, the doctor could not chance that Louis might harm him. Thinking, if he probed his injured friend, would he be better for it? "Louis, are you feeling well enough to travel? I will give you enough percon demurral for the pain and dressings for the time."

Kolezy turned the table, "Anton, I require that you accompany me. I promise you that I will not harm you. I have to go to Budapest tonight, or at the latest, tomorrow. You will continue to tend to my wounds. After that you can return to Houston."

Now believing he was in danger, Horvath's heartbeat, deeply, "Louis, I implore you. It is impossible as my patients need me tomorrow. How can my housekeeper know what to do if I am not here to tell her the duties? What about my wife, when she returns and finds me gone, what will she think?"

Kolezy casually ignored his friend's pleas and reached into his slightly blood stained Bill Blass slacks, retrieving a vial of a white substance, taking a pinch of it, he sniffed it up the right nostril and then to the left giving off a surprised but pleasant look on his half shaven face. Then he reeled in his chair for a few moments, as though to come back to Horvath's question. The doctor's mind was ablaze with confusion on his issue. Now, he had a wounded druggie on his hands, wanting to flee to Hungary.

"Louis, how are you planning to go to our homeland? I am positive that the police are waiting at the airports."

Kolezy, still in a nanno second haze, looked at Anton, "I am going to phone my people who will come and run interference for us. You will drive my BMW and meet up with them if this area around Rice University is impassable."

At that time, as the television was on but the sound considerably lowered already tuned to Channel 77 with the roving reporter, Tom Zizka, announcing the day's events surrounding the shooting of Tibor Szilanyi. Horvath picked up the remote to increase the volume on what Tom was saying. "Earlier today, there was a shooting at The Eldridge Town Homes off Memorial Drive. A Eastern European man was shot by a distraught woman protecting herself and her roommate. Witnesses, notably the next door neighbor, a devout Jewish man named, Jerry Koch, gave a blow by blow detail as to what led to and during and after the alleged break in by a Tibor Szelanyi and Louis Kolezy. Melanie Magassey, the step-daughter of Houston's high profile attorney, Louis Kolezy, reportedly, shot Szelanyi numerous times. Kolezy was also shot and fled the scene in his BMW. Based on Mr. Koch's eyewitness to the break in and shooting, the attorney and dead man were at the townhome in an attempt to abduct the women. Further, Kolezy is a person of interest for a murder in The Montrose area, where Houston Police found the body of Mark Carlson in an empty field. Louis B. Kolezy, was last seen at Eldridge and Memorial driving a late model BMW with Texas personal plate, 'ATRNY 1'. Houston police asked that if you have any leads to this killing and the whereabouts of Louis B. Kolezy, that you call 713-HPD-0000. In other news...the cost of a tank of gas..." With that Horvath clicked off the flat screen. Turning to his old friend, shocked by the news...

A blank look swept across his face as Kolezy knew Horvath was going to lay into him. "We have both come a long way, Louis, in my heart as a physician and you as a prominent attorney. Yet, you need treatment for more than your gunshot wounds. You need to seek others skilled in assisting your mental problems. It is impossible that I accompany you to the airport as I am vital here to my family and the community. I cannot go to Budapest. You will have enough medicine that I will give you and after you arrive in Hungary, I am assured you can seek the follow up medical needs there."

Kolezy's face reddened with anger that his friend would not leave with him. As he began to rebut Anton's statement, the back door of the kitchen slammed and a voice rang out in broken English of a European woman, "Hello, Dokter Hervath, are you here, sir?" It was Hannah, the housekeeper and cook. "I have returned from vizithing my neece in Alvin. Are you hungry?"

Kolezy was slightly confused, "Who is that, Anton?"

"My housekeeper, Hannah. She is a longtime friend from Szeged."

Kolezy sneered, "I wonder if she knows Ilona's late aunt, the Queen of Paprika?"

Anton did a double take, "What?"

Kolezy shook his head negatively, "Forget it; I do not care about Szeged. If you do not go, she dies! "Meghalt, krual, Hanou"

Horvath's eyes popped, disgusted at Kolezy's ultimatum, "Disno!"

Kolezy reveled, "You look down upon me and call me a dirty pig! How can you? Do as I say, she is nem to dem." At that point he reached into a nearby jacket and pulled out a .22. "It may be small but it is mighty. One or two shots in the heart and Hannah dies instantly."

Horvath backed down as he had little choice in the matter, "Put the gun away, alright?"

They began to go outside the doctor's office from where the housekeeper threw off her coat and began a systematic dinner without any regard to an answer, as they passed her in the kitchen. Kolezy saw her large buttock and wanted to squeeze it but only blurted out, "Yo estae, Hannah, hood von?"

She knew by the brogue he was of her area, " Elig, You, feum." Hannah was a full figured woman, in her 60's, gray haired, with lines across her face, as she had taken on more than the normal woman in combating the number of times she had to haul her husband out of many a bar and cabaret, shit faced and puking. One of those women, who did not wish to divorce her unfaithful man, only to bring shame and disgrace to her and her family, but to admit she was not able to hold onto him as a female should.

Kolezy had slipped his coat over the bandaged area. Hannah never suspected any wrong doing.

Alute nem, Hannah!" voiced Louis.

Hannah, looked at Kolezy, "It iz too early for bedtime. Vould you and the Doktor enjoy a late night meal of my Hungarian stuffed cabbage and noodles in butter or hudka and galuska vith steamed potatoes?

Remember, too, Doktor Hervath ve have that special vintage Tokay vine you have chilled in the vine room. That would go vit thiz meal."

Horvath was wishing that the housekeeper would shut her mouth and not become a potential victim that Tom Zizka spoke about on his newscast as the backbone of that Channel 77 network television outlet. The doctor found a way to get his housekeeper away from the Grim Reaper of Kolezy, "Hannah, better yet, please go over to Spec's Liquors over on Shepherd and pick up three or four bottles of Romany Merlot, vintage 2006."

Kolezy knew his friend wanted the housekeeper out of the home and figured it would be easier since she was not aware of his being wanted.

Hannah removed her apron from her ample girth, then stopped," I theenk you vould be better to go vith the Tokay, sir." She turned to Kolezy, "You, sir, Jo' este't."

Kolezy replied, "E's maga. Also, a good night, Hannah."

Momentarily, Hannah knew something was different with Doctor Horvath.

The doctor looked at Kolezy, then to his housekeeper. "No, I insist, we have an account over at that store so go now, please!"

She really did not wish to go, but decided, due to her employer's tone, to do as he wished. "Okay, as they zay in Amerika, "You're the doktor!" With that she hustled, apron less with her trench coat on, out the door.

Horvath had a relaxed feeling. "Alright, Louis, I will go with you but let me pack a few items for the trip and more medicine for your wounds, also, to leave a note for Hannah."

"I'll come with you, Anton, to your bedroom and back to your office."

"What, Louis, you don't trust me?"

"It is that and I want to leave quickly before she returns and if she had any suspicions that might lead her to summon the police. Even if that is not the case, you would not wish her harmed. Correct, Anton?"

Horvath had thought of escaping but that idea disappeared quickly.

As they ascended up the stairs to the master bedroom Horvath knew what he needed to do. Upon entering the suite he left Kolezy to look at family pictures on the wall as he went into the closet to pull a suit case off the shelve. There concealed behind the case was a loaded .45 automatic pistol. He brought it out, confronting Kolezy. "Louis, leave my home immediately!"

Kolezy's eyes popped wide open as his mouth dropped. "Anton, you really have surprised me tonight. First, deftly getting Hannah out of the home. Now pulling out that gun. I don't believe you would shoot me. How would you explain to the authorities that you bandaged me up and then gunned me down?"

Confident now, clicking the automatic, the doctor strode two paces toward the crooked, murderous lawyer, "Easy, my former, good friend, you held me under duress while I attended to your wounds and when you became aggressive, I killed you. And...Louis, I will do that. So kindly turn around, do not reach for your weapon, and move out of my home, NOW!"

Kolezy did not have any choice and started to go out and move toward the stairs with Horvath behind him. He wanted to reach back and hurl the doctor down the steps but his injuries were too new and would open up, so he obeyed. As they reached the foyer and front door, he stopped. "You are correct, Anton, I should not involve you. I thank you for binding me up. Will you at least give me until sundown before turning me in?"

"You have seen too many John Wayne movies, Louis. Get in your car and leave to turn yourself in to the police. I won't wait until sunset."

Grimly, Kolezy turned, leaving the home and got into his car. As he sped off, Hannah returned with the wine.

Murray pulled into the crowded parking lot at Houston's famous Rudi Lechner's German and Austrian Restaurant on Gessner, in West Houston. He scheduled to meet Michaeleen at 1:00pm for lunch and was running a few minutes early. Searching the lot he found her 2008 silver Mercedes sedan with personalized license plate, VNTURA, and parked next to it. With everything going on and Sheryl safely away, his thoughts turned to their young benefactor. Her phone call was strange. It was almost as though she was planning to relate a bottled up problem and wished to unburden herself. There was a deep sense of urgency in her voice, unlike anything she previously ever revealed. As he entered the front of the restaurant, Rudi met him at the greeter's stand. He shook his hand, while pointing to a booth in the corner of the restaurant where Michaeleen was just being served by Rudi's best waitress, Greta. He approached Greta, a longtime friend, and gave the slender, blondish woman a hug, ordering a gin and tonic, the favorite house cocktail.

Greta Kleyhons, with her husband, the late Hans Kleyhons came to Houston from Austria and at one time owned a European restaurant in northern Houston. When that became more than they could handle, the couple sold the establishment. Rudi knew of their experience and hired Greta. Hans became ill and could not work for many years prior to his death. This day, though, Greta pulled Murray aside, "Miss Ventura, has been here for about an hour and is working on her fourth dry martini. She has been crying as well, it appears. I don't want to be a busy body, but maybe with you being here now, she will be more relaxed."

Murray had to manage a laugh at the 'more relaxed' part of Greta's view, as having four dry martinis which were almost like doubles at Rudi's. It would cause anyone to float away without a care. Murray experienced that same vision years back and swore off that drink. That memory seemed to increase his fear of Michaeleen's apparent problem.

He came up to Michaeleen as she looked up at him. He knew from her red eyes that something was very wrong. Touching her with an easy, almost tickle to show he was there for her. As he seated himself across from her, with a candle between them, she clutched her drink. Looking for some consoling words on a yet to be known apparent problem the young CEO had gnawing at her. "I guess it is my turn to come to your rescue, if it is at all possible. It is apparent that you are in a quandary. You are such a strong and vibrant woman, but if I can be of assistance in this hour in need it will take precedence over this Kolezy thing."

Michaeleen layed her right hand on his, which was slightly cold from her holding the continuous round of martinis. "I apologize for all this, Anthony."

An alarm went off, as she always addressed him as Murray, once she really became acquainted with Sheryl and him. Murray attempted to shrug off her saddened and borderline overwrought condition. "Hey, kiddo, that is okay, honest. You do need to tell me what all of this is about, so I can get in with both hands and feet to solve your situation."

"First, Anthony, I heard Tom Zizka's report on Melanie Magassey's killing one of Kolezy's Hungarian Mafia and that the crooked attorney was with him and was shot as well. You most likely, were there?"

Murray then related the events from details that were not in the news.

Michaeleen stammered, "I cannot think of a more troubled family than the Magassey's, although what I am about to say to you could ..."

At that moment Greta came to deliver his gin and tonic. The experienced woman looked with concern at the young gal sitting there and did not want to offer her any more to drink. "Will it be a few moments before ordering lunch?"

Murray thanked her for his beverage, "This is a great gin and tonic, Maurillo, the bartender, can really whip up a good one. Give us some time on the food, Ok, Greta?"

In a mood breaking effort she encouraged, "Yes, no hurry, the band will start soon and liven up everyone's table."

Michaeleen knew from her comment that Greta was attempting to cheer up the young woman. "Yes, we shouldn't be maudlin over things. Thank you, very much, Greta."

Murray was waiting for the young woman he had grown to know the past three plus years, to explain what was going on and wanted to tell him. Was she pregnant by a Casanova he did not know about and ditched her because of it? Not possible as Michaeleen was too tough to be crying over some a-hole walking out.

As she relaxed in her chair, taking the three olives out, the sometimes tough as nails, young woman, cleared her throat looking over at another table where two would be lovers were gazing at one another. "I have a very difficult item to face, still stirring her drink. "Family like in Adam's case is important; it is to me as well. I wanted to tell you about this as I totally value your opinion and friendship. It is about my mother and father."

"Michaeleen, I am not sure what you are trying to explain to me, your mother was very special. I did not know your father or what type of a man he was."

Her uncharacteristic approach to this left Murray greatly puzzled. But she began, again, with tears in her eyes, fidgeting with the silverware "Actually, ah, well, you see my dad, the one who raised me, Brett James, he was around my mother. Brett adopted me as she told me that my father was elsewhere. Then she and Brett were killed in a car accident outside Burkburnette. Carol Sue, took over as my guardian and raised me."

He thought, 'Why was it Burkburnett, again? Did her real father come back into her life? Actually, he was acting as though she owed him an apology for allowing him to believe Bobbie Jean was her mother. He asked. "Whatever happened to your real father?"

Before she could answer, Murray's cell phone rang. He attempted to disregard it as Michaeleen was attempting to make her point. The ringing stopped and began again, causing her to become frustrated with explaining an important issue with him. He glanced at the caller ID it was Carol Sue. He hesitated in answering and then it stopped. His thoughts ran by him, it kept hammering that Michaeleen had a step father. 'Who was her father?' That may have eliminated that one in a 100,000 chance of his impregnating Bobbie Jean. This time Michaeleen's phone rang. Speak of the devil. It was Carol Sue.

The girl was too fraught with tension as she answered." Hi, what's up?" Her eyes narrowed "What! Of course, I'm alright. Sitting here with Anthony. Yes, Murray, as you call him. We're at Rudi Lechner's on Gessner. You want me to come over to your place in East Memorial. NO, I have not been kidnapped. Nor even an attempt. What is this all about?"

Murray's views of adoption and Bobbie Jean disappeared at that moment, as his heart began to pound excited that maybe Kolezy was on the loose and attempting to take hostages. His thoughts ran ramped.

Michaeleen remained silent listening to the one sided conversation from Carol Sue. The CEO of Ventura Oil was at an impasse and just replied, "I am coming over right now."

Murray wanted to know. "What was going on?"

She looked up at Murray, "Anthony, I have to leave and see her, at the East Memorial home. We will have to table this for another time. She needs me, desperately!"

Murray got up threw a Franklin on the table, and at the same time, leaving the restaurant, grabbed Michaeleen's arm. "What did Carol Sue tell you that caused you to be so upset?"

"She, she, received a message on her cell that someone took me and was holding me for ransom. She thought the voice on the phone had a foreign accent. Possibly, a Hungarian."

Murray began to put things together, "No, wait, it sounds like a trap. We need to get Bill and Rich on this. Before that, I need to call Lieutenant Cavazos and his brother, Zeke, to get over to East Memorial." With that he hastily dialed up the Lieutenant.

"Lieutenant, Kolezy is planning to go over to Carol Sue's place in East Memorial."

Cavazos responded, "You are too late, I am on my way to her place now. Gotta run."

Murray thought that was a quick response by the Lieutenant. "He's already on it, heading to her mansion in Memorial."

Michaeleen looked at him as they were getting in their respective cars, "Don't you realize the two of them are very close and she contacted him immediately then called us?"

Murray understood but wanted to come back to what the young woman wished to bestow on him in the bistro. "I know we want to head over to her place but you had wanted to tell me something that was urgent and now... Let's take my Enclave and you can tell me on the way."

Michaeleen only declined. "I'll go by myself, we have to be alone and not in a situation like this. Right after the supposed danger is over. I promise, although this incident may explain it all."

Murray was confused by her statement and wanted to delve into it but she raced to her car, hit the starter and sped off. He then dialed Bill and explained the latest probable Kolezy plot. St. George agreed to round up Rich and Tanski and head over to Carol Sue's Memorial mansion and meet his friend there. Sev and Ernie were alerted and were going there, in a separate SUV.

What about Adam? He thought. He then phoned the young man thinking that since Carol Sue was more than a buyer of MABB that he would want to be told as well. Adam was caught off guard by the possible maneuver of his stepfather, yet knew it was the Hungarian Mafia way to do things.

"Murray, we'll be right over to East Memorial, Brian and I will go there now."

Kolezy was still aching from his near fatal shooting ordeal but had the pain pills to bridge himself through it and to pursue his plans to kidnap Carol Sue. After calling his men, they met at a parking lot north of East Memorial near Voss Road. Dimitri and Drago pulled up with Joe Molnar, who had been bailed out by them earlier. A stressed out, Gabor Szilanyi, now learning of his brother's killing and wanting to seek retribution against anyone connected to Melanie. Gabor believed that Carol Sue was behind it, even though her only connection was with the therapist, Kerry Yanek. He believed the psychotherapist was the catalyst using Melanie, who thought of starting a new life away from Kolezy. This fueled additional hatred for her stepfather and anyone employed by him.

Dimitri also had an update on another operative, "Louis, we have someone else we can count on, Lupe Perez. He is a coyote, bringing in illegal's to work in Houston restaurants.'

Gabor shook his head, "Damn, Perez. Luka is in jail but might get out. Drago had Bela Kiroly, our good attorney who thinks the State has a weak case against Luka and will release him on his own. My brother is dead. Galgany, well .... What can you say? Now we are down to a Mexican landscaper who may be married to some gypsy woman to qualify for our Hungarian group? Louis, have we sank that low?"

Kolezy had enough on his mind and shrugged, 'What are you talking about?"

"He might be a fuckin illegal that screwed some gypsy bitch and is passing himself off as a new Hunky. So we are down to six Hungarians, now that we have Molnar, and a Mexican who cannot speak our language?"

Kolezy had enough, "We must forget about Perez, He can be our driver and we can abduct the women and take them to Budapest, but we need to proceed."

Drago was elated. "Bela sprung Luka and our boy is at that Winter's home. He texted me that she and that therapist are together. Yes, we must quickly go there and take them."

Kolezy drifted into his childhood. "Yes, I want to be back in my old home outside of Budapest and have those memories with me. The ripe pickings of those East German women attempting to make up for the shortage that came to them as The Wall came down. Now they are like prostitutes."

Dimitri was overly concerned, "Louis, I don't' have an abundance of forints to bring in those women."

Kolezy reared his head and was enjoying it all in, "Don't be concerned, Dimitri, we have a unlimited supply of Hungarian and United States currency that is in our vault on Andrassey street, in Budapest, near one of our clubs. Oh, Dimitri, I dreamt of being there now. Dipping into the Danube and being in the arms of my beloved."

Drago nudged Kolezy, "Hey, Louis, we need to go to that woman's home."

"Kolezy agreed, "You are right and I am reliving as a, lofus, a dumb ass, about the past. Let's swiftly journey out, now!"

At that time, Carol Sue and Kerry were enjoying a Macallan single malt scotch together.

Kerry was an adopted stepdaughter of Bobbie Jean when Carol Sue's sister, was married to Brett James.

After the car accident where he and Bobbie Jean perished, Donna, the mother of Carol Sue, took it upon herself to raise Kerry, as her own. Donna did this until the girl finished both undergraduate and graduate school, turning out to be quite a woman. Smart, intuitive, and very knowledgeable. Carol Sue toasted Kerry. "You helped so many people", as she sipped down another scotch on the rocks.

The long legged woman only smiled as she raised her glass to Carol Sue, "You have done very well, yourself, raising your own two children, and two that were not your own, Bobbie Jean's own flesh and blood. Michaeleen, who has grown so much and a head of two companies, while her brother, David, is a lost soul, somewhere. He is not your fault."

Carol Sue was struck by that as she also raised her glass. "Yes, I was deeply saddened by his disappearance. David has changed his name, took his inheritance, vowing to turn his back on all of us. He blamed everyone for the death of his friend, Lauren, who worked for my father, Tex Miller. David also had that secret life of drugs. Michaeleen tried in vain to have her brother seek help for his addiction to whatever." Carol Sue, at that point, closed her eyes, placing her drink down. "I was totally devastated by David's disappearance." Choking back the tears, Kerry offered her a handkerchief, she continued, "In a way I see the same traits in Adam Magassey. His addiction was sexual, but he raised himself out of that and assured me and Murray of wanting to go the straight life. Now I've heard that Adam may have a young man from Las Vegas. Murray desperately wanted me to cougar Adam, who was actually a joy in bed." She smiled coyly on that.

Kerry was peeked in interest, "OH? Can you relate me some intimate details," showing a look of raising anticipation of the juicy womanly gossip.

Carol Sue liked to embellish some of the reality. "He ripped my clothes off and had a pair of handcuffs ready. I was not positive which way to go. He threw me down on the bed and 'cuffed' my hands behind me. I was helpless and whispering to him, to not hurt me. He asked if I ever was dogged while unable to resist? I started to cry a little... while he stripped off all his clothes. He was very well endowed; at least, so help me, his dong was over eight inches at rest. "

Kerry, was extremely happy in her marriage to Jon, and did not require that type of spice in the bedroom. Certainly not this way out experience as she knew Carol Sue enjoyed exaggerating some of her over the top sexual adventures.

Suddenly, Carol Sue switched subjects, "I miss David...", as she turned a joyful moment to a sorrowful one.

Kerry, true to her profession, sprung to assess Carol Sue's mood. "Do you blame David's lost whereabouts, on Adam? Did you believe he was intimate with him? You related to me, one time, that Adam had a stable of young men, entertainment for high paid executives who were lonely. David being one of them?"

Defensively, "I never asked Adam during our fling if David actually worked for him. About six months ago, David, came over to my home and in a less than sober evening. He was feeling contrite for being a total butt head and confided in me about someone he knew in this adult business but never admitted any intimacy and they were only close. For some reason, David enjoyed solace in their relationship after losing Lauren. David did reveal that the man had a restaurant in

Montrose and was very well off."

Kerry was riveted on this, "How did David live? Inheritance? That could not last forever."

"After Bobbie Jean's death, both Michaeleen and he received a trust fund on their 21st birthdays. Until then they were under my money. The trust enabled each to receive $15million dollars. David went through most of it while Michaeleen used her money on lucrative investments and paved a way to marry Ventura and.... well, grab hundreds of millions. Yes, Michaeleen made the most of her inheritance. David pissed it away on cars, travel, art, jewelry, young naïve girls, and a bunch to some seedy men who wore gold medallions around their neck and in my opinion, around their dicks. Michaeleen, though, yes, a mother of a cute son and beautiful daughter and she dotes over them."

"You are obviously proud of her."

"Yes, as I am of Wes, my son, and talented daughter, K'Lynn. My very, very own." she hesitated looking at a family picture of Wes, his wife, Gina, their two children and K'Lynn. Then she snapped, "No, at first when Murray came to me on buying MABB from Adam, an adult business, I wanted to smash that kid. Ruin his fucking, beautiful ass, even though he may not have been the reason David was lost and he wasn't responsible for it. Just because of the business. The night at the Merriam that we were together, he told me of a young man, whose name was David and who he repeatedly attempted to turn to a straight path from wanton sex and drugs. Not knowing of my connection to David, Adam almost broke down telling me of his ways to convert him, but David was always pigheaded and would not change or listen as that inheritance blew him away. I think David is like his father, stubborn. I could not find Adam at fault, at that point. I wanted to buy MABB for whatever price Adam wanted and he was sooo great, Kerry, in the sack. I melted before him." She quickly switched subjects back to Michaeleen. "Now when I say obstinate, that is Michaeleen. They both have their dad's stubbornness."

Kerry was questioning that last part of Carol Sue's statement. "Brett was stubborn then? I thought he was pliable and laid back? And... he wasn't their biological father...like who was?"

Carol Sue thought for a half second and started to correct herself. "Oh, there were times; you know how men are, Kerry? Your own Jon can be that way. You know, not wanting to bend at times. Isn't that the way?"

Kerry looked at her adopted aunt. "But that Brett wasn't their father. Still I always pictured him as more passive, as I grew up." She then switched to another thought, "Then you have forgiven Adam?"

Carol Sue wanted to change the subject. "Ah, would you care for another scotch on the rocks?"

Just then a noise ensued in the rear of the home, near the kitchen.

Both women looked at one another, slightly startled at the sound.

Kerry was worried. "Didn't you say that you had that strange call about Michaeleen being kidnapped and you contacted your Lieutenant and he was coming over?"

"Yes, and so was Michaeleen but I figured it was a crank call. If it was from Louis Kolezy, he has most likely taken off because of that shooting that has been all over the news. He certainly would not risk coming to my home and threatening me. He has a lot more to be concerned about and I am not worried."

There was a thud and the sound of broken glass. Carol Sue's face turned pale with fright as she got up from her chair, joined by Kerry, as they froze in the room. Before Carol Sue could reach her purse for her twin pink .38's, Kolezy and Drago appeared with guns drawn.

Kerry's eyes widened. Her face wore a panic look.

Carol Sue now gained her composure and became angry, "Get out of here, immediately! We have called the police and they will be here at any moment!"

Although hurting somewhat, from his flesh wounds, but regaining his courtroom swagger, Kolezy managed to egotistically return her volley. "You have no idea, woman, whom you are addressing. You can be assured that no one will be coming to your rescue."

The fear of being subjected to his tortuous way, further left itself, as the memory of David and Kolezy's apparent involvement in his possible disappearance, pushed Carol Sue's will to fight him. "Don't flatter yourself, you ambulance chaser, I know who you are. Your face has been on every news channel. Only it was too bad that your stepdaughter missed hitting your worthless balls. You are a wanted man, besides being a horse's ass or lofus, in Hungarian. Lofus fits you, you damn dipstick! The police will hunt you down and you will wind up in Huntsville waiting for justice to be served!"

'Kolezy loved a fight from a woman who he considered a likely opponent against his fencing and desiring to patronize her. "You're a lovely and feisty woman. Very sensual and I cannot wait to be with you in every way possible, Vixey."

Carol Sue was deeply surprised at Louis' knowledge of her nickname, considering only those in Katy, twenty some miles away knew it and Murray who loved to tease her with it. No one in her upper crust circles of associates and friends were aware she had a more common life. "How did you know my alias?"

Kolezy, smugly, approached the women closely. "I know much about you and some about Ms. Yanek."

Kerry was studying his motives and ready to kick him in his groin if he attempted to accost either of them. "Mr. Kolezy, you are only a few steps away from being taken down. Carol Sue phoned the police and I would not be surprised if they were setting up and surrounding this home as we stand here wasting your time to depart in a hail of bullets."

"Are you feebly trying to scare me, Ms. Yanek? I will deal with you in good time. You have caused all this by dealing in lies about me to my wife and lovely Melanie."

"I am not afraid of your worthless intentions, Mr. Kolezy. I just freed the pent up spirit of Ilona and Melanie. I, as well, hoped your manhood, what it is worth, was severed. The day is not over with."

Kolezy ignored Kerry's statement. "As to knowing what some call you, Ms. Winters or Miller whichever you choose to use, I have been studying you since you chose to buy MABB from my beloved stepson, the eminent porn star who is attempting to be a CEO executive. A misplaced joke. But you lead two lives, how very interesting. A patron of the arts in East Memorial, driving a Cadillac Escalade and Mercedes. Then you switch to ride a motorcycle, driving a Corvette with a personalize plate, 'Vixey' on it. When we are alone you will be sipping Dom Perrier and munching on Beluga caviar."

He then turned his attention to Kerry. "And to my comely lass, the last time we met, it was all too brief," as he brushed lightly with his backhand on her lightly tanned face. "Again, you turned my wife and step daughter against me. You were so busy doing that, you had no time for your husband, Jon and son, Devan. I can attend to your needs. Now, we can adjourn to Ms. Winter's bedroom attending to one another's desires. I will reward you so that no matter how well your husband had performed, I will surpass your expectations by my outstanding actions."

Even though the current atmosphere was a little dire, Kerry had to cup her hand in front of her mouth in total amusement. "Don't flatter yourself, Mr. Kolezy. And, when was the last time you used mouthwash?"

Drago was angry at her rebuff of his master. "Lady, you are fortunate that you got away with your car at your office, or I would have beaten you and done a great harm to you as you are disrespectful to Louis."

Throwing her head back, Kerry, laughed out loud, "You were too out of shape to run after me. Not even a challenge."

Dimitri came in, wearing a worried look across his scared face. "The police are surrounding the area, Louis."

Kolezy's heart pounded, rapidly, as he walked to the front and peered out the front window, where he viewed three Houston Police cars and two more were joining them, "Where in the hell are Perez and Gabor?"

"They are by the cars in the back", Dimitri responded in a guttural tone.

"What are our chances of making it to the cars, Dimitri?"

Looking at Kerry and Carol Sue, "With these two women as hostages, the police won't shoot and we should get away."

Kolezy flashed a slight smile, "Good. The police certainly will not chance killing these two comely females. Ms. Winters are you on board?"

"You haven't been great at doing things correctly, Kolezy. Cannot figure you as the top attorney of the year. The way you have screwed up things, it would not surprise me that Kerry and I get our derrieres blown off."

Kolezy went up to her, touching her chin, "You better hope they don't shoot and hit your voluptuous asses. You two will be our shields."

Kerry mocked the three, "Big men, you need women to protect your worthless hides."

Kolezy pulled his Rugar automatic to check the clip. "If you don't believe they won't shoot you, I will, though."

At that warning the women sat back on the couch.

Meantime, Murray pulled up and climbed out of the Enclave as Bill, Rich, and Tanski arrived. The Cavazos brothers were already there preparing their officers. Harris County Sheriffs and deputies heard the call and sent two squad cars. Along with eight HPD cars and a swat team, they were prepared to take down the Hungarian Mafia.

After an exchange with the Harris County Sheriff, Lieutenant Cavazos declared loud and clear that he was in charge, along with Zeke as second in command. Quickly, Dimas dispatched a half dozen lawmen to the rear as he and Zeke with additional six were taking charge of the front.

Murray, St. George, Rich, and Tanski had their guns drawn waiting to cut down Kolezy. The Lieutenant did not want citizen bounty hunters horning in on his capture. "Murray, you and your band of men stay put. You are amateurs, who could screw up everything. We have plenty of fire power here and don't need a bunch of citizens shooting innocent folks."

Murray knew that the Lieutenant wanted the entire glory of bringing in Kolezy without their assistance.

Dimas blew out his warning, to his men, holding up his hands, "Remember, don't discharge your weapons unless it is necessary and I tell you to fire."

St. George almost began to tell Cavazos to go to somewhere, and then reconsidered in favor of a lighter comment. "Well, Lieutenant, I am sure that you don't want us to go 'bang, bang', right?"

"No, you damn Hungarians, I just am advising HPD. I don't want to kill innocent bystanders from you vigilantes shooting up the area!"

St. George just shrugged his shoulders, "Fine, Lieutenant, it is your show. If some 'citizen' gets shot it is on your watch, not ours."

The Lieutenant just ignored St. George and grabbed a bull horn, "You folks in that house. We are with the Houston Police Department. You are to come out one at a time, without your weapons and with your hands over your head!"

Just behind Cavazos were two more Houston Police squad cars that were not dispatched but wanted to get into the action and were in the neighborhood. To the rear of them was a silver SUV with Sev and

Ernie. Adam and Brian screeched in Adam's new BMW sedan. The former adult star quickly jumped out. Sev, semi amused at a quivering Brian who was slow in alighting from the vehicle. "Hey, boy, don't you wish to say "'Hi', to your father who is held up in that house?" Brian was unsuspecting of the new environment by the former Las Vegan resident and now exposed to the gentrified Texas area.

Brian blinked as though a giant light blasted in his face, being a novice on the Lone Star State's weather and other aspects of life. "Not really", in an almost inaudible voice.

Sev turned the knife a little, 'After all, Brian, he would love to see you and I really do mean 'love''

Brian stuttered, "I...I want you to...to kill that son of a bitch, bastard."

"Well, kid, that term fits another person here. One who hates Kolezy."

Brian realized who it was; after all, he was a damaged goods son, himself, done by the dishonored attorney, who now was on the run.

Ernie and Adam nudged up to Murray who was brandishing his five shot Taurus Judge. Adam volunteered, "Murray do you have another weapon I can use? If Louis gets past the Houston cops I want to blow his worthless son of a bitch away and not even give it a thought!"

Murray reached into a bag and brought out a semi-automatic .22 and handed it, loaded, to the bent on kill stepson, who seethed hate for his stepfather, as a worthless piece of manhood.

Before anything could take place, Lieutenant Cavazos interceded, "Murray you and your men stay out of the way. Just leave it to professionals. You don't want to get killed. Do you? I'll let you know when I actually need you." With that he strutted away, anticipating the capture of Kolezy.

Murray yelled out after Cavazos, "It appears that you believe twenty men will take down Kolezy and his gang. Lieutenant, it will take more than that!"

The Lieutenant scoffed and gave a gratuitous wave.

Murray thought otherwise, "You have what, six in the back, and the rest up here. I don't believe that Ms. Winters or Miller cares to have her front door shot up."

Zeke came to Dimas' rescue, "If you and the rest of these guys are trigger happy, we don't need that here. You are a group of wanna be vigilantes. If that by someone in a million chance Kolezy and his merry men come your way, take your best shot. Which if it happens, I won the Power Ball lottery."

Dimas liked it, "Well Bro that was sage advice."

Inside the large home, Kolezy was contemplating his next step for escaping.

Dimitri was dripping wet, worrying as he surveyed from the front window, seeing six police cars with the bubbles running and heavily armed swat officers taking their stances. "Louis, we should go out the back now as the police seem to be ready to storm the front of the home."

Drago, backed up his partner, "Yes, my mentor, our SUV's are parked in the rear of the house. We need to leave now!"

Kolezy concurred, "Alright, we will move to our cars and Dimitri, call Danika, our pilot, to ready the Falcon as we fly to Budapest."

Dimitri responded, "That damn woman is always trying to get me into bed."

Carol Sue thought that was hilarious, "You in bed with a woman? Ha!"

Dimitri was red faced. "Well, I have my moments."

Kolezy then turned to the two ladies, grinning with pride, "Have the two of you been to my beautiful city and viewed the lovely Danube, under the stars?"

Carol Sue, sarcastingly replied, "If it is anything like Houston and Buffalo Bayou, we can stay here, I have to figure, it is dark and murky, just like you."

Kerry giggled over that, "I have been there and parts of the city, while beautiful, are dark, dangerous, and full of people like you, Louis. A man in the shadows, beckoning young men to enter his house for no good."

Kolezy was stunned, "You know my city. Then when we all leave from the airport, completing our getaway from here, you will enjoy the fruits of all the pleasures bestowed by both men and women. I feel you would like to take full advantage of each."

Kerry was accustomed to many of her clients confidentially spewing out some unusual fantasies, but not involving her. "I am very content to have you release us at the airport as you disembark for your destination."

"No, I think both of you women, with long, limbs and slender bodies would enjoy my 'friends' as they will want you. I can almost promise that they won't even eat you...very much and those young men, yes, they will be beckoned to enter my home and you can watch, and even partake in it."

Kerry wanted to look at Carol Sue for reaction but dared not and only stared out the back.

Suddenly Gabor came in brandishing a AK15 automatic rifle, as he anxiously waited for orders to start using it.

Outside, Murray, Bill, Rich, and Adam all were equally getting antsy for their concern about Carol Sue. Adam, even though he apparently had been overthrown by Carol Sue still had feelings for her. Did Murray? They were unaware that Kerry was an unexpected guest of Vixey.

As the guys were checking their ammunition, Michaeleen's Mercedes sedan came to a halt just behind the yellow ribboned crime scene. Out stepped, the harried young woman, ducking under the ribbon and past an unsuspecting rookie HPD policeman who was outmaneuvered by the determined young exec. "I attempted to call you, Anthony, but your cell phone did not answer."

Murray threw up his hands, "That damn cell phone company! Their towers must have had a burnout or something. I'm going to change to another provider after all this is done! Or whatever! Anyway, I know you are deeply, deeply worried about your aunt. Unfortunately, sweetheart, she is held hostage by Kolezy."

Michaeleen held her head, pleading to Murray, "Oh, no, no! Can't you do something about all this?"

The others viewed all this with surprised curiosity as to her mini fit.

Murray attempted to calm her down, grabbing both of her shoulders. "Lieutenant Cavazos and his men are going to take care of this and assure that Vixey, er, Carol Sue, and is not harmed."

Rich budded in, "Murray, Jon Irion, your pilot, is at the Sugar Land Airport. Two things. One, Kolezy has a Falcon F 7 Dessault ready for takeoff. Secondly, unfortunately, Jon spoke to his wife Kerry, earlier; she is also in the house with Carol Sue."

Murray grimaced, "OH, crap, I gotta let Cavazos know that there are two women." He made his way through everyone to the Lieutenant, now joined by The Texas Rangers, a squad that Zeke was part of a few years before joining the HPD. They were there to back up an old colleague. Murray found Dimas. "I need to talk with you, Lieutenant."

Dimas abruptly turned on his heels, already stressed over the fact that his new lady friend was held, apparently against her will and just having an aggressive situation, made him over the top in anger and wanting to tear Kolezy apart for holding her hostage as his ticket to escape. "Whaaat? What do you want, Murray?"

"Lieutenant, Kolezy has a plane ready for a takeoff when he gets to the Sugar Land Airport. He has two people in the house. Carol Sue and Kerry Yanek, a psychologist."

Cavazos, half listened. "Who the hell is Terry Coning?"

"No, it is a woman. Her name is Kerry Yanek. She is a psychotherapist AND the wife of my pilot, Jon Irion. She is a VERY close friend of Carol Sue."

Dimas, becoming slightly overwhelmed, was being reminded of his own closeness to Carol Sue and now another woman who was in harm's way. "Ok, Ok, Murray, get the hell back to where you came from. We have to go in, no matter what...." Then the cop grabbed the bullhorn. "Kolezy! We are not waiting and coming in!"

Dimitri was going ballistic. "Louis, you have to do something. The police are coming to break down the front door!"

Kolezy looked at his second in command, disappointedly, not paying further attention to the hysterics, slowly walked to the front, peering out the tiny glass in the front door. He opened the door slowly, and sent out a warning, "We have two woman held as our hostages. You come closer we will kill them. We have nothing to lose. We want safe passage to our vehicles. You have one minute to decide."

The Lieutenant did not want the women murdered and especially Carol Sue. He looked over to Zeke who knew what his brother was thinking. "Dimas, you cannot take a chance of lobbing tear gas in and storming the house. Let them go for now and if Kolezy and his crew are open targets, kill them!"

Suddenly, two shots rang out in the house. Louis poked his head out. "Those were warning shots in the ceiling and if you don't agree to our terms the women get a bullet in their head."

Murray stuck in his opinion, interrupting the two police brothers, "Remember, I told you about his plane at the Sugar Land Airport. He is not aware that we know he is probably heading there from here. We can wait and surprise them, free the women and take the Hungarian Mafia down, dead or alive! You have your sharpshooters waiting and voila! One less dirty attorney!"

Lieutenant Cavazos had a change of opinion for Murray and his band of what he considered, 'vigilantes'. "Yeah, it might work, as much as I hate to admit your being here. "

Rich offered further confirmation of a positive kill. "Lieutenant, Ron Tanski was a top marksman in Nam and later Somalia, as well as in a Banana Republic place or two. I was with him in Bolivia when he knocked off two gorilla soldiers with one shot a piece a half mile away."

Zeke was skeptical, "Yeah, Tanski misses and then our guys are behind the eight ball trying to target Kolezy. Remember, we are not doing a Bruce Willard movie, citizens."

Murray defended his actions, "Hey, I like Bruce Willard. He has the balls in real life to do what no man would ever do. My sister-in-law told me that the town he grew up in, Penns Grove, New Jersey, had great stories about him. Someone said he ran naked down the street, while in high school for some football stunt that the team dared him to do. Of course, he got suspended for doing it. So they say. Of course, I was not there but, he is like me, left handed."

Dimas mopped his brow with his back hand, "Whew, for a minute, I thought you were going to run down Memorial, NAKED. We have to answer that sucker in the house."

Once more grabbing the bull horn, "Okay, Kolezy you can come out with the women and we won't fire on you but don't get any ideas that we are going to let you run a long leash."

Kolezy yelled back, "You better cut the leash or these gals will be thrown from the cars, dead!"

St. George had another idea, so he turned to the Cavazos' brothers, "Anthony, here, has his co-pilot, Arnie Kaplan, with a helicopter at the airport, he can trail Kolezy's group. It is a plain gray one, not like the blue ones HPD has. We can get him to fly over. Maybe stall Kolezy for a while."

Murray was wasting no time as he cell phoned Arnie to rev up the copter and fly to the scene. Lieutenant Cavazos agreed and got back on the horn.

"Kolezy, I want to see the women first. Have them walk to the door so we know they are alright."

It took five or more minutes for Kerry and Carol Sue to appear, apparently unharmed as they both waved. Dimas had a relief appearance on him upon seeing his newfound lady friend.

Suddenly, they were pulled in and Kolezy barked out a warning, "You better not get any more ideas or they WILL be dead. "We are going out the back. Savvy?" With that the fallen attorney slammed the front door.

Dimas turned to Zeke. "Bro, did your guys place those homing devices on their SUVs?"

Zeke smiled, "Our blue's did it when Kolezy's drivers drifted back to the house, Dee, In case the copter deal doesn't work, we GPS them."

The Lieutenant now, more than ever, believed he could get Carol Sue back without harming her, and of course, this Kerry woman.

Kolezy and his men pushed Kerry and Carol Sue ahead of them as they walked from the front of the home through the kitchen, going out the rear door of the home. As the five inched out the back, Kolezy surveyed if any of the police had a sharpshooter visible, as they moved toward the waiting cars. Finding no police, they continued toward the cars. Kolezy held a gun to Carol Sue as Drago and Dimiti did the same to Kerry. Molnar and Perez manned the wheels. This took an extra fifteen minutes, enough time for Arnie and Jon, who were just about to cruise over ten or so blocks away, not giving away their part in the plot to follow Kolezy and his Hungarian Mafia to the Sugar Land Airport.

Michaeleen had witnessed all of the events, frustrated, visibly upset, as she confronted Murray and the others. "You are not going to do anything? Carol Sue is in so much danger! Anthony, please do something!" The distraught young woman broke down in his arms.

Murray grabbed her and could not answer the trembling young woman, unable to come up with any reason that this entire nightmare was unreal. "Michaeleen, honey, we will free Carol Sue and Kerry from these wretched, evil people. They will not get away with this, I promise you. Right now, Lieutenant Cavazos has chosen not to use any gun fire or a sharpshooter."

As Murray held the distraught young woman for assurance, more HPD cruisers and the SWAT team's van pulled up. Two local news helicopters began circling. There was also a new official in charge, Captain James Short, a 30 year veteran in law enforcement. He was the Cavazos' brother's commander at Reisner St. "Fill me in, Dimas and Zeke. What is going down?"

Dimas replied back strongly, "Captain, we have it under control. Kolezy is taking the hostages, but we will get them at the Sugar Land Airport. We cannot take a chance on shooting the main suspects without injuring the women."

"Okay, Cavazos, you better be right. I'll try to cover for you."

As the Captain walked back to the SWAT team, Zeke dropped his cigarette butt on the ground, in distress, "Yeah, Dee, you take the fall for all this but he'll try to cover for you. I'll do everything to make sure that we get that cock sucking, fucker, Kolezy and pin his balls to the wall!"

Lieutenant Cavazos was strongly determined, "WE will get them, Zeke. I have to. I am going to free the women if that is the last thing I do."

An HPD officer came up to the brothers, "We have the fix on the GPS dial on both the BMW and the Mercedes SUV. We only need them to move out and we will follow on our screens."

Zeke was relieved that in the event the two suspect's vehicles were lost in traffic or if Murray's helicopter could not keep up with them from above, the GPS signals would pinpoint their position.

Dimas and Zeke ran around to the rear of the home's drive to survey the fact that both Carol Sue and Kerry were on board the getaway SUVs.

SWAT shooters, stationed on roofs and strategic spots waited for the signal to take out Kolezy and his gang. Because both women were exceptionally tall, a clear shot was not available and the signal to shoot was not given. Both women looked terrified not knowing their fate as they were pushed into the rear seat of the SUV. At the back of the BMW appeared Luka. Both Dimas and Zeke were speechless, as they ran closer to the rear of the home. Captain Short was just behind them.

The Lieutenant caught Captain Short, "Hey, Captain, is that Luka at the back of the Beemer?"

Short hung his head, "Yeah, sorry, Dimas... we could not hold him."

"Great and you tell me you cannot help me if this goes down wrong. Fuck it, Captain!"

The two cars were now loaded with the nine as they sped down the drive and away. Murray called up to Arnie and Jon who were hovering in the company helicopter to find out if they were ready.

Jon was calm as he asked Murray how Kerry may have been doing, as she was caught up as an unwilling participant in this unplanned event. "Murray, do you know how Kerry is? Was she or is she, hurt?" His voice beginning to crack in deep concern coming from a man who flew forty missions in the Iraq crisis and now flying a helicopter enroute to probably save his wife.

"Jon, Kerry seemed to be holding up as well as expected. She's a trooper. This nightmare will end in Sugar Land. I will do everything in my power to protect and remove her from the clutches of Kolezy. Are you and Arnie ready?"

"We're on it!"

Murray attempted to give assurance to Michaeleen. "Sweetheart, we'll get your aunt back safely. He then turned to Bill, who knew it was, at best, a 50/50 proposition. The two of them climbed into the SUV with Ernie, Tanski, Adam and Rich, as Sev slide behind the wheel of the silver Chevy Suburban screeching out toward the Sugar Land Airport. The Cavazos brothers sped by in their patrol car. Brian stayed behind not wishing to become involved.

Michaeleen was left standing next to her car, holding back tears of both hate and love, worrying about Carol Sue, dialing Wes and Gina to give the latest update as they had been vacationing in their favorite playground, Playa Del Carmen, Mexico, and were attempting to get the next flight back to Houston. As she got into her car she looked over at the cowering Brian. "I don't know who you are or why you are here, the police will take care of you. I need to catch up to the others."

Brian only nodded and headed for a police cruiser.

Murray received a call from Sheryl. "It's all over the news. Are you in the middle of all this, Honey?" She was almost gasping for air trying to hold back her overwrought emotions.

"Relax, Sheryl, my love and one and only. We are heading for the Sugar Land Airport to stop Kolezy from flying out of the country."

Sheryl quizzed, "Is he trying to go to Mexico or the Caribbean Islands?"

"NO, we think it is Budapest, Hungary."

She laughed in a relaxed way, "Well, we wanted to go there last year when we were in Switzerland and Germany and then another business problem came up and we flew back to Houston. Why, if everyone knows that, will their police arrest him? Can Kolezy come back here?"

"He has connections here and in other spots. Whether the police can get extraditions from Hungary takes time. He can jet off to the Czech Republic, although, they may be worse on co-operating with the United States on criminals. He can avoid authorities indefinitely, change his identity, do plastic surgery, and then re-enter the U.S., maybe live in South American or Canada. He speaks Spanish, as well as Czech and Hungarian. We have got to nail this no good. "

Knowing full well he had a mission but still wanted to ask, Sheryl beseeched her husband. "Oh, honey, do you have to go? Let Lieutenant Cavazos take him out, please!"

"I have to do this. Strike a stunning blow to his type of person who did this to me. I love you very much. You are the very best thing in my life."

Sheryl was resigned to the fact that her man had to do what he was seeking, making this a closure for him as well as for Adam. "I love you very, very much and wait for your return!"

Adam caught the conversation, "Louis wanted me to do a lot of things and, at the time, pushed me into what I became. From what you said, Murray, it was age nine. Welcome to the fraternity of those who are molested. You were able to come back because you did not have a live in person screwing you on a daily basis. Louis was always only twenty five feet away in another bedroom. I should not make excuses for what he did and had I been stronger then, like you, led a straighter life."

Rich, Tanski, and Bill looked over at a calm, Adam, who they started to view in a more positive light as he opened up to Murray. The others were stone silent, especially, Sev and Ernie. And what puzzled them was the dialogue their old friend leaked to Adam about his past experience, as the younger man gave credit to Murray for his early childhood bad experience. It was an awkward time as the seven were driving toward Sugar Land down Highway 6 to intercept Kolezy and free the women. The other five men, without any conversation, each understood, for now, to forget what they heard.

Murray looked in the rear view mirror at Bill, who was directly behind him. "You look like you have something on your mind, Billy?"

St. George shifted gears, quickly, "What are the chances, Anth, on our getting this jack ass at the airport or are we going to fly out to Hungary if it comes down to it? You have to think that Kolezy has international connections all over that part of Europe. He may fly to an unknown airstrip in Hungary or the Czech Republic since the

Interpol or Hungarian cops are going to hear from Texas law folks and may arrest him."

Murray was up to it, "That is why we have to prevent him from taking off, with or without the gals. If need be, partner, we will take the Gulfstream and tail him to where ever he lands. I want to take him down."

Rich nudged St. George. "I have a feeling we are taking an eleven hour trip to Goulash Land. Something says he flies off and we follow. We will have to keep him in view at 35,000 feet. Weather, loss of time he has on us, and familiarity of landing some place we are foreign to, in that part of the world."

Sev looked in the mirror, briefly, as he drove over the speed limit, "Rich, that is why we have to get Kerry and Carol Sue before he attempts his takeoff. If he takes her with him, being Carol Sue is the main buyer of MABB; he can throw her off the plane and get rid of the roadblock to the sale. She would be bait to the sharks if she lived after being thrown out."

Adam clenched his teeth as he swung around to face Rich and St. George. "I think if she is forced aboard, Carol Sue will take care of herself and knowing what I do, she may drive him off the plane. I do not want her killed. She is one hell of a ..... piece of ass."

Rich smiled, broadly, as he heard rumors of the sexual encounter at the Merriam. "So you really think she is that cool?"

Adam's feeling for Carol Sue stirred inside almost in a hurricane force. "I don't want her injured or worse, murdered by this lower than life viper. We have to catch Louis, as he may torture both of them, killing and then ... he loathes women. My sister was his plaything, enjoying his domination over her weakness. My father would not have permitted this. He knew Louis hated women.'

Tanski was lost, "You were, what five years old? How can you even know, and I take your part, but you could not have learned that Louis was what he is today?"

Adam felt like lashing out but held back, "Tanski, even at five and one half, I knew he was evil, although I was unable to do anything about it. My mother would not listen to my young pleas. She had no one to turn to as the Russians still occupied parts of Hungary and a young major was, as you might say, screwing her. Somehow, he made Louis have sex with my mother's sister. My step father was drunk at the time telling me this, after a night of humping. He hated his own parents for what he became. That supposedly was his reason for abusing me, Ryan and Melanie."

The three men were speechless, stricken from what they heard as their heritage was the opposite of what Adam encountered, even Murray as to what he endured as a boy was taken back. They were getting an armchair view of what Kolezy was like. Murray wanted to ask more of Adam but getting his stepfather came first.

Lieutenant Cavazos radioed to the Sugar Land Police and West Bend Sheriff of Kolezy's intent to fly out and that they placed a GPS monitor on each of the two fleeing vehicles.

In their police cruiser, Dimas turned to Zeke, "This is going to be touch and go. If we lose this shit head here, he could fly off to Budapest or Bundganistan or what the fuckville. I want to shoot that mother ass whip and his son of a bitch dick head gang. God, though, I don't want Carol Sue or Kerry harmed.'

Zeke looked over at his brother, "You really got it bad for that tall, platinum blond, and tight butt, broad."

"Zeke, she is one of a kind woman."

"Brother, my best hope for you is that you finally found the happiness you have been searching for after two failed marriages."

"Yeah, you might be right, but at this time we have to stop Kolezy." Murray's group trailed at a safe distance behind the two vehicles carrying the GPS monitors, thus throwing the Hungarian Mafia off the track by not appearing to be following them to their destination. Soon, the Lieutenant and his brother were joined by two West Bend County Sheriff's cars and a Texas Department of Safety patrol pickup, each containing two heavily armed officers.

Inside the Mercedes SUV front seat Kolezy turned to the two almost calm women and in a disgusted tone, "You both have made my life miserable. Ms. Yanek, you are the main reason that I lost my wife and stepdaughter by filling their heads with nonsense about me. And you, Ms. Miller or Winters, whichever name you choose, at whatever time, encouraged my stepson to sell MABB to you. Was it that night at the Merriam that turned the trick? Hmm, talking about turning the trick. That is a favorite term used by prostitutes. Did you prostitute yourself to gain his co- operation?"

Carol Sue, in an uncharacteristic moment, "Go fuck yourself, asshole!"

"I cannot wait to savor that moment with you, Carol Sue."

"Not going to happen, mother fucker!"

"We will see what unveils in my chateau outside Buda, my feisty wench."

Kerry wanted to cut in as she heard enough bodily functions, "Do you actually believe that your wife and stepdaughter caused your downfall? Louis, all your underhanded dealings brought you to this point. Ilona and Melanie were the last part of the puzzle that did it. You left a trail of rape and murder just to satisfy your way. Should you be fortunate to board your plane, fly numerous hours, and land in Hungary, the local police and Interpol will catch up to you. Now is the time to stop the car, surrender to the locals here and let us go. Life in prison is better than dying in some foreign land."

Kolezy scoffed at Kerry's remarks, "I plan on going to my heritage. The beautiful and rolling hills and valleys of Hungary. I wish to visit my parent's graves, the places I grew up, visit old friends, and stomp on the ground where the Russian soldiers trampled my family's garden. It was all the Russian's fault of what I became. No, Mrs. Yanek, you and Mrs. What's her name, Winters or Miller will accompany me back to my wonderful country."

Both Carol Sue and Kerry looked at one another, each thinking that this maniac would not get rid of them immediately if they played along, humoring him, living a little longer, perhaps until they are able to plan an escape.

Kolezy turned around, relaxed as the Benz SUV rolled down Highway Six toward The Sugar Land Airport. He began speaking to the windshield, not caring if he was listened to or not, "Yes, I am returning to my homeland and will become the top attorney in the country, there I will control the largest adult entertainment empire in the world. So Mrs. Miller, for now, neither of us has gained MABB. Women, ah, oh," as he smugly chortled. "Yes, we men are still superior to you females in every way. There is a definite place for each of your fairer sex. Most of our men would pay dearly for an evening with both of you. I would have you team up on a tandem. Your luscious, hot bodies, sizzling on and under gold, satin sheets. Kerry, you will most likely be the favorite with those long and sinewy legs of alabaster."

Kerry gleefully responded, "We are not even near the airport. Do you really believe we will be allowed to leave on an airplane, much less seeing my long and sinewy legs of alabaster? That is your downfall, Louis, you are a dreamer."

"I will dream of you occupying my bed as we travel in not just any airplane, but a Dessault, F7 Falcon which will rocket us at nearly 600 miles an hour. The seats are baby skinned leather from Chennault in France. By the way, Carol Sue, I know you collect French art work. I wish I could have gazed at the famous paintings you collected. I have millions of dollars of art work. A Matisse over my bed where I can gaze as I penetrate you. You have never experienced such unforgettable, sensual love before our times together."

Carol Sue only wondered how this man has survived and become a spirit in the community?

Carol Sue was ready to respond when Kolezy raised his hand, looking back down Highway Six and to the left and right of the any near intersections, "We are at our destination at the Sugar Land Airport and no police are in view. We have fooled the very smart police." They cruised to Hangar 29 where the Falcon was readying to fly out. As they all began to alight from the vehicles, Perez, cried out, "Patron, see! All around ez the puleez, vee are going to bee stopped." He gasped at the barrage of authorities with the bubble lights and sirens blaring.

Dimitri was dumbfounded, "Louis, how did they know? Our vehicles were hidden in the back, guarded."

Kolezy was undaunted, knowing that it was too easy, as he felt taken by the police preventing his attempt to leave the country. . "Dimitri, my ingenuous friend, I am certain they placed some homing device on our SUV or the BMW. No matter we have two beautiful hostages and their friends will not endanger them by any foolish actions."

Both women were horrified, fearing for their safety, as the vehicles pulled into the hangar, somehow thinking they could escape, but how would it occur? The police shooting it out? Would they survive?

Murray and his group pulled behind the Cavazos duo and their heavily armed men. Zeke and Dimas pulled within 25 yards of the Mercedes SUV and the BMW.

Outside as the Falcon began to rev up the Rolls Royce engines, Drago appeared to be rattled upon seeing the bevy of police and barricades seemingly blocking their way to fly to their homeland 5700 miles away. "Louis, can we actually make it to the plane and will we have enough fuel to fly to Budapest?"

"Drago, I thought you had more faith in me. The police will not shoot while we have these shields and, yes, the Falcon has a 6700 mile range. Danika, our pilot, with her co-pilot, Bridget, will pull away and we will sail into the realm at 35,000 feet. A pleasure of inner sanctum wiped across his face.

Lieutenant Cavazos halted the squad car to a stop almost equal to Murray's vehicle. Dimas garnered the bull horn as the other police vehicles began to surround the plane in an attempt to prevent the plane from entering the tarmac and eventually the takeoff strip. The Lieutenant shouted instructions to the 30 plus other police officers and deputies from the various departments "Close the circle tight so the plane cannot move! Be ready on my command to begin shooting if they open up on you from their vehicles!"

Kolezy needed to devise a quick plan. The plan to ditch the police and get to the plane and take off was now thwarted without his shooting his way out. He spoke to his men in the BMW. They were to pull next to the SUV as close as possible as he was going to use the two women as their cover to the plane. "We will use them as boarding passes to the Falcon. The police will not shoot us, stay close."

Gabor and Perez dove low from the Beemer to the side of the Benz SUV as Drago opened the door for their cover.

The Lieutenant was about to issue another warning via the squawk box in his hand when the West Bend Sheriff, Ed Lachowski, roared in with three more of his patrol cars spinning their bubble lights and blaring their sirens. It did not take long for the Sheriff to swagger out and head for Dimas. "You realize Cavazos, that I outrank you and you are on my turf! I want these guys as much as you do, Lieutenant."

Dimas was getting feed up with Lachowski's high grandstanding. "Look Sheriff, I know you are the law here in Sugar Land, but we followed these criminals here and the DPS and your locals joined in without any hesitation as to who was in charge. Hell, if you want to take over and start pouring lead their way against Kolezy with your guys, go ahead. He has two women hostages in that SUV and the intentions are to board that plane we have boxed in. We have to free the two women and then shoot it out with him and his mafia gang. Do you want to give the orders to start shelling the car and kill the women?"

Lachowski stood back, "Well, no. Ah, hmm, maybe go ahead and see what you can do to get those two gals to safety. I have to warn you, Lieutenant, if your tactics fail, I will not hesitate to take immediate action. Is that understood, Lieutenant?"

Cavazos was resigned for the moment. "Yes, Sheriff Lachowski."

Nearby, Jon Irion, the husband of Kerry and the pilot of their Gulfstream jet, had just landed the company helicopter at the rear of the hangar. He came up to Murray. "I cannot live without Kerry, what can you do to prevent her from being taken by these monsters?"

Murray looked at his pilot and close friend, "Jon, I will try my utmost best to prevent her from being taken by Kolezy."

"Murray, she and I have been together for twelve years and now we have a six year old son, Devan, to share our lives with. I would not know what to do without her and how it would affect our son. "His emotions increased, becoming the better of him. "Please, bring her back to us, safely. I have been through a number of close episodes in the past, flying, but they could not compare to this."

"Jon, I know and understand where you are coming from, I love Kerry, in a different way, of course, and am going to save her and prevent anything occurring to her." He knew, in his mind, that it was, at best, an even chance in preventing Kerry from getting on that plane. "Jon, Kerry will come out of this without a scratch. "

Lieutenant Cavazos was ready to storm the cars. He gave a last warning to Kolezy to release the two women, and surrender to the police.

Suddenly, smoke bombs were tossed from Kolezy's SUV, clouding the area from any view. Kolezy had prepared for this possibility, in the event they were needed. He and his crew with the women scrambled out of the Benz toward the plane's open door.

A number of police yelled out they were going to fire into the maze of smoke.

Lieutenant Cavazos was now ready to breach the aircraft. He wanted to issue the orders to go after Kolezy and shoot to kill... then he held back. "No, hold your fire! Stand down, men!" As the smoke cleared, Kerry was huddled by the rear left of the quarter panel of the SUV, crying, uncontrollably. Jon had jumped the police barricade, without caring for his own life, somehow finding her. They wept together on the tarmac as he pulled her up and ran to the safety of a police car where two DPS patrolman shielded them from any potential gunfire initiated by an irate Kolezy or one of his men.

Dimas started toward the plane as the cloud of smoke subsided showing a struggling Carol Sue being pulled into the rear door of the Falcon, its Rolls Royce engines now fully revved to start the move toward the runway blocked by five patrol cars.

Zeke yelled out over the din of the engine's noise, "Dimas, they intend to blow past our blockade!"

Ed Lachowski, yelled out to his men, "Get ready to start shooting, West Bend officers!"

The Lieutenant knew that if the Falcon attempted to hit through the police vehicles, it could result in a catastrophic explosion killing everyone on board, including Carol Sue and quite possibly, many of the responders. He bellowed through the bull horn "I don't want the plane to blow up, move the cars! Sheriff, hold your fire! Pull all vehicles back, NOW!"

The police vehicles screeched back in seconds as the Falcon screamed by heading for the runway and their eventual escape to Hungary.

Dimas, his head down, dropping the bull horn, realized that he might never see Carol Sue, alive, again. She was someone, who started to make his turbulent life make sense, now gone, possibly forever.

Murray, himself, disgusted at the current outcome, but knowing this cop, now more a friend after all this turmoil and strife, needed his consoling. "Look, Dimas, we will find Carol Sue and you can collar Kolezy in the process.

Without any extra warranting, the Falcon with Kolezy, Carol Sue, and his group took off and circled back over the airport as a sign of defiance and superiority the attorney bestowed upon the crowd below. Some of them shook their first and most shot the finger back at the wing tipping jet rising up and over the late afternoon horizon heading toward the East and a date on the Danube.

Ed Lachowski came up to the crest fallen Dimas. "I am sorry, that this shithead got away. I know if we started to blast away, that hostage would be dead. Carol Sue Winters seemed like a nice gal. Too bad for her. What is your next move, Lieutenant?"

Dimas, saddened, and temporarily lost on his next move to get his lover back. "I don't know at this time, Sheriff, but will think of getting that bad news attorney, one way or another."

The West Bend Sheriff nodded affirmatively, "If you need our help, please call on us, Lieutenant Cavazos." With that they shook hands as Dimas knew that Lachowski was attempting to ease the loss of Kolezy and Carol Sue. Devastated, the Houston cop, head bowed, started back to his cruiser to radio Captain Short of the happenings.

Short answered. "Yes, Dee saw the plane take off. We are going to alert the Hungarian police. When Kolezy lands, they will pick him up and free the hostage. He will be sent back here to stand trial and get the maximum sentence or the needle. You don't need to be concerned, we have this covered."

Murray came up to the cruiser, listening to Short's message. Turning to Dimas, "Well, that is why your Captain is paid the big bucks. No problems, right?"

The Lieutenant wore a worried look. "Carol Sue is going to be used as a human shield."

Murray knew the cop was right but attempted to lighten the situation. "We have to go after them in our Gulfstream. Somehow figure a way to free Carol Sue as Kolezy is probably flying to Budapest. The local police or Interpol can arrest him after he lands and before he has an opportunity to try something. It's a shot, Dimas."

As the Lieutenant contemplated Murray's plan another option appeared.

As everyone on the ground felt a kick in their stomachs, Arnie Kaplan, the co-pilot of Murray's Gulfstream rushed up to his boss. "A, a, do, do, want to know, ha, ha, where they are going, ha, ha?" Arnie's mouth was crunched up as his nose twitched like a kid who was in on a secret and could not wait to tell everyone about it. Dancing like a child who could not keep that secret. His nose now squeezed into his glasses, bouncing up on his bulbous nose. Murray was accustomed to Arnie, who was an excellent second seat pilot and would forgive him for his unusual dance like movements. In the three years of his ownership of the Gulfstream, he had Jon as his first chaired pilot and Arnie, the co-pilot, as they were both reliable. Dimas appeared interested and came up to them.

Murray took a breath, "Arnie, we are a little preoccupied for now. What is it? Please, as time is ticking. What is it that you are attempting to tell all of us?"

Arnie was partially stuttering with the news, "You, You know what I heard about the plane that just took off with the bad guys and that blond ? Huh? Huh?"

The Lieutenant was bewildered and did not know what to make of all Arnie's antics and hand waving." He actually pilots for you, Murray? Really?"

Murray closed his eyes and nodded, "Yeah, it's true. He IS an excellent navigator and co-pilot. Never gets us lost in the air. Sometimes on the runways. "He then grabbed Arnie by the shoulders, "Hey, Arnie, kindly focus for us! What do you know, tell us quickly, alright?"

Arnie's eyes saucered and then crossed, "They're flying to Istaviz Field at Solizy near Budapest. Isn't that where we went last year? Well, you, Sheryl, and the rest of the family were to go, almost."

"Yes, Budapest. We had a company thing that prevented our going. "You're, positive, Arnie? Istaviz Field by Solizy?"

The co-pilot squinted up his face, "A buddy of mine at the terminal overheard Kolezy's female pilot, Danika, tell someone who spoke a funny language that they were going there. That is the name of the guy who got away. True?"

"Murray agreed, "That is the name of the guy who just flew out. Go on..."

"Well, Kolezy's pilot, who is a knock out, because I caught her behind as she was leaving the terminal..."

"Okay, Arnie, good work. We are going after them. Have the plane ready and ask Nikki Bridges, our hostess, to have the food and drinks ready. I'll clue Jon in and make sure he is alright to pilot, first seat."

Arnie was excited, "You mean we are actually flying to Hungary?"

"Yep, I gotta get our guys together. We have a connection in Budapest. Our good friend, C. W. Roberts, was an attaché at the embassy there for two years. Sheryl told me the other day that C. W. was dispatched to go back there to take care of some government loose ends. He can assist us on this, as well."

Lieutenant Cavazos was anxious to take off and follow the Falcon as Murray made it sound like he had everything in place. "When can we fly out, Murray, and catch up with those Hungarian bastards? I'll get Zeke. We have extradition papers that were prepared at Reisner Street as you believed that Kolezy was heading for his homeland. Yeah, and I know what you're thinking. I am going to rescue Carol Sue. We have to tell the Budapest police that there may be a change of plans since Kolezy isn't flying into their International Airport, but to Istaviz. I will let Captain Short know, the local police can cover both places...in case. Oh, Carol Sue, I am coming for you!"

Murray was somewhat amused that she had this effect on the crusty cop who had already been down the aisle twice. "Well, Dimas, it won't be easy, although it can be accomplished, as long as she remains cool with Kolezy. We'll get Vixey back. Get on board when you are ready."

Lieutenant Cavazos knew that it was going to be a struggle in a foreign and unchartered area of the world he had never known, yet, strangely, he had faith in Murray and his vigilantes. He went back to his police cruiser and dialed 61 Reisner with the new information.

Murray suggested some light packing for the trip to Hungary as Zeke lived close to the airport. They could pack enough for the trip. Then he went back to brief the news to St. George, Rich, and the others to advise the trip would take 11 hours. As he finished with them, Michaeleen came up to him, gripping his arm tightly. Tears welded up as she puppy dogged him.

"What's going on, sweetheart?"

"I want to come along, as well. You don't know how much it means to me. Believe me, it is vital."

Murray did not want her to come, "It is much too dangerous, Michaeleen. Even though I realize how you feel about Carol Sue. We will free and return her, unharmed."

The young woman was insistent and would not be denied, "Please, I will not be in the way. You just don't know everything and I am not positive this is the time and place to explain it to you."

The way she said that prompted Murray to ask more, yet, it was not as important, at that time, to pursue what she meant. He only thought for a moment and said, "Okay, but you have to follow our instructions on not getting in on any action where you would be in danger. Understand?"

"Yes, you won't need to be concerned about my getting into anything. I want to be there for Carol Sue."

"Just be ready. We are taking off in thirty minutes! Need passports and all that stuff!"

"I always come prepared," as she held them up.

Just as everyone was getting prepared for the journey, Tom Zizka, Channel 77's venerable reporter, landed in his helicopter, 200 feet from them.

He pushed his way through a growing group of police, holding back the bystanders. He finally saw Murray. He yelled out as he approached Michaeleen and Murray. "Hey, Murray, we heard about the police attempt to capture Louis B. Kolezy, but he got away. He abducted two hostages as he, literally, flew the coop."

"Yeah, Tom, a play on words. Our barrister left short one hostage. Her name is Kerry Yanek. Somehow she was able to get away." Then Murray introduced the freed woman, still in shock and tearing at what could have been her last moments on earth.

Kerry held up her hand to both Murray and Zizka. Tom flipped on the microphone as he had a scoop that the other stations did not have and with his trusty cameraman rolling, "You're my favorite newsman, Tom," she uttered, wiping her face with a handkerchief, Michaeleen slipped her, "It was a miracle. Yes, maybe God saved me. I can only tell you and the rest of the world as I was being pushed in the dense smoke, almost ready to choke and held tightly by a man called Drago, I was wrenched from his grip and a gigantic light guided me away from him, back from the SUV we were in and gently placed me down on the ground. It seemed that my body was still held by that man, yet my spirit was pulled away to safety. An out of body experience. Something I may relate to my patients...Tom, oh... it was something that makes you want to believe that a force greater than evil put it all down. There is a higher being that we need to thank."

Zizka was in heaven, so to speak, on catching all this on tape. He cut the interview, thanked Kerry, Murray and smiled at Michaeleen, thinking maybe he had another story. Just about to ask her what she was doing there and figured she could add more to this almost fatal event, "And you're, a witness as well, Ms.?"

"It is Michaeleen Ventura, and my, ah, aunt, is the person who was abducted by Louis B. Kolezy. We are all going to depart from this airport shortly, on Mr. Murray's plane to catch him and release my, anyway..."

Tom sensed that she was about to break up and pulled back on his questions, instead thrusting the microphone into Murray's face. "Where is the flight going? And what is the aunt's name?"

Murray spit out, "Budapest, Hungary. Kolezy will rue the day he did what he has done and the other unspeakable times. HPD has warrants for arrest and extradition, if needed, for him and his Hungarian Mafia. The Houston Police are coming on board our company jet. Her aunt's name is Carol Sue Miller from Katy."

Zizka pressed, "Some say that you and your friends are vigilantes. Is this the reason you are going after Kolezy? What is this Hungarian Mafia story? How does this Miller woman fit in?"

"We do not like violence. That is why the police are coming. We are only seeking justice for people we care about. Our group is only going as a subliminal support group. Louis B. Kolezy established this Hungarian Mafia to get what he wants. Anyone who stands in his way is eliminated. Carol Sue Miller was just an innocent bystander. That's all, Tom."

Zizka really knew that there was more to all this..."Murray, what are you referring to on "other unspeakable times? Is it a part of this Hungarian Mafia?"

"Tom gotta leave, when we return we will give you the story first. You're our man!"

Zizka turned away and into the camera, "There you are folks, you heard it straight from Anthony J. Murray, CEO of The Murray Companies at The Sugar Land Airport that the chase is on. Tom Zizka, live."

Murray knifed his way back to an ever increasing crowd of bystanders who knew something sinister had taken place and the wanted a piece of it. On the way, he was grabbed, almost accosted by Wes, Carol Sue's son. Red faced with anger, "This is all your fault, Murray! How can the father of my wife drag my mother into all this? She may be killed as we stand here! All over that damn company, MABB!"

Murray whirled back, "Listen Wes, we are going to retrieve your mother, alive and well. It was, after all, her doing to be involved with Adam and MABB. You know how stubborn she is. Carol Sue could have easily backed off. Besides, Wes, I don't care for your blaming me for everything that goes sour with you and Gina. It is your business and I want you to keep it at your doorstep. Coppice?"

"She is such a shopper, though. Gina can run through ten thousand a month, just on household crap, especially repainting our home."

Murray rebutted, "Our daughter is at every meal, social function, taking care of your daughter, Lila Grace and your growing son, Noah Grant. She is wearing three hats, Wife, mother, daughter as well as running three homes and taking over your company's HR department. God damn, boy, what the hell do you want? Think! We need to get your momma back."

Wes stood stoic and thought for a moment, "You are right on, but I want to come along and bring my AK15 and gear."

Murray gave it another moment as it appeared he had already been already pushed by Michaeleen to go on the journey. Both she and Wes had a huge stake in it and he did not wish to block their enthusiasm. "Alright, Wes, there's room, for you and your weapon, just get on board. Only, please don't shoot Arnie with it as I know how you feel about him."

St. George was within listening and strolled up to his longtime buddy, "This saga is getting too much. Adam, at first, then Michaeleen, now Wes, finally Kerry getting away. Hell, I am surprised Tom Zizka didn't want to hitch a ride to Budapest."

"Knowing Tom, if he could have wrangled it from the station, he would be on this flight."

"Betty is deeply concerned about me, like Sheryl is about you. I just don't know on this MABB selling and Kolezy and his Mafia group?"

Murray placed his hand on Bill's shoulder, "I just hope C. W. will be able to pinpoint Kolezy's landing in that obscure area outside Budapest. Jon and Arnie are starting up the Rolls Royce's on the Gulfstream 560. I have my Judge and are you packing your trusty pair of forty-fives?"

"You got that right, Magyar man."

As they all boarded the Gulfstream for the ten plus hour pursuit to bring back Carol Sue and Kolezy or at least take him out, all the passengers were silent. Adam had a huge score to settle with his step father for killing his brother Ryan and abusing Melanie and his mother, Ilona. This did not include the four attempts on his life and the eleven years of physical abuse he unwittingly endured while living in River Oaks.

Michaeleen was feeling calmer, although still teary eyed, as the plane elevated to 35,000 feet. She attempted to stare out the window into the soon fading light and clouds.

Lieutenant Cavazos finally found a woman he wanted to be faithful to and love for the rest of his life, only to have her swept up by Kolezy.

Tight lipped, Wes Winters, left his wife Gina, behind with their two children, Lila Grace and Noah Grant, to hunt down the unwilling abduction of his mother, perpetrated by the man everyone on board despised. Clutching his AK 15 and staring straight ahead, only thinking of His mother, Carol Sue, and why she became so caught up with MABB.

Sergeant Zeke Cavazos remembering his wife Janie, and their talk of his early retirement from dodging bullets, the city and superior politics over the past 30 years, the arresting of drug dealers, bank robbers, murderers and endless hours of stakeouts, almost ruining their lives. The couple began to buy a Mexican restaurant in nearby Texas City and would have their offspring's run it until he fully retired. For the moment, he was on a journey zooming along at 565 miles an hour in a cylinder, packed with a dozen others traveling to an unfamiliar land. It was not unlike what he and his brothers, Dimas and Lupe, did fighting in a Viet Nam rice patty or jungle many years ago. Now, he and Dimas were going to another foreign land and a language, neither of them understood.

Murray sat across from the others, looking out the window as the red and orange sunset disappeared into the clouds, thinking back to an evening that March night when he and Sheryl found the tied up and naked, barely alive, Adam. Then how their new life of the past three and one half years had become overshadowed by the past five plus months of this, unwanted and, at times, a dangerous ordeal. Restless, he got up from his seat, passing a snoozing Bill and Tanski, and watching Rich, Sev, and Ernie playing gin rummy or was it liar's poker? Anyway, he wanted to visit with Jon, to be sure he was recovering from the trauma of the near hostage taking of Kerry just a few hours before.

Nikki Bridges, their flight hostess, who bore a striking resemblance to Murray and Sheryl's eldest daughter, Renee Goehring, was taking food and drink orders. Murray stopped her and whispered," I could use a George Dickel Number 12 and Diet Coke, when you have a chance, just to take my mind off of things."

She smiled, batting her blue, slightly outspoken eyes, "Yes, in a jiffy"

"What is on the menu tonight?"

Laughing," Arnie tried to order pressed duck, but all I have is a bar-b-que chicken or beef sandwich with the fixings. That and he attempted to order a pitcher of Miller Lite. You would think he was at some bowling alley in Katy on a team. Ha, ha. We only have Coor's in cans and Shiner Blondes long necks."

"Well, a Shiners Blonde with that bar-b-que will hold me until morning", as Murray did a mock belch.

Nikki looked up the morning offerings, "Looks as though, it is microwave Blue Ribbon sausage and egg beaters with biscuits."

"Blue Ribbon Sausage, Bum's Brand", Murray responded, fondly remembering the famed Houston Oilers head coach, O. A. 'Bum' Phillips, who turned pitchman for various local products in the area, including the tasty sausage offerings.

She laughed softly, "I'll bring both, the Dickel and Shiners."

Murray slipped past her, "I'll check with Jon. He is attempting to come down after the near miss of Kerry being ferried off 5700 miles."

Jon was steady as a rock, even in the face of this near disaster that he and his wife narrowly escaped. He was a Lieutenant Colonel in the United States Air Force having flown many missions in the Iraq War. "Murray, you do not need to worry about me, I can handle everything. Kerry is safe at her sister's and her husband's home in The Woodlands. Our son is there, as well."

Arnie attempted to butt into the conversation, "Jon, what are we going to do about that system, the one, weather people are calling Tropical Storm Ike?"

Jon agreed, "When we return, in a few days or so, the Gulfstream will probably need to navigate around a possible hurricane, if it approaches the Texas Gulf Coast."

Murray had totally forgotten about any weather bulletins or early warning. Now he had a dual concern, "Sheryl had to contend with the possibility of closing their home on Galveston's West beach. She could go to our younger daughter's place in Austin and take Gina and the kids with her. I will call her after we arrive in Budapest. Meantime, I need to get hold of C. W. Roberts who was a special attaché to the Hungarian ambassador, Lazlo Kupas. Arnie, get C.W. on the phone, please. He flew out from Houston two days ago and should have arrived in Budapest, yesterday. He goes by the name, Robie, to his friends."

Jon asked Murray, "How can he help us on this?"

"Jon, C. W., for many years, had been a U.S. State Department rover of sorts. Not quite a diplomat and not quite a secret agent. He has a lot of contacts in Hungary, Germany, Czech Republic, Switzerland and Poland. Maybe even a few in Russia. He is a cognac drinker and there is a lot of Remy Martin that flows around those countries. That and he was a major in our Air Force, stationed in Dusseldorf, Germany. If anyone can locate Kolezy, he is our best choice. Not bad for a raw, skinny kid out of Stephenville, Texas, becoming a whiz at diplomacy and secret bull shit stuff."

Arnie got C.W. on the line, Murray asked, "Hey, Robie, we are traveling in this glorified twin engined, tens of millions of dollars tin can coming to your part of the world. Should be there in nine hours. Need to know is Istaviz field near Soliz? We're on the trail in hot pursuit of that crook, Kolezy. Call us back on our radio frequency 9211006 256, ok. Rob?"

C. W. dialed back almost immediately, "What is up or Whatses Slooss? As the Germans say. "

We need to locate this schmuck, Louis Kolezy, ASAP."

"Don't you want to go to The Balaton on Andrassy Street first for some kolbaz, hudka, chicken paprikash, stuffed cabbage with such a strong aroma that flies will be perched on the outdoor screens of the building? I'm already for that now."

"Hey, Robie, that sounds fine after we wrap up this gig. Kolezy took off over an hour ahead of us. The number on his plane is NK36505, a Falcon Dessault F7. Black in color just like his heart."

"I can rustle a couple of jets to shoot it down. Know this Light Colonel, in the Air Force. He owes me a favor."

"Can't do it Rob, Kolezy has a hostage on board."

"Ah so. Whom may I ask is it?"

"It is our gal, Wes' mom, Carol Sue Winters-Miller."

"The plane may crash with the way she acts. I remember her with the handcuffs at the wedding reception for Gina and Wes. There were five guys willing to do whatever....that night."

"Kolezy is too clever to go for that."

"How did he grab her?"

"Long story that we can kick over dinner when we can relax before returning to Texas. Just need that airstrip locale and maybe you can get some firepower so we don't get ambushed."

"I have an airline pilot from Holzkirchen that knows a lot about these off the beaten path strips and he has a couple of people we can trust that can back you up."

"Great, get back to Jon and Arnie, our pilots, and have them zero in on the location."

"Hey, Murray, after we take down this ass hole, we can go to a couple of places that have....?"

"Let me stop you there, C.W., your wife, Renate, the German bar maid, would skin your hide and Sheryl has gone through too much shit on all this. I don't wish to put her through anymore. Ok?"

"Yeah, you got it. Just a quiet dinner and we can talk about some old times in Houston at The Sears store, on Main Street, where we both once worked."

C. W. wanted to do his usual teasing, more like agitating, "Sheryl and Renate won't mind if we sample a few of Budapest's favorites..."

"You are full of shit at times. See you at the airstrip. "

Arnie looked up from his normal squint, questioning the one sided conversation, "What the hell was all that about?"

Murray stared at Arnie, and now Jon was a little curious as he swiveled around in his seat. "What WAS that all about?

"C.W. is a crazy bastard, always stirring up some crap to get my ass in a crack. I'm going back to my seat to grab some 'z's'. Wake me when he calls. I know he is up even though we are seven or eight hours difference. He is likely playing games with the internet jockeys he plays poker with at all hours of the night."

As Murray went past the front section to his rear seat, everyone appeared to be asleep or squirming in theirs, except Michaeleen, listening to her IPad headset and gazing out into the darkness as they flew over the end of the U.S. and into the Atlantic. He decided to stop and sit on the edge of the table in front of her, not saying anything just waiting for a response.

Sleepy-eyed, she looked up, "How much longer will we be before arriving in Budapest?"

"About nine hours, maybe less, you may want to get some shut eye. If you wish to, you could freshen up a bit in our immense bathroom facilities. Then let's talk after that. You are deeply concerned about Carol Sue. I know how close you are to your aunt."

She still had her mojito cocktail and took the last swallow as to gain some mode of confidence. "That is what I need to discuss with you." She leaned back in the beige and leather seat. "You may want to pull in closer after all this."

Murray thought for a moment that perhaps he may want to belt down a beverage, but pulled even closer to her, waiting for the hammer to drop. "Yes Michaeleen, back at Carol Sue's place I knew, well, the way you acted....yeah, tell me. "Then he thought for a second, "It concerns the three of us?"

She was surprised at his comeback, as her lips puckered and then parted, “Yes, how did you...?”

Just then Arnie tapped him on the shoulder. “Your call came in...”

Not knowing if he felt anger or the pang of suspense, his heart began to vibrate in his chest, “Michaeleen I have to take this call, it is my contact on where Kolezy is going to land his plane. I’ll be back shortly. Maybe Nikki could make you a Nigerian Cabdriver cocktail?” She did a possible double take on that, as it was Carol Sue’s favorite cocktail, next to McClallens scotch. He then bolted to the cockpit for the call.

Arnie was taking down the co-ordinates that C. W. was giving him on the airfield at Soliz. Murray leaned in, “Hey thanks guy, just meet us there with some firepower, but be careful, Kolezy is a wily one and like a wolverine will claw at you.”

C.W. replied, “That does not concern me as the people I will be with are stone cold individuals that The State Department here put me in touch with. They gave me the lowdown on Kolezy and his large web of pornography. He is operating in both Budapest as well as Prague. This Kolezy is a blight on all of us in the States. We will help in any way we can. He has an office off the main street. We can take you there if we lose him at the airstrip. Also, his mansion overlooks the University there. For now get some rest. See you at Istaviz.”

Murray was greatly appreciative to his friend, “WE have to go to that Baliton café for some schnapps’. Over and out!”

Jon looked up at him as C.W.’s conversation was on the speaker. “This scoundrel, Kolezy, seized my wife, holding her against her will, and now we are chasing is more than bad news. It appears he is heading for safety there. How’s your Hungarian?”

Murray shook his head,”’Kechi’. That means little of hardly anything. Ernie and Sev are fluent in the language. Bill holds his own but Adam is a whiz at it. I believe we will be fine, as English is universal. C.W. gets by in Hungarian as well and can speak German and some Polak.”

Dimas was awakened by the speaker, as his seat was just in front of the cockpit door and heard most of C.W.’s conversation. He sprung out of his seat like a Jaguar, bumping into Murray as the plane swayed with a mild turbulence. “I heard your buddy give you information on Kolezy. You know, Murray, anything you find out is mine.”

Murray wanted to play a little on the cop. "I was hoping you would say 'Cosa Nem', Lieutenant."

Dimas looked confused, "Coors goosing them. Who are you goosing? Me? You have been on this Kolezy fella too long. He is the King Gooser!"

The three looked at the Lieutenant and busted out laughing by what had happened that day which affected everyone on the plane. This small outburst by Dimas was welcomed.

Murray corrected himself trying not to knock the man who was unfamiliar with the European language. "No, Lieutenant, that only means 'thank you', in Hungarian. Yes, we are going to nail this bastard. You Lieutenant, and your brother, Zeke, will bring him in. Both of you will get a commendation for doing it and HPD should promote the two of you!"

Dimas wanted to contact his captain at HPD to see if he could connect with the Budapest police and Interpol. "Murray, can you get your crew to patch me to Reisner Street and Captain Short for a contact with the locals?"

Murray directed, "Arnie, get the number from Dimas and contact whomever he needs to at the local police."

The Lieutenant's jaw locked. "I want to hunt that pecker down before he kills someone else."

Murray knew where the cop was heading. He looked at the deeply involved man. "You really love that woman, don't you?"

"You, in your way, do too!" he spun back." Carol Sue talked a lot about you. "You have history with her. She appears to have certain feelings about things."

Jon knew his place, "Arnie, take over and put on the headset, I need to use the can."

Murray was more relaxed as the lead pilot slid by him and Dimas, not saying anything as Jon started back to the rear of the plane. "Dimas, I had a thing for her late sister, back when I was an Air Force Lieutenant. There is nothing between Carol Sue and me. You are welcome to go for her full bore. I only know she is a fighter and can handle herself. I want her safe for Michaeleen's sake. Nothing more. Is that something unheard of?"

Dimas silently looked at Murray, knowing where he stood, nodding in the affirmative.

C.W. gave Kolezy's office address, "It is 18 Balog Street. That is supposed to be his headquarters and movie studio for Romany Pictures. I need to head back and talk with Michaeleen."

As Murray went to see the young woman, he found her sleeping. Sitting on the table across from her seat, wondering what she wanted to tell him. What was so important and what did Carol Sue, she, and he have in common? As far as he was concerned, he knew Michaeleen was the one most responsible for Sheryl and him to live the great life. It was, at times, a fantasy they could hardly believe recalling, once again, the previous three and one half years when she walked into their office making them instant multi-millionaires. Why suddenly now, now? It could wait until morning, as he picked up the navy blue wool blanket and draped it over her. Murray admired her very much for what she accomplished, but felt a strange love for her that momentarily terrified why he had that feeling. Backing up, he just figured it was all due to the happenings that day. Not something a normal day would ever offer to him. He started back to his seat and needed sleep knowing that the next eight or so hours were to be filled with even more consternation in the hunt for Kolezy. As he went by, Wes held up his hand.

The big man, his son in law, cleared his throat. "Lately, things haven't been great between us, Murray." Now in a conciliatory tone, Carol Sue's son uttered, "Due to all this. Here I am with this gun, along with a bag full of magazine clips and a Glock. Maybe it is the third gin and tonic, Nikki made for me but I am seeing things much clearer now. I can't fault you or even Adam for bringing my mother into all this. She is a grown person and knows better, yet Mom has always done things here way. Nothing any of us said to her, or had done, would have made a difference."

Murray took the seat next to his son-in-law. "Guess that is your way of patching things up between us Wes. We have always been slightly distant, mainly because of my past association with The Millers and your mother. Your grandfather, Tex, took away what was rightfully mine. I was never greedy. Mike Miller, the great-grandfather you never knew, brought me in for ten per cent and drew up an agreement. He gave me a signed copy that was for the Back Forty Burkburnett Strike. I invested the money to get in. Granted, it was Mike's lending the cash, leading me to hit it big on that airline stock and selling it, then putting the profits into The Strike. Twenty grand was a lot of dough back in those days. When Mike died I went to the local judge and he threw it out stating that Mike was not in his right mind. The judge was in Tex's pocket. I really believe he got rid of his own father in that fire at the ranch, burning up all of Mike's papers and agreements except the will. It stated that Tex and his brother, Jack, would inherit seventy-five per cent of Mike and your great-grandmother, Lulla Belle's estate. Lulla Belle, from what Michaeleen learned, never believed the fire was an accident and she overturned the will with another judge. The revision only gave Tex and Jack five percent each of an amount that was over a billion dollars and that Burkburnett deal was worth three or four billion. Lulla Belle left her 80 percent to Carol Sue, Bobbie Jean, your uncles, Russell and Millard. Donna, Tex's wife and your grandmother, was given a stipend to live on, as she was separated from her husband and Lulla Belle felt sorry for her. When Tex committed suicide the day Michaeleen found him in his Wichita Falls office building it ended a great deal of grieve he cast upon a lot of folks. Michaeleen researched it, found how I was cheated and made things right. Here I am standing in a multi-million dollar luxury airplane. It was all because of that lady sleeping over there that made it possible. Of course, she took over a revised Miller Corp. and doubled it making the company you are in charge of today."

Wes never knew the entire background of this behemoth company. He blew out his breath, "Whew, so that is what happened. My mother would only sketchily tell me when I asked the why's and how's and when's. I had no idea why she never discussed any of this, especially, Tex's greedy part."

"Just figure she could be protecting the memory of her father. Tex is fortunate that he met his end, as he could have faced jail time for embezzlement or even in the death of his father. Tex always thought that he was above the law. I don't really curse his worthless hide as another door or two opened up for me even before Michaeleen entered our lives."

"With all the double dealings I can see why my mother was tired of the business that is why she elevated me to CEO of Miller Corp."

"I believe she saw a lot in you. You are not like Tex. That is why in all this, freeing your mother should not bring you into shooting up the place. Allow us to take down Kolezy. We will bring her back. I know she does not want you to do any dumb thing to endanger your life or your integrity, landing you in jail away from Gina and your children, our grandkids. They need a dad. Gina needs you and so do Noah Grant and Lila Grace."

"I am here, too, as she wanted MABB badly and for some stupid reason I Ok'd it. For the life of me I cannot put my finger on why she loves gay porn. That is what MABB is all about. The video stores, the magazines, porn movies with guy on guy, woman on woman, clothing, resorts that cater to gays and lesbians on an island in the Caribbean or in Key West, hotels, clubs and restaurants...Why does she go that way?"

Murray defended her action. "She is a business woman. MABB is a cash cow. Money maker. It has been proven that women ages 22 thru 65 like this sort of entertainment. They view it, initially, the majority buys. They like two women, sometimes, but really enjoy two men making it, unlike a guy on a gal, pumping off. Carol Sue sees it as a new wave. She lost a lot when Miller Corp. was broken up and sold. She wants her money back and this could be the ticket."

Wes did not say a word as he knew what his father-in-law said was totally correct. "I better get some rest. But believe me, if everyone fails to bring my mother back, I will do anything possible to take care of things."

Murray agreed. "Go get em, son!" With that he got up and walked away.

As Murray started to get settled in his seat, Tanski buttoned holed him. "Hey, Murray, all the time at our high school, Cathedral Latin School, in Cleveland, you never let on how much you loved adventure. You know, after this, we can grab my wife, Ruby and your lovely, and head to Nairobi to shoot some tigers. You shoot left handed, right? I have a left bore on a 30/30 and all it would take for you is aim and fire. Those Bengals charge and I just stand my ground and bring them down, one shot. There is a great taxidermist there. We have it FED Exed to our winter get away in Colorado, mounted and all. Must have over thirty heads! "Ron brought his arms around in a mock rifle position. Smiling at the thought of being on the plains of Africa. Doing a mock, "pow, pow, pow."

Murray laughed, "It took three shots to get that last one, Ron, to bring that last cat down. Didn't you say you could shoot that charging whatever? You always say one shot and I can kill anything."

Tanski fell back, "You know you're right. Of course, it could have been that third bourbon shot that Nikki prepared for me that caused me to squeeze another shot or two off."

Murray attempted to answer a man he was depending upon, after learning of Tanski downing three bourbons on the rocks, "You realize, Ron that we need you clean and sober on this deal or whatever we want to call it. Don't want you to wind up like your friend, Hank, who drank too much and went out in the woods and accidently was killed by hunters, as he did not wear his bright colored forest clothes.

That set off a warning light to the veteran. Tanski attempted to straighten up, as he did, the empty Wild Turkey bottle that Nikki left rolled across the aisle of the plane to a zonked out Sev. "I'll be fine when we get in, Murray. I can hold my liquor, unlike Hank. You can definitely depend upon me to bring down that ass hole. Kolezy, at 250 yards. I am not anything like Hank. He was a drinker. Confidentially, this Kolezy shit has me spooked a little. We are up five plus miles trailing this dip stick, who has that platinum blond, ex-model, wild ass broad, on a motorcycle. We had some clear shots at her home and at the airport but everything got fouled up. I would not have allowed him to fly away. I saw that broad, 'Wadna Dupa'. In Polish, means a beautiful ass. She is one hell of a fuckin' piece of ass. Anyhow, those so-called sharpshooters did jack shit, no balls. One shot, like JFK, through the skull. Hell, I was a young kid, back in Dallas that day. Saw the rifle in the Book Depository, sun hitting the barrel. Too late to do much. It was like Hank," as he became a little emotional, uncharacteristic for this man of fortune, hands trembling, "Did not want it to turn out that way. He was a decent guy who had his share of problems."

Murray caught all that, "Look, Ronnie don't press, lay back, I'll get Nikki to get you some 'joe'. Get some rest..."

"You don't understand, we were in the line shack. Hank was drinking too much and got on me for leaving my first wife, Jane, who he secretly loved and thought I ruined her... I told him to sober up and get the hell out of the cabin. He tore out with a bottle of Old Grand Dad. Minutes later, I heard a shot. Some dimwitted hunter put a slug through his chest. I went out and saw it. The hunter came out and we cell phoned for an air helicopter to come and pick him up for the trip to the nearest hospital. By the time the 'copter landed in a clearing a 150 yards away, the medics tried their best. Hank was gone. I blamed myself for all that for a lot of years. Now I'm not sure if I am here to get Kolezy or join Hank in the Hunter's Boot Hill!"

Murray, temporarily lost, mentally kicking himself for opening up the subject. All these years Tanski kept this inside and now he was on the edge of his life. In all the battles, small or large, did Ron want to even it all up? Were those men he shot in Cleveland two years ago justification for Hank's death, somehow, and now would his friend go off center? Murray just walked back and got into his seat, attempting to get comfortable. He questioned himself, 'was he there to get Kolezy or rescue Carol Sue or to get the attorney to admit he had a hand in Troy's death'? Was their son another victim just like the others? He would make Kolezy admit it at the point of death?' Or, if the King of Hungarian Porn was not dying, he would blow him away with the Judge, emptying all high caliber shots into his worthless body. Then he thought of what Lieutenant Cavazos told him about Troy's death. It may have been at the hands of a woman, a redhead. Murray went back in his mind about those last months that Sheryl and he had with Troy. The young man had girlfriends and they liked the last one, Skylar Locke. She was a redhead and slightly overbearing. Troy proposed and gave her that ring only to call it off. No, she could not have been the one in that dive of a motel. Then, he had a close relationship with a Jewish guy, Saul. They were tight, Troy would go over to the house where Saul lived with his parents, went to barmitzvas, bar-b-ques, the wedding where Saul's sister got married. He and Saul, each broke the glass and threw it in the fireplace together. Troy broke up with Skylar shortly after that. Troy was an altar boy, honor student, college grad, as he and Saul attended Stephen F. Austin in Nacogdoches together as did his sisters, Renee and Gina. Murray went blank, as all the chaotic events of the past twenty four hours were crushing. His main goal was to get Kolezy and if he could get him to admit the connection with Troy and of course, free Carol Sue.

Across the aisle was Rich, all six foot, three inches stretched out past the seat. He wanted to talk, and although Murray was almost mentally spent he still wanted to hear from a guy who was a friend, though not as close as Bill and Tanski, but a person he admired and respected for his past service and devotion to his country, serving in a Secret Service capacity and then FBI operative. Rich began, "You know I want this low life guy just to show the Bureau that they made a mistake on pushing me out. They thought I was washed up and getting long in the tooth. New regime at the top, hiring young, 'Joe College' types with fancy resumes who think God sent them to defend the country and squash all the insurgents. This Kolezy would be Public Enemy Number One if they ever got it right. I want his European Ass."

Murray agreed. "Rich, hell, we know you are not over the hill. You are a brilliant tactician and hunter of the worst kind out there. I'm glad you are on our side. That deal in Cleveland showed me the way you work. We would not have gotten those bastards who were terrorizing our old friend from our childhood Hungarian neighborhood. YOU were single handedly responsible for getting the Cleveland cops to arrest all of them. Least the ones, Tanski and Sev did not shoot. The cops were fumbling trying to help Les Monostory, who had his shop on Buckeye and constantly was broken into and terrorized."

Now, Rich was sitting on the edge of his seat, "I only pinpointed the culprits after that last robbery. You, Bill, Ernie, Cousin Sev, and Ron, over there, laid it on those former DP's or their grandkids."

"Yeah, after the DP parents came over from the late fifties from Hungary, their kids grew up alright. The kids, the next generation became thugs. Never fails, the hand is bitten by those who are given a free ride in this country," Murray contended. "As far as breaking up the gang, I was there for the ride. A backup. All of you did the heavy stuff. Bill and you cracked a few heads on those Hunkies."

"Well, I owe Tanski. A couple of those Third Generation Freedom Fighters had me in their gun sights. He blew them both away. The Cleveland cops never even asked or checked who shot who. Must have given them a reprieve on having to shoot and make out a report. Now, Kolezy is in my crosshairs."

Murray eyes began to droop as Rich continued, but the words faded as he drifted off, until St. George shook him.

"Anth, this whole thing is getting very edgy. We're not talking Buckeye Road bandits here. Sev there, of all people, is planning to shoot a grenade at Kolezy. He has a half dozen in that duffel bag, along with a launcher in the cargo hold."

Almost in a drunken state from lack of sleep and the two George Dickels on the rocks, he managed to think out loud, " Well as long as.., wait.. he can't send a rocket launcher; we need to get Carol Sue away from that bastard. ...and I have a few questions to ask Kolezy. What the fuck is Sev thinking about?"

Rich laughed, "That's the way us Fedor's do things. Sev won't endanger 'The Blonde Bombshell'!"

Bill looked down the aisle at Sev who was catching some needed rest, "He confided in me, Anth, that he wants revenge for what the attorney did to a former friend of his, in the Green Berets, who was killed by Kolezy's body guard, Drago, the scar man. She disappeared a few years back and was found strangled. The police were unable to get Drago to come into Reisner Street and sit down for questioning on it. He conveniently went overseas and was unavailable. An attorney from Kolezy's practice gave the police a supposed deposition stating Drago was in Nebraska when the gal disappeared."

Murray was astounded about the connection and that Sev never let on about it. "Rich's cousin signed on to hunt down Kolezy, but I figured he was doing it more for the Hungarian connection with Adam, just like that Cleveland thing we fought over. Ha, I guess it seems like everyone has reason to be aboard. What is Ernie's reason?"

Bill smiled, "You won't believe this, but he is writing a novel about all this."

Murray's sleepiness seemed to disappear on that. "No shit, you know with all this crap going on I did see he had a miniature tape recorder, 'yakking' into it now and then. Meant to ask him but with all ..."

At that point, Arnie called on the intercom, now at the controls taking over from Jon, who was getting much needed rest in the aft pilot's compartment bed. "Oh damn, what the hell does he want now?"

Murray stretched as he went towards the cockpit, Sergeant Zeke Cavazos, grabbed him enroute."Hey, Gringo. Are you ready for all this? No second thoughts?"

Murray looked down at the slightly overconfident Sergeant, "You bet nerves of steel", as he held up his non-trembling left hand with the other slightly flinching. "And you, Zeke? This is not a tamale run or a rousting of illegal's at a Mexican run business on Navigation, in East Houston."

Zeke let out a full blast of laughter that caused most of the sleeping group to momentarily awake then resume their slumber. "I bring this guy in dead or alive and I am back as captain on HPD. Maybe even run for office in Houston or Harris County. Maybe, Sheriff."

Murray thought for a moment, "Yeah, Sergeant that would make anyone's day. Just remember to duck those bullets...I need to see what our pilot, Arnie, wants..."

Arnie, in the right seat, was intense at the controls, oxygen mask on, and wearing the headset, as Murray tapped him on the shoulder. He jumped almost a foot off his seat... pulling the mask off, "Whew, you scared me! I knew Jon was in the pilot's aft section taking a siesta."

Murray was unsure of his co-pilot, at times. "Just who did you think I was, Louis B.Kolezy or the masked intruder of the skies?"

The edgy co-pilot displayed a concerned look on his cherubic face. "You know I have never flown on a dangerous flight before. Never was in Iraq or one of those banana republic places that some pilots fly for the money. In all my 26 years as a pilot, never had any close calls. I know all of you have your mission to accomplish. I just need to be assured that Jon and I will not have to shoulder a rifle or carry an automatic weapon?"

Murray flipped the left seat around as he sat in it and placed his hands to his face almost in an attempt to smooth his fifty plus features devoid of any wrinkles or laugh lines, which was a way to think before giving an answer, "Arnie, I certainly won't get Jon or you in the middle of all what's going to happen. Your jobs are to get us to our destination safely, secure the plane in some protected hangar, and do some night life, if you wish, in Budapest. We will have the backing of the Budapest police and Interpol. We may not even have to draw our own weapons. Maybe we will do some questioning and a little surveillance. Advise the authorities where the culprits are, then they can tell the cops where and they can arrest or kill them. The Lieutenant and his brother, Sergeant Zeke can bring the gang back in cuffs or in bags. If alive, they will stand for murder at their trial."

Arnie's face squelched up more as his lips quivered, "Jon and I know these men are bad and maybe murderers." He reached up and touched Murray again and again.

Murray drew back to avoid the almost relentless light jabs by Kaplan who was unconsciously doing it because his mind drifted to a time he experienced in his youth when he witnessed a robbery gone bad resulting in the murder of a neighbor. Later he was called upon to testify and that he had to leave the state to get away from the murderer's friends who threatened him.

"I, I, Ah, Ah, cannot go through seeing a killing."

"Don't get your shit in an uproar, okay? You and Jon, again, as I told you, are not involved on that part. "

Arnie seemed to relax. "Alright, I believe you. My past had something like this."

Murray had enough, not wanting to delve into Arnie's past. "Look man, I am going back to my seat for needed sleep. I'll catch you later. One thing before I go, you do have the co-ordinates for the airfield at which we will land, right?"

Arnie fidgeted. "Of course, I do."

Murray was convinced for the time being that they were on target. "We already have the police alerted in Budapest and they are going to meet Kolezy's plane when he lands. The authorities will arrest him. Meanwhile, Lieutenant Cavazos radioed his superiors in Houston and they in turn have a squad of FBI personnel coming to back up this whole deal and to take back Kolezy and what is left of his band of merry men."

Arnie leaned back in his seat, "Whew, so it will be over without any hassle? But, I heard you talk with the Lieutenant and he said, said, ah, ah, dead or alive."

"Well sure, that is his game, although the local Hungarian cops and Interpol, it should not go down that way. Kolezy will not back off easy but knows, if cornered, he might take his chance with the Houston courts and surrender and be brought back to Texas. Just think of this as a 'milk run', as combat pilots termed it during their tours over some bombing run."

He was still not convinced, "What, what if this Kolezy fella has to come on our plane, for, for, for eleven hours and he tries to pull something?" His voice raised untold decibels enough to wake up Rich in the rear of the plane.

Murray winced, but gained control, "Look, The FBI will take him aboard another plane that their agency supplies. Maybe even using an Air Force plane. The Feds take over the arrest and don't want us to be a part of it; sooo, you and Jon are out of this. We fly back with Ms. Winters and have a party on the way."

Arnie sighed, "I guess my mother would have a heart attack if she knew her son was involved in all this."

Murray seemed wrung out over the co-pilot's act of over anxiousness. He patted the pilot on the shoulder, "You will do fine, just fly the plane and make positive we get land at the right place near Budapest. Okay?"

Arnie bobbed his head up and down as though he had five Red Bulls before gaining control of the plane, placing the oxygen mask on and stared straight focusing on navigating the plane over the horizon.

Murray let out a deep breath and headed back to his seat for that needed sleep.

Again, though prevented for that moment, by St. George. "You okay, Anth? Arnie is a real piece of work. Have you thought of cutting him loose for some real co-pilot?"

"Naw, Billy, he is a seasoned flyer. He cannot operate as second in command and be on drugs. Besides, he needs the job. Arnie always is pressured to pay his way on numerous family things that his wealthy mother insists he attend and pony up the money. He has always passed the drug tests, physicals, shit like that the past three years we owned a plane. Both he and Jon have always been dependable. Like you heard me tell him, we have bigger concerns once we land."

St. George was worried a little about his friend. "Anth, are you going to make it through this? You know this is not dealing with some Buckeye Road hoodlums."

"Funny, you should say that, it seems like I heard that before. Kolezy is no better than those Freedom Fighter's grandkids that turned out to being tough guys. He only has a degree. We are journeying to our heritage land. It is still foreign to me, at least, to take down a murderous, porn king. Sure my stomach has turned over a few times, knowing that maybe it won't work out and we may be in over our heads. Sheryl has texted me twice. I need to hit the head, and then check back with her. You'll have to excuse me, it may be The George Dickel#12." With that Murray comically jabbed his friend on the arm and moved toward the restroom.

Kolezy's Falcon F-7 leveled out at 35,000, with Carol Sue still strapped in her seat, the smug attorney sauntered up to her. "Well my dear Ms. Winters, we have a lot of time to get re-acquainted. Perhaps you would like a martini, not too dry, I assume? Then we can talk about the future for each of us. You will enjoy the nightlife and the beautiful day bathed in sunshine. My mansion overlooks the city on one side, and the back, the fertile valley with gorgeous flowers and trees turning the color of fall. It definitely is not like the flat, dismal area you would find in Houston."

The woman looked up at the Cheshire grinning Kolezy and dryly responded. "If you even make it to your house on the hill, Louis, it will be your last glimpse of freedom before the police get you and return you back to flat, dismal Houston to stand trial for all your crimes. Of course, if you go peacefully and not in a body bag."

Kolezy sat down next to her touching her soft uplifted cheek with his hairy hand. She turned away, choosing to look at the cabin wall. His eyes widened as he placed his hand under her jaw, pulling it toward him. "Carol Sue, you cannot get off this plane. That is, unless we throw you off and that may well be an option come to think of it. Certainly, you have sacrificed yourself in the past to survive, haven't you? It would be a shame to see your beautiful body floating down."

"Look Kolezy, you want to make time in this tin French crate of an airplane with these disgusting sea foam colors? You would be required to drop well below 10,000 feet to open the doors and you cannot afford that time. Plus you would hear me invoking The Hungarian Curse on your family...as I fought off your goons. Besides, I am a descendant of Enni."

Kolezy drew back, in an uncharacteristic actual shock at what he just heard. "The Magyar Curse? Enni? You heard of it? You know of her? How? How?"

Unknown to him, Adam related the story at The Merriam, the night they made love telling of the Gypsy Curse. Kolezy was semi superstitious and that story always terrified him, as told to him growing up by his parents when they were in the Old Country. If she ever needed to use a weapon on his stepfather, her life would be spared. Now, sitting in his getaway cylinder, Louis was almost delirious, as his mouth gapped open in a semi shock. He got up and slipped down the aisle, catching himself on empty seat, looking back at a different type of woman he thought that would be putty in his hands, riveting a terrified look at her as she cast a damn, 'I not afraid of you' type, gaze into his frightful eyes.

His henchmen were bewildered at their leader's sudden loss of composure to this woman, seeing him in a sweaty loss of control state. Their strong mentor almost reduced to a down trodden peon. He staggered to the plane's liquor cabinet and wet bar, grabbing a glass and pouring himself a Patron, three ounce straight up gulp. "He murmured to a nearby Dimitri, "She knows of The Curse, The Magyar Duna!"

Hungarian folk lore of the late 19th Century when Hungary and Austria were one. St. Elizabeth was the patron saint. Louis Kossuth came later in the twentieth century and was the revered warrior and soldier, fighting for the cause. Those who grew up in either time were told the story of the Magyar Duna.

Louis sat down as Dimitri and Drago came up, but the one most interested in the tale was Luka.

Luka, almost pleaded to Louis, "Please, my master, tell us of the story of Magyar Duna."

Kolezy's eyes rolled, bulging; as his breathing became shallow, just to relate the thought of The Curse, his voice so low that his disciples grew near to hear the story. "The Curse is of a tall, beautiful, and captivating woman with long golden locks of hair cascading around her nebulous shoulders, the color of her ocean blue eyes made by a higher being. She had an affair with Andrew, a Cusack soldier that ended in a tragic triangle when Lazlo, a peasant farmer, from the region of Szolnak, Kerestezy, just south of Monsor found them making love, both totally naked on the lush green foliage. Lazlo loved her from afar and he tried to speak to her but being a peasant she did not want him. The woman named Helen, known as Enni, was married to an older rich farmer that she never loved. She rode a large, white horse. Lazlo was a worker for that man and he coveted the young beautiful woman. He attempted to engage her sexually but his advances were always thwarted. When he found the two having sex, he grew angry and killed them with a cleaver he used in the fields to clear brush and weeds. Stabbing them numerous times, he stopped, gasping for breath, as to the deed he performed. Horrified and in terror as to what the law would do to him, he cut his throat and fell upon the couple next to the Danube.

Luka's curiosity enlarged, "Then, Louis, why the fable of a curse?"

Kolezy laid his hand on the impressionable lad, "Each time a couple would embark on love making near the Danube, the man would feel as though a sword was piercing his balls and stabbing him in the back. There had been many suicides at that same spot where the tragedy took place. Never has a man and woman married after visiting there. Some people have even seen the ghost of the three people appearing at them, one of which is the woman and as she appears to me. It is her, Carol Sue! Now I know why she is called 'Vixey'. She is a vixen!"

Dimitri had enough, "Louis is that the reason you did not get rid of her when we first leveled off on our flight and you had the opportunity to throw her from our plane?"

Kolezy drew back in a low tone, not to have Carol Sue hear him, " I wanted to take the woman back to the bedroom, enjoy my carnage with her and at 10,000 feet, cast the bitch out below thus, ending any strife that she caused me. Now I envision all the people I have wronged due to this Curse. She has brought this on our journey and I am powerless to do anything with her. She must be protected.

As their leader was still shaking, Luka became more interested in how she knew anything about the story. "Louis, how would this woman even know about the Curse?"

Louis, still numb and unclear in his thinking, he muttered "I believe she is a descendant of Enni Kerestezy. She mentioned that name and was a great, great, great granddaughter of Enni. I was totally blind and should have known."

Dimitri shared his fear of the blond woman. "We must get rid of her, push her out the plane's door, Louis. Do it now before we crash."

Luka was struck with terror, "No, no, she must be preserved until we land. She is a witch. She will place a spell on our plane! After we land, Louis, take a spike to her and pound it through her heart."

Kolezy looked over at Carol Sue who appeared to be sleeping, although she was actually listening in glee at the stupid interpretation of an old superstition that no one was positive even existed. Adam was right. It worked. Kolezy's stepson was a great lay and he actually saved her life with this old wife's tale. Knowing everything was going for her, she knew she had to remain quiet unless Kolezy might begin suspecting that she was not a descendant of this Enni, what's her name.

Kolezy went past the woman barely acknowledging her existence as he stumbled toward the bar for more Patron. His men were at an impasse unless he changed his mind, that of getting rid of this siren.

After nearly eight hours into the flight and sleeping like her young grandchildren, Carol Sue got up, stretched and headed to the rest room. All the men watched from afar as she entered and locked the door. Louis was stoned drunk, partially passed out, from emptying the Patron bottle.

Gabor humoring, whispered to Luka, "You and Louis are correct, she is the woman on the white horse."

Luka agreed, tossing his head in an upward motion, "Yes, yes, you, Gabor, can see it, too!"

Gabor laughed at the lad. "Luka, may you buy that underwater lot in Szeged I want to sell. I think that Louis has lost it and you are a naïve child. She rides motorcycles, throws darts, plays poker, drinks and swears like some Russian sailor. If I were in charge, I would rip off her clothes and show her what a real man could do. She would be in ecstasy, as she never experienced love like that before. I would not throw her out of the plane because we would be making those magic times throughout this flight. For now I need a Uricum drink. You want to share one, Luka?"

"No, that is bitter Hungarian brandy. I enjoy other palinkas, like Alma, the pear brandy."

Gabor chided the youth, "Ah, that is a child's drink. Let us drink Zwack Uricum. It will make you feel wild and exhilarated. Yes, wild to plunder the depth of Enni Kerestezy's supposed relative," as he eyed the somber Carol Sue who looked his way, as she returned from refreshing herself. "Enni", he called out, "I have some Hungarian brandy you must try."

Carol Sue waved off, "I am not into brandy."

Louis' semi hangover was disappearing as he came up to Gabor and Luka. "Leave her alone and besides, we may require her if the Hungarian authorities respond to our arrival in Budapest. Danika, our lovely pilot, has received a phone message just now. The government has been alerted that we may be on our way there, flying into Ferishesy International Airport. No, we will be landing at the airfield that is close to my mansion. I must talk with Mrs. Miller or Winters, whatever, and ask her why she wishes to buy MABB so badly." Locating another bottle and ice, he staggered with his Patron on the rocks, now, an almost more sober Kolezy sidled up to a prone Carol Sue who only wanted to get rest.

She looked up at him, "Had to go, could not hold it for three more hours, Kolezy."

"Well your highness, you have big ears after all." He, again, began to touch her face with the palm of his hand. "How about a Patron on the rocks or are you into some other hard liquor? I know you do not care for brandy, nor do I."

She deferred, "No thank you. Your hospitality is overwhelming," as she pulled further away from his reach.

"Tell me now, since you will be unable to buy MABB, what was your interest in it?"

"Strictly business that will make me countless millions. AND, I have a better opportunity to get it than you."

Kolezy was still interested even though he felt she was only dreaming about obtaining the company. "Tell me, Carol Sue, why?"

"Alright, you see two gay guys or even straights acting gay banging one another. Women see it much differently. They are the big buyers into all this."

Kolezy laughed out loud, "Really Carol Sue, you and I can really partner up on this. You go ahead and buy MABB and I can have hunky boys with my Romany Productions. You can use my Hungarian houseboy, Herbak, and I can even get you Ryan Anthony, my Adam."

The woman thought it all humorous. "A houseboy and your stepson. You are dreaming, Louis, you have had too many Patrons. You have a better chance of getting a life term than that."

Still not deterred, "Carol Sue, you are such an expert, how do women view gay porn? I cannot believe that they are such a large segment in buying that?"

The woman was very confident in her situation, as she knew that it would be easy to convince this low life attorney. "Louis, two women can have a sexual encounter. Take lesbians, men like woman on woman. In the man on woman, she is normally the submissive one. In man to man, both can be dominant. It is a common fantasy a woman has. Most of them enjoy it. Gay porn works on many levels. The general public does not know that women love it. So few admit openly sharing their interest. There are internet gay porn websites that attract legions of female fans. Man on man is girl on girl in reverse. Gay men tend to be picky about aesthetics. Their star leads want to be better looking and immaculately groomed, not always true of their so-called, straight actors. Straight porn casts, for the most part, male leads that have large penises and their ability to ejaculate on cue. That lends to average porn film delivering a leading male whose only attraction is a functioning set of balls and, sometimes, a nice ass. Normally, it is the same pudgy guy with a tattoo, and a mullet driving home into some ageing donkey with a bad dye job. On the other hand, the gay performer gets the gal's vote all the time. Great for advertising a product too. Look at it this way, Louis, have the one guy with a Ralph Lauren emblem on his shirt as it is being torn off by his male counterpart, or display the Jack Daniel bottle next to the bed. It shows that our guy wears that brand and/or drinks a special alcohol, maybe even, Remy Martin or Courvoisier cognac, not that crappy Alma or Zwack Uricum. Expensive cologne, Ralph Lauren, as he sprays himself waiting for that special person."

Louis wondered, was there more. "And what else, my dear?"

"Another advantage, are female views don't need to suffer feelings of gender betrayal that comes as a result of watching a pneumatic bimbo pretending to be a French maid unconvincingly begging for a double penetration in an Eastern European scene. It all leads for both the man and the woman, or the bed participants, who view the video, to a great deal of fantasy, in their own minds, as they become sexually aroused. It makes sex more of what sex should be...."

Kolezy was almost in agreement, as he was momentarily aroused by her description of what sex could be, not what it may normally turn out. He then came back to reality "That's what I like about that part, over straight Eastern European actors and scripts. Americans are more open. Take my stepson, Adam AKA Ryan Anthony. He is brilliant in that, and yet, refuses to allow me to come on board. So to speak, and buy into his company. We were so close. I don't know what has come over him?"

Carol Sue had to bit her tongue on that lie, but wise enough to let it pass as she attempted to buy more time for herself. "Louis, I need my beauty rest." With that she switched off the overhead light and turned her back to him.

He agreed, "Yes my dear, we all need that." He left her, sensing that he had an ally in this woman. Returning back to his seat he thought that he had a potential duo, Danika, his he-she pilot that stood six feet, blond, feminine voiced, but had all its male parts. Yes, Kolezy dreamed of highlighting both Danika and Carol Sue in his flicks which would sell throughout the free world and even where freedom was non-existent.

As Kolezy was settling in, feeling that everything was going his way, Danika came back and told him that his partner, Imre Rabb, was on the plane's phone. Louis went into the cockpit. "What's up Imre?"

Rabb, his Budapest front man for Kolezy's Hungarian operation, told him that their contact at the Budapest police department, was warning that Interpol and local police were waiting to arrest them as the plane landed at Istaviz Field. Rabb paid his contact, Sergeant Cheheck of the Budapest police, in both Hungarian forints and U. S. dollars to only have the authorities, in wait, at the main city airport, Feretezyi International. Rabb guaranteed that the Falcon could land at Istaviz Field without any police intervention.

"Thank you, my friend, that is a relief as much has occurred. I will see you at the mansion and we can toast our success with the best Hungarian brandy."

Hours later, the Falcon approached the airfield. As the plane landed and the door opened, Kolezy's operatives met him and they all went to the office next to the airstrip to pick up some packages, they then embarked to the mansion overlooking Budapest. Carol Sue was at first dazzled by the late afternoon charm of the new land she had never been exposed to in her life. While the others were rummaging through the packages, she found some paper and scribbled a message on what she overheard Kolezy tell Drago. As they departed the office, she tacked the note to a computer, hoping that none of Kolezy's men would see it and if, by chance, rescuers would see it and come to her aid.

Kolezy commanded Danika to taxi the Falcon, to a small patch of trees, about three hundred yards away, and hide the plane, under a green tarp until it was needed.

The Gulfstream circled the near empty airfield a scant hour and a half after Kolezy's landing. Except for a few small aircraft and no Falcon in sight, the area appeared to be cleared of any major aircraft. They all peered out the plane's windows, sighting a half dozen small, metal buildings and no hangars. The group had munched on Nikki's sausage, biscuits', and Puerto Rican coffee, content on waiting for the next chapter of this saga. Murray had overcome his George Dickel #12. He glanced over to Michaeleen who was silently staring out the window. Murray wanted to be certain that his friend, C. W. and his crew were waiting and had swept the area of any thought of an ambush as their plane landed.

Murray, went up to the cockpit, as Jon slowly circled, "Arnie, get me C. W., please!"

Moments later C. W. Roberts responded. "I see you circling. Our group is here, at the airport, scanning the buildings now to see if any of Kolezy's men are hiding in ambush. So far, as they signaled me there is no sign of anyone armed or otherwise. All looks safe to land. See you soon."

Murray instructed Jon to land the Gulfstream, then returned to rear of the plane and advised everyone to strap in their seats as this was the final approach. Perhaps, at the Sugarland Airport someone planted the idea of Kolezy landing here, only to throw everyone off the track and he really flew to another destination with Carol Sue. He prayed not.

The plane touched down without any problems. It rolled up to a cluster of three metal structures, one of which was a weather beaten building with a lone light in the window in what passed as a main structure. A set of fuel pumps were in front of it, almost like a rural gas station. Everyone on the Gulfstream had their eyes riveted to the office, where that light glowed in the Hungarian sunlight.

Lieutenant Cavazos stirred from his seat casting off his blanket. He yelled out, "Hey, Murray is this what you call a Mud-Yar welcome? Where's the band, the catering trucks, dancing girls?"

Murray was tired already from the long flight and as he rubbed his eyes. He responded, "Lieutenant, you want to run out there in the event Kolezy and company have AK 15's, ready to mow down everyone? If you want girls and a band get your fill in town. They don't have food trucks like we do, either."

Lieutenant Cavazos agreed, "I am not rushing off to be shot. We can always wait on the other things. Didn't you tell me a State Department guy you know would be here to assist us?"

Murray started. "My friend, C. W., is already here with some of his people. He is almost 100% positive that we are safe, had our plane in sight, and checked out everything before we could land. C. W. is bringing enough SUV's to load us and our gear to a hotel where we can operate in Budapest. Ernie and Sev, along with Adam are going to be our interpreters."

Lieutenant Cavazos was a little confused. "Don't you speak the language?"

"Not really, I am one of those who did not want to take the class in summer so I could converse with my grandmother in Hungarian. She would have told me to fuck off, anyway, of course, in her Magyar way."

Suddenly, three Mercedes SUV's rambled down the side road next to the narrow asphalt strip, as the occupants in the Gulfstream still cautiously waited at the windows.

Jon yelled back to Murray, "Is that your friend, C.W.?"

Murray ran up to the cockpit looking over his pilot's shoulder as Arnie was shutting down the plane. "Sure hope it is, Jon."

At that moment, Murray's cell phone rang out. It was C.W. "Hey, man, that has to be you and your drivers? Yeah, we'll gather our stuff and be out as soon as you and your bunch run up with your vehicles. Wait! Can you and your folks poke around the corners, once again, since we're unable to and don't wish to be shot, just in case our wayward attorney has the devil in mind? Oh, your guys are already armed and doing that. Great! We'll be visible in a few minutes."

Adam tugged on Murray. "I have a friend here in Budapest that can help track down Louis. His name is Szilard Szabo. I already texted him to meet us. He is connected."

Arnie turned in their direction, nose squeezed up, eyes squinting and in an almost trance like uttered, "By chance, is he a male prostitute?"

Acting slightly offended by that question, Adam dryly responded. "No, his father is well known as an executive at his own factory in Pest. Did you require a man for the night, Arnie?"

Arnie appeared to disregard the retort and returned the volley, "Do they make widgets?"

"Pottery ware. It is something I heard that you are interested in. If you are a good boy, he'll take you through his father's kiln shop. That is, if you don't get your ass shot off doing all this!"

Kaplan hunkered down in his co-pilot's seat, pretending to click off the controls that he had done earlier. He looked up at Murray. "I thought you said Jon and I would not be in any danger?"

Murray gave Adam a mock evil eye, "There you go again, telling Arnie a bunch of bull shit. Arnie, you and Jon are our ticket out of here and we cannot have you taken out. So cool it!"

Dimas was anxious to begin the journey, "How long are we going to wait before getting out of this, whatever, we call this engine rocket? When do your people come and take us away?"

"Right at this moment Dimas, they are rechecking out the buildings and hangars so we don't get cut down by Kolezy's Mafia gang. Hang in there, okay? Even you know that is regular procedure."

C.W. then squawked, "Hey, guys, we made positive all is in order. This place is totally clean."

Murray relayed the news then advised, "Okay, folks, get your gear together. We are heading out to the beautiful place called Budapest."

As everyone scrambled out with their personal effects, Murray pulled Adam aside, "You never mentioned this Szilard person before. Where did he come from?"

Adam was clear, "Well, he and I were together. I followed his contests and met him in towns, both here and in the U.S."

Murray frowned, "What type of contests? For what?"

"Szilard is a rich kid and was bored, but he possessed a dynamite bod. God given, without much of a workout schedule. He got into body building. Won contests a zillion times. I visited a few and we connected."

"Has he worked in MABB or other movies for you?"

"As a favor, he has done a few. Doesn't need the dough. Doing it for kicks. His co-stars were in Heaven as he fell in place in the scenes without any coaching. The flicks we put him in sold abroad and were a woman's dream. They became a fantastic sellout. If he was not a close friend, I would push him into doing more MABB. The women like his techniques."

Murray knew that everyone was fooled by Adam's previous description of Szilard. "So you snowed Arnie and everyone on this Szilard fellow being in the pottery business."

"His father is, but Szilard is not interested in crack pots. More of what women have to offer."

"Oh that is good, you know a straight guy, of course, besides, the ones on this plane."

Adam showed a sly smile. Szilard can go either way. I bet one or two on this plane can do the same."

Murray shrugged, "I cannot believe that, but let's take care of things for now. So you have your stepfather's haunts and we should be able to track him down, to at least, one of them? Just pray that he has not done away with our blond bombshell."

"Yes, I know the places Anthony. I am not totally concerned about her. Carol Sue is an up and over female. It is, if Louis is still breathing, after she has had HER way with him!"

The group led by C.W. moved toward the buildings for a last chance of anyone leaving evidence of their being there. Dimas and Zeke were following close to them to see if any clues were there.

The Lieutenant yelled out, "Hey, hold up, we're going to check out the office to see if there are any leads we can use."

Murray, St. George, and Adam raced behind the two policemen. Upon reaching the building everyone had the same motive in mind to seek some scrap of evidence that Kolezy was there earlier. The door lock was already forced and broken. Murray reminded Lieutenant Cavazos that it was probably done by C.W. or one of his men when they made an early investigation of the premises before their plane landed.

The small office had a single bulb illuminating it, accompanied by the noon sun radiating through the dirty windows. The contents, except for two desks, three chairs, and a desk top computer were all that appeared to be visible.

Lieutenant Cavazos and his brother, the Sergeant, started to look through the desks, "Dimas called out to Zeke, "Let's see if an arrival log or something can be found indicating Kolezy was here."

Stuck to the computer, was a scribbled note that Dimas found, 'I'm ok. check out Red Cat Club tomorrow nite.'

Dimas handed the note to C.W. as Adam was peering over his shoulder. "Do you recognize this area, Mr. Roberts?"

C.W. had been in and out of Budapest over the last five years and only recently returned. "Lieutenant, our embassy was over on Lechfar Street and I never frequented places like the Red Cat Club but I will check around."

Adam interrupted, "Lieutenant, I know where that place is."

Zeke figured as much and agreed to that statement, "You probably would. It sounds like some shady meat market."

Adam snorted back, "You better be prepared to go full bore on that place. It is Louis' base of operation and I have seen enough of Carol Sue's handwriting to know she wrote the note."

Dimas was not sure, as his mind was full of concern for the tall blond. "What makes you so positive, Adam?"

"Carol Sue had written up the rough note on buying the company from me and I totally recognize her handwriting. That is, if she was not coerced into writing this to throw us off."

Murray come over and looked at it. "Yeah, I know it is her hand writing."

The Lieutenant was totally relieved and wanted to proceed. "This is all new to me in this country. I have to think that Hungary is not all bad guys and the police will want to put away someone like Kolezy."

Murray wanted to back up the Lieutenant, "We are all sure that the Budapest cops don't want him around corrupting their citizenry."

Adam was not in agreement, "Anthony, Szilard confided in me that bribes are, sometimes the thing, for the local gendarmes. Maybe getting rid of a witness or two. Even though the government supports democracy and the so called right thing we enjoy in our own country."

Murray became anxious, "Lieutenant, who is your contact in the city?"

The Lieutenant drew out his special notebook. "It is Inspector Toth. Magassey, does that name mean anything to you?"

Adam pondered for a moment, "Not offhand. I can dial up Szilard to see if he knows Toth."

"Szilard. Adam. Yes, we are heading in for our hotel. It is The Hotel Estavan at 129 Baross Street. Our guide, so to speak, C.W., made the reservations but did not realize it was in the middle of a sketchy area. That is what my stepfather would have in mind. We got lucky. How about an Inspector Toth? Do you know him?"

Adam listened intently and nodded, as Szabo was filling him in. "I will see you very soon, my friend."

Magassey had some important information from Szilard. "The hotel is close to the night life where Louis hangs out. His Red Cat Club is nearby as well. He will show up at Dream Island that is frequented by a lot of 18-20 year olds. Louis loves to hang out there and pick up some future stars in his productions."

The Lieutenant put down the information but wanted more. "How about this cop, Toth?"

"Szilard knows him. Tough cop but has his soft side. You decide when you met him. Meantime, Szilard will try to meet us at the hotel to fill us in on the Red Cat Club."

The ride from the air strip to the hotel took less than an hour as C. W.'s Hungarian chauffeurs drove like they were at LeMans or at a Monte Carlo rally, narrowly missing other vehicles on Budapest's busiest, narrow streets.

The Hotel Estavan was sandwiched between Hungary's version of Macy's and a large video book store with questionable characters lurking in the doorways. Murray was amused that a quality hotel and fashionable department store would share its block with a bevy of shady appearing people, but that may had been the charm of Budapest. After all, what did he know of his heritage, living in the safe environment of his old world neighborhood in the sixties as a dumb ass, or in Hungarian, who yea, kid from Cleveland, Ohio? Back then he cared less of what actually went on there. He wanted to know what else was in the world, besides hudka and goulash.

Their entourage was quickly led to their suites by older, typical Hollywood type stereo bellhops with round, coffee can hats strapped to their chins. The hotel halls were a touch dingy and ill lit with old Las Vegas type carpeting in dire need of change. The good part was that all of them were located on the same floor within walking distance to a loud ice maker and a vintage, faded red colored, Coca Cola vending machine that surprising took U.S. dollar bills.

Nikki had a room to herself next to Jon and Arnie who shared a pair of double beds for their accommodation. The others were housed two to a room. C.W. had seen to it that Michaeleen had what might pass as her own suite that comprised a saggy queen bed in an enclave housing a settee that rubbed up against a brown cabinet that held an old mini Frigadaire.

Murray had his own queen size bed that was well worn from countless, apparent, one-nighters and a bathroom that had two LED lights that kept flickering. As he set his vitals down on a slender slab of sink and table top next to an old Kohler toilet with a wimpy handle, he hoped it would flush without his having to pour water from the nearby pitcher. A gentle knock came upon his door. It was Michaeleen.

"Come on in." He knew that she tried to tell him something that appeared difficult for her. A deep secret, Maybe! We haven't had the chance to discuss what's on your pretty mind. Can I offer you some Hungarian brandy? Don't think it is the best. They brought this up and said everyone in Budapest loves it! We'll see." He then retrieved two long stemmed flute type glasses and opened the Alma brandy, pouring it into the two crystals, giving one to Michaeleen.

She stared at the glass, breaking her silence, "I'm not positive this is the best time to tell you and you may not wish to hear it but it is the truth, so help me." Now half in tears she took a strong drink of the brandy and made a disappointing face.

"Jesus!, Michaeleen," seeing her emotion taking over and tears rolling down her perfect make-up face and wanting to break her tightness she appeared to portray. "I wish we had something better to drink that would not make you cry."

"Actually, it is not that, Anthony. This really tastes fine, for this moment of truth", as she fell back in the leather upholstered chair that looked like an antique going back to the 18th Century. He sat down in a rusty colored imitation leather chair, took a deep swig from his glass, anticipating some shocking news, that maybe Kolezy was a relative or Tex abused her or...then she blurted out. "Carol Sue is my mother!" She attempted to hold back a flow of water from her eyes, yet could not, based on the circumstance.

He was in semi-shock and did not know what to do or say. His thought was to place his arms around her for some protection, but it was awkward, at first, as he placed his glass down on the end table that separated their chairs in a 'V' position. Instead, he reached for his handkerchief and bent over to give it to her. Her words wore off as she looked up and took his offering, wiping her eyes with one hand and holding the glass with the other. She finished it and placed the empty glass on the table. She began to dab her blue eyes and face. Strangely, the young woman was temporarily unable to speak. Silence filled the room. Murray did not see this coming. This was totally unexpected, and then his mind kicked in. Finally, he sputtered out what came to his mind, "Oh, wow, I don't know how to take this kid. Carol Sue never told Wes and Gina that she, ahh, ah, hmm, had another daughter. Gina would, at least tell Sheryl, I guess. Gina, if she knew, has never let on. I really don't think Wes and, I don't know, K'Lynn. Mothers always confide in their daughters. Shit, I don't know? When did Carol Sue tell you?"

"I always felt that she was more than an aunt. One day I found two birth certificates. One with my, now, Aunt Bobbie Jean, and one with Carol Sue's name on the other. That one appeared to be an original. I always had a Xerox copy with Bobbie Jean as my mother. I need to talk with her as she is unaware that I may know, although she may suspect it."

Murray was relieved that, as strange as her story was, revealing in some way it unburdened him and now he could clear his mind on a subject he had pushed back in his mind, one that he had about Michaeleen even remotely being his daughter. Carol Sue was the mother of this female savior who turned him and Sheryl's life 180 degrees around making them independently wealthy. He had always thought that Michaeleen's benevolence was strange even though he was deserving of the money that Tex had withheld from him. He was finally resigned with the idea that she did it to correct the wrongs her family bestowed dishonestly upon everyone connected with the oil and gas finds for those 400 acres in North Texas.

Michaeleen could see that he was in deep thought, "Anthony, are you alright?"

"Sorry, Michaeleen. "Who is your father, then?" He rubbed his chin, slowly still partially thinking of his moments with Bobbie Jean, now finally dismissing it as pure bravado or was it to even the score with The Millers?"

"I believe my father is Lawrence K. Potter, The Third. A First Lieutenant in the Air Force stationed at Wichita Falls. The original birth certificate for 'father' was blank. It was on another document I found. Don't actually know if he is or is not my father? I have not been able to locate him."

Murray was still in a semi trance listening to the young woman detailing whether this Air Force Lieutenant was her real father when a knock sounded at the door. As he got up to answer the door his mind was still abuzz, opening it. There stood C.W. and St. George.

The two men saw the scene. Murray was ashened and Michaeleen had red, puffy eyes.

C.W. had to know. "Are we interrupting something?"

Murray had great empathy for Michaeleen and distraught for the moment, grabbed the lapels of Robert's sports jacket. "We have to find Carol Sue! Now! You hear me!"

St. George was aghast, "What about Kolezy? He's...What the hell is up, Anth?"

"Nothing, Bill, yet everything!" as he turned to a trembling Michaeleen. "Yeah, we have to get Kolezy and .... Sure. "C.W., when can we strike out into the city and locate him?"

The slightly muscled, shorter, mustachioed former U. S. Government official pulled on his light colored mustache. "I can lead you to the Red Cat Club on Andrassey Street. Maybe this Inspector Toth will meet everyone there. In speaking to Lieutenant Cavazos, he has the FBI behind him and they should be arriving very soon..."

Murray looked to St. George. "Bill, I am not sure of all the answers. Have you spoken to the Lieutenant about all this?"

"No, Rich may have as he's been down this road before being FBI and with the Service. Inspector Toth most likely wants the warrants to be in order before the take down begins."

C. W. had been in on a few of these before. Most, involving small time drug dealers or smugglers. He wished to set it straight, "These Hungarians, not you people, but the ones in authority here, won't get into any mess if things are not in order and our State Department personnel will only backup so much."

Murray could not believe it. "What the fuck do you mean? Our U. S. Government won't go along and extradite this slime ball over some wording on a document! He's a killer, a kidnapper, and Christ, what else hasn't he done?"

Bill, again, saw that Michaeleen was totally silent and wanted to know what she was thinking. "Hey, Sweets, what is your story? You are pretty quiet there and we know you are concerned about your Aunt."

Michaeleen just handed Murray his handkerchief. "I'll be alright. And Carol Sue is NOT my aunt. She is MY mother!"

Bill stepped back a couple of paces, stunned by the latest news, looking at Murray. "Yeah, I see where you and Michaeleen are coming from on getting the show on the road. I don't know what to say, hell, let's go, C.W. and round up everyone to get Kolezy and Carol Sue."

Louis knew Carol Sue was stretching the truth on The Legend of The Magyar Duna. He wished for his own enjoyment, to protect her from the others as they lounged at his pool.

"My dearest, Carol Sue, here's your Scotch whiskey", as he handed her the glass, as she was still clad in her slacks and shirt, while he was sporting a bright red, Speedo bikini.

She sniffed the glass, not trusting her host, and placed it next to the brown table by an old, worn, couch.

Louis smugly came up and sat next to her, "You don't trust me, my dear, Carol Sue? Actually, I would not wish to poison your drink or even enter a truth serum in it. I already know what is important. You are not in that equation."

"Louis, it is not that I don't trust you. Here, take a generous sip of this delicious libation." She handed him her scotch.

The slippery attorney took a large amount and handed it back to her. She smiled and could not miss the moment to comment, "Of course, you may have an antidote close to you."

"Carol Sue, Carol Sue, if I wanted to get rid of you when my men were concerned that you were a witch or some bad omen, you'd have gone out the plane's door into the Atlantic. Woman, do you really believe I fell for that invoking of the Magyar Duna?"

Carol Sue gave a coy look over to him as she took a drink. "And I thought I had you going. You seemed wide-eyed over that bull shit, Hungarian legend."

Louis agreed, at the humor of her story. "You're very clever but don't figure for a moment I may not really require your partnership, although we are very much alike. Remember, I could have shoved you out the Falcon's door."

"And I could and would have pulled your butt with me. Besides that, Louis, you still need me."

Kolezy was slightly puzzled. "Oh! Why? To make love to you after my men strip you naked and handcuff you to a stake, taking turns at overpowering you with their emotions."

"And, Louis, you would not want to sample the nectar first? You'd allow that Dimitri and scar faced Drago, to enjoy their pleasure before you had your lust?"

"The time will come when you wish you would've been sent out that plane's door."

Carol Sue was getting bored at his rhetoric. "That is all well and good, Mr. Kolezy, with all the threats, you should be looking over your own shoulder as the Houston and Hungarian police are probably coming for you."

"That is why you are alive. If they come and surround me, you will be my personal shield."

"Well until that comes along, I need to freshen up since you did not give me much of a chance to pack a suitcase and know you don't have women's clothes that I can change into."

Kolezy kidded, "We have some stores that are like that. I will send my houseboy to fetch you some clothes. Size, hmm." He surveyed her figure. A ten, extra-long or you have the shortest dresses in your closet. Short and tight. Panties, thongs, most likely, black lace, of course. Bra, if you chose to wear it, 36C. Eights in shoes."

Carol Sue was duly in impressed. "Just about sounds like you are describing your wardrobe."

Kolezy amused. "No, but my houseboy does have some of those clothes in his closet. Here he is now."

Carol Sue viewed the linen clad twenty something, dark Eastern European boy-man, with a slight built. "I bet he does, too.....and you even borrow from him?"

Louis was smug at her question, returning her volley "Not my size. A little too small. Let's get on with this as you are coming with me to the Red Cat Club tonight to show you around. You'll see up close, the people who enjoy what you were trying to buy at MABB."

She shrugged, and repeated "Oh, Trying To buy, ha. You act like it is already in your shopping cart. Look, I'll go along with you showing me off as eye candy but be assured, Kolezy, no hanky-panky. I bite hard."

"Feisty one, aren't you! Your bite is not as good as your bark and I am not positive what part of me you'd prefer to bite. I need my private parts. Perhaps you would like to know it is large as we stand here and when aroused, increases three more inches. I would start with your beautiful mouth and work down."

"Kolezy, you are such a romantic! More a dirty old man that jerks off in your houseboy or some eighteen year old, uneducated, young man you would pick up!"

"If I was not in a hurry, we could start caressing to ease our relationship, although I am getting that aroused feeling I mentioned before."

"You're not that much into women, are you? Perhaps your houseboy would be more accommodating."

Undaunted by her suggestion, he launched into the past. "When Ilona, my wife, was younger even after giving birth to her four children, she was a magnificent looking woman. My former law partner, here in Budapest, was very fortunate to have her. That is, until, he was killed in an accident.

Carol Sue seemed to agree and then cut into him, "Fortunately? Yes, that he was killed? You might call that killing two birds with one stone. He dies mysteriously and you wind up with the entire practice, his wife and four kids to screw. Wasn't she enough to make love to? Why the kids?"

Anger leapt from his eyes. "You can't prove anything like that? Anthal was my partner and how can you say I hurt my children? More wild tales..., like Magyar Duna, from Adam?"

"You're denying it all. How fortunate for you that you can push unwanted events out of your mind."

She kept focusing on his young houseboy. "Eleg yow. Feui?"

The boy looked at her as she winked at him...

Kolezy caught the flirt. "Oh you picked up a little Hungarian. Most likely from my wayward stepson, I assume. And now you want to take my house boy, Herback, to bed?"

"Not exactly, he may have some clothes in his closet that would fit me. Come, Herback, and show me what you have."

She grabbed the startled boy by the hand and guided him, "Show me your bedroom, you young hunk."

Kolezy was at an impasse. "If the clothes don't suit you, he will get them from the shops. Adam lied to you about Magyar Duna and Anthal's death."

Carol stopped, whirled around, "Knowing what I do about you, it is more than likely true. Just another murder. You could give a hairy fuck. Did you know David Potter?"

Kolezy was startled by her asking about that name and looked away. "Ah, ah, why did you bring up that person's name? My dear, how would I know him?"

She attempted to hold back her true emotions but unable to do so. "He is my ...ah ah, nephew... Disappeared in The Montrose, eighteen months ago. Was he another statistic done by people in your business?"

Defensive, he fought back to the woman, "You believe that your gay nephew was kidnapped by my people. Adam has filled you with lies and innuendo along with my killing his father and his brother, Ryan."

"I never inferred that David was gay. Explain the fact that Adam's brother was mysteriously hung in a closet from a chair that was three inches short of his feet and with abrasions on his wrists. It does not bode well for you, Louis. Adam's father died under mysterious circumstances. Do you want to discuss that?"

Kolezy did not wish to debate further with Carol Sue. "I did not have anything to do with your nephew, David's disappearance. You should watch your tongue, woman. I am positive your feet would touch the chair very easily."

Her eyes narrowed and taking a deep breath, snapped, "I need those clothes, now."

Murray finally fought off his struggles after Michaeleen dropped the bomb on him regarding Carol Sue. As he spoke to St. George, Rich, and Adam, his mind began clearing up to what their real mission was in the beginning, that was to take down Kolezy. "Tomorrow, we can go to the Red Cat Club. It has been a long day. Let's meet with this InspectorToth. Before that, let's set up the plan. The Cavazos brothers have been in touch with him and Toth is going to find a way to capture Kolezy and freeing Carol Sue. Adam, what does your friend, Szilard Szabo have to tell you about the Red Cat Club and Kolezy? What is his connection to your stepfather?"

"Only that Louis' partner, Imre Rabb, wanted to recruit him for his Players Club that is upstairs from The Red Cat. He promised lucrative salaries and commissions if Szilard would bring him more 18-19 year olds for various jobs?" At that Adam raised his eyebrows.

Being on the Houston Police Vice Squad for a time, Rich was intrigued. "How far did your Szilard friend go on the deal? As you know procuring prostitutes, and that is how it sounds, is a felony. At least, back in The States."

"Rich, Szilard is well off and did not need the money, although it is not treated like a major issue here. Sorry to say, my homeland is not like living in The U.S. My friend would not return Rabb's calls after they had their first and only visit at Players. Szilard is straight, although he has favored me by being in a few of my MABB productions. Even Carol Sue told me about seeing him in a production we had, 'Au Natural'. A huge seller for us. He is a doe eyed, well groomed, dirty blond, and is nicely proportioned, who actually can act. He earned top dollar per scene then he turned the money over to the Hungarian Relief Fund For Molested Young Men."

Bill did a double take on that. "You mean to tell us that Hungary has a fund for that? C'mon, Adam!"

Half gloating, half smiling, "That's what he did."

Murray said, "Okay, if the deal falls through at The Red Cat Club, I hope his well-groomed, dirty blond, nicely proportioned body won't be shot. Can he lure Kolezy and his crew where the police can nab him?"

Adam was not positive, although he attempted to put on a confident appearance, "Szilard is very smooth in tough situations and there should not be any trouble."

Murray felt that Adam was more bravado than talking sensible, "Sure, like he has been in the middle of sting operations before. Let Dimas and Zeke check him out. Well, speak of two of Houston's finest, here they are!"

Lieutenant Cavazos and his brother were wearing frowns as they approached the group, and Murray decided to jab their favorite cops, "Hey, Misters Cavazos, do you have a plot in mind on using Adam's friend?"

Dimas hit the side of his right ear. "What am I hearing, Gringo? You said something about Adams 'friend' or something to that effect?"

Rich spoke up, "Thought you would like some type of trap for Kolezy where we use this Szilard guy as bait. He has had some dealings with Kolezy's partner, here in Budapest, and this fella is supposed to be a heart throb of sorts that the partner likes. Maybe talk with Inspector Toth to set it up."

Zeke looked over at his brother, "You know Bro, these citizens may have come up with a good one."

The Lieutenant was a little skeptical, "I don't know, Zeke. Let's see what Adam's friend is like before we try to spring something on this wayward ambulance chaser."

"Crap, Lieutenant", Murray pushed, "This so-called lover boy is supposed to melt Louis' heart from what Adam tells us."

About that time, a rumpled gray haired, man dressed in a well-worn black sports coat and red slacks walked up to them, "I'm Inspector Toth and I heard about you being from Texas and vant to arrest this Kolezy person ..."

Murray was caught between the two cops. "What do you say, Lieutenant, about Adam's friend, Szilard Szabo? Using him to set up Kolezy? The Inspector figures we are typical Texas' types."

Dimas thought for a moment, "Inspector, we don't ride horses but if this Szilard Szabo character will go for it, we can rustle up some horses here, in your city. We can nab our wayward ass hole. I'm in", shrugged the Lieutenant.

Toth's eyes lit up at that suggestion. "You vere talking about Szilard Szabo? Ohhh. Egan, yes. I agree, for vhatever you have in mind, Lieutenant."

C.W. strolled in. " I am on the outside, but from what goes on here in this city, let me suggest they set it up at the Kuylari Baths which is three blocks from The Red Cat Club. You can fool them by wearing only bath towels. No guns that way. The Houston police and our local, InspectorToth, along with the FBI come in with the papers and Louis is on his way back to Texas to stand trial."

Murray liked the idea. "I guess your stint at the State Department may have paid off." He gave a high five to his friend, C.W., and then he wanted Adam to come into the plan. "Where is Szilard, now?"

"Anthony, I suspected that we were in need of his assistance. I just finished speaking to him and filled him in that we could use his services. He is okay as long as the police are in breathing distance. This Rabb chap is trying to size him up for a one on one deal."

"The Au Natural film did it for Rabb. When we will know on his connection for all this?"

"He's calling Rabb now."

St. George wanted in, along with the others. "How are Rich, Sev, Ernie, Tanski, and I going to fit into all this?"

The Inspector pulled on his coat lapels for a minute. "You hunkies from the United States, as they zay in Hollyvood mofies, 'No Vay, Jose'. You are not geeting into these and shoot them up. Not in my Budapest. My own men and this FBI and the Lieutenant Pancho Villa, over there along vith our own puleetz are going to do the arrest. I vill be in total charge."

At the reddish stone estate of Kolezy, not far from the middle of this now, thriving Eastern European city, Louis had changed into street clothes and was entertaining his European partner, Imre Rabb.

Rabb was sipping an apricot brandy, Barack, as he slid down on a nearby sofa, holding up his glass in triumph, "I just heard from Szilard Szabo! He wants to meet us at Kuylari Baths, late tomorrow afternoon. He will be a gem in our Romany Production films. He is a Hungarian beauty. He is oh, so ...hmm. I cannot contain my feeling for him. He will earn a nice profit for us."

Kolezy was eager to hear this. "So, Imre, is he an all-star performer? If then, I want to sample him tomorrow."

Rabb was overjoyed in dreaming of the encounter with Szabo. "Yes, he is. One other thing, the baths are very shielded. We will have the privacy in our own cabana. He will walk in and then drop his cloth. You will be enamored with him and he will be yours for the entire day and night. Szilard will do it late tomorrow afternoon as he has other plans tonight."

"Imre, I am anxious after your description of this young stud, as they say, in America, but first I must attend to Ms. Carol Sue who is dressing for an unforgettable evening with me as Herback brought her some clothes. Perhaps, it is better that we do not meet, tonight, with this young man. She will need my total interest and it would most likely extend to the early morning."

Rabb knew of his partner's sexual appetite. "Louis, do not use all your energies on that woman. Remember Szilard has needs, as well."

Swaggering around the room, "I will not disappoint either of them." He then started to unbutton his silk blue shirt walking toward the Tiffany chandeliered foyer and up the gold and white spiral stairs to the bedroom Carol Sue was to occupy. As he reached for the butterfly, gold door knob, he found it locked. Tapping gently on the door, he uttered, "Carol Sue, will you let me in."

Carol Sue had been busy. She tricked Herback into stripping his clothes and then tying him up in what he visioned as a sexual encounter with her. As Carol Sue heard Kolezy's approach, she found and grabbed Herback's motorcycle keys and headed for the French doored balcony. Thanking her daily workouts and natural athletic ability, she climbed down on the downspouts along the front of the two story mansion, locating the houseboy's Harley parked to the side of a brick overhang. She slipped the key into the ignition, kick starting the cycle.

Meanwhile, Kolezy continued his attempt to enter Herback's room. There was no answer. He began to get angry and pushed up against the white lacquered and gold door, putting his full weight against it as he banged on it four to six times. Backing up in one bold move he kicked the door open, breaking the lock and striker. Now increasingly aggravated, as she was unavailable, he screamed out, "Carol Sue, where in the fuck are you? You damn bitch! No one locks me out in my own home! Melanie tried it and lost. You will as well!"

Stumbling through the clothes strewn room, he searched the adjoining bathroom to find it empty, except for a note pinned to the mirror bearing large lettering , 'Louis, it was great being with you. Ha, Ha! Thanks for the new set of clothes. See you, very soon, in Houston, for your court appearance. LUV, Carol Sue'.

As he tore off the note, the sound of his house boy's motorcycle outside filled his ears. He raced out the bathroom, through the bedroom to the French doors, out to the balcony, to see Carol Sue revving up the Harley 1450. She looked up and shot the finger at him then raced down the circular drive and onto the street. He walked back into the room, head down; he started dejectedly out the bedroom. From the closet he heard a thumping sound, opened the door to find his houseboy, naked, gagged, and tied up. Removing the gag, the boy gave the story that Carol Sue promised him sex in turn for her new clothes. She found his keys on the floor after he returned from the clothing store. The houseboy told his master that she started to undress and suggested the tie up to him with some leather straps he had hanging in the closet. Naively, he accepted the bindings, and then surprised him by stuffing his mouth with a tattered t-shirt, as he bent down she kicked him into the closet, closing the door on him.

"I should leave you here for Drago and Dimitri to pummel your worthless body, but we have work ahead of us." He then untied the leather straps, as the youth lay shameful among his cross dressing garments. Louis, disappointed, vaulted from the room to announce to his Mafia soldiers of Carol Sue's escape.

Given his sometime superstitious moments, Kolezy had purchased the Club years before but thought that The Black Cat Club had too many hidden meanings for him and thus, changed the name to The Red Cat Club, making it luckier for him. He even attempted to change his often abused stepdaughter, Melanie's name, as it meant, 'darkness'. Ilona would not hear of it. A warning he should have heeded as the girl, her mother, and Adam were instrumental in the start of his eventual downfall from grace.

Imre looked at his business partner, whose anger was overshadowing everyone in the room. "That tall bitch escaped, thanks to my dimwitted houseboy."

Imre encouraged the moment, "You're referring to that lady you spoke so highly of, what, two hours earlier? I thought you had your thumb so securely on Carol Sue?"

Kolezy continued his rage, "Screw you, Imre! I seemingly cannot depend on anyone since Hector left."

Robb wistfully recalled him. "Yes, Hector. He was such a good one. Then he left for Brno, in the Czech Republic, going over to our rival studio, Prague Productions, romping with their guys in scenes that so many women enjoyed. Yes, Louis, we should have made him a star in our own Romany Productions, but you demanded too much personal time from him. He was jealous of your love for your stepdaughter, Melanie. You talked longingly for her when you were away from Houston."

Kolezy mumbled back, "She was just as the Americans refer, 'handy', no more."

Imre did not believe that lie. "You had designs on her as your emails to me were more in print that she was a beauty, and at no time, did you say she was 'handy'. That has never been a part of your verbiage."

Kolezy changed the subject, "You tell me that we now have this someone, Szilard Szabo, that you thought was the next Johnny Masters, the top male porn star in Europe!"

Imre boasted, "That and more."

"If, Imre, he is half of what you believe he is, will he be as demanding as Hector, that dick sucker?"

"He will and I bet Hector was, too!" laughed Imre.

"Whaat? bellowed Kolezy, You don't know, yet you judge!"

As Rabb, uncaringly walked to the wet bar to pour himself a Slibivitz on the rocks. "Whatever, Louis. Never mind, we will journey tomorrow afternoon to The Kuylari Baths. Forget for now, Hector and that woman."

Louis agreed, "You are correct my friend, we will attend to her later. Carol Sue will deeply regret her disobedience to me. She will beg for her life and there will not be a Magyar Duna story to save her from her fate."

Imre gasped at the last sentence, "That's a wife's tale. You don't actually believe in it?"

Kolezy sheepishly admitted for a moment, "No, well, she did extend her time by telling me she knew the fable. I am not concerned about her. She does not speak the language and is probably lost on the streets. I am confident she will fall in the hands of slave runners. They will take her to The Black Sea and have their way with her."

Back on the streets as Carol Sue zipped around corners as those seeing the tall blond caught many an eye, unexpectedly, as the locals dined at their sidewalk Kave Café Houses sipping Slibovitz and Barack to go with their plates of pigs feet, capostash, hudka and kolbaz. As she zoomed the Harley by the bistro the men looked at her, and all smiled broadly. They all raised their glasses of brandies and Tokay wines to her.

On the next block, she spotted a young looking policeman on the corner. He observed her graceful lines straddling the 1450 as the cycle screeched to a halt within five feet from him next to his police cruiser.

Rattling off excitedly, "Do you speak English? I am looking for the nearest police station as there are killers who are after me!"

Startled somewhat by her outburst, and also by her beauty, he half stuttered, Miss, ah, ah, you, Americon? Bey sulock Magyar do? Then he gained his authoritative confidence, again. "Vat is your name, Miz and how can I ezzizt you?"

Carol Sue was at a disadvantage for her first time in many times, as Vixey was not in charge or able to connive her way out. "I am in danger, please..."

The young cop kept looking her over and finally came to his realization that the goddess needed protection. "I am ezzured that I can help you, Nani." Then recognizing her as a U. S. American, he asked, "But Americon liedy, do you have any Marlboroz or Camelz zigarettes? I can pay you in our forints currency for them?"

Vixey did a double take, "Cigarettes? Honey, I quit smoking but I desperately have to go to your police station. You understand?"

"Politeetz almsmus, egan, Politz Ztatshun. Of course, I can take you there."

"Yes, she repeated, the police station. I want to go there now!"

The policeman forgot he asked, "ET magyarul, Do you zpeak Hungarian?"

Losing patience while looking around to see if Kolezy was watching all this, amused by her futility to make the policeman understand her situation. "No, I don't speak or understand it. I am a Texan in a big, God forsaken city, Can you hurry? Take me to your superior, sergeant, chief or whatever you call them in this country? Please! Kindly!"

Just then another police cruiser came up as a crowd of curious onlookers started to swell nearby. An older, almost American looking policeman stepped out of what appeared to be a Yugo police car. Even with all her problems stacking up, she wanted to make fun of the vehicle but thought better of it in the face of her situation. Exasperated, she blurted out to the older cop, "Can you kindly help me? I was kidnapped in Houston, Texas and brought here against my will. I escaped and need to tell the police about these monster people. There are others from the United States who are probably here. My cell phone was taken away by these bad men."

The older cop attempted to take care of her concerns "Don't worry, Madam, I vill take you to my zation." He then pointed to the Yugo, "Pleeze get into my polize zcar." Then he went over and started to open the passenger door of the smallish car.

Carol Sue waved him off, "Thank you officer, but I will follow you on the motorcycle." She then mounted the two wheeled hunk of power as he started toward his car, looking back at her and smiling as it appeared he had never had the fortune to escort a pretty woman to his precinct station.

She yelled over to the Yugo, "Officer, I'll be right behind you!", as she revved the Harley, blowing out dark smoke. It took only five minutes to reach Budapest's version of 61 Reisner Street. Carol Sue and the policeman arrived at the same time Murray and company were pulling up as they accompanied Lieutenant and Sergeant Cavazos to check out the police facilities, as Adam knew where the station was located. Carol Sue's son, Wes, had accompanied them in a plea that he asked Lieutenant Cavazos and Murray to be at the Kuylari Baths as they arrested Kolezy. He was overjoyed at seeing his mother dismount the Harley. Son and mother ran to one another in an unashamed embracement and tears. His eye glasses popped off as she squeezed him so hard. Each recalling the past nearly 48 hours where she thought and he did as well, that they were never going to re-unite as a family.

Murray, St. George, Adam, Dimas, and Zeke conveyed right behind Wes at the Uras Street scene outside a non-descript building which passed for their major police outpost.

Dimas appeared as happy as her son in this reunion. He hailed her, "Hey, babe, glad you made it! Hell, I don't know how you did it but who gives a damn, you're here!" as he grabbed her by the butt, they kissed, unashamed.

When she had her breath back, she wise cracked, "I got away from Kolezy because his houseboy thought he was going to find his Thrill on Blueberry Hill!"

The group thought it was hilarious but were happy that she had fled the clutches of Kolezy.

The freed woman was now serious. "Hey, ya'll, I know how you enjoyed that, but I need to be able to contact Houston and Michaeleen?"

Murray looked over at Adam who was largely ignored in all this. The young guy knew he was the odd man out, once more, and figured her tryst with him that night at The Merriam was only for business purposes. The table top sex they had at her place came out better for him as his price for MABB was met and she showed him a good time. He just could not figure out that day at her Katy place when she was so horny and they did it on the dining room table. As he kept reliving all that. Dimas, her love, rushed to the scene. The cop came out okay as she swooned into his arms and Adam knew that she wanted someone older and more to her taste. Yet, the younger man got a good taste of what a woman like her desired. Could the Lieutenant compete or would she still like him for his youth?

Murray already was privy to Michaeleen's secret and knew that Carol Sue might be seeking her newest daughter. Murray interrupted the joyous reunion placing a comforting touch on her arm. "I want to speak to you, Vixey." He pointed to a quieter place.

She looked at him quizzically but somehow knew it was about Michaeleen. The others were standing there unable to figure what was occurring between the two of them as they walked out of hearing range from everyone.

Murray broke the air. "I'm positive that you wanted to get together with Michaeleen. She is here at The Hotel Estavan, Suite 508. She has already confided in me that you are her mother. I was thrown for a frickin' loop. Obviously, Wes and Gina are unaware of her being your daughter. Does K'Lynn know about all this?"

Carol Sue was apprehensive, "Michaeleen found out with good detective work, and I should have confirmed it with her, but screwed that up. Now, I have some major work with not only her but with Wes and K'Lynn as they do not know they have a sister, and if we can ever locate, David, a brother. Yes, I am both their mother. What was her reaction to it? Was she overjoyed by that even though I kept it from her in the beginning? I'm afraid Murray, what she will eventually think of me. Did she uncover anything else?"

Murray did not know how to respond. He was in a buzz as he did not know his own feelings. "What are you referring to about 'uncovering anything else'?"

"Oh, I don't know. It is not that important."

He felt that there was more to that comment but decided he already had enough on his plate. "Okay, Michaeleen was upset, but I think in her way you being her mother is something she will come to grips with eventually. Why didn't you tell them from the get go?"

"Anthony, it is very complicated. I have to sit down with Wes, first, and try to explain it. I need a ride to the hotel and on the way, will tell him. Then go to Michaeleen...and.... I really appreciate your not saying anything for now to the others."

"That is a little too late, as Bill and another friend, C.W., were there when Michaeleen told me. They promised not to say anything to anyone, especially, to Wes. I'm still in shock from this. Good luck, with your son, as well as your new found daughter."

The blue-eyed woman cast a strange look toward Murray, then went over and pulled Wes from the others. "Guys, really no words can describe what has gone on and you're being here to track down that cockroach, Kolezy. Have at 'em. Wes and I need some R & R from all this. Will see you soon! Adios, Amigo," She threw a kiss to Dimas who was beaming with pride and later anticipation of a rendezvous, after all this was over.

Wes and his mother strolled off arm in arm as Rich hailed a taxi to take them to the hotel.

In the cab, she fumbled at first, "Sweetheart, I have a confession to make to you. It is something that you will not completely understand at first, but I really, really, really love you and K'Lynn and hope you will forgive me for waiting this long..."

Wes was thrown for a loss. Confused, he looked at his mother, putting on his glasses. "What do you mean, Mom?"

"We have to sit down, the three of us, now to talk about this."

Wes was unclear, "You mean, K'Lynn is here in Budapest?"

"It is not K'Lynn. Ah, god, I wish I could hide for the moment. Here it is. Wes. Remember, I really love you and don't hate me for what you are going to hear."

"Mom, I cannot hate you. You raised me to be open and be even handed with everyone and set me a pattern of doing things right. Treating people the way they should be. Not unlike my grandfather, Tex Miller. Even at an early age, I saw what he was like and you broke away from that, so tell me."

Carol Sue took a deep sigh, "You have another sister. It is Michaeleen. And... a brother, David. I realize it is going to be a difficult thing to absorb so fast, even for you. You, me, and Michaeleen are going to sit down and talk things over."

Wes removed his glasses and leaned back not saying a word, staring straight at the oncoming traffic. Finally after a minute, he looked at his mother who did not know what to expect. "Wow, Michaeleen...and a brother... God, I guess you will fill me in on the how and who the dad is. Do I know him?"

Carol Sue inhaled deeply as her insides started to settle down believing that her son was on the way of accepting his new found siblings. "Let's take one step at a time." They traveled to the hotel and walked in, taking the elevator to room 508.

Back at the Hotel Estavan entrance, the group returned from the police station and interjecting their feelings. Murray, though, wanted to soothe the soul of Adam for his romantic loss. He pulled the young man back, "Don't give this deal a second. There are other people who you can covet."

Adam shrugged it off, "Vixey figures me like everyone else around here. 'Damaged Goods'. She had her shot and doesn't want to get dirty."

"Forget it, kid. We, both, have other fish to fry."

Bill caught that old saying. "Anth, you are saying Kolezy is the fish that has to be fried?"

Murray looked at his longtime friend. "Yeah, he is a whale."

Almost on cue, a Jaguar convertible rolled up and out stepped a tall, late twentyish man. He was model like, dark skinned, most likely from daily tanning, sporting a thin goatee, wearing leather pants and a silk button down shirt. Adam immediately parted a huge grin on his face and turned to the others, "It's Szilard!"

Smiling back, Szilard, acknowledged his upcoming star status, but riveted his attention on his longtime friend, offering a Western salutation, "What's up, Adam?"

Magassey formally introduced Szabo to everyone.

Murray turned to Szabo; I heard good things from Adam about you. We really could use your help in bringing down Kolezy and his mob."

Szabo was puzzled somewhat, "I know you saved my good friend, Adam. I am here to serve you and do whatever is necessary to stop this monster, but what is this term 'Mob'? What is that?"

Murray and Bill thought it was almost hilarious that the main attraction was not familiar with that term. He appeared to be Americanized with almost no European accent. Bill wanted to make it clear, "Szilard, 'Mob', means a group of bad people who have a sole purpose in life. That is to take you down for their own good. We cannot have that occur. You follow what I mean, Szilard?"

Szabo, finally, knew what was at stake at that moment. "Egan, botchie."

Tanski thought it was another episode of Hungarian humor. "Egg and who?"

Murray clarified it. "Szilard was just saying 'Yes, Mister'. Look, everyone, we need to start out fresh tomorrow as it is set up at the Kuylari Baths in the afternoon.

The following day, the group gathered to bring down Kolezy and his Hungarian Mafia.

They all held up their thumbs in unison as to going to a final game, as men do like in touch football or the last game of a sandlot baseball game between two would be teams, running on to the field of a make believe Super Bowl or World Series Game. Little mattered to them that a pigskin or baseball were not involved, the group were dedicated in their search and capture of a person who needed to be taken out.

Lieutenant Cavazos, Sergeant Zeke Cavazos, along with three FBI Personal went ahead, driven by a local policeman who knew the area. C.W., Sev and Tanski piled into one SUV while Murray, St. George, Rich, Adam, and Szabo were in another. Ernie, for unknown reasons, chose not to go on this venture and was absent. All of them appeared grim, knowing that the end of the trail was bringing down Kolezy as they journeyed to the Kuylari Baths. Without getting out of his police cruiser, Inspector Toth saw that Szabo was with Murray and waved to him. He then continued with four city policemen taking the lead, ahead of Cavazos Brothers and the FBI. Murray and his group had Adam at the wheel, who knew the way to the location. The Inspector had wanted to speak to Szabo but not in the presence of the Americans. He would wait until arriving at the baths.

St. George saw that his boyhood buddy, Murray was uneasy. "Anthony, you have been screwing around with your Judge. What is going on?"

"This is more than the Cleveland episode nearly two years ago. The airport deal at Sugar Land was close but Cavazos and the West Bend police did their jobs. Actually, not for Carol Sue but then, again, she is okay .... There have been some close calls, Billy, when the Szilanyi Brothers broke into our Memorial home and at the hospital." He thought there was a time that he could have used Dirty Harry.

Bill knew he friend was uptight. "Anth, I know you are concerned with all this. Don't worry; you might not need to pull the trigger."

"I never shot anyone before, Bill."

"It never is... easy... don't worry, the others will do the dirty work and you can back it all up. If you need to, just shoot over their heads."

Murray felt offended, "I don't want to sit on the side lines and let the others do the so called 'dirty work' Bill, it sounds like you are letting me off easy. I don't want that, not now."

St. George looked out the window, as he knew what his friend was capable of and did not wish to pursue the pluses or minuses of what was ahead.

Rich Fedor was listening to the two and broke the eerie quietness after St. George went silent. "No, it is unlike Cleveland. Growing up in that neighborhood, I thought we knew how it all was; the immigrants came in and went to work at The Mills for Republic Steel or Harshaw Chemical or even at the stamping plants at Chevy and Ford in Parma. Our lives were simple and protected by those men. We are going back too far. This is 2008, not 1968."

Murray was taken back at all of that as the memories were brought back to him.

Bill just looked over at Murray, "You'll be fine, Anth, and will do the right thing."

Murray thought it over. "I got all of you into this. My goal is that we get Kolezy in the next few days without any of us getting killed or shot. I realize this is not Cleveland. That hunky attorney is ten times more dangerous than our 1956 DP's grandkids that turned sour after our families' extended their money, homes, and food to them when they did not have anything other than the clothes on their backs. Actually, our attorney guy is just a version of an upscale DP. When I use the Taurus Judge, it will be to shoot him between the eyes!"

They arrived at the front of Kuylari Baths. Upon seeing a group of men in vehicles, a Budapest policeman hailed them and wanted to know why they were there?

"Rich responded, "We are with Inspector Toth."

The policeman waved his hand and at the same time said, "Enspecther Toth vants everyone in the back of the baths. You go down that zmall ztreet ."

With that the group drove their vehicles down an alleyway, pocketed by dark, unknown businesses with an assortment of men and women loitering about.

St. George remarked, "Kind of questionable looking characters lurking around."

C.W. observed the entire situation and turned to Murray. "This is more than I bargained for. I saw a cab a block back. Sorry, Murray, I got you here and I wish you good luck but I am heading back to the hotel and work with Ernie on some Old West stories. Be safe."

Murray agreed. "Can't blame you. We'll be fine. See you back at Hotel Estavan." With that they high fived as C.W. got out of the SUV, then hurried past a group of vagrants back down the alley to the main street to hail a taxi and return to the hotel.

Rich put it in perspective for the rest, "Well, guys, we are here, seedy or not .I here is Inspector Toth preparing to read the riot act because we are here."

As everyone got out of their vehicles, Toth saw Szabo and walked toward him. "Hello, Zilard. Vee need to talk, now. Hgyvan, Zabo, ur?"

He responded in English, "Very well, thank you. It has been awhile, Inspector. When I do this thing to bring this Kolezy Litche to you, we are, as the Americans say, 'even'."

"Szabone, Its besze lunk." The inspector wanted to be clear, "

Zilard, ve are talking here, man to man".

Szilard shook his head in agreement, "Egan, yes, but I wish to speak in English, though. It is not good to use our Hungarian language in front of non-speaking Magyars."

Inspector Toth concurred," Egan, egan, yez, yez."

As Szilard wanted to make his own point across to the Hungarian cop, "My part in all this, Inspector is only to meet Kolezy and Rabb and cause them to be arrested by you and the American FBI."

The inspector, at first, was non-compliant, then spoke, "You are the only vay ve can make Kolezy confess, Rabb, yoi, nehez."

"Yes, Inspector, Rabb is difficult but with all of you at your posts close, it must work. I am told by my friend, Adam, Kolezy has two, three very dangerous men. Drago by name with a scar on his forehead. Then a ubutka, round man, Dimitri, both backed by Gabor, a ruthless man, who carries a knife in his boot. They are killers. We must take them before they have the opportunity to re-act."

Toth stared at Szilard, half listening but appeared to be more interested in the young man's current address than what was at hand. "Egan, feyou. Meg szivesen meg mindig a re gi lakusuken laknak?"

"Yes, Toth, I live in the same flat, but no visiting after this. Recall what I told you, 'we are even'."

"I understand", he uttered solemnly, lowering his head. "You vill go to The Baths, change to your cloths as Kolezy and Rabb vill and they not suspect any trap. You vill walk away. Ve vill take them into cuztody. It vill be eazy. Ve vill go in the back of the baths and place the polize van there to pick up thez people."

Szabo drew a deep breath, "Egan, yoi, yes."

Meantime in the rear of the bathhouse Murray was searching. "Where are the FBI people? The Budapest police? Maybe we will have to take down Kolezy ourselves. I believe I'm up to it!"

Rich in his easy former Secret Service and FBI drawl, "Our guys are around. The Budapest cops? Who knows? Toth seems more interested in Szilard than catching our Hungarian lawyer creep. I can't answer for everyone, Murray, maybe they took off out the back way."

Adam breathed heavily, "I am deeply worried about Szilard. He disappeared with Toth."

It was Murray's turn to calm someone, "Adam, Szilard is probably with their police and the FBI, being briefed and wired."

Even in the tenseness of the situation, Bill found some humor in that statement. "Anth, are we sure, Toth is not removing Szabo's briefs?"

Rich was shaking his head at St. George, "Remember in Cleveland, you found something funny about the food deal. I remember you were about to throw a pan of strudel at that dumb fuck kid, Elaysh, but picked up a tort then put it down since you thought it was more expensive and they weren't used to the better things in their face. So you threw the strudel at him when he walked into the bakery."

Murray agreed, "Yeah, we ate the tort later with some fank and that strong coffee they imported from Kuziad."

Rich cut it, "No, guys, Szabo is not being wired. Knowing what this job is, I figure he is dropping his clothes and can't wear a microphone. Besides, Kolezy is a fugitive, anyway, and really don't require any more incriminating evidence to get his worthless hide back to Houston."

At that time, Inspector Toth emerged from the back.

"Let's find out from Budapest's finest on what is going on." Rich offered. "Hello, Inspector Toth, Where is our star performer, Szilard?"

"Hees vit my men, Zargent Cheheck is taking him and your FBI people. They vare in charge and ve are the arrezting party. You Americanz stay back. Lieutenant Cavazos and Szargeant Cavazos, I vill accommodate, as they, along vit your federal people and our polize are the only von authorized to use the veapons, if it is neceζζary. I requeszted another zquad. Ve have zix men on the front side. Cheheck will vait for my call on our radio. "At that he produced a mobile one type cell.

St George quipped, "Let's hope, Inspector, you won't get a dropped call from your sergeant."

Toth's eyes squinted, "Drop call? Vat iz zat?"

Bill decided not to pursue it, "Ok, it's really nothing, just giving a little jab...", as he gave a 'what the hell he doesn't know' look.

The Cavazos brother came up shivering, Zeke uttered, "I thought the weather here was supposed to be warm. It was 80 degree something when we landed, yesterday, now today it seems like 40 degrees!"

Toth did not attempt to hide his contempt for the Mexican cops. "Vell thez iz not Laredo or El Pazo or even Houzton. You may vant to eat some of that hot zauce you dip those deep fried pieces of vhat? Hard cheeps? Vhatever those are to make you varmer. Budapest is not like the Mayan Rivera."

"Thanks for the encouragement, Inspector!" countered back, Zeke. "Like you ever went to a place other than Siberia."

The Inspector reminded everyone, "Remember American'z, you are to stay back. Ve vill brink out Kolezy and he vill go to the police station and he be zent to your Texas."

Murray yelled out, "Egan, Polizeman!"

Bill was astonished, "Anth, you are beginning to pick up our native tongue. I am really proud of you!"

At that moment a police van pulled in. It appeared to be a converted mail truck marked with POLIZE. It probably was to take Kolezy and his group to their jail after the capture.

Murray began to wonder about why everyone was in the rear of the bathhouse? "Lieutenant Cavazos why are we back here instead of the front of this place?"

Dimas shrugged, "Toth wanted it that way. We have to get going."

Adam wished the Lieutenant and Zeke safety, "Be careful and return!'

They turned around, with a slight smile on both of them. Zeke held up his hand, Thanks, Adam, we will."

Adam turned his attention to Toth, "Ve jas, bothche!"

Toth looked over his shoulder, clenching his fist, "I vill be careful, Mr. Magazzey. Kolezy and Rabb are mine!"

Sev grimaced at the same time, "Yeah, right, what do you want to do cousin Rich? You have been on stakeouts and rumblings like this before."

Rich had a soft spot for the unwanted hero. "Murray, you brought us here, although I have been on a lot of these smokers and such before, it is your move."

This was a big decision for a guy who basically was a backup in

Cleveland and in Sugar Land. It was a chance to prove something even though he did not need to in the eyes of his fellow Hungarians. "I'm for pulling our guns and going in following close to where the locals and FBI are. If it goes down the way they're talking, ok... We won't fire a shot but if the shit hits the fan we drop Kolezy and his gang. Are ya 'll in with that plan?"

Rich was the most experienced in this going wrong and having to improvise to save the original plan. "I have to agree with him. We don't want to go busting in unless there are hostages taken or Kolezy gets a bug up his ass and starts blasting. Only, let's don't get killed, just fire enough to keep the bad guys away and maybe take one or two out."

Murray turned to Adam. "Are you okay with it? After all, he is your stepfather and would you want to kill him?"

"Even though Louis is my stepfather and right now married to my mother and if we do wind up killing him, it will not bother me. He murdered my brother, Ryan. Blood is thicker than water, right?"

St. George agreed, "Absolutely, kid. Will you be the one who drops him?"

Adam gritted his teeth, "Watch me Bill, I am hardly a kid. Kolezy robbed me of my innocence."

Murray was well aware of that statement. He was again, recalling back to his innocence and the times he was subjected to unwanted sexual involvement. Murray wanted to push ahead. "Alright Rich, where do you want to post our bunch?"

Rich responded, "Since the police and Cavazos Brothers went in the back, we should stay back here, as well. Murray, Bill, and Adam stick closer to the SUV's for protection. Tanski, get close to that police van. I'll take a spot by the back door with Sev. Rich brandished a .357 Magnum with Sev clutching Wes' AR15 automatic rifle. They all took their places, nervously awaiting the outcome and the supposedly capture of the dangerous Kolezy and his Hungarian mafia.

Murray was concerned, "Bill, we only have side arms. We sure could have used another AR15."

"Anth, Zeke had one. Adam has a .22 but I have a .357 and you have the Taurus Judge. With that gun, it should be plenty of fire power. Just don't be too edgy with The Judge."

Murray shot back as to hide his concern, "Don't worry, I am not edgy as you think. I'll be okay when the bell rings. Only this back door idea, it doesn't seem right."

Bill was not that worried about his friend and shrugged it off, "Whatever, on this rear exit strategy. And, Anth, shoot at Kolezy. O-Kay?"

Inside, the Cavazos brothers and Toth weaved their way through the bathhouse. Szabo was already in the area where he kept a locker. Wearing a long coat, Zeke hid his AR15 from sight. There was a man dressed in lounging pajamas playing the cimbalom, a Hungarian version of the piano. It was a reminiscent of Barry Mammilowe who began his career playing in the New York bathhouses where he once accompanied Bettey Mindler, the now famous singer and movie star. The thing missing was the female singer in these premises. Men were in various modes of dress, half talking among themselves, some, even listening to the cimbalom player. He was not 'Sam' from the movie, Casablanca and 'Rick' was not around at the bar.

Zeke and Dimas were witnesses to many things on the streets of Houston but this did not compare. The Inspector was very nonchalant about all of it. Of course, this was not button down Texas but the free and easy attitude of typical European dark life. Toth caught their looks, "Gentlemen, this ez vhat you Amirikans might call,'nothing'. Vait until ve go to the Greek area or the pool."

The door attendant noticed they were not carrying any type of workout attire and stopped them from entering the area. Inspector Toth flashed his credentials and the attendant allowed them through into the workout room. As Toth and the Cavazos brothers went forward, the men mainly undressed, surveyed the full clothed trio.

Zeke did not know what they were in for as he elbowed Dimas, " Bro, I' m a little uneasy with these Hungarians seemingly sizing us up for something on a platter, and it is not enchiladas with rice and beans."

"I'm with you, Zeke. This is not the McAllen YMCA where we went as ten year olds. "Say, Inspector, just where are we going on this?"

The Inspector held a finger to his lips, "Talk quiet, Lieutenant and

Zargeant. Kolezy and hez people are in here and may ve around the next room. Szabo advized me that he vould ve in the Greek area to meet them."

Zeke was still in the dark, "That is the second time you said something about this place. What is The Greek area?"

'You Amirikanz are not going to like this, it ez a place vhere men are vorking out, naked."

Zeke shrugged on that, "Oh shit, like who needs this?"

As the three turned another corner there was a set of lockers where two unclothed men were fashioning a sash to a small piece of cloth no larger than a cheap motel's bath towel as they fastened it to their waists onto a cloth tie belt. The two, thirty something men looked up and smiled at the cops. Toth gently pushed the two Houston cops forward to the next bank of lockers, where Dimas spied Kolezy, Drago, Dimitri, and an unidentified man, presumably Rabb, who were getting dressed in their loin cloths.

Zeke had to hold back his glee filled feelings. "This is going to be easy pickings. No guns or knives to carry. "

Just then, Kolezy reached for a medium sized gym bag.

The Lieutenant cautioned his brother, "Don't be so sure, Bro., he whispered, that bag has got to hold their weapons of choice, it appears to be heavy. If we grab it before they can reach in and use whatever fire power they have, then we got them."

Szilard tapped the Inspector on the back; he had changed and was ready to enter the fray.

Toth looked at Szabo, clad only in the tiny cloth. "You look very, very available, Zilard. Pleeze be cautious zo they don't cut off your prized part."

"Inspector Toth, I am too partial to my manhood and won't allow a knife to come close to me."

"Yes, ve vould not...."

Zeke and Dimas looked at each other, again, both thinking 'what was that all about?'

The Inspector then came to life, but in a low tone, "Lieutenant and Zargeant, are you both ready? I vill szignal our men and your FBI now to come in the other doors as Szabo goes in."

Szilard viewed the three men with some slight consternation, "Alright, but just don't wait very long once I drop my cloth and they do the same, rush in, please." With that Szabo slowly walked toward Kolezy and his men. Toth and the Cavazos brothers swung behind another set of lockers directly across but still hidden from sight, guns now drawn. Toth whispered, "Vhen Zilard drops his cloth ve vill make our vay toward them before they have time to react."

Rabb's eyes lit up as Szabo emerged toward them. "Oh, my Szilard, I wish for you to meet Louis who is from Texas. He has been waiting anxiously to see you in person as he knows of your movies."

Szilard held up for a few moments, then offered his hand. "I have heard about you from Imre."

Kolezy's eyes widened,"My instinct tells me you and I will be together for a long time." He uncharacteristically was almost drooling over the young man. "I want you to show me the other parts of you. You appear so innocent, yet, you are an Adonis and so tan. No lines on your face... Is that green eye shadow you are wearing?"

Dropping his voice to a lilted volume, "No, just the poor lighting but I would love to see your jewels. Louis, show me yours first and I will show you mine," as he batted his round brown eyes with eye lash extensions. Looking over at Drago and Dimitri, as well as Rabb, "Okay everyone, on the count of three, drop your clothes."

Dimitri was ready to leave as his ample stomach hung over the minuscule cloth. He looked over to Kolezy, "Do I have to Louis?"

Kolezy responded, "Yes, you are in great fortune to view our next star at Romany Productions!"

Rabb was already getting aroused looking at Szilard. "Please, everyone, do as he says."

Kolezy waited. "Well, my young friend, you go and we will follow."

Szabo eased a bit, "No Louis, please do the honors and I will follow."

Kolezy tugged at his small white napkin, looking over at the young sting artist. "He finally pulled down the small covering showing his prized possessions as the others followed daunted by the option of showing off their bodies to a stranger or, actually, one another.

Louis was momentarily caught off guard, "Szilard, I confess, as I am not sure why you have not uncovered what makes you so enduring to others."

Seconds later, Toth was next to him, holding an automatic to his ear. "Vee finally meet, Kolezy. I am Inspector Toth, Budapest Polize". Dimas and Zeke drew their weapons and were followed by two FBI personnel, emerging, holding guns to the others.

Szabo forced a smile, "Too bad, Louis and Imre, neither of you will see my emeralds. All of you will have time to think of this moment as you await your fates in prison."

Noticing no restraints relieved, Kolezy retorted, "No handcuffs, Toth?"

"Mr. Kolezy, ve vill have our weapons pointed always in your direction."

Szabo turned to the four ready to be incarcerated men and laughed, "You moo mocks, dumb Hunkarians, falling for this. You deserve to be kept in captivity forever, ha, ha, ha."

Drago bristled at this. "You god damn fucker, you are fortunate that I cannot reach your hanging balls to twist them in the wind!"

Murray and his group, now accompanied by the local police and FBI waited for the capture and arrest of Kolezy unaware of Perez, Gabor, Luka, and Molnar, who were fully armed with automatic weapons, waiting outside. They perched in an alley loft, between the two entrances of a neighboring warehouse, overlooking the rear of the bathhouse. The police van was waiting for the authorities and their captives.

Inside, Kolezy and his crew were trapped and in process of arrest. While not wearing clothing, Louis still presented a brave front as Lieutenant Cavazos, acting as a Roman conqueror, following Toth, with his head in the air, wanting to show the attorney that his time had come. "Kolezy, we always knew you were guilty from that time we visited you in your office and now we have you."

"Alright Cavazos, so you really believe you have me. Don't count on it, you Mexican flatfooted underpaid and overworked centurion of Houston. Do you really think you gained anything today by taking me in? I pay ten times my yardman as to what you are worth. You are nothing but window dressing for the mayor. Do you actually care what they think of you at City Hall?"

Dimas was seething at all this rhetoric, "Look, ass wipe, I am going to read you your rights, then you will need a good attorney, unlike yourself, to pry your fucking hide off the holding cell at 61 Reisner. I am sure there are some former defendants of yours that you ignored that really would like to have you alone for an hour. Judging by your limp dick, some of them will be looking for some sharp sheave to cut it off. If you make it through the arraignment, you will be prosecuted and sentenced, waiting for your fate in prison."

Kolezy was not finished, "Good luck, on getting me to Houston, and that Szabo fag, "Hey, chicken bait, I certainly won't forget your betrayal. You aren't nearly as good as Hector, anyway!"

As the Lieutenant read them their rights, they were joined by two FBI and two local policemen. After that they were allowed to put on their clothes. Dimas turned to Kolezy. "Yeah, you will be flying no class, away from the good folks on the plane. The FBI has a plane waiting, with your name on a seat, to take your sorry butt back to Houston hot shot, mister lawyer."

Kolezy started to eye their gym bag that was a few feet away.

Dimas was ahead of him on it. "Kolezy, don't even think of moving toward that bag."

Zeke picked it up, unzipped it, and found four weapons. Laughing at the Kolezy and his crew, "Ha, Mr. Attorney, you thought you had us. Too bad, dickhead!"

Louis had a down look on his face as he looked at his men. They began to dress, knowing that, at the moment, Toth, Dimas, and the good guys had them by the short hairs.

After they finished dressing, with the assistance of his men, Inspector Toth and the FBI began escorting Kolezy and the other three, out the rear of the building to a waiting police van parked in the back. Szabo was finishing up and he shot a Cheshire look over to Imre and Kolezy.

Still not in handcuffs, the arrested quartet began the walk outside the bathhouse, toward the van with Kolezy shooting the finger at Szilard.

Adam saw Szilard walking out ahead of the group. He ran up and hugged his close friend. "Oh, thank god, Szilard, you are unscathed from this ordeal." They each broke open, emotionally, planting a kiss on one another's cheek.

Murray and St. George stood by, in semi-shock, as all this occurred, Bill was the first to comment. "You always told me that Adam wanted to go straight, get married, have kids, live the normal life. Yeah, he went straight alright, straight to Szabo. I Guess, we don't need to leave the porch light on for him tonight."

Murray felt at a loss to defend Adam's latest act of emotion. "Hell, if I know. Maybe they are doing the French thing. You know, kissing each other on the cheek. He and Brian Davis were at it in 'Sin City'. Adam swore he would have him circulate among his friends, then this. Bill, one minute he's rolling in the sack with Carol Sue, next he is doing the same with a guy. Let's just say, he may be still a little confused at this moment."

St. George levitated his hand, shifting it in a rolling motion, "AC/DC. Confused? He should be kicking his stepfather in the balls, but here he is... Oh, by the way, where is the platinum bomb shell?"

Murray did not want to open that avenue, "Back at the hotel with Wes and Michaeleen. They needed to hash what you and C.W. already know. Maybe, business, maybe not. She has a lot of PR'ing to do with telling Wes about his new brother and sister. For the moment, we have some business of our own. Let's be certain that Toth and his merry men don't fuck this arrest up. I never knew that a number one killer or fugitive, like Kolezy, would not be wearing any handcuffs."

Bill agreed, "Yeah, I 'm looking at that, too."

Tanski left his post and came up to them, hearing their comments. "I am doubly disappointed, guys, with this entire mess."

As the four men were about to enter the rear of an old converted UPS truck, turned police paddy wagon, shots rang out. Murray, St. George, and Tanski, who began walking toward Adam and Szilard, quickly pulled their guns as fire balls rang out from two directions in elevated spots.

Tanski got a bead on their locations, "They're about fifty, sixty yards up on those buildings."

One of the Budapest police man was felled by a barrage of bullets. Kolezy was the last one to attempt entering the police van as the hot lead flew around. He abruptly kicked the unsuspecting policeman who had charge of the four, dislodging his Glock automatic, as it fell to the pavement. The policeman bent over to retrieve his gun, Kolezy kicked him in the groin and pushed him away picking up the weapon, the cop hugged the pavement in panic.

Next, Drago rolled out of the van elbowing his guard, who was distracted by the latest firepower, then placed a choke hold on him enough that the scared face man wrenched the .45 automatic from the cop just as another Budapest policeman came up. Drago pulled the trigger quickly and placed two shots in the chest of the unsuspecting cop who bloodied the side of the van as he collapsed to the concrete.

Imre and Dimitri, unarmed, retreated from the van, looking for Louis and Drago.

Murray gasped, as he never witnessed the carnage. Momentarily in a freeze pattern, this was not Cleveland. Nothing like this ever happens in Northern Ohio. "Bill, Tanski, did you see anything like this fucking mess of local cops standing there acting like statues? He uttered in Hungarian, 'Yesus Madia, Jesus Christ, They killed that policeman! He never had a chance to use his gun."

Drago looked in their direction as the three drew near the van, raised his gun, where St. George pushed a targeted Murray to the ground, temporarily, losing his Taurus. Tanski was accustomed to broken plays and with his Sig Sauer fired off three rounds as he tumbled to the ground breaking the windshield of the van with his bullets.

Drago took their attention away as Rabb and Dimitri fled from the van's side... Kolezy, quickly aimed the Glock and fired at Murray and St. George, sending a bevy of shots toward a policeman and an FBI man turning them each, wincing in pain as the policeman's mouth opened in agony, blood poured out. The FBI man clutched his side, falling to the pavement.

Murray surveyed the area, with its deafening 'pow, pow, pow' sounds. It turned swiftly to muffled moments caused by the rapid fire of three or four pockets of gun fire emanating above by the semi-automatic rifles stationed above the bloody battlefield strewn parking alley. He crawled back to his Taurus Judge as St. George opened up with his .45 Glock not hitting any of the culprits. Inspector Toth scurried to the aid of his fallen comrade, turning him over and looked away as he knew it was too late. Lieutenant Cavazos did the same to the Bureau guy, only to find out he was dead. Kolezy had two notches and was now a murderer in a foreign land. Murray saw what death brought to this group, staring him in the face, slamming him in the stomach and, asking himself, in disbelief, "what was he doing there"?

St. George pulled him away as they both huddled by their rental SUV. St. George, turned to his friend, "Well, Anth, you wanted to get into the action? Is this what you figured it would be like?"

Disgusted at the current events that were occurring, Murray shook his head, "I wanted a clean pinch of Kolezy, HANDCUFFED. What a damn blunder by Toth and the FBI or was it intentional? Hell, I don't know, Bill, would you have believed twenty plus years ago when you were short stopping for The Yanks, you'd be in some god-forsaken alley in Budapest?"

"Anth, forget what and where. We have to survive this ambush!"

Just then Tanski ran toward them, ducking a barrage of AR 15 fire. "God damn, guys, this is Nam all over again!" His tone was almost grateful that he was, once more; in a gun battle with the make believe Viet Cong or some other insurgents. He shook his head, "I wish I had a pineapple to throw at them and blow their asses away"

Murray blinked for a moment, "Oh, pineapple. You mean a handgernade?"

"Yeah, civilian, one of those you pull the pin and lob into their cave or truck. Just like Da'nang."

Tanski's eyes seemed to glaze over thinking about the conflict he was in as barely a man in a hot jungle, almost forgotten war when he carried his semi-automatic hunting down the enemy.

Murray looked over at St. George, shaking his head negatively. Then he said to Tanski, "Figured you would have a bandana on your head and a Bowie knife between your teeth by now?""

Changing the subject for a moment, Bill agreed, "Anth, you're got a point. I think the cuffs on those four would have saved a bunch of this shit and maybe not get a few of the good guys killed. What bothers me is how did these gunsels above us to station themselves in the back and not the front? Something eats at me that this screw up was all intentional."

Murray thought it was strange, as well. "This whole mess smells like a setup."

The Cavazos brothers had opened up with their automatic weapons with little success, as Kolezy and his men fired back randomly. His men, who were firing from the buildings, came down, closer to the action. Three who were cold blooded killers, Perez, Molnar, and Gabor, along with an unlikely murderer, Luka, who was more afraid of not freeing Louis, continued their barrage of gunfire.

Murray and Bill saw that their own HPD men were unable to contain the fight. Murray was getting restless as the bullets kept whizzing by their vehicles. "We need some kind of distraction and then come out shooting. I haven't done crap with my Taurus Judge."

Bill recalled a Newman/Redford movie. "We could be like Sundance and Butch Cassidy fighting the Mexicans at the end of the show. They are all bandaged and have only the ammo in their guns and stand up and start firing at the Federales."

Murray contradicted his old buddy. "You have a point their except, technically, Butch and Sundance were in Bolivia robbing banks and shooting a few people now and then. I don't think I want to stand up and start shooting like them. Do you, Bill?"

"Bolivia, eh? Guess we'll wait and crawl over to the next car."

Nothing appeared to work as Kolezy and his crew seemingly in command waiting for their escape. Out popped Carol Sue...on a borrowed Harley with a near forgotten Adam clinging to her back end roaring down, unexpectedly, on Kolezy and his group who were frozen and totally unexpecting this turn of events. She tore straight toward them, as both Carol Sue and Adam extended their legs out at a 45 degree angle tripping a gaping Rabb and Dimitri as each of their borrowed weapons hit the pavement. Drago grabbed the handlebars of the cycle swirling Carol Sue and Adam off the bike sending it forward and hitting the bathhouse rear door as they each fell into a pile of trash. Adam got up and ran to Carol Sue as she was slow in coming to her senses, but apparently cleared the cobwebs from her brain, realizing where she was and hugged an unexpected Adam.

Molnar, who was crouched on the edge of the SUV, stood up with his AK 45. At that moment Zeke fired a dozen rounds hitting him below the eye causing the Hungarian to drop his weapon back into the car almost squeezing off a dozen rounds as Luka grabbed the gun. Molnar, wide-eyed, fell still across the young guy, momentarily as Luka pushed off the dead man. Luka, still holding the automatic rifle, scampered back, opening the BMW's door.

Kolezy, Rabb, Dimitri, and Drago made it to the BMW SUV, where Luka and Gabor had jumped in, still firing their weapons, with Perez at the wheel. The four scrambled into the waiting car as it was a distraction to Toth and the Cavazos brothers who, like everyone else was startled by Carol Sue and Adam's intervention, but definitely saved the good side.

Dimas and Zeke re-entered the conflict and began empting their weapons at the BMW as it drove past them, almost unscathed from the shelling. Tanski got off a half dozen shots from his Sig Sauer. Gasping in frustration. "Fuckin' gun is off. Did not hit a lick with it."

Murray ran up, finally pulling the trigger of The Judge, as the shots careened off the top of the black SUV. "Those shit heads got away, Damn! Where are The Cavazos brothers?"

Tanski looked over at the van, "Both of them are checking out the other FBI guy who was wounded. They're behind the truck. "Murray wanted to get the posse going and searched the area for the others, "Bill, let's get Sev and Rich, along with the Lieutenant and Zeke to go after Kolezy now!"

Adam walked up, as Carol Sue limped in. "I know the streets, Magassey offered, let's get in the cars and follow them."

Murray looked at the somewhat dishelved tall, platinum haired woman, "You saved us, Vixey. It was a brave thing to do, riding in like that. Even though they temporarily got away, Kolezy's bunch had too much fire power and would have taken us out. Thanks." He gave her a long look as though for that moment, going back in time with Bobbie Jean and her. "See you around, Vixey."

Carol Sue seemed to return his thoughts and murmured, "Yeah, hey, be safe going after Kolezy."

He silently nodded, giving a faint smile back to her.

Dimas came up and grabbed her, "Are you okay, Carol Sue? You did a dumb thing but probably kept us out of further harm's way. Words cannot describe it. We all have to thank you for it. You're amazing. How know where to find us? Whose motorcycle did you get, this time?"

"Wes and Michaeleen were safe at the hotel and I was getting antsy. Wes told me about The Baths and the plan to get Kolezy but being I was out of danger her did not wish to get into any shoot out. I asked the hotel clerk where this place was. He gave me directions and I paid some Hungarian guy $200.00 off my ATM card that I luckily had tucked into my bra back in Houston. Saw Adam who wanted on and the rest is history!"

Dimas was totally captivated by her, unashamedly wanting her, not caring about those around or even Kolezy's departure. The couple drew closer.

She fell into his arms for a brief few seconds as they locked in an almost inseparable embrace. Dimas was now in another world like it was the time he bid farewell at the station to his first wife. "We are off to war, woman. I will savor this sendoff from you as I hunt the enemy." Now releasing her as his heart was beating faster, torn between his burning love for this tall damsel and the pursuit of Kolezy.

The woman knew he had to go and hunt down the wretched murderer. Carol Sue threw a kiss, as she did her famous slow handed release to her man. "May the God's be with you, my darling!"

Adam stood there, coming in second again, as he thought his actions with her might re-open the door to their relationship. Being as worldly as he portrayed, he was just a wet behind the ears school boy when it came to female emotions and their meanings.

Rich yelled out, "Let's get rolling after Kolezy; this is not a Hollywood movie. The trail is going to get cold fast!"

Toth radioed to another police car in the vicinity, Kolezy's BMW SUV and license number so that they would be on the lookout for it. Moments later they confirmed that they spotted the car on Kochsis Street near them.

With that Toth and two of his men joined Dimas and Zeke in one SUV as Adam, Murray, Bill, Rich, Sev, and Tanski piled into the Mercedes SUV, picking up a left behind AK 45 from Kolezy's mob. The two vehicles screeched out of the alley way and went on the streets, careening around the corner from Balaton Street to Al Kotaqs Way toward Kariniky street and Kochis toward the Danube where they caught up with the BMW and the other Budapest police car. Sev was a former wanna be car racer in his youth, and savored the moments, to drive, as the wild chase began down the streets of Budapest. Toth's driver roared past their counter pointed patrol car with Murray's Benz almost bumper behind, blurring, seemingly blending into one car.

Kolezy turned around in his seat as the sirens began blaring twenty five yards behind the BMW. He barked at his men, "Gabor, Drago use the automatics through the sunroof. Perez, stomp on the accelerator. We must out run these police! Dimitri, fire from the side window." With that Gabor and Drago opened up on Toth's lead SUV, where the top of their car and windshield became peppered by the gun fire, causing the police car to pull back.

Sev hit their SUV in higher gear, like he was still at those Sunday amateur race tracks he always raced in as a young man. He virtually got out of his seat and pressed the gas pedal to the max as their car swished past Toth's and was within five feet of Kolezy's back window. Murray turned to St. George, "I know this sounds crappy, but I love this."

Bill thought It was funny, "Anth, you amaze me at times."

Tanski had visions of Nam and Cleveland as he grabbed the AK 45, yelling at Sev to open the sunroof where he prompted getting up and took aim as Gabor came back up with his AR15. Ron yelled out, "Punch it, Sev!" He let go of a barrage of bullets striking Gabor in the chest and face, his blood spewed down to his fingers as he catapulted from the top of the SUV pulling him out of the sunroof, still firing his gun into the air as he landed on a passing grain truck.

The BMW lurched to the right and left attempting to avoid further gun fire. Drago peered out of the sunroof, firing wildly, with his Lugar at the pursuing Benz.

Meanwhile, the Cavazos brothers in the Toth SUV, poked their guns out, with Dimas' 45 ringing out 3-4 shots as Zeke, from the other side, ran his Glock and puked 4-5 shells hitting the rear and passenger side window of the BMW showering glass and causing a blood flow within the interior. Perez, who was driving, clutched the back of his neck as dark liquid poured from his body, losing control of the SUV. The Beamer hit the bridge with such force it careened over the rail. The pursuing SUV's and police cars all screeched and swervered to a halt. They jumped out of their cars, nearly trampling one another to get to the rail, only to witness the car landed, roof down, in the water.

Murray, St. George, Tanski, Adam, Rick, Sev, Lt. Cavazos, Sergeant Cavazos and Toth all gripped the ancient bridge rail at the same time. Disappointing silence fell over all of them.

Sev, initially, was the first one to mock the moment of disbelieve as he blurted out, "Holy shit! Who is the first one to go in and save those poor bastards?"

Murray looked over at Bill, who in turn looked at Tanski, who in turn looked at Rick, who turned to Lieutenant Cavazos, who turned to his brother. Zeke's response as everyone seemed to be numb with the outcome, "Hey, it's been years since I did diving at McAllen, Texas in high school, but no thanks, everyone."

There was disappointment that not even one person volunteered to jump into the dirty, slightly polluted Danube. Another apparent victim of The Magyar Duna!

Toth went back using his cell to call the water police for the search and recovery of the survivors or victims.

The River was bathed in the bridge lights below the avenue, designed to guide shipping and river crafts. As the car sank in a 'whoose', the bubbles cascaded on top of the car as it went down having the Danube claiming Kolezy and his gang. The river was once more placid.

Adam was in remorse. "I never had the chance to confront him about Ryan."

Murray agreed, as he too, wanted to ask Kolezy about Troy's death, yet attempted to console the young man. "Well, your stepfather got what was coming to him. Least, let's figure he was caught inside with the rest." Then he yelled back to Toth, "Inspector, how long will it be for your River Cops to do their thing? Like diving and pulling up the car?"

Toth appeared confused. "It vill take time, I don't know. You are velcome to jump in for yourself."

Murray did not care for his nonchalant answer. It was getting cold and the early evening turned into late in the middle of some unfamiliar part of the world. He went over to the old cop, "You know, Inspector, I am not in law enforcement but it all was downhill when Kolezy and company were not handcuffed. Why didn't you do it? Also, how did Kolezy's bunch know that you were bringing him out the back?" The Lieutenant looked over in agreement as he was not the senior officer on the pinch and had argued, in the bathhouse, on the non-use of the bracelets, and now questioned how Kolezy's Hungarian Mafia knew where to station his men.

Toth was enraged. "I lost two of my best men at Kuylari Baths. You have the nerve to queztion me on getting Kolezy? Ve had him. Only, only... he HAD hiz men, shoot at us from above and distracted everyone. I cannot ezplain how Kolezy had hiz men there.."

St. George joined in, "You are a real spin doctor, Inspector Toth. You screwed this up by not having them handcuffed and not having your men check the adjoining buildings."

Toth defended himself, "You and your Texaz cowboyz vere there!"

"We did not know that his guys were there and you told us to stay out of it."

Toth was at an impasse, "Ok. Ve vill vait on the River Police... it vill bez early morning. Now let me be."

Zeke was holding back his disapproval of the Inspector, as he looked over at his brother. "Toth is in charge, Dee. Kolezy may well be dead and case close. Guess we will have to freeze our asses off until morning. Do you think this burg has any late night Mexican enchilada palaces ready to serve up some rice and beans to go with the Jose Cuero?"

.

Tanski ran back. "Ya'll, there's café a block back that stays open all night. All the Americans hightailed it with Ron to the place for whatever was available. Most needed a john to take a piss.

Murray thought back as he settled in a booth at The Rathskellar café. "Carol Sue and Adam, we should thank you and her for the intervention back at the bathhouse."

"I did not want Carol Sue, who just came up out of the blue on that cycle, to go it alone. She did the thumbs up and I hopped on.

Dimas listened in. "Glad you brought her up. She just texted me that the police were cleaning up the scene and the ambulance arrived. Unfortunately, taking away the two policemen and FBI agent who did not make it. The attendants wrapped her bruised ankle. Otherwise, ok."

Adam feigned a positive response, "Well, that is fine news about her. She is quite a ...a good gal."

Dimas realized the young man's words were of a man who came in last in the contest of winning the hand of a fair maiden. Of course, Carol Sue did not quite fit that description and Adam was better off without her. He just did not think of it that way at the time.

The hours went by as the hudka, kolbasz, and the palenckinka pancakes were washed down with Barack, Tokay, Kimmel, and the ever present strong Hungarian coffee, which most of the group made faces over it. Sev was chomping at the bit to find out as the dawn broke, if anything was going on at the bridge. He hurried back with the latest news. "The river cops found two bodies that just popped up."

Everyone returned to the bridge as the morning sun rose and traffic was being routed around the crime scene. Toth was found looking over the rail as he spoke to his men on the cell phone, directing them to more strategic positions. Murray was anxiously awaiting the word of who the divers found. "Inspector, who are they bringing up?"

Toth only replied, "The Legend of the Magyar Duna has arisen!"

Murray exclaimed "What is that about?"

Adam chimed in, "It is that old wife's tale. Only dumb assed Hungarians buy it."

Toth was taken back by that. "Doom azzed?"

St. George laughed it all off, "Toth just had too much, Tokay or Kimmel."

The divers started to bring up the bodies. "One of the divers, hollered to Toth, "kate fee you , meg halt, muutud!"

Murray asked Adam, "What was he saying?"

"It means, two men, found dead, in the car."

Rich asked, "Do they know who they are?"

Toth heard the question, "Itz too early to find out who they are."

Bill put his hands up, "Probably going to find all of them and then we will know, that no one could have survived the hundred foot fall."

Rich observed, "Bill, the current in the early morning hours with the lights shining down on the dead guys, the others, I bet, were swept downstream."

Murray was intrigued, "Rich, do you believe that, they made it after the crash?"

The tall, slightly bald, man took off his glasses and pulled out his handkerchief wiping the lenses. "The time I had one was when I was going after a drug dealer in Indiana. The car crashed on the Wabash River. Same type of deal like this. The locals found the bodies two days later ten miles down from the original entry where they flipped in. So, it is the same scenario. I am positive a 100 foot drop. Maybe we poured so much lead into that car they may have been all dead by the time the Beemer hit the bridge and careened into the river."

Zeke was listening intently to all this and wanted to put in his view. "I remember we chased some hombres to Buffalo Bayou, in downtown Houston. They dove in fully clothed, around the North Main bridge and drowned. One was a gringo, the other maybe a Puerto Rican or San Salvadorian, fuck, I don't remember. They speak Spanish, maybe a little high or low in dialect. Anyway, they bloated like a blowfish. Pale skin, butterfly lips, eye balls that bugged out of their sockets. Their last meal was coming up even though they were dead."

Murray winced, his face squeezed up. "I get it Zeke. Maybe the Hunkies will take pictures and we can ID them that way. You know when they lay them out. Don't need an indigestive bull shit post mortem thing."

The Lieutenant was eating this up as Murray wanted to let it go. "You know Murray; you can take the pictures of Kolezy. That ass hole won't be bothering anyone, anymore."

Adam interrupted. "My gut feeling, guys, and sorry to put a damper on your celebrations, but Lieutenant, Louis is a cat with nine lives. He told all us kids, when he was here growing up in Pest. He almost drowned by another kid. Another time he was shot in the stomach in a hunting accident. He made it through a plane crash about fifteen years ago. The pilot and two others perished. Louis spent ten days in ICU. Actually, we were glad he was immobile. He did not have an opportunity to fondle us. Too bad, he made it through all that. Now it is de je ve all over again."

St. George was a shade disappointed in this. "You realize, don't you, who is writing a journal on this? No takers? It was Ernie who decided to stay at the hotel because of his avoidance of violence."

Murray could not get over Petrovich' s reluctance as to why he was with the group on the plane, yet failed to get involved at the bathhouse?"

Sev came to Ernie's aid. "Ernie wanted to get the flavor of the hunt, then interview us on the battle, not wanting to be in danger since he was not packing. Plus, he and C.W. had an interest in Petrovich's love of old westerns, especially, Louis Lamoure novels. They decided to hang at the Hotel Estavan and exchange notes. Who figures? You know?"

Murray was still trying to tie up loose ends. "You know, guys, we landed at that airstrip. What happened to the Falcon? We know they landed there as Carol Sue left us the message that lead us to the Kolezy. You realize if that plane is available somewhere, and if he is alive, that son of a bitch is hightailing it somewhere in the world on that jet and it goes a long way and can hide at any non-descript place. We need to find that F-7!"

Tanski had enough and could not resist throwing in a zinger." In getting back to these corpses, let's pray that Kolezy is alive! Okay? He can be brought back to Houston to stand trial."

Sergeant Cavazos came unglued at the Soldier of Fortune, Nam Vet,

"Are you fucking crazy, Tanski? We may have saved the Harris County folks in Houston, a couple of million dollars in legal fees not to try and convict that hoodlum. That is not to say dragging folks into court and being hounded by the media wanting to know all the gory details of how they knew him and how he killed those young guys for control of this god damn company Magassey owns. Plus we'd have to wait in this part of the world, in this god forsaken city, and their jail with rats and smelly Hungarians and Czechs while he dried out after being fished out of that polluted, so called beautiful river. No sir, I am happy that he ran out of lives!"

Toth had just was informed that the two men had ID's on them. Solemnly, he gave the news to all in listening range, "Ve have been told that thesz men are not Mr. Kolezy."

Lieutenant Cavazos demanded, "There were six men in the car and you only could locate two and have determined that Kolezy was not one of them. Where are the others?"

Toth calmly retreated two steps, "Our vater polize zay all vindows of the car vere broke. Many bullet holez in the exterior of the car. Bodiez vent out the vindows vhen they vere zhot. These two vere caught by the veight of the car and vere found. The others ve vill find zoon. You must ve patient. It iz much different here than in your country."

As he began to leave, another plain clothes policeman came up to the Inspector and whispered to him.

Bill was at a cross roads of lack of sleep and coldness, he voiced his discontent, "Why in the hell are you being so secretive? You can easily talk in Hungarian so most of us would not understand what you are telling each other."

Dryly, Toth responded, "Mr., it iz no zecret. Our men found one more body, two hundred yardz downztream from zee bridge, caught on the rocks. Lieutenant Cavazoz, you muzt come to the zcene. And you do underztand Hungarian, yez?.

Dimas had enough and comically responded, "Zay Vhat?"

The Inspector shook his head in disgust.

Adam looked at Murray, "I still believe Louis will not be among the three when we view all of them. He is slippery as a snake, and for some reason, has led a charmed life.

Murray agreed and added, "Maybe, he is lucky or because he is a believer of the way these cops handle things here. All this time and trouble, dragging the river when the locals, here, could have cuffed Kolezy and the other three and had better preparation, knowing they were dangerous."

The Inspector caught those cutting remarks, "Mr. Murray, it haz yet to be determined that Kolezy iz not in the river and ve did vhat ve thought vaz bezt as I had enough men and your FBI people vith me."

Bill murmured, "Seems like we are bombarding him a lot and he can't handle it, Anth. Relax. This is going to be over soon."

Rich took to the defense of Toth. "Look, Bill and Anthony, Toth has a tough job. Sure, our guys may have handled it a lot differently and may have some sympathy for him but he has a half dozen civilians poking their noses, with guns, into all of this."

Murray still was defiant, "Right, but the Budapest police were pinned down at the bathhouse, along with the FBI. We backed them up, chased Kolezy, attempting to rid the world of a slimy bastard, mother fucker and his gang. So the Inspector's pissed off at us. We should be the ones awarded a medal of honor."

Bill thought it was all comical by Murray. "Anth, how about hanging a Hungarian Hudka sausage around your neck. The medal of sage, rice, pork, and garlic, as the Hungarians would say, 'a variety of spices'."

The Cavazos brothers were amused by this non-Hispanic bull corn, journeying back to the café. As the six finished off their breakfast of coffee and local leckvar and Danish, Dimas sprang some undisclosed news, "Adam, you may be in luck. One of the water cops told me that he thought the information off the last stiff may be your beloved stepfather. You know him the best and need you to ID him."

Zeke broke in, as he wiped his face from devouring the third pastry, "I was told he is a little skinned up and his clothes are almost torn from his body. Since you have seen him naked so much, you probably can confirm if it is your stepdad."

Adam was dealt a low blow by Zeke's comment. "Yeah, Sergeant, you think because I have been naked with him, what, fourteen years ago, I can positively tell you he IS Louis B. Kolezy?"

Zeke took a long sip from his coffee, "You have to do it. I never went to bed with him."

Bill and Murray were embarrassed for Adam and only shook their heads.

Bill tried to save the day, "Okay guys, let's go and finish up this crap."

With that they left The Rathskellar, walking 200 yards, where now, three bodies were on display under a green canvas. They all were covered in grime and splashes of blood as the river did not wash it off. The Inspector stood over them as a triumph of catching these dead villains. .

Adam breathed deeply and looked at each one. Recognizing him from the motel that night when he was taken down. "The one on the end is the kid that set me up at the motel, Luka. Next to him is the Mexican looking guy, probably Perez. The other fellow, from pictures Louis showed me ... Yeah that is Imre Rabb, his partner, here in Budapest. Unfortunately, none are Louis."

Bill attempted to comfort Adam. "Thought we had that snake in the grass... Sorry, kid."

"That is about what I figured. Louis is not dead. Believe me, he still has four lives left."

Murray was more drastic, "Find him, skin him alive, then shoot him! No one can go through what they did, have the car go into the river and still live."

Toth only made the parade and shook everyone's hand. "Vell, you Amerikan's if Mr. Kolezy iz ztill alive I vill alert you and zend him over to Texaz."

Sev looked down at that, "Yeah, we're sure. And not in handcuffs, either."

Tanski counted out three, "That leaves, Dimitri, Drago, along with Kolezy. With their plane somewhere, hell, who knows where they could wind up? "

Murray thought out loud, "If Kolezy did make it through all that, he is going back to his place or the Red Cat Club. Carol Sue knows the layout of his house. The cops can take the club. Let's go to the hotel and get her now!"

The Lieutenant concurred, and added, "Gringo, that sounds like a plan to go to Kolezy's mansion. Inspector Toth probably will go to the Red Cat Club."

Adam added, "What, we are not checking out is Romany Productions? That's Louis' movie company and he has stashed money there before. He confided in Melanie, one night, that he wanted to take her to Budapest and then to the Hungarian Rivera and the Black Sea for fun and frolic on the beach. He had a vault there. With the way he likes to play it all up, Louis will need the money. The house and the movie company, yeah, that is where he is."

Zeke glanced at his watch. "That car went over the top, nine plus hours ago, let's think he swam away, got dried off, called another of his dip sticks to pick him up. Go to his mansion or what did you call that company, Rome productions? He got his shit together and headed for wherever that plane is hidden and takes off for parts unknown. Dee, we can't wait to pick up your girlfriend, Carol Sue? Toth hits the club. We go to the movie spot and mansion. Might be too late in both places. That fucker, Kolezy, may have screwed us over."

Rich was faster on the draw, "Look, everyone, what we all did at the Secret Service and Bureau was fan out when everything was evident immediately. We should have had Plan B in place, except we depended upon Toth."

Lieutenant Cavazos rubbed his face with both of his hands. "Yeah, Rich, you are right, we may have been had by that low life. I had too much faith in Toth. Let's get into our cars and head to the hotel after I call Carol Sue and pick her up to take us to Kolezy's place."

Toth stopped them. "My informants gave me the addrezz of Mr. Kolezy'z place earlier and they vent there. The house boy, vas co-operative and told them that Danika, hiz pilot, vas at the houze and gone into his office. Kolezy vas not vith them. "

Dimas looked over at Zeke, "He may not have made it as we thought. That son of a bitch... has nine lives, like Adam said."

"What about the airstrips around here, Inspector?" questioned Murray.

Toth was suddenly on top of the hunt for the elusive, wayward attorney,"Ve have all of them covered. "

Tanski and Sev tried to suppress their surprise by joking at it all. Tanski started it. "Appears that the Inspector drank a lot of brandy and ate a plate or two of that Hungarian grub to realize he fucked up at the bathhouse."

Sev was right behind, "He is thinking that his boss is going to kick his fat ass off the force and needs to atone for screwing up a layup arrest."

Toth almost bristled at the comments, "Vell, you people!"

Zeke handled it, "Look Inspector, just go and see if Kolezy paid a visit to his movie company or whatever."

Lieutenant Cavazos lamented, "It appears that, Mr. K may still be in the Danube River. Let's hit the hotel, clean up, and get some rest. I don't know. We can't wait on the cops to drag the River."

Adam knew what Dimas was actually thinking, allowing his emotions for the woman take over, "You really mean to see if Carol Sue is available. Not wait on picking Louis out. Truly, I feel he made it."

Dimas could care less of what Adam and the others thought, "Well, kid, you just may have that right."

Adam had another arrow thrust through his heart, as he walked away.

They all took the advice for whatever it was worth and wound up at the Hotel Estavan for needed R& R and to contemplate what their next move was. As the group walked into the high storied lobby that looked like a 1950-ish place, Ernie and C.W. greeted them.

Bill did not know what to make of Petrovich's absence at The Bathhouse. "Erne, we just spent the last twelve hours in a shootout and a wait out for eight hours to find if that shithead, Kolezy, was still alive. And...you ditched us."

Ernie was taken back, "Bill, I left you a note with the desk captain. You know me. We have been friends since age 10 on 130th and Buckeye in Cleveland. I never actually enjoyed confrontation and violence. I knew you, Rich, and Sev could handle all that. I had enough in Cleveland. Besides, C.W. and I are going in on writing about The West and some characters he met in Cisco, Texas as a young man."

Bill was satisfied at the explanation from Ernie. "Well, it is what it is, Erne. As long as you're happy with whatever, but you should have been there..... Oh, damn, whatever..." He walked away and headed for the elevator but was stopped by Murray.

"Toth just had his men blanket the house, club and Romany Productions. Kolezy's bunch were already there and cleaned out his safes. And the airstrip we landed at, the guy there, said a Falcon F-7 took off at five o'clock without filing a flight plan. He did mention a tall, European woman in leather pants that appeared to be the pilot. No indication if Kolezy was with her."

Bill gave a deep breath, "Sounds like that Danika bitch, Adam told us about. Well, Anth, we knocked off five of them and did not lose anyone in our group. Toth and the FBI had losses but they may be expected. They fucked up. Guess it is back to Houston. "

Murray was in a sarcastic mood, "Yeah, we did fly for eleven hours, cramped in a plane, met some Hungarian gigolo, named Szilard, saw how the Budapest cops handled things when it came to handcuffing a murderer. Hey, that midnight dinner and breakfast was a highlight and seeing Vixey on a motorcycle, well, I wish I had taken pictures of her on the cell phone, but was too busy shooting my Taurus Judge.

Bill managed to hold back a large snicker, "Anth, hate to inform you, but when you shot your fabulous Taurus Judge, besides the windshield, it hit a couple of light bulbs in the alley of the bathhouse.

We had less light to work with, but what the hell, it was not your deal that got us in a bind. It was Toth and his group. He would not listen to The Feds or Cavazos. Can't get in his damn ass Hunkie head as to why he did that?"

Murray reasoned, "Bill, most likely, he's on the take. It is too late to do anything to him and we cannot prove it, but head out tomorrow, or whatever, and fly back to Houston."

Rich heard some bad news from Houston. "Another guy was dumped in Montrose. Same deal. His name was Justin White."

Murray thought out loud, "Maybe that lets out Kolezy and his mafia. Looks as though we have some weirdo out there. Did you tell Adam?"

"No, Adam came back with us but Szilard pulled him aside, maybe they are saying their 'goodbyes'."

"Yeah, it has been a large rocky road with him from the time we picked his ass out of the ditch while going to our home."

Rich was consoling. "You and Sheryl saved his life. That is something."

Murray lamented, "I lassoed the six of you in helping him and we wind up with three dead fishes in the water and one at the bath house, and another flipping out of the sunroof. I'm also getting indigestion from the food at the Ratheskeller. We're 5700 miles away. Was any of this worth it?"

No one answered, perhaps thinking the same thing.

Zeke wandered up to them in the lobby. "Well, my chances to get my bars back went out the broken windows of the BMW. We can't even get Mexican food here. Then Tanski is complaining about not getting something named pear old geez. Has to be something the Polaks eat. "Hey Polak, get over here and 'splain what that shit is you were looking for."

"Zeke, my man, they are called pierogies and a delight to behold. Only imagine, an old woman in the neighborhood, you know, the place where we Polaks grew up on the east side of Cleveland or maybe Chicago or wherever. This gray haired woman is in an old dress with high heels and white socks putting the delicious ingredients in them and ..."

"Tanski let me stop you. Do you know why Mexican have refried beans?"

Ron was a cross between tired from no sleep and his hunger for some native Polish food. "No, Zeke, lay it on me."

Zeke was almost hiccupping with tears in his eyes, "It's because, the Mexicans can't get it done right the first time. Ha, ha."

Tanski shook his head, "I still hunger for pierogies! I am heading to the room, Sarge!"

Murray had heard enough and as he hit the button on the elevator to his floor, Michaeleen came up to him. "I know you are very tired, Anthony. Adam phoned Wes and told him about the outcome. Looks as though, Kolezy is on the loose."

Murray was in a light delirious state, "Yes, and we think he might head back to Houston on his Falcon. It only means we are going to fly back there. Found out there was another young man who was murdered like Adam's buddies were. Kolezy was here, so maybe that lets him out.

"I need to really tell you something I just found out and you need to know. It is not involving this mess... I spoke to Carol Sue...my mother." The girl grabbed his arm.

Murray did not want to go up to his room as Michaeleen was looking at him strangely, and he could not discern her intentions. "Michaeleen, let's grab a drink at the bar, get into a private corner and you can tell me the rest of the story." When he held her hand, it was pounding.

She looked up at the half asleep, somewhat confused Murray, by her actions and what had already taken place in the past 48 hours of this bustling city. "I need to explain another part of all this. Explain may be too vague a word."

Murray could feel her pulse rising as they entered the bar. Not far to their left were Dimas and Carol Sue. Both he and Michaeleen gave a courtesy look and half smile to them as they acknowledged their being there but not beckoning a welcome to their table. Murray looked at Michaeleen, clearing his throat, "I imagine Vixey, that is, Carol Sue, your mom, is laying it on the Lieutenant. He may need something stronger than that Hungarian beer he's pretending to like after she tells him about you."

The young woman wanted to break the ice, "Why do we always refer to her as Vixey? Seems as though we all have reasons to call her that."

As they sat down at a corner table, he rubbed his face as a prelude to the story of Carol Sue's nickname. Just as he started, the waiter came by. Michaeleen ordered a double martini. He wanted George Dickel number 12, 90 proof, White Label. The waiter gave him a 'meazz'? Like in what are you talking about? "Ok, buddy, how about Jack Black, double, straight up?" The waiter gave thumbs up on that and disappeared.

"The reason we call your mother, Vixey, it is a slang term for Vixen. She enjoys being the center of attention. Carol Sue appears to enjoy that part of adulation. She always has to be loved. Well, you should have been there to see her ride in on that motorcycle and startle Kolezy and company. She saved the day for us and we were able to rebound to get the upper hand, but they got away. You and I have to discuss your relationship with her as your mother or, do you call her, Mom, now?"

"It will take some time to get to the MOM part. Wes took it in stride. His twin sister, my step sister, K'Lynn was not surprised as she always had a soft spot for me and she liked David. When we see one another she will welcome me with open arms... just need desperately, to find David...if he's still alive."

Murray touched Michaeleen's arm lightly, "We will find him."

Michaeleen had more to add. "I need to tell you something even more startling. Perhaps, we should wait for our drinks. You may need a triple."

Murray's heart raced. He thought, 'What now'? "Michaeleen, what else can you lay on me?"

As the waiter brought their drinks, he took her hand, "Look Michaeleen, David is just out there and probably safe. He just wants some time to himself. I will try, myself, to find him. Meantime, you have something more to tell me, right?"

As she started to down the double martini, looked over at Murray. "Maybe you should have ordered a double, double on the Jack Black."

"You're scaring me, once more, just like at the hotel room, young lady!"

"Sorry about all this, the actual reason I came back into your life," Then Carol Sue limped up.

"What are you two, up to? I found out that Kolezy survived the fall on a bridge, fell in the Danube and most likely swam to safety. That son of a bitch! That is his method of operation, to get rid of somebody and take off."

"How's the ankle, Vixey?"

"It still is attached to my leg."

"Your daughter has filled me in on you."

Carol Sue's lip quivered, "And did she tell you everything?"

Murray questioned that, "Everything? What do you mean, Vixey?"

Carol Sue looked at Michaeleen, "You did not tell him, my daughter?"

Michaeleen was laid to waste by Carol Sue, even with her status, trying to drain the remnants of the double martini. "No, er, Carol Sue, ah, Mom, I was just bringing it up to him."

Carol Sue, laughed, gloated by her next spew of her version of the truth, bending down to Murray's face, "Not only is Michaeleen my daughter, and remember back about those thirty plus years ago, Anthony J. Murray, that stuffy, Burkburnett motel, with the bad air conditioning, that afternoon in room 102? You were with me, not Bobbie Jean, and we made hot, passionate, sex and you chose not wear a Trojan, wanting to make love to me to bring our kids into the world. Remember that? She let it all out, "Michaeleen and David are our bundle that day you chose to go bare backed and gushed into my 'sensuous hole', as you termed it."

Michaeleen rose up swiftly as she knew her place was not there at that moment. "I will let the two of you sort all that out. From now on I am calling you, Dad, even though My Mother is not very tactful."

He jumped up, in a delirious state, and picked up the girl by the shoulders, almost crushing her in a tight bear hug, "I love you Michaeleen, my newest daughter!"

Murray then fell back into the leather bar chair, half surprised at the revelation, yet he managed a small smile which broke his face. It could have been the Jack Daniels. He faded back to reality and that motel day in Burkburnett when Tex and his sons broke in; ruining his romantic time with whom he thought was Bobbie Jean. Or did he? Dialing back those years he remembered that neither of them had protection as they savagely ravaged one another. Ecstasy was their passion which flowed that afternoon, as each of their love was consummated in the motel. He vividly recalled using the exact words that just haunted him, all of it Carol Sue was only too glad to remind him of. He only recalled her dashing, naked into the bathroom only a moment or two before the hard knock on the motel door took place.

Carol Sue was reveling in the fact that Murray was caught in between the nouveau riche and finding out he had another daughter and son. "Bobbie Jean really liked you but I saw you as a young Air Force kid who wanted more than a government position. I told her that day that you went to Fort Polk, Louisiana and would call her when you landed at Leesville, at the base."

"What a great person you are, Vixey. You are one .... Whatever you are?"

Murray, got back up and managed to pull himself together, "Maybe it is because I have been up for over two days with little or no sleep and had this crap with Kolezy go down the tubes, yet none of that should matter because if I am hearing you right, I have a privilege of being in the company of a wonderful, young woman, both Sheryl and I think is extraordinary. Add to that a son, in David, which I will do my utmost to find him."

Carol Sue laid her head on Michaeleen's shoulder. "I wish to find David as well. We are a family!" She abruptly departed, Michaeleen trailing slightly behind, both women looking back.

Still in a semi shock, he uttered, still not fathoming what was told to him moments ago. "I will see you both on the plane, right?"

Carol Sue gave a wry smile, "Of course, nothing could stop me from being there."

Murray took a deep breath, feeling that the dying hand of Tex Miller reached from Hell and was going to make his life a purgatory, wanting to shoot the finger at Carol Sue but did not wish to act like a sore head that just got one upped. Maybe he wasn't?

Michaeleen drifted back to her dad. "I am terribly sorry that she told you before I had the chance. She related it to Wes and me, an hour ago. I was in complete shock."

Reaching out for some place of confidence to his new daughter, "It is alright, you attempted to, only your MOM was bent on beating you to the punch. Same ole Vixey!"

"I was beginning to put it all together before we left from the Sugar Land airport. There was not enough time to confirm it with Carol Sue or Mom, so when I got together with her and Wes, I confronted her. She never told you but, the physical difference between Bobbie Jean and now, my new found mother, is a tattoo of the butterfly just above her butt. Bobbie Jean did not have one. Did you know that?"

Murray closed his eyes in silence, remembering their bed actions at the motel and his making a sexual remark of how the butterfly seemed to shift as the now, Vixey, gyrated up and down to his pulsating movements in her as she acted like a stripper on stage.

"Yes, Michaeleen, I recall the butterfly."

"When I came to you and Sheryl at your office three and one half years ago, I was not aware of any of this, only something strange inside of me began the mission to come into your life and make things right. My grandfather, Tex Miller, cheated you and I was determined to give you a better life. I told you, Vixey, was instrumental in assisting me on getting you the money. I know she just laid one on you but it is her way... Now I have to make adjustments as we always do not see eye to eye. You know what, Dad? I kind of like the nickname you gave her. Vixey, definitely, fits her!"

Murray felt better as he was shaking off the drink, the lack of sleep, along with the failure to bring Kolezy to justice. He now had an older daughter to love and possibly a son, along with the three wonderful daughters; he and Sheryl have Renee, Karen, and Gina. They had to be told of this wonderful news. Yet, he had not heard from Wes' wife, his middle daughter, Gina. "Michaeleen, has Wes told Gina of all this?"

"I asked him to hold off until I gave you the news, if we can call it that?"

"That was deeply appreciated. I am going to ask that he waits until I can tell Sheryl and then, Gina, Renee and our Karen, in that order. After that, we have to see if Bill and the rest are interested in searching for Kolezy. They will have a lot to say about all this as well."

Michaeleen looked over at Carol Sue and Dimas who was smiling now at his lady. "They appeared to have ironed out things."

All this danced in Murray's head causing an uneasiness. "I have to get a pretty hot iron myself to explain things to people who are close to me."

"I would not worry very much, Sheryl is understanding. I just wish David was here. My 'new' mother asked Kolezy about him and the man swore he did not know my brother. Dimas seems capable of going after Louis. Maybe you, Bill, Tanski, and the rest will find David."

"You know, daughter, I was just thinking that same thing. Right now I want to head back to the room and get a full eight hours of rest as we are heading back to Houston tomorrow. Murray was still curious about a certain item. "Michaeleen, what puzzles me is how did you find out I was your Dad?"

"Have you ever looked at me and found that I favor you quite more than you want to admit?"

"Well, they always say we have an identical person in the world, maybe I did not want to admit our similarities."

"When I met you in your office, it struck me but I pushed it aside as the transition of the money to you was daunting. After Carol Sue, mom, gave up and was honest about her being my mother, something more clicked in about you. There were things she said about you over the years which made it more possible that you could be my own flesh and blood father and not Brett or Potter. Vixey admitted to me that you and she had sex at their favorite place in Burkburnette and based on the date and being David and I were born nine months later... She swore that she did not have sex with anyone for three or four months after that."

Murray thought that was funny, "So Vixey, Carol Sue, was trying to be a nun without going into the convent. That is rich. Well I better get going, but for now, let's keep this under wraps and I hope your Mother will do the same. I want to catch up to the guys and have an early dinner then get a good night or days sleep."

He gave his daughter a kiss on the cheek and left for the bar where the rest of the group were unwinding after the grueling past incidents in this European country. After a round or two of drinks in the hotel they made their way to the Balaton Room for an early dinner and then to their rooms as the plane was pulling out in mid-morning for Texas.

Carol Sue clouded everything. Adam was not with the rest of the guys, neither at the bar or The Balaton Room. Then he spotted the young man with Michaeleen, heading to the elevators. She was casting a moonstruck look at the former adult star turned CEO mogul. Murray thought upon seeing Adam he wanted to know. 'He's with my daughter and what the hell is going on'!

The couple saw Murray racing toward them and stopped. Adam sensed a possible hostility knowing he was Michaeleen's father. The young man knew he needed to deal with Carol Sue on issues of their past as well as his knowledge of David, her son. Michaeleen did not have a problem with her brother and any relationship he had with Adam.

"Murray, Michaeleen has filled me in on things...She and I."

"Wait, Adam, that is not what I wanted to talk to you about." He stopped short then began, once again, "You were saying, 'She and I'. What about... Have you slept with my daughter?"

"NO!"

"Whew! That's a relief!"

Michaeleen giggled.

"Adam, since you appear to be aware of things, namely Carol Sue and me, are you also romantically involved with my daughter?"

Michaeleen held her breath, waiting for a positive response.

"Well, sir."

"OH, Shit! The 'Sir Thing'. I have heard that three times with our other daughter's pre-husband's launching into asking me for the hand in marriage thing."

Adam gulped. "Yes, I am."

Murray was shocked. "Adam, you slept with Vixey. Remember that incident? You thought about K'Lynn, Wes's sister. And your relationship with David?"

Adam was flustered by Murray's intense barrage. He did not know how to respond.

Michaeleen came to Adam's defense. "Dad, you're not being fair to him. I know what I am getting into. Vixey was a fling, he did not repeat. He attempted, as I did, to reach out to David and help him break his bad habits. I hate to say this but David may... be a lost cause."

"I am not convinced, daughter, not yet. I have not seen or spoke to David. I cannot judge him. He is my own flesh and blood. Your twin brother."

She wanted to move on. "Dad, I love Adam. He loves me. When we return to Houston I know we have a lot of things to settle."

Murray remained stunned. "This has happened so very soon. I need time to figure all this, hon." With that he hugged his daughter and looked sternly at Adam, as he walked back to the elevators and his room.

Early the following morning C.W. had the SUVs waiting to take the group from the hotel to the airstrip and their plane. Murray bumped hands with his old friend, "Well, C.W., Ernie was telling me last night you are cleaning out your desk and flying, compliments of The State Department, a first class flight back to Texas and retirement."

The red headed, Central Texan, concurred, "Yes, they gave me a package I could not pass up, and my wife, Renate, will enjoy the time with our daughter in Austin, who is finishing up at Texas with your kid, Karen. They want to work for Governor Perry, now that he has thrown his hat into the ring for President."

"Well, we will see you there. Thanks for your help here."

Murray and his band of Hungarians boarded the black Mercedes SUV's on their journey arriving almost an hour later. As the men discussed their past four days in a new land, Murray started for the Gulfstream to check out that Jon and Art were ready for the long trip back. As he neared the plane, Dimas, sidled up, slightly amused as Carol Sue related the latest and he was seeking to get a rise from him, "Guess you have some things to discuss with certain folks in Houston? Unless, Murray, you have already called your wife and your family, relating the great news?"

Murray, after having a full eight plus hours of sleep was up to the task of undoing the Lieutenant's swaggering approach. "Oh, you are referring to bringing back those Hungarian souvenirs, surely, not that Kolezy with all the misguided assistance from the HPD, FBI, and Budapest Police allowed him get away. And no one bothered to see if he made it back to his home or the club and eventual disappearance?"

Dimas went on the defense, "Hmm, well, ah, ah, you know Zeke and I would have had him cuffed and ...I told Toth he was to go that way, as did the FBI. Well, The Feds did nothing to secure Kolezy and his gang."

As the cop struggled to distance himself from the botched arrest, the others starting coming up to the plane. Murray knew, though what Dimas was getting at, gigging him on the Carol Sue and Michaeleen revelations. After all, they were not the cop's family and he thought it was okay to turn the knife, good-naturedly of course, a little into the gringo, as he termed the harried Murray.

Murray had the chance to light up the cop as he headed up the stairs of the silver and blue cylinder where Jon, Art, and Nikki greeted the cast of characters with hugs as they passed out drinks.

Jon pulled Murray aside, "I heard from Ernie that Kolezy was not found and may have swam ashore from the Danube crash."

Murray could only shrug his shoulders, "Yes, Jon, unfortunately, it appears that way. Of course, we are not sure. He may have drowned. Kolezy is like Teflon. Inspector Toth of the Budapest police promised, if you can believe it, that he would keep us informed through Lieutenant Cavazos and Sergeant Cavazos if that slippery attorney shows up at the Red Cat Club or Romany Production Studio. Toth promised, this time to clap the cuffs on Kolezy. Meantime, my good and capable pilot as soon as everyone is in their seats let's take off for Houston. How's Kerry?"

"Thanks for asking. She is almost over her ordeal and when I called, she was ecstatic over the fact that Carol Sue was safe."

Finding the 'safe' was funny. Murray forced out a laugh. "Not positive that we rescued Carol Sue from Kolezy or he was rescued from her. She mowed them down at the bathhouse coming in on a motorcycle with Adam on the back. Together, they both saved the day but we will fill you in on that later. For now, we need to get everyone on board this rocket plane, provide food and drinks for everyone, get rest, and land in our beloved State of Texas in the next eleven hours."

Murray moved past the empty seats and found Michaeleen, placing an arm around her. "We may not have put Kolezy away for the time being but mine was a mixed bag that I don't want to get into at this time. I not positive that everyone on this weird journey found what they wanted in Budapest. The three of us have to discuss things. And...I am saying you, me, and Adam, not Vixey."

As each of the others came aboard, Ernie was finishing the end of his journal to this unfulfilled trek to follow Kolezy and arrest him. Tanski and Sev, somewhat similar in their ways, thought the entire project was just another adventure waiting for the next episode in an unending chapter of their travels, perhaps a Kolezy manhunt. Rich did not see any fulfillment from all of this. He received a cell phone message from a former colleague at the Secret Service, who needed his expertise on a Los Angeles case that centered on an internet mogul which was a similar Kolezy deal and required him to gather important evidence. Wes was elated that his mother had made it through all this and was still focusing on adding a sister and brother, David, to their family, as well as the odd turn of events on Murray now being his stepdad. That and the closing of the deal on MABB. Mostly, to get back to his wife, Gina and their two children. He hugged his mother, who was sitting with her new love, although giving a jaundice look at Dimas. Michaeleen had not confided in Wes about her love for Adam. She wanted to spring that on him and her beloved mother when they landed in Houston.

Jon and Arnie revved up the engines as the Gulfstream took off for Houston with the cast of characters falling into place.

St. George looked somewhat tired as he, Sev, and Ernie were up playing poker with Zeke and C. W. the night before. His take on the trip and the past six months since Murray strode into his office and sought the assistance for Adam was 'I came along for the ride' attitude as he held up his thumbs up to childhood friend, Murray.

The Cavazos' brothers knew they brought an end to The Hungarian Mafia or at least derailed further incidents that they caused. Zeke, putting on his seat belt, felt confident of a promotion to Lieutenant taking his brother's spot as Dimas was angling to be Captain. As for the Lieutenant, if the promotion did not happen, he at least, wound up with the girl in this soap opera saga, named Vixey.

Adam was disappointed in not capturing his stepfather and bringing him back to stand trial for Ryan's apparent murder. He was satisfied with the eminent sale of MABB to the vixen, Carol Sue, and planning a new life which did not include either Szilard or Brian, he had his eye on someone entirely different and would complicate a few others's lives in the weeks and months to come. He was deeply surprised and saddened that another of his friends was murdered but still believed Louis was responsible for it, and wondering how he could prevent further murders.

Michaeleen had a huge stone lifted off of her and gained the lives of two people she admired. Only her mother did not know how much she loved Adam.

Carol Sue looked at Michaeleen and Adam, wondering what was happening but not wishing to get entangled with another problem yet. She knew, as a woman, that her new found daughter may be falling in love with a man she was not through with.

As for Murray....Nikki informed him that Hurricane Ike was heading for Houston. Another thing for him to delve into as he had to talk direct to Sheryl about the events he learned about in the past days. The hours went by as everyone finished their meals and drinks, falling asleep in the now dim lit cabin, with an occasional snore from Tanski.

Upon awakening, Murray wanted to see how Carol Sue was doing as she was up in the cabin heading for the restroom. He waited for her to come out as he surveyed her new beau, the Lieutenant, totally conked out in blissful sleep.

"Hey, Vixey, Are you feeling better that you hit me with the news?"

She sat down next to him, "No one has called that since..."

"Yesterday...as he finished her sentence.

She uncovered her ankle. "See, it is getting better. That's what you meant, right."

"Actually, I thought you had a tattoo on that part of your body, like the one on your lower back."

"You want to revisit that afternoon in Burkburnett where you thought Bobbie Jean was in that bed?"

"I am having a hard time believing you wanted to be with me, for whatever you had on that mind of yours. You lied to your own sister that I was in Louisiana at Fort Polk. Actually, you knew that it was an Army base, not an Air Force one."

"I always wanted what she had. You were her number one guy, yet, when you went away..."

"The Went Away, Vixey, was Tex, your brothers, and your doing, not mine."

"I did not have a choice. My father realized it was me and not Bobbie Jean in room 102 at the motel and he went over the edge. I wanted to stop it all but could not."

"Is that the reason you helped Michaeleen and our money to make up for not stopping Tex and your brothers?"

"That money belonged to you."

"What other reason, Carol Sue?

I thought it was the legal thing to do."

His ears started to clog up from the change of pressure in the plane as Jon was angling the Gulfstream into the eastern Gulf of Mexico. Then he noticed Michaeleen looking blankly at the two of them. "Vixey, I wanted to tell you something now that you admitted things. Bobbie Jean and I had made love at Room 201, the day before; I know she did not have the butterfly tattoo above her ass crack."

Carol Sue was finally one upped at that moment. 'YOU KNEW ALL ALONG? You did not wear a condom with me?"

"When you came into the motel room in those tight rolled up shorts and tied denim shirt showing your pierced navel...things went out the window. Bobbie Jean had an allergy reaction and never wore even pierced earrings, only the clip-on type. I knew from the 'get go' it was you and wanted to wallow your body like no man had ever done before just to show you I was not some dumb fuck, Second Louey."

Carol Sue almost lost her breath and got up to sit next to her still, sleeping new boyfriend.

Bill came over seeing the debate between the couple. "You and Vixey appeared to have had a major discovery. Were you going back those past three and one half years when you were just Tony Murray, attempting to make a living as an insurance agent?"

Before Murray could answer, Arnie ran up to them, "Look out the windows... that's, that's, Hurricane Ike and it is going to hit Galveston and Houston!"

Murray told St. George, "That is nothing. Hurricane Ike is only the half of it. Maybe the storm will be a blessing to take the edge off of what I have to tell my family. As for your question before Arnie interrupted us, I finally screwed over Carol Sue's mind on some, as you called it, a major thing. Ha, ha."

Not totally knowing what he meant, St. George felt that his friend came out of it on the plus side. Or did Murray concoct that episode to blow her away and make her believe it was true?

Murray looked over at Carol Sue who stared at the ceiling, seemingly, totally in awash, attempting to grasp what she just learned from that episode of over too many years ago in that motel. Not surprised, he spied Michaeleen and Adam almost sharing the same seat as they appeared to be discussing serious plans for the future. It was more than their interest in MABB... and he was going to need another George Dickel to settle his thoughts over that, as he ordered a five ouncer, straight up from Nikki.

Nikki was back in a short time. Taking some generous sips, Murray smiled faintly, closing his eyes as the George Dickel #12 was taking affect. He thought about those 33 years. Now Michaeleen, a product of it. What would Sheryl think about both her, David, and Carol Sue, as being a part of their own lives? But more than a hurricane, Kolezy was another wound that he wanted to get back at. Was Troy a part of Kolezy's doing? Or did someone other than Louis take their son's life? Dimas cast doubts on it. Was it a red headed woman that caused their son's death? Skylar Locke was a red head. What part, if any, did she play in their son's death? He wanted to find her to ask a lot of questions. Foremost, where was she that night Troy died? And...who was actually responsible for those murders in The Montrose? Was it some woman jilted by a man? He even thought it might be someone who was close to him or Adam. But who? This trip? MABB? Kolezy's Hungarian Mafia? Carol Sue's shocker to him? Michaeleen finding out who her mother and father really were? It all began that night, finding Adam and bringing all this together. A hurricane might be a well meaning masking of his problem from all The Damaged Goods.

ABOUT THE AUTHOR

J. X. Alexander, has been in the insurance industry for over 30 years in both Texas and California. While working as an underwriter, living in his native Cleveland, Ohio, he was mentored by the late Peter B. Lewis, CEO of Progressive Insurance.

Alexander and his wife have three grown daughters living in various parts of the United States.

The author has touched upon the story's reality from personal experiences from his own life.

Although a fictionalized work, many of the tragic events did occur in their character's lives.

J. X. Alexander and his wife, currently reside in Texas where they actively counsel and protect their very valuable insurance clients with proper guidance. He is currently writing the second novel to this trilogy.

by J.X. Alexander

www.ingramcontent.com/pod-product-compliance
Lightning Source LLC
Chambersburg PA
CBHW071637260626
47170CB00001B/133

* 9 7 8 0 6 9 2 7 9 4 8 1 4 *